The GENTLE INFANTRYMAN

W.Y. BOYD

ELTON-WOLF PUBLISHING

The GENTLE INFANTRYMAN

Cover design by David Marty
Text design by Jeanne Hendrickson

Published by Elton-Wolf Publishing
Seattle, Washington

ISBN: 1-58619-048-2
Library of Congress Catalog Number: 2003105382
07 06 05 04 03   1 2 3 4 5

First Elton-Wolf Publishing Edition August 2003
Originally published in hardcover by St. Martin's Press
Originally published in softcover by Capital Books, Inc.
Printed in Canada

ELTON-WOLF PUBLISHING
2505 Second Avenue Suite 515   Seattle, Washington 98121
Tel 206.748.0345 Fax 206.748.0343
www.elton-wolf.com info@elton-wolf.com
Seattle • Los Angeles

To all American combat infantry
past and present

★

FOREWORD

I want to share my reactions on reading *The Gentle Infantryman* by William Y. Boyd.

First, I found it to be authentic. Early on one can't help thinking that the author is in fact "The Gentle Infantryman" and is recounting his World War II combat experiences. Having fought in that war as an Infantry Lieutenant and Captain, I found it right on the mark—exceptionally realistic.

Second, the story captured my interest. I can identify easily with the feelings of the principal character, as I feel sure many others will also. Many of us have had similar experiences and though nearly fifty years have passed by, I was moved and probably always shall be by the heroism and devotion to duty and contry exhibited time and again, day after day, by the infantry soldier.

Third, the book has great acceptability. Those who were there will enjoy reliving what is undoubtedly the most significant chapter in their lives. Those who were not there will find a valuable addition to their study of the Second World War.

I commend the author for an outstanding portrayal of one of many gentle infantrymen.

John J. Hennessey
General (Retired) U.S. Army

PROLOGUE

———◆———

The ground war on the mainland of Europe began on D–Day, June 6, 1944. After the initial ferocity of the Normandy invasion came the summer's grim deadliness in the hedgerows. The subsequent Allied breakout and dash across France was followed by the battles at the gates of Germany that occupied the entire autumn of 1944.

Winter set in. Spring promised a new Allied assault that would sweep into Germany from the west. But the Germans did not intend to wait for spring.

In the middle of December, they struck with three panzer armies in the Ardennes. The attack was swift and unexpected and drove a "bulge" into the American line. The bitter winter turned brutal as armies surged back and forth, leaving trails of blood in the snow.

The Germans struck again, this time in Alsace. They hit hard against a thin line. They attacked with panzers, SS infantry, and crack paratroops. Again, the Americans fought back with a valiant desperation, throwing in all their reserves. Now, in the first days of January 1945, they had emptied their infantry replacement depots from Le Havre to the Ardennes and from Marseilles to Alsace. Everything they had was on the line.

BOOK

1

AT MIDNIGHT IN SOME FLAMING TOWN

1

A United States Army truck jolted and jarred its way along a
rutted road in France. On the horizon ahead, a dozen pillars
of black smoke rose in the windless sky, like the columns of a ruined
temple. In the rear of the open truck, infantry replacements shivered
in the January cold. Their eyes and noses were red and runny; their
faces reflected the sullen fear they felt.

Eighteen-year-old Private William Pope's teeth were
chattering. He heard the thumping of artillery and wondered if it
was German or American. "Incoming" or "outgoing," he corrected
himself. The man sitting next to him sucked in his breath. Will
patted the man's knee, and the man turned his face toward him.
Will smiled, the smile cracking his chapped lips. The man nodded,
and Will felt better for having comforted a fellow sufferer. Yes, he
thought, I'll need all the good deeds I can get.

Then he wondered if he'd done the right thing. Maybe he
should act tougher. After all, he was an infantryman on his way to
the front. Yet, he'd always been nice to people. Always tried to
please—to do what he thought he was supposed to. Sometimes, he
fell short, of course. He didn't make the high school football team
like his father had wanted him to—he was too awkward, he'd
grown too fast. Maybe he'd do better when he went to college—
play on the freshman team, then the varsity. His dad would like that!
Will started to smile but his lips cracked too painfully.

He hadn't thought he could face going to war, either. But after he was drafted, he didn't have any choice. He'd tried to get assigned to the navy or the air corps, but they were putting everybody in the infantry now. A sergeant had explained that that's where all the casualties were. So, Will figured, that was that. He was going to die at eighteen, and there wasn't much he could do about it. He knew he should at least act tough, but he felt absolutely terrified. He realized his hands were trembling; he tried to think of other things. He knew three men on the truck: Jim Mahoney, who was his best friend; Gary Mills and Buck Gawalsky, both of whom he knew only slightly. They had taken basic training with him and Jim on the 57 mm antitank gun. Will had never seen any of the other men until that morning at the replacement depot when they had all been assigned to the Fifteenth Division, but, from their conversation, he knew they were riflemen.

Now the artillery firing was louder and sharper. It sounded close. The men in the truck began to be alarmed. Voices rose above the growl of the truck's motor:

"Hey! That's shellfire. You hear? That's shooting!"

"Those're guns! They can blow us up, you know! You know that!"

"That's the front, ain't it? We're close. You hear? We're close—"

The sergeant sitting in the seat beside the driver turned and shouted, "Okay, you guys! Settle down, now, dammit! That firing's a long ways off, and they got better things to shoot at than a truckload of replacements. So dammit, settle down!"

The murmur died. Jim Mahoney, sitting opposite Will, must have been as cold and uncomfortable as everybody else, but as soon as the rest fell silent, he threw back his head and sang at the top of his lungs:

"Born in Kentucky,
Bred in Tennessee,
Went to school in Georgia,

Gonna die in Germanee."

The other men smiled. Jim Mahoney could joke about anything. To him, life was a joke; the army was a joke; the war was a joke.

For Will it wasn't; he just pretended it was. Actually, he worried a lot. But he was six feet tall, homely and plain, and people expected him to be funny, so he tried to be. Besides, when he joked, it seemed to make other people more friendly. Yet, he couldn't understand how Jim Mahoney could not take anything seriously. Will shook his head.

Jim Mahoney was as handsome as Will was plain. Not just handsome, striking. Jim's green eyes and black hair were set off against a paper-white face that had just enough freckles to look healthy, and his features were straight and well proportioned. But Mahoney went to great lengths to keep from being a "pretty boy." He was so careless of the way he dressed that he always looked sloppy. He seldom combed his hair, and he let his teeth get discolored from sheer neglect. And he said and did anything he pleased. Will envied him for that.

Will smiled until his lips cracked again. Jim saw him smile and shot out, "What're you grinning at, Will? Thinking of all the fun you're gonna have shooting Krauts like they was turkeys?"

Startled, Will recovered quickly. "No, Jimbo," he drawled. "I was thinking about all the fun you're going to have getting shot at by every Kraut in France. How long do you think it'll take before one of the bastards hits you?"

The men managed to crack their lips again.

"The first time one of them Germans shoots at me, I'm quitting this here army and going home," replied Mahoney.

"The hell you are," said Will. "Getting shot at's what you get paid for, dogface. That's why they're trucking you all the way up here to the Alsace, you dumb hillbilly."

Mahoney started to reply, but changed his mind. The cold and the long, exhausting journey on the boxcars and through the replacement depots made kidding around too much effort, even for Jim Mahoney.

Will looked out at the white fields with black skeletons of trees silhouetted against them. He knew the war had passed this way, but the snow had covered the scars. The truck was getting closer to the smoke and the firing now, and Will saw there was a town ahead. He shivered from the cold.

The sergeant in front turned and yelled, "That's Damen, that town. That's where we're going. That's where we'll find the First Battalion of the 555th Infantry Regiment, which is gonna be your new home."

The driver turned to the sergeant. "Damen? Damen, Sarge? Hell! Nobody told me we was going to Damen! Jerries're at Damen already. The tanks been fighting there all morning. Got their ass shot off, too. Let's go back."

"No," replied the sergeant. "Let's get in there and unload. Then let's get the hell out as fast as we can."

For a brief moment, Will Pope thought seriously of jumping off the truck and running away.

The town of Damen was larger than a village—its mud-splattered houses showed marks of shrapnel, its unpaved streets were rutted. The civilians had long since departed with whatever possessions they could carry with them.

The truck came to a creaking stop in front of a large, two-storied building. It had once served as the town hall, but it now bore a sign that proclaimed it Headquarters of the First Battalion, 555th Infantry Regiment, Fifteenth Division. The sergeant jumped down from the front seat, calling, "Okay, you guys! Everybody off! Everybody off!"

The replacements climbed down, stiff and cold, wondering what was going to happen now. They didn't have to wonder long. Sergeants from the line companies of the battalion stood waiting for them. They quickly read names, counted heads and led men off until only four were left standing by the truck—Will and Jim, Gawalsky and Mills. A Jeep splashed them with mud as it bounced down the street. Will tried to wipe off his field jacket and trousers but only succeeded in spreading the mud all over them. The other men didn't try.

The sergeant was looking around, obviously impatient. "You guys're going to the antitank company," he said. "They're here to help the First Battalion defend this damned town."

A captain came out the doorway of the headquarters, and the men snapped to attention. The sergeant saluted.

The captain was short and stout, and he needed a shave. He looked tired. Will could tell from the way he stomped out of the building that he was not in a good mood.

"Your replacements, sir," said the sergeant.

"Whaddayamean? There's only four guys," snapped the captain.

"Yes, sir," replied the sergeant, swinging himself back up into his seat in the truck before any further conversation could develop. As the motor coughed itself into a steady growl, he made a motion that was supposed to be a salute, but the captain was already reading the replacements' names on the clipboard he held.

He shook his head. "Dammit," he said. "Regiment grabs half my men to fill in for their rifle company casualties, and when a panzer division shows up, they send me four replacements. Four. What a way to fight a war!"

He looked at the men standing in front of him. "At ease. I'm Captain Colina, commanding officer of the antitank company of the 555th Infantry. It says here that you guys've trained in antitank. Is that right?"

"Yes, sir," said all four at the same time.

The captain smiled. "You men know from your basic training that an infantry regiment's antitank company consists of three gun platoons of three guns each, a mine platoon, and a headquarters platoon. Right?"

The men nodded in unison.

"Well," continued the captain, "we still have all nine of our guns, but we got less than half the men we need to man them and defend them."

Colina looked at his clipboard. "What the hell do I do with four men?" he asked himself. "Okay. Mahoney, you go to the First Platoon; Gawalsky, Second Platoon; Mills, Third. Pope, you go with Gawalsky to the Second Platoon."

Will Pope felt a pang of anxiety at the prospect of being separated from Jim Mahoney. They'd been together ever since they first met in basic training. He started to say something but closed his half-opened mouth before he could put his foot in it. He remembered just in time that officers don't like privates to give them suggestions on how to run their outfits. No sense in starting out wrong—he'd wait until later, then see what he could do to get back together with Jimmy. He knew Mahoney wouldn't give a damn where he went.

"Hey, Captain," said Jim Mahoney, "Pope and me's buddies. How about keeping us together?"

Colina looked up from the clipboard. His expression indicated he hadn't grasped what Mahoney had said. Then he nodded slightly and looked at his clipboard again. Will realized the man was exhausted and had much more on his mind than the four replacements who stood before him. Now the captain was rubbing his chin, but his thoughts were far away.

A young lieutenant came out of the headquarters. As the cold air hit him, he pulled his scarf tighter around his neck and at the same time took in the scene of the captain standing in front of the four new men. He smiled.

Colina seemed glad to see him. He said, "Hi, Dave. These are the replacements. All of them."

The lieutenant nodded and bit his lip.

"Two of them are yours," continued Colina. "You can take them over. I thought MacAllister could use a man and…"

"Yes, sir," replied the lieutenant. "I think we'd better get going, though. All hell's going to break loose any minute, and I want to be with my platoon when it does."

The lieutenant was fair, small, and wiry. He drove his own Jeep and, for a road as bad as the one they soon were on, he was driving it fast. He turned to Will, sitting beside him, and to Gawalsky in the back seat and said, "I'm Lieutenant Sommers, platoon leader of the Second Platoon."

"I'm Will Pope."

"Gawalsky, sir," came the voice from the rear.

"Welcome to the Triple Nickel," said the lieutenant, and Will saw him smile. That made him feel better, and Will liked the nickname of the regiment, too, "Triple Nickel." He turned the words around in his mouth a couple of times. Yes, they sounded jaunty, saucy, like a regiment of infantry should.

As the Jeep bounced down the road, he wondered when he'd get his division shoulder patches. The Fighting Fifteenth was a famous division. Its patch was the Roman numerals XV in dark red against a neutral background, and in the First World War, General Pershing had stated, after a particularly bloody engagement, that the XV of the Fighting Fifteenth would for him always stand for Extraordinary Valor, and the division was officially named the "Extraordinary Valor" Division. But nobody ever called it anything but the Fighting Fifteenth.

The Jeep followed a dirt road that went along the edge of a woods that lay beyond Damen. "Our line's the other side of the woods," said Sommers.

They left Gawalsky at his gun, and Will and Lieutenant Sommers continued on their way to the next position, where a lean, tired-looking G.I. came out of the woods to meet them.

"Hi, Mac," said Sommers. "This is Pope, your new replacement. Pope, Sergeant MacAllister."

MacAllister looked disappointed, but all he said was, "Thanks, Lieutenant."

He ducked under a branch and went into the stand of pine trees. Will followed.

They entered a clearing and Will saw three other G.I.'s and a well-camouflaged 57 mm antitank gun. The gun had a clear field of fire. It overlooked a shallow, snow-covered valley that stretched out until it came to a pine forest. Will wondered if there were Germans behind the far pines. The long, straight barrel of the 57 pointed that way. There was nothing in the valley except some dead-looking trees.

MacAllister said, "Boys, this is our new replacement, Pope. Pope, meet Jones, Hayes, Faulkner." He gestured at each. They nodded at Will.

All four were so well bundled against the cold that they looked like fat barrels on legs, each topped off by a pile of wool scarves and a helmet—only their eyes and noses showed. Their jackets and trousers were dirty and stained with grease spots and looked like they'd been worn for a long time. Will felt conspicuous in his new gear and was almost glad he'd had a little mud splashed on it.

Off to his right, Will could see the foxholes of a couple of rifle companies. They were newly dug, and there was fresh dirt around them. Will could see G.I.'s sitting in them. He could hear them talking to each other as the wind caught a word or two.

To the left there were more foxholes, and beyond them Will could spot the rising columns of smoke he'd seen earlier from the truck. He pointed and then turned to ask what they were. He didn't have to.

"There was a hell of a tank battle this morning," said Faulkner. "Those are burning tanks. Ours."

"After knocking out all our tanks, the panzers pulled back," said Jones. "We figure they'll hit us again. But we don't know where. Just pray it ain't here."

"Yeah," said MacAllister. "Antitank guns're okay against one tank. Or a couple, even. Or armored cars. But they don't have a chance in hell against a full-scale panzer attack. Don't know if we'd have the guts to try to stop them or not. We ain't never deployed our guns like this before, though, all strung out along the line."

"You hear all the firing?" asked Faulkner. "It sounds like the Third Battalion's getting hit hard. So it'll be our turn next."

"Look," said MacAllister, "if we have to go into action, I'm gunner, Jones is loader, and you three'll pass ammunition to us as fast as you can. We fire three quick rounds, then we move. Fast! After three rounds, Jerry'll have us spotted and zero in on us, and I hope to be long gone."

"Yeah," said Hayes, speaking for the first time. "We got a second position picked out over on the right. We got six rounds of ammunition there. We got three rounds here. The rest is out by the road." Will nodded. Hayes was obviously the one who did the work of hauling ammo.

MacAllister said slowly, "Since you ain't worked with us, I think we ought to dry-run it."

The practice drill went smoothly, and Will became more confident. His training had been good, and his actions were reflex. He breathed deeply, with a certain satisfaction; he'd arrived. He was a member of an antitank gun crew on the front line.

And, so far, nobody had shot at him.

★

The dull thumping of artillery on their left reminded Sergeant MacAllister of something. He turned to Will and said, "Pope, you'd better dig yourself a hole." Will nodded. He had seen the four shallow foxholes nearby.

He started to dig, but the ground was frozen. On his knees, he chipped and hacked away at the concrete-hard earth with all his might. Jones told him that as soon as he got through the top layer, it would be easier digging.

Will liked the men in his gun crew. They had been friendly and helpful. But he couldn't stop thinking how much he was going to miss Jim Mahoney. He wondered if Jim was digging himself a foxhole right now, too. And if, maybe, sometimes, Jim might even get as scared as he did. That made Will wonder how long it would be before the Germans attacked. He tried to concentrate all his mind on chipping at the earth with his small shovel.

As he continued to dig and think, he decided a great part of his anxiety was due to the fact he didn't know what to expect. He'd never been in battle before. "Oh, God," he thought. "I can be dead in a few minutes. Dead." The word sounded so final. Once again he tried to pry his thoughts away from the ordeal he knew lay ahead.

It was the first time he'd used the shovel. It was a good one, and the hard work he was giving it was taking off some of the new-ness. Will knew he'd been well trained; he had been well equipped, too. And with a catch of his breath and a flip of his heart, he realized he was about to fulfill the sole purpose for which he'd been so well trained and so well equipped.

2

Will Pope became aware that the babble of voices and the clank of metal had ceased as the other members of the gun crew stopped talking and tinkering with the gun. When he turned his head, he saw them squatting beside the 57, staring at something on the other side of the valley. The other men's matter-of-fact attitude had begun to relax him a little bit. Now he became tense again, just as suddenly as if somebody had thrown a bucket of cold water in his face.

Jones turned and called hoarsely, "Hey! Pope! You want to see some real, live German soldiers?"

"Cut that out, Jonesie," growled MacAllister.

Even though his "hole" was only a series of notches hacked in the ground, Will got up and walked over to the others. He knelt beside Jones. At first he didn't see anything at all. Then he saw movement. He saw men drifting across the snow-covered valley toward them. A lot of men.

They were still on the far side of the valley, and they were wearing white parkas. Now, against the snow, Will could distinguish the darkness of their faces, the rims of their helmets, and the silhouettes of their rifles.

The German soldiers were not running. They were walking in extended squad formations.

Attempting to gather his thoughts above the thumping of his

heart, Will tried to count the advancing German squads, but there were too many of them. And more kept streaming out of the far woods. Will's mind froze. He licked his lips nervously.

MacAllister turned and said, "Well, here they come. Let's pray they don't bring panzers with them."

The others nodded.

Will thought, "Well, this is it." That's what they said in the movies—it sounded brave and fatalistic, but Will felt like crying, and a voice inside him kept repeating, "I want my mama; I want my mama." He was able to still the voice and stifle the urge to sob, but he couldn't stop his body from shaking from the cold.

Faulkner was saying, "In a minute, they'll start to shell—"

But he never finished the sentence.

There was a sudden, loud shriek like a railroad train coming into a station, fast and out of control, with its brakes on full. It grew louder and louder until it ended abruptly in a dull explosion.

It took only a few seconds for the German shell to scream in and blow up somewhere down the line. But in those few seconds, Will Pope felt a terror he had never felt before.

Another scream. Another explosion. The men of the gun crew had thrown themselves into their holes. Will Pope lay in the open all alone, his hole not even properly begun.

The screams of the shells and the explosions increased to a crescendo. The earth shook. Will didn't dare look up. He didn't dare move. He felt naked under the incoming artillery shells, petrified. And the shells kept screaming in and exploding. He lay face down in the indentation he had made. With his arms over his helmet, he pressed his body as deeply into the ground as he could.

In the distance, where a line company G.I. got hit by shrapnel, he heard the cry, "Medic! Medic! Over here! Medic!"

Will's terror became acute. The German gunners were shooting at him. They were bound to blow him to bits. It would happen any minute. It would happen with the next shell. Fright was turning to panic.

He couldn't stand it. He had to get out of there! He had to run away. Right now!

But nobody else was running. Nobody. They were enduring the rain of steel and fire. If they could stand it, he could stand it, or, perhaps, he didn't have the nerve to run away. He didn't know. But one thing he did know: he was going to stay and just pray he didn't get killed.

As the shells continued to scream into the positions around him, throwing up dirt and snow and jagged steel fragments, cutting off branches and uprooting entire trees, Will stayed. And he prayed for his life as he had never prayed before.

Suddenly the shelling stopped. The other men of the gun crew were out of their holes and beside their gun. Will joined them quickly, even though his legs shook so badly he thought he might fall.

The German soldiers were closer now. They had moved across the valley while their artillery had kept the G.I.'s deep in their holes.

"You okay, Pope?" asked MacAllister.

Will nodded. He realized, with shame, that he must be showing the fear he felt or MacAllister wouldn't have asked the question.

And then he saw them. Panzers!

They had emerged from the woods across the valley. Will could hear the steady roar from the motors of a couple of dozen German tanks, the clank of metal, the squeak of treads. Now the low-slung, mechanized monsters were rolling forward behind the soldiers of the German infantry.

Will heard MacAllister say, "Tiger tanks. My God! Tiger tanks. And Tiger Royals!"

Will's heart thumped hard. He heard a Jeep on the road behind them. A voice shouted, "Hey, Mac! Do you see them?"

MacAllister rose and took the four or five steps necessary to reach a point where he could talk to the man in the Jeep.

"Yeah, I see them, Lieutenant." MacAllister's voice came with difficulty. "What do you want me to do?"

Sommers replied, "If we open up on them, they'll blast back at us with every 88 they've got. But nobody ever won a war without doing some shooting. So when they get in range, open fire! Our guns are all we've got to stop them with, now."

MacAllister walked back to the gun. He knelt beside his four men, and they stared, dead-eyed, at the valley and at the German panzers creeping toward them.

The battalion's line companies opened fire with their machine guns, automatic rifles, and M-1 rifles.

Will saw Germans drop in the snow. He saw Germans fall, jump up, and run forward, then fall again. He didn't know which ones were hit and which ones were throwing themselves down in the snow to make themselves more difficult targets for the American riflemen.

American mortar shells began exploding among the enemy soldiers. Will heard the dull thudding of bullets hitting trees behind him. The Germans were shooting back.

The Tiger tanks continued toward the American line, and the German infantry now fell behind them for protection. But there were a lot of Germans lying in the snow who did not get up again.

On his left, Will heard the sharp report of an antitank gun; it was followed by several others in rapid succession. Will Pope was shaking badly and there was nothing he could do about it. More 88 shells were zipping through the air. There were more explosions now. The panzers were firing into the American line.

A shellburst made Will jump. It was close. The snow fell from the pine branches overhead, and spattered on his helmet. He heard three more sharp reports. Another antitank gun had opened up on the panzers.

Will saw a German tank slew around off one of its tracks—at the same time, its turret began traversing so that its 88 could continue firing at the American line.

Three more sharp reports. Another gun had opened fire.

One of the German panzers in front of Will's position jolted to a stop, jarred as if it had hit a solid wall. The turret cover flew open, and a flame shot out of it, followed by another. But the second flame jumped off the turret and began running and Will saw that it was a man completely ablaze, burning to death as he rolled and thrashed in the snow.

Will knew he was going to vomit. Now he could see two other flaming bodies. One came from under the disabled tank, ran several yards, then fell, still on fire, and lay there. The other dropped from the turret of the panzer like a ball of burning wax. He hit the snow and lay still.

Will realized with a shudder that these were human beings like him, who were enduring the agony of burning to death; dying by inches as the flames engulfed them.

He felt cold and clammy as he fought the nausea. He felt dizzy. Then he knew he was going to faint.

"Where you hit, Pope?"

Will heard the words through a haze. The world was still swinging in circles. He still had the urge to vomit.

"Where you hit?" the voice asked.

"Put his feet up and his head down. He's in shock," another voice said.

"Yeah. White as a sheet," said the first voice.

Will opened his eyes. MacAllister was bending over him, looking worried.

Now he could hear the sharp reports of the antitank guns, the crackling of small arms and machine guns, the zipping of the 88s before they exploded, blowing up in the earth.

He struggled to get to his feet. MacAllister pushed him back, gently but firmly. "Where you hit?" he asked again.

Will was too ashamed to answer; he just lay there. He reached out, took a handful of snow, and rubbed it on his face to try to wake himself up.

A loud, whining swish was followed by a louder explosion.

Snow came tumbling on them in chunks. MacAllister turned around to face their front. He jumped up and bounded to his gun.

Fighting off nausea and dizziness, Will rose to his feet. As he stood there, swaying slightly, the rest of the crew were already in firing position.

MacAllister was leaning into the gunner's cradle with his eye to the gunsight. Jones knelt beside him.

Will tried to speak, to say, "I'm okay now," but he couldn't. He was still fighting to keep from vomiting.

The sound of a Jeep on the road behind them made MacAllister turn his head quickly. He saw Will standing and asked, "Pope, you okay?"

Will nodded as the sound of the Jeep motor faded in the distance.

"Okay, get set!" said MacAllister. "I'm gonna concentrate all three shots at that lead son-of-a-bitch."

"Up!" yelled MacAllister.

"Up!" shouted Jones, ramming a shell into the breech with his fist.

Bang! exploded the shot. The gun leaped in the air as it fired.

MacAllister's eye never left the gunsight—his shoulder stayed pressed tightly to the gunner's cradle as he rode the gun into the air and back down again as the carriage recoiled and the breechblock dropped, ejecting the spent shell casing.

"Up!" yelled MacAllister.

"Up!" shouted Jones.

Bang! went the gun again.

"Up!" yelled MacAllister.

Bang!

The three shots had been so close together they could have been one. The smoke choked Will. His eyes burned from it. The smell of cordite and gunpowder stung his nostrils.

MacAllister and Jones had already snapped the gun trails closed, and they all grabbed the gun and started running toward the new position.

Will was amazed at how light the gun was and how fast they could move it. It had seemed so heavy and slow in basic training. From the position they'd just left, he heard shells crack, blowing the now empty space to pieces. He was flung to the ground. The ground shook. Pine needles, branches, and snow showered on him and around him.

The five men got up and kept running with the gun until they got to the new position. They were breathing hard.

Will realized he had stopped shaking. The horror he had felt had left him. Now he felt excitement. The fear was still there, but it was a different kind of fear—an exciting kind that comes from facing danger with action, not the helpless terror that paralyzes.

MacAllister was already leaning into the gunner's cradle with his eye to the gunsight.

"Up!"

"Up!"

Bang!

"Up!"

"Up!"

Bang!

"Let's go! Got the son-of-a-bitch!"

Again the gun trails were closed. Again the men pulled the gun out of position; the gun that seemed to Will as light as a feather. He was running so fast, he felt he was flying, his feet barely touching the ground. Yet they were crashing through small pines, through snow and fallen branches, rushing to flee from the devastating return fire from the panzers' 88s.

Again the ground shook beneath Will's feet, but he kept going forward. Jones and MacAllister, guiding the gun, swerved to avoid running over three dead G.I.'s sprawled in the snow. Their blood had just begun to spread a steaming red stain in the snow around them. Will felt clammy again.

Beyond the dead G.I.'s, MacAllister guided the gun among some pine trees. It looked like good cover, even though there was no clearing here, just pine trees. The gun's long, straight barrel stuck out between two of them.

Will tried to catch his breath. He heard firing on all sides of him, and explosions. Explosions of incoming shells. Explosions of mortars landing on the Germans.

Hayes had carried the four shells that remained. He put all four down by the gun, but MacAllister did not lean into the cradle as quickly as he had at their last position. Instead he turned to his men and said, "We got two of the Tigers! From our angle up here, we can hit the bastards good."

Again MacAllister leaned into the cradle.

Hayes said, "We got four shells. Want me to go get some more?"

"No. Can't spare you. Pope!"

"Yes, Sarge!" Will yelled.

"By the road, right behind our second position, you'll see a tarp. Under it are a bunch of 57 shells, still in the cartons. Bring as many as you can carry. Now, move!"

"Right!" shouted Will as he turned to run to the road.

He heard MacAllister say, "We'll shoot twice from here. Save the other two rounds for the next move."

"Up!"

"Up!"

Bang!

Will ran fast. He was afraid he'd have trouble finding the tarp. MacAllister had shown him everything he'd need to know about their situation except where the extra shells were. But they were right where he said they'd be. Will lifted the tarpaulin. Under it were the black, cylindrical cartons. He took four of them in his arms and started back, but now he was trotting rather than running. He didn't want to drop any of the cartons, and they were a lot heavier than he'd ever imagined.

"Up!"

"Up!"

Bang!

Ah, thought Will, I'm almost home.

Just ahead of him Will saw the bright flashes of the 88s exploding in the pine trees.

At almost the same moment, he heard three cracks that sounded like lightning hitting close by.

He dove into the snow.

Metal thudded onto the ground. He thought he heard a scream.

He got up fast. A large branch floating down from above knocked him back onto his face. His helmet bounced in front of him.

He got up again, more slowly this time. The black cylinders were strewn around him. He picked up his helmet without thinking, put it on his head, and began gathering up the antitank shells.

With his arms full, he trotted forward toward the gun, toward the trees the 88s had hit.

The first thing Will saw was the gun, its flash shield riddled with jagged holes, its tires flat, and its barrel so out of line that it almost pointed sideways.

Then he stopped dead. His mouth fell open; his eyes widened. The black cylinders tumbled from his arms.

His four companions lay sprawled around the gun. Drops of red blood dotted the snow. No one moved. MacAllister had been flung on his back with his legs across a gun trail. Jones lay face down near him, and both Faulkner and Hayes lay face down beyond them. All four were steaming from ragged, bloody holes in their jackets and trousers. With a shudder, Will realized the steam was caused by warm blood pouring out of their bodies and hitting the ice-cold air.

The popping of small arms and the exploding of shells continued, but Will was oblivious to the noise of battle.

He did not know how long he stood there, believing everyone to be dead. It was clear that the German 88s had hit tree branches over the position and showered shrapnel on the antitank gun and its crew.

Faulkner moved. He rolled over onto his back. His helmet had fallen off and his face was gray. He opened his eyes, but they showed no expression. Not of pain, not of fear, not of anything. At the same moment, MacAllister groaned and flung out the arm that was resting on his chest.

Will was petrified. He glanced at Jones and Hayes. Both were steaming a lot, which meant they were losing blood fast and must be dying.

They were in shock or unconscious from the impact of the shrapnel. What shall I do? What can I do? Will asked himself as bullets thwacked against trees and as the battle continued unabated.

He began fumbling with the first-aid kit on his cartridge belt as he knelt beside Faulkner, but his slung rifle kept sliding off his shoulder and hitting Faulkner on the leg. Faulkner groaned and tried to motion with his hand. He was breathing heavily. He managed to gasp, "No. I've had it. MacAllister."

Will crawled over to MacAllister.

MacAllister lay on his back. As Will approached, Mac said, "Don't."

Then his voice cracked as he said, "I think my back is broken. Can't move."

Both Faulkner and MacAllister were riddled with shrapnel, and there was no way Will could stop their bleeding. Jones and Hayes never regained consciousness—now they had ceased to steam, so he knew they were gone. Then Faulkner slid away. He lay with his mouth agape and his eyes open. His labored breathing had stopped.

Will heard a Jeep motor. He whispered, "Sarge, don't move. Help's coming."

He jumped up and ran to the road behind their position. Lieutenant Sommers's Jeep was coming down the road toward him.

Will stepped into the road and waved his arms; the Jeep swerved to a stop, almost skidding into the ditch.

Will told the lieutenant, "Everybody on our gun except me and MacAllister's killed, and Mac's in a bad way. Can you get us a medic?"

Sommers said, "Let's get MacAllister in the Jeep."

"I don't think we can, sir. His back is broken."

"Good God," said the lieutenant, turning off the Jeep motor and springing out.

Will followed Sommers as he ran toward the gun. But when they reached the position, none of the bodies was steaming anymore.

Lieutenant Sommers knelt beside the still body of each man. After he had examined MacAllister, he got up and said, "No. They're all dead." His voice sounded so sad, Will thought he might burst into tears. Then the lieutenant looked toward the enemy. "I think we've stopped them," he said slowly, as if he didn't really believe it.

Will saw the surviving panzers pulling away—there weren't many. Most of the German tanks remained on the field, sending up great clouds of smoke. Several were going around in circles. Others sat still and appeared unscathed, but inside them, their crews lay dead, killed by armor-piercing shells.

The lieutenant said, "By God! We've turned them back."

The German infantry was also in retreat.

The lieutenant turned to Will and said, "This gun's knocked out. You'd better come with me."

Will nodded. He couldn't speak. He had just watched four men die, men he'd liked, men who had been alive and active only a few minutes ago, now dead in the snow.

It couldn't be true. It couldn't be. But he knew it was. Four men had been slaughtered like—like what? You don't even butcher animals like that.

The pain he felt was worse than any physical hurt he'd ever known.

Had MacAllister known this would happen? Had he? Did he send me to get extra shells when he knew he wouldn't have time to fire them? Did he? Will felt his lower lip tremble. Will Pope had never felt so dejected in his life. Then his mind began to go blank in an effort to shut out the anguish.

He was numb now, but he followed the lieutenant. As they got into the Jeep, Sommers said, "We lost number three gun, too, but Randolph's was working a few minutes ago. Let's go to it."

Will wondered about Gawalsky. He had been on number three gun.

It was getting dark. As the Jeep drew to a stop, a soldier stepped into the road. Will gathered it was Sergeant Randolph.

"Our gun got four of their tanks," the sergeant said. "The rest turned tail. What do we do now?"

The lieutenant said, "I'm going to find out."

"I think they're coming back," said Randolph.

"So do I," said the lieutenant. "Do you need any more men?" He nodded toward Will.

"No," replied Randolph. "We have a lucky crew. Let's leave it like that."

The lieutenant nodded and was about to start his motor when another Jeep came tearing down the road, swerving from side to side as its tires lost traction on the ice and the driver fought the wheel to keep it from going into the ditch.

Beside the driver sat the unshaven captain of the antitank company. After the vehicle slithered to a stop, Sommers jumped out of his Jeep and strode toward his company commander. Will got out and stood in the road.

There were no preliminaries. The lieutenant's voice was urgent. "Lost number one and number three guns. Randolph's all I've got left. We knocked out six or seven of their Tigers, as near as I can tell. Broke up the panzer attack. Stopped the bastards good."

The captain nodded. "Our other platoons knocked the hell out of the Tigers, too, but I don't know what we've got left.

Randolph's the only one for sure. Communications are out all down the line."

"What do you want us to do?" asked the lieutenant. "I can work with Randolph and try to gather up any other guns we've still got and deploy them as a platoon."

"We're going to defend Damen with the First Battalion," replied the captain. "Regiment thinks the attack this afternoon was a probe. Their main attack'll come tonight, after dark. Able and Baker companies are already moving out of the woods into Damen. Charlie and Dog'll cover them, then move back to the town. I'm sending a truck to haul in Randolph's gun. You wait with him and position the gun to cover the north road, then report back to me at battalion C.P."

As he was standing by the side of the Jeep, Will's numbness wore off while he listened to the two officers talk. He was aware of being cold again, a sensation his fear had relegated to insignificance. He shivered and tried to beat his arms against his body to get warm, but his rifle fell off his shoulder and clattered onto the road. He picked it up. An hour ago he would have been embarrassed and flustered at his clumsiness. Now he didn't care.

He wondered if Jim Mahoney was still alive, or Gawalsky or Mills. Or any of the riflemen who'd come up with them.

Will Pope breathed deeply. Just being alive felt good. Suddenly he realized he didn't care who else had made it through the day. He had survived. And that was all that mattered.

3

The tall, gray-haired man who strode down the corridor of the State House was maturely handsome at forty-eight. He greeted every person he passed with a cordial nod and a pleasant, "Good morning," to which they responded with a smile and the inevitable, "Good morning, Governor Pope."

The aides who followed him took their cue from the governor, bowing and murmuring, "Good morning" as they proceeded at their chief's brisk pace.

George Pope was a Franklin Roosevelt Democrat who had won his last election by the largest majority of any of his state's candidates in living memory. And that January morning he should have been particularly pleased. He had just convinced a select committee of the state legislature to approve several bills that were important to him; yet George Pope was a troubled man.

He was aware that one of the men with him was speaking. "What did you think of the meeting, sir?"

"It couldn't have gone better," replied the governor.

"Yes. I thought so, too, sir," said another man.

"You were very convincing, sir," spoke up another. "You tore their arguments to shreds."

"You were brilliant, sir," said the first man.

They arrived at the door to the governor's private offices, and his subordinates expected him to invite them inside, as usual, to review the conference they had just attended and plan their future actions. But that morning, George Pope stood silent for a moment, then said, "Boys, we'll get together later on. I've got some urgent matters I've got to take care of right now."

With a chorus of Yes, sir's and Yes, of course's, the other men departed, and the governor entered his office. Now he could concentrate on the thoughts that had been distracting him all morning. The headlines in the newspapers had not been good for the past several days. Ever since the middle of December, the fighting in Europe had been particularly bloody, and now the Germans were rampaging into Alsace. American troops were being killed in countless numbers, and George Pope didn't know where his son was.

What he did know was that the army was rushing infantry replacements to the front as fast as they could get them there and that the last letter he'd received from his son, Will, was from Camp Kilmer, New Jersey, a port of embarkation, saying he was going overseas as an infantry replacement. The shock had almost paralyzed the governor into inaction. The news had been so unexpected he hadn't had time to do anything about it. By the time he was able to think clearly enough to telephone Washington, it was too late.

George Pope let his leather-covered chair spin until he was facing the picture window that looked out onto the capitol mall with its snow-covered vista that always delighted him. It gave him no pleasure that morning.

He'd been pleased, though, back in July, when his only son had been drafted into the army. That was his kind of democracy. There were no privileged ones. If the son of any ordinary citizen could get drafted, so could the son of the governor of the state. One law applied to all, rich or poor, high or low. Equality under the law was what democracy was all about—that's what it meant!

The sweat broke out on George Pope's forehead. Back in July he'd never dreamed of Will going overseas so soon. For some reason, he'd thought Will's training would take longer, that in all likelihood the war would be over before he finished it. He'd never even considered the fact that his son would go into actual combat as an infantry private.

"Damn! I should have paid more attention to what was going on! Hell! I could've asked how long infantry basic training took. I could've found out what happened afterward. Will wrote that he was in an IRTC, and I never even asked him what that was! He'd have told me it was an infantry replacement training center! That's what it is! And I sure as hell could've figured out what that meant! Dammit!

"But, no. I never asked. My damned logic told me he was in basic training and that some sort of specialized training would come after that, and then assignment to a unit... Who in hell would have figured the goddamn army gives these kids four months of infantry basic training, then sends them overseas into battle?"

George Pope put his hands over his face. "If I'd only asked a few questions. If I'd only thought. Dammit, I could've gotten Will into officers' training—that would've taken a few months before he got commissioned. Or I could have gotten him transferred. There are lots of other branches of the army that aren't anywhere near as dangerous. Before he ever got on that boat, I should've stopped it!"

He got up and began pacing back and forth, thinking, What can I do? What can I do now? He stopped in the middle of his rug and shook his head. He knew it was wrong for him to do anything. It was against all his principles of democracy; because George Pope was governor shouldn't entitle his son to any special privileges. It would amount to using influence, something he was against. He should do nothing. He clenched his fists. "To hell with that! Dammit! If I can do something to save my son's life, then, morally, I must! I'm his father! That comes first!"

He frowned. Sam Reynolds' son, Jack, had gone into the army a month or so before Will. Sam was George Pope's best friend and most loyal supporter. Sam's money got Pope elected the first time he ran for office. If it wasn't for Sam, George Pope would probably still be clerking in his father's law offices.

Sam had never asked for any special treatment for his own son, and he could have. George Pope owed Sam a lot of favors. Young Jack Reynolds had gone overseas right after his basic training in November. Yes, thought the governor, November. He sat down again and leaned back in his chair, pensive. That should have told me something, he thought. Now my own son's on his way to the war, too, the same as Jack. Good God, how stupid I was not to see it!

In Will's letter from Camp Kilmer he'd told his parents not to worry about him; he was in an antitank outfit, and antitank was part of a regimental headquarters, so he'd be in no danger, even if the war still was going on when he got there, which was unlikely.

Will's mother, Cecily, had pounced on that. "Isn't it nice, dear," she'd told George. "Will's going to be in a nice headquarters in the rear someplace. Oh! I do hope it's not Paris! He's so young…"

George had said he was sure it wouldn't be Paris, so not to worry. He didn't want to upset his adored wife, but privately he was pretty damned sure an infantry antitank outfit was not in the rear someplace.

"Hell, no, it's not in the rear someplace! Infantry antitank. It sounds awful." The governor swallowed hard. He blinked his eyes a couple of times, then rose from his chair and raised his fist and hit the top of his desk with all his might. It hurt, and he shook his now open hand to restore the circulation.

Poor Will. The vision of his gangling, awkward son rose before him, just as homely as ever. As far as he knew, Will had never done an unkind thing in his life. The governor shook his head slowly. "Will was always too damned nice, if you ask me. And all I ever did was pick on him." The governor winced. "It wasn't his fault he couldn't do the things I did when I was his age. We're made differently. That's all. Dammit! I should have been glad he liked to read Shakespeare and all that crap. Besides, he tried; God knows how hard he tried to please me…"

Alone in his office, the last pretense of the calm self-assurance he'd exuded all morning disappeared, and if anybody had looked in on the governor at that moment, they would have thought they were seeing a man in terrible physical pain. His face was twisted in anguish. He was remembering the times he and Cecily had gone off and left Will alone with his grandmother when he was a little boy and they were out campaigning. "No wonder he kept trying so hard to please us. He was afraid we'd go off and leave him for good! Being left alone so much made him self-reliant, though," but George Pope knew he was beginning to rationalize. He shook his head. "If he were only here with me now, I'd take him in my arms and hug him and tell him how much I love him…"

It suddenly occurred to Will's father that he'd never done that. He should have, he thought, but do fathers ever do that sort of thing? He didn't know the answer.

His thoughts shifted. He remembered Will's letter from basic training saying he'd made "expert" on the rifle range, with the highest score of anybody in his company. Will was so proud! Locking his fingers together, Governor George Pope raised his face to the ceiling and said, "Lord God, please help me. My only kid must be scared to death somewhere in Europe right now. And he's a good kid, God, but he's just a kid; he won't last two seconds in infantry combat. He's not tough enough, God—he's gentle. And who in hell ever heard of a gentle infantryman? You've got to help me save him. I've got to think of a way right now, before he gets killed or crippled…"

George Pope became aware that his intercom light had just flashed on. Strange. He'd told his secretary, Mabel O'Connor, he didn't want to be disturbed, and she was a bulldog when it came to protecting his privacy. The light went off just as it had come on, silently. Mrs. O'Connor had changed her mind. Now there was a soft knock at the door. It opened a crack and the governor said, "Come on in, Mabel. It must be important."

Mabel O'Connor was agitated, which was unusual. The plump, gray-haired secretary was normally a model of calm efficiency. While George Pope sat looking at her, she blurted, "Oh, sir, I know you didn't want to be disturbed, but the Reynolds just got a telegram, sir. Their son, Jack, is missing in action in Europe."

For a minute, George Pope didn't speak. He sat still, as if he couldn't grasp or didn't believe what Mabel had just told him. Finally he said, "It'll kill them. It'll just kill them." And his voice had a quality of sadness and sincerity that made Mabel stop wringing her hands and stand perfectly still.

The governor continued to sit without moving. Sam and Sara Reynolds adored their only son, and why shouldn't they? He was handsome, tall, popular. He'd been the captain of the football team of the local high school. Pope had always wished Will were more like Jack Reynolds…

Finally George Pope rose from his desk and walked over to his closet. As he put on his overcoat, he said, "I'm going to the Reynolds's house. I won't be back today."

Mabel nodded. She knew that whatever important matter the governor had been working on, he had put it aside.

What she didn't know was how close to home her news hit.

✪

It was dark when Sommers's Jeep got back to town after positioning Randolph's gun. Will followed the lieutenant through the front doorway of the First Battalion's headquarters, which led directly into a large room. The only furniture consisted of a few wooden tables and chairs and two or three army cots. In a corner, tarpaulins covered cases of rations and ammunition.

The radio operators were using the largest of the wooden tables. Two officers, talking in urgent tones, sat at another, which was covered with papers and maps. There were windows on three sides of the room. They were covered with blankets and ponchos to keep the light from the candles and kerosene lamps from being seen by the enemy outside.

In the middle of the room stood a tall, calm man wearing the insignia of a major. He was giving orders rapidly and without hesitation.

Will knew this man was the battalion commander. He wore no helmet, and his brown hair gave off a few flashes of silver as the candlelight caught it. He had a strong face and was about thirty-five years old. Men addressed him as "Major Rankin."

As Will and the lieutenant crossed the room, Will heard machine gun fire in the distance and also small-arms fire, and a few minor explosions he supposed were grenades. The lieutenant went straight to Captain Colina, who was standing by the radios, and once again came right to the point. "Randolph's gun'll stop anything that moves up the north road."

"Good!" exclaimed the captain, hitting his open hand with his fist, "Joe Sumeric's gun is back in town, too, covering the east road. Whitey Woodall's gun survived the panzer attack okay—I got him on the road, but the gun never made it. A German artillery observer must have spotted him—the Krauts blew hell out of the gun and the truck. Crew jumped clear, though, thank God. They're filling in as an extra squad with Charlie Company."

The captain looked down at the floor. When he looked up again, he said, "That's it, Dave. We're down to two guns. And the fight's just started."

Will didn't have to strain his ears to hear the rapid bursts of machine gun fire and the almost constant blasts of grenades. The sounds of battle were getting closer. The German assault on the town of Damen was making progress.

The radios were busy. All the companies of the First Battalion were under severe attack. But Major Rankin did not look worried; Captain Colina seemed calm; and Lieutenant Sommers, apparently unconcerned by the conflict outside, had begun to study some maps on the table. Their composure was the only thing that kept Will from being frightened out of his skin.

Men began trickling into the command post, singly or in pairs. Captain Colina sent them over to where Will stood at one side of the room, and they waited with him to be told what to do.

They didn't talk very much, and when they did it was in low tones, but they made signs of recognition to each other and stayed together. They were a subdued group.

These men, like Will and the lieutenant, were so bundled up Will couldn't tell one from the other. They wore helmets and had their rifles slung on their shoulders. Their scarves were pulled around their necks and faces, sweaters bulged under their field jackets, and cartridge belts stretched around their waists. And they remained standing.

One of the men who had just come in found himself so close to Will he couldn't ignore him. The man's field jacket and trousers were ripped and dirty. His face was plump, and the scarf that encircled it made it look even rounder.

He said, "My name's Ceruti. Mike Ceruti. What outfit you from?"

"I'm Will Pope," said Will, sticking out his hand. "Antitank company." He'd had to think for a second before answering.

"What gun?" prompted Ceruti.

"Sergeant MacAllister's. We got knocked out." Will was trying very hard to sound tough, the way a hardened veteran ought to.

"The hell you say!" exclaimed Ceruti. "What happened?"

"During the panzer attack," replied Will. "Don't know whether it was a tank or artillery, but something blew the gun to hell." He thought that sounded tough enough. Real off-hand, like it happened every day. But he wasn't sure whether he'd gotten away with it or not.

"What happened to Mac?" asked Ceruti. "And Jonesie and the rest?"

"They were killed," answered Will. His pretended composure almost cracked that time.

"Oh, good God! Oh, no!" gasped Ceruti. "All of them?"

Will nodded. "The lieutenant brought me back in his Jeep after we got knocked out." Will thought the soldier was going to break down.

"What lieutenant? Sommers, Second Platoon?" asked Ceruti, obviously struggling to keep his voice even.

Will nodded, pointing to the lieutenant. He tried to say something, but his own voice broke. No sense trying to sound tough now. But he couldn't let himself cry, either.

"Yeah," said Ceruti. "That's Lieutenant Dave Sommers."

"Captain's named Colina," croaked Will. That was better. More natural, he thought.

"Right," replied Ceruti. "Captain Colina."

At this point, the captain and the lieutenant walked over to the group. The captain looked at them, recognized Ceruti, and asked, "What happened to your gun, Mike?"

"Our first shot knocked out a Tiger. Direct hit. So we started to move to our second position. My job was to carry the ammo. I'd already taken off with my arms full when I heard the 88s. Captain, they blew the gun and everybody with it to pieces. There wasn't nothing left... nothing... just pieces. It was the awfulest thing I'd ever seen..."

The captain nodded. Then he spoke to several of the other men. Their stories were similar—they were the survivors of knocked-out guns. They were dazed and bewildered; grateful they had been spared, sad that their friends had been killed, and apprehensive of their own immediate future.

There seemed to be about seven or eight of them, as close as Will could tell. Jim hadn't shown up among the survivors, nor had Gawalsky or Mills. But Will was too dazed to think about it. The captain faced them and said, "Okay, you guys are now the antitank mine platoon." He turned to Lieutenant Sommers and continued, "I'll coordinate Randolph's gun and Sumeric's. Dave, you take over the mine platoon."

"I ain't going in no mine platoon," said a man the captain had addressed as Gruber. "What do they take me for? That's the lousiest deal in the army…"

"Screw the mine platoon. I'm a gunner," said another man, named Sark.

"Not me," said a man they called Carrington. "I'll go to hell first."

Most of the others just cursed.

Ceruti asked, "Captain, what do you mean, we're the mine platoon? Where the hell is the mine platoon? They got bored and went home or something?"

The captain didn't answer him, but he gave him such a stern look that Ceruti shut his mouth for a minute, then whispered to the man next to him, "What happened to the mine platoon?"

One of the men standing behind him moved over and whispered, "Where the hell you been? Artillery caught them in a minefield. They was trapped. Nobody made it out. Not one."

"I didn't know," said Ceruti. "Mamma mia!"

"I'm damned if I want to be in any mine platoon," said a man they called Kilbride, who had taken longer than the rest to come to that conclusion.

Will didn't relish the idea either, but he kept his mouth shut.

Captain Colina and Lieutenant Sommers ignored the grumbling and continued to talk together, planning their movements. When they finished, Sommers turned to the men and said, "Let's go."

Silently they followed him through the doorway of the C.P. and into the night.

The lieutenant located the mines in a trailer half a block from the battalion command post. He spoke rapidly. "I don't have to tell you guys things're getting rough, and the Krauts have panzers, and we don't have much to fight panzers with. But we're going to try to stop them by laying antitank mines across the streets."

Will watched the other men start to unload the mines. They were exactly like the antitank mines the engineers had shown them in basic training—round, like large plates, each mine was about four inches thick and contained twelve pounds of TNT.

A man named Cohen turned to Sommers and asked, "Lieutenant, do we have fuses?" Until somebody screwed a fuse into the top of the mine, it was fairly harmless. After it was fused, it was lethal.

Sommers nodded. "I brought a couple of boxes from the C.P."

A few minutes later, with a mine under each arm, the men set off, hugging the sides of the buildings. It was pitch dark, but the flashes of explosion made momentary vision possible.

As they came around a corner, Will saw that part of the town was in flames. He saw figures running, silhouetted by the blaze, but he had no idea who they were, friend or foe.

"Halt! Password!" Even above the noise of battle, the words were sharp and clear. They made Will jump. Sommers gave the password and asked for the countersign, which was given. Then he went forward to talk to the soldier who had challenged him.

In a minute, he was back. "Okay," he said. "In front of this outpost, we lay some mines. We'll put three across the street up there by the corner, then three about twenty yards back from it. The outpost can protect the mines with their machine gun."

Will noticed that the road was icy. He could hear small-arms fire from all quarters of the town. Beside a building they grouped together in the shadows and prepared to lay their mines. Then one of the men took his two mines and strode out onto the road. His action was so unexpected, nobody had time to stop him.

He had just gotten to the middle of the street when he threw up his hands and went dancing backward, as if he were receiving a series of hard body punches from an invisible foe. When he hit the road, he skidded on the ice and lay still. His mines and his rifle clattered onto the street with him.

As the little crowd gazed in horror at the result of the enemy's quick reaction, the man named Cohen slid out onto the road, flat on his stomach, clutched the foot of the dead man, and dragged him back behind the building.

"Damn!" said Lieutenant Sommers. "What the hell made him do that? Those mines weren't even fused."

The man named Gruber said, with a hint of cynicism in his voice, "That dumb Kilbride. He could never think things out. He was showing off for you, Lieutenant."

The two mines lay not far from where Kilbride had dropped them. One had rolled a few feet to the side of the road; the other was lying in the middle of it. Cohen slid across the ice slowly and recovered the mine at the far side of the road. He picked up the one in the middle on his way back.

By now, Sommers was fusing a couple of mines. Cohen took them. Thinking better of it, he put one down and said, "I think this is the way we should do it."

He slid out onto the road again and gently left one of the mines about two feet from the far edge. He inched back and, without leaving the road, took another mine in both hands and slid to the middle of the road, where he laid it. He came back for his third mine, which he deposited two feet from the near side of the road.

Will wondered if any of the other men felt sorry for poor, dead Kilbride. If they did, there was no time to express their grief, no way to. Combat was like that. Without saying a word, they all moved back twenty yards, where Gruber positioned three mines; they took the remaining mines and went to the next street, where Ceruti laid them.

They kept this up all night, as both American and German infantry fought desperately for the town. The same buildings changed hands several times in several hours. Houses burned. Walls were crumbled by panzers, blown apart by shells, wrecked by grenades.

Will remembered hugging the side of a building as two German paratroopers ran down the street screaming at the top of their lungs and flinging grenades as they ran, until some unseen G.I. cut them down with an automatic rifle.

Only the fact that he had a job to do kept Will going. He was so tired he could hardly stand. Scared to death, he kept taking his turn sliding onto icy roads to leave mines strung across them. Occasionally he heard the sharp reports of antitank guns. Later they would run across Tiger tanks, blazing, lighting up the night like huge flares. One, he remembered, kept being racked by repeated explosions as its ammunition blew up.

Will was too exhausted to think about it, but when he crawled out into the middle of a street to lay a mine, he was conscious of bullets hitting all around him. Of Germans shooting at him in the dark.

Just before dawn, they were back at the battalion command post. Will was so tired he did not believe he could stay awake. His mind must have been asleep for the past hour, because he didn't remember returning to the C.P. But he was there.

Lieutenant Sommers looked at his men. There were now five of them: Will, Ceruti, Gruber, Cohen, and Sark. He said, "Kilbride got it at the first road, but what the hell happened to Carrington?" There was no answer.

"Where's Carrington?" Sommers repeated.

"Don't know. Don't think he got hit. At least I didn't see him get hit," replied Gruber.

"When's the last time you saw him?" persisted Sommers.

"I think it was that last Jerry tank, the one that kept blowing up."

Sommers was still standing. He said wearily, "Okay. I'll go find him."

Gruber said, "He was in my outfit. I'll go with you."

As Sommers and Gruber started out, Will noted that the sounds of shooting had died down. Apparently the Jerries had mounted their all-out attack and been unsuccessful, so he started to hope this meant the battle was over.

Then the four men sat down, took off their helmets, and began snoring, asleep before they hit the floor.

4

When Will opened his eyes, it was daylight. Gruber had returned sometime during the night and was sitting beside him, wide awake. The sounds of battle were close by.

"Did you find Carrington?" asked Will.

Gruber nodded. "By the side of the house near the Tiger tank that kept blowing up. He had a bullet right through his head. He never knew what hit him, and none of us saw him go down. Probably just a stray shot."

Will wondered about Gruber. He was a loner who didn't seem to want to have much to do with anybody else. Yet he'd volunteered to look for Carrington. "Were you a friend of Carrington's?" ventured Will.

"No," replied Gruber. "But he was in my platoon, like I told the lieutenant."

Will nodded.

"I was surprised the snotty, stuck-up little son-of-a-bitch even took the trouble to go look," continued Gruber. "Them officers don't give a good damn for us enlisted men, and that's for sure. That's why I went with him. To make sure he went."

Will glanced at Gruber. He was a nice-looking guy. Average in every way. But Gruber's cynicism made him nervous. It was like sitting next to somebody with a bad cold—he was afraid he might catch it.

Will tried to keep his voice steady as he asked, "How's it going out there?" jerking his thumb toward the street.

"Rough," replied Gruber. "But some guys from the knocked-out guns've come back in. They sent them to the rifle companies. They need everybody they can get."

"Any of the new guys in the group they sent to the rifle companies?" asked Will. "A guy named Mahoney, maybe?"

"I don't know," replied Gruber, shaking his head. "Who cares, anyway? We're all gonna die here before long, so what difference does it make?"

Will sighed. If some of the others had made it, maybe Jim did, too. He brightened. "Maybe they'll put us in a rifle company. Then we'll be out of this damned mine platoon. Do you think they will?"

"No chance," replied Gruber. "Now that they got us in the mine platoon, you can bet your sweet ass they're gonna keep us here."

Will didn't really want to be in the mine platoon, and he knew nobody else did, either. He supposed it was because it was so dangerous, working with high explosives under enemy fire. But could it be any worse than a rifle company? More hazardous than the antitank guns? The company lost seven of their nine guns in a few minutes yesterday afternoon.

Then he remembered that the mine platoon had been completely wiped out. What had the man said? Artillery caught them in a minefield. What a sickening thought. It was no wonder nobody wanted to be in the mine platoon. And he was in it.

He turned to Gruber again and said, "If we stay in the mine platoon, what'll we be doing if we ever get out of here?"

"I'll give it to you straight," replied Gruber, with a hint of a sneer. "We'll clear mines in front of our attacks, so our armor can come through. Or, if we retreat, we'll stay behind and lay mines to slow up the Jerry tanks. That's the army. They'll screw you any way they can, okay?"

Will nodded. He felt so depressed, he couldn't trust himself to speak. It was all he could do to keep from bursting into tears. Now that he was in the mine platoon, he figured he didn't have a chance. In his despair, he kept asking himself, "Why me? Why me? Why me?"

Above the other sounds, a sudden, dry *crack!* pierced Will's eardrums. He jumped even though he was sitting down. That was very close. He threw himself on the floor of the command post.

There was smoke in the room—plaster was falling all around him and he saw everybody else had fallen flat on the floor, too.

Captain Colina was the first on his feet. "What the hell was that?"

"An 88—and it's close!" somebody yelled.

Several G.I.'s and an officer went out the side doorway to look. A sergeant grabbed a light .30-caliber machine gun, put it on a table by an open window, and stood ready to do battle for the C.P. Two other men were putting a bazooka together.

Will's heart sank. Butterflies fluttered in his stomach, and he had no idea what he should do. Then he heard the distinctive squeaking of a panzer's treads.

The G.I. at the radio stood up and shouted to the major, "A Tiger got past Able Company! They couldn't stop it! It's headed this way!"

Major Rankin turned to the men who were putting together the bazooka and said, calmly, "Hurry up. It's getting close."

By then, one of the men had already inserted a bazooka rocket and was attaching the wires to the triggering mechanism. The light machine gun began firing fast, evenly spaced shots one after the other as the spent brass shells tinkled onto the stone floor.

The squeaking and rattling of the tank stopped. Although Will could not see it, his one day's experience in the line told him that the barrel of the tank's 88 must now be turning toward the machine gun, which he was sure the tank had spotted.

There were shorter intervals between the machine gun's bursts as it jumped up and down on the wooden table.

Then the machine gunner, as if by instinct, threw himself onto the floor. So did everybody else.

The *crack!* made Will's ears ring. It felt as though somebody had hit him hard. But the armor-piercing shell had passed completely through the building without exploding. Had it been high-explosive, it would have killed everybody in the C.P. In the excitement of battle, the German loader had, somehow, reached into the wrong ammunition compartment, and the command post was spared by a stroke of pure dumb luck.

The machine gunner was immediately back at his gun. It jumped around on the table once more, filling the C.P. with its chattering and its smoke. Will saw the two men with the bazooka run quickly out the side doorway.

The tank rumbled toward the command post. Its next shot would blow them all to bits.

Will heard the swish of the bazooka rocket leaving its tube. There was a dull, hollow explosion.

"They got the son-of-a-bitch," said the machine gunner.

Major Rankin was already on the radio talking to Able Company. The conversation was short. He nodded once or twice and called to a lieutenant, "Able doesn't have any bazookas left. Send them a couple, right now!"

He turned to Colina. "That Tiger went right through the mines. Wilkes up at Able thinks it didn't touch them."

"Then we've got to lay down more mines," said Colina.

"In the middle of the day?" said Gruber out loud to nobody in particular. "Jerry'll cut us to pieces. What is this? Some kind of dirty joke or something? I can't believe it. Even the stupid army wouldn't—"

Colina turned to Lieutenant Sommers, standing beside him, and said, "Dave, I want you to lay more mines in all the streets so the Tigers can't thread their way through them."

"Okay, Captain," replied Sommers. He turned, and there was authority in his voice as he called to his men, "Let's go."

The five of them got to their feet and followed the lieutenant out of the C.P. In the street, not thirty yards away, sat the Tiger tank, smoking and black. Will looked the other way.

There were bodies everywhere; Gruber turned to Will and said, "Damn glad it's winter. That's the only good thing about this place. If it was warm weather, this town'd be stinking to hell by now from all the dead stuff lying around."

When they arrived back at the trailer, Sommers told them, "Okay, since it's daylight, we'll stay behind buildings, or anything else that'll protect us, and we'll just slide the mines onto the roads from there. I don't want you to expose yourselves to enemy fire. And remember, after the mines are fused, be real easy with them."

The men of the new mine platoon learned to gauge the distance a mine would slide on an icy road. Before the day was over, they had gotten expert at it. No panzer could thread its way through the mines that now stretched irregularly across the main roads of Damen.

The operation had taken all morning and most of the afternoon, and Will realized, through the numbness of exhaustion, that it was beginning to get dark again.

A light wind began to blow. It seemed to freeze everything it touched. Exhausted, cold, and scared, Will wondered how long he could keep it up. How long he could endure it.

Will did not know how long he had slept when he felt someone kicking the soles of his boots—not hard, but not gently, either. He got to his feet. Sommers was rousing them all.

Will noticed that there were only three or four people in the C.P..

"Where is everybody?" asked Gruber. "They all done took off and left us here to die, I'll bet. We been deserted, right?"

"Everybody's out fighting Jerries," replied Sommers. "They're all over town, and we're going out to protect our mines."

The men of the mine platoon crouched low and darted from wall to wall as they made their way through the debris-filled streets of Damen. Buildings blazing out of control, rifles and machine guns crackling, and exploding grenades emphasized the desperation of the struggle. The fighting in the town of Damen was war at its most vicious and most merciless. No prisoners were taken by either side. The thought of giving himself up to the enemy to save his life never occurred to either German or American. When they met, they fought to the death—it was that simple. If a man was wounded on ground his own people held, he was looked after. If not, he died.

It was freezing cold. *Zing!* A bullet hit the wall above Will's head, and a chunk of the building rocketed off his helmet. He hit the ground, his heart pounding in his throat. Somebody had shot at him, and he hadn't the slightest idea where the shot came from. The whole town was full of firing.

Up ahead, Will saw Sommers duck into the doorway of a small house. In front of him, Ceruti scrambled to his feet and headed for the same doorway. Will almost ran over him on his way in.

For a moment or two, nobody said anything. Everybody just stood breathing hard and trying to size up the situation.

The house they were in had only two windows facing the street. Standing well to the side of one of them, Will peered out. He could see the mines lying on the street where they had left them. Gruber was at the other window, well back in the shadows. The lieutenant and Cohen were checking the room, and they both seemed uneasy.

Lieutenant Sommers said, "They told me there'd be some guys from Charlie Company here. Hope we're in the right place."

"We'll have to go through this whole house, Lieutenant," said Cohen. "Can't take any chances."

Sommers nodded wearily and replied, "Yeah. I know."

As Will turned his attention to the road, he became aware of a slight movement. He thought he saw a silhouette of something moving onto the road toward the first row of mines. It could be a man, but Will wasn't sure. The only light came from the flames of the burning town.

Without turning, Will whispered, "Lieutenant! I think I see a Jerry. What'll I do?"

Sommers looked over, shrugged his shoulders, and said, "Oh? Shoot him."

Will sighted down the barrel of his M-1 rifle until he thought he saw a movement on the road again. He squeezed the trigger. His rifle jarred against his shoulder. The noise of its report startled him. He had hit something. The figure involuntarily raised himself in pain. It was a man! Will squeezed the trigger again, and the German jerked. Then he lay absolutely still.

"Get him?" asked Sommers.

Will said, "Yeah! I got him."

"Good work," said Sommers.

Even as cold and numb as Will was, he realized he had killed a man. Actually shot a man to death. But the dead man was a German, and he was supposed to shoot Germans; that's why he was here. Lieutenant Sommers had said, "Good work." Will knew he should be proud of himself for having killed an enemy. But he was disturbed by the thought that he'd killed a man, and even more disturbed because it had been so easy. All he'd done was pull the trigger a couple of times.

As he thought about it, he kept his eyes on the road he was guarding. The flickering light had an almost hypnotic effect on him. Suddenly he saw what looked like shadows darting in and out of the doorways of buildings, but coming closer with every dash they made. He called softly, "Hey, Lieutenant, somebody's coming down the road, and I don't know who they are."

"Could be a patrol coming in, but I doubt it," replied Sommers "If they're coming from that direction, they've got to be Krauts."

When Will got another look at one of the figures, he saw the man was wearing a white parka. Will began to turn his head to say, "They are Jerries!" But before he could move, Ceruti and Gruber began shooting. Each fired the eight bullets in his clip so fast Will heard the pinging of the metal clips ejecting from the M-1 rifles almost before the firing stopped. In a fraction of a second, fresh clips were jammed into the breeches, and eight more shots were fired.

They heard shots from the building across the street.

"Who's over there?" Will yelled.

"What's left of another squad from Charlie Company!" the lieutenant yelled back.

From the other side of the wall behind them, they heard the rapid fire of an automatic weapon. It chattered twice in two long bursts, then fired three single shots.

Good Lord! thought Will. Somebody's fighting right here in this house!

The lieutenant and Cohen already had their rifles pointed at the door connecting to the next room. A voice from the other side of the door yelled, "Don't shoot! We're G.I.'s!"

Will heard the words clearly and realized the firing in the street had stopped. As the men of the platoon watched, silent and still, the door swung open, and two grimy, well-bundled-up soldiers stepped cautiously into the room.

"We heard you guys when you come in," said the first man. "But we was waiting out them bastards. We know'd they was there. They come in through the roof the last time the Krauts tried to rush this place. They figured to hide and shoot us in the back with their burp guns while we was busy with them bastards you just drove off. But we know how to play that game, too—as soon as they made their move, *Zap!* We got the sons-of-bitches good. Ain't no more in here as far as we know."

Back at the window, Will saw that the firing from both sides of the street had driven the Jerries back. At least, he could not see any more movement, and there were several bodies huddled beside doorways.

By now, both of the grimy G.I.'s were sitting beside Sommers and Cohen, and all four were digging into cold K ration meat cans.

The G.I. sitting next to Sommers looked up at Will and said, "Hey! You want to use my grease gun? Might be better for covering that minefield. You might want to spray a little."

Will thought, What the hell's a grease gun? Aloud, he said, "I don't think I've ever used one."

The G.I. got up and walked over to Will. In his hand was a short, all-metal gun. Will saw it really did look like a grease gun, the kind they use in a garage to grease automobiles. The G.I. showed Will how to insert the clip full of .45 slugs, how to pull the bolt to half cock and ready, and how to flip the safety catch.

"You gotta watch it climbing. It's just a cheap, lightweight Tommy gun," said the G.I. "Somebody told me they costs about thirty bucks apiece to make. Not bad for laying out a lot of lead— they'll really tear up anything they hit, but they're not accurate at any distance of more than five yards or so."

"Thanks," said Will. He jammed the heavy clip home, pulled back the bolt, let it slide, clicked off the safety, and was ready for business. Now, where the hell were those Jerries?

None came, but it was easy to imagine them. The shadows cast by the flames conjured up imaginary storm troopers all over the road. Finally he could stand it no longer. Will decided to let loose a couple of bursts at the shadows, just to see how his new grease gun would fire. He squeezed the trigger. The gun went off loudly and kept firing steadily as long as his finger pressed the trigger.

The gun jumped in his hand like something alive. He squeezed off several bursts, and each time he finished one, the muzzle of the weapon was pointed at the sky. So that's what he meant by climbing, thought Will.

He let off another burst. It was a short one, and after the last shot, the bolt stayed back. His clip was empty.

Will had not realized it, but his firing had brought everybody to the window to see what was happening. The G.I. looked at him as if to say, "What the hell was that?"

Will said, "I thought I saw Jerries coming up in the shadows."

Everybody continued staring at the road. Nobody moved. Will took out the empty clip, turned to the G.I. and asked, "Do we have any more clips for the grease gun?"

"Sure," answered the soldier. "In the other back room, under the tarp."

Will went into the next room. The roof had burned off, the windows were open, and the fires in the town lighted his surroundings. He began looking for the tarp. Then he stopped, and a sudden lump rose in his throat. Along one side of the room, laid out in a straight row, were the bodies of ten or twelve G.I.'s. They were covered with ponchos, blankets, or field jackets, but an occasional foot or arm stuck out.

Will gave a convulsive shiver that was so hard his whole body jerked; then he gritted his teeth and turned to look for the clips for his grease gun. He quickly found the open metal container of Tommy gun ammunition. He took three clips, shoving one into the gun and the other two into his field jacket pocket. When he returned to the front room, he saw that Cohen had taken his place by the window, so he sat on the floor with Lieutenant Sommers and the two G.I.'s.

Sommers turned to one of them and said, "Where the hell's the heavy attack we came to help you fight off?"

"Aw, shucks, it was all over before you got here," replied the man. "Them Krauts you shot was just a little patrol activity, is all. Hear the firing now? It's over on the other side of town, where Able's holding. Maybe the Jerries was just probing to see if they could come through us, and seeing as how they couldn't, now they's probing someplace else."

One of the men at the window yelled, "Halt!"

A voice outside gave the password. Then, without waiting for the countersign, a G.I. came through the doorway.

"You guys the mine platoon?"

"Except for two guys from Charlie Company," replied Sommers.

"Okay," said the newcomer. "I got to bring you back to headquarters. The Jerries got too damn close. Everybody's out fighting Krauts, so you're coming back to guard the C.P." Then he saw the bar painted on Sommers' helmet and finished his sentence, "Uh, sir."

Sommers nodded.

Without realizing it, Will had focused his attention on the messenger from the battalion. His mind was digesting the fact they'd have to make it back to the C.P. through the hell of this flaming town, when, suddenly, without warning, the street outside came alive with shouts and shots that were so close they seemed to be inside the house. The Germans had crept up and were attacking them. The men at the windows were firing as fast as they could pull their triggers.

Behind them in the shadows, Sommers and Will, together with the messenger and the two G.I.'s, spun around as one man, their weapons pointing toward the fighting, which was now desperate. A German grenade flew in through the window. Will could only gape at it, paralyzed by the knowledge that it would blow him to pieces in the next second.

With one quick motion, Phil Cohen scooped up the explosive and flung it out the window. As it blew up in the street, the front door banged open, kicked in by a German storm trooper who stood there with a blazing machine pistol jumping in his hands.

Startled into action, Will whipped his grease gun's short barrel in the direction of the German and squeezed the trigger. The impact of the heavy slugs lifted the German off his feet and hurled him through the doorway into the night. The door swung back and forth until Phil Cohen leaped forward to slam it shut and secure the bolt.

Behind him, Will heard a groan. The German's shooting into the darkness of the room had done its damage. One of the G.I.'s lay on his back, writhing in pain. Beside him lay the crumpled body of the messenger from Battalion. Will was both sick and scared and felt his knees start to shake. The sound of voices brought him back to the action. Cohen said, urgently, "I'm taking this guy and covering the back so they don't come in at us through the roof. I'll yell if we need help."

"Go. Go quick!" replied Sommers just as urgently.

Gruber was pitching hand grenades into the street as Sommers moved up behind him, firing rapidly at the flashes in the dark.

Will knelt beside Ceruti and let loose a burst from his grease gun. German bullets buzzed in through the windows and imbedded themselves in the wall behind him.

"They're clearing our mines!" yelled Gruber. Sommers shot off a full clip of ammunition in the direction of the minefield. As he ducked back into the shadows to reload, Will raised up and fired at the shadows darting in and out around the mines. When his grease gun stopped jumping in his hands—its bolt back, chamber empty—he heard the sound of a Tiger tank coming down the street. In another few seconds it was so close he could see it distinctly, pressing on toward them, menacing and deadly. It stopped to wait for the German infantrymen to remove the mines. Gruber stood up and hurled a grenade with all his strength at the minefield.

The chain reaction of mines blowing up all over the street was more awesome than anything Will had ever seen before. Every living thing in the immediate area of the blasts was blown to pieces. The concussion killed the rest. The sounds of the Tiger reversing gears and revving its motors came clearly through the night as the panzer backed away as fast as it could move.

There was still firing in the distance, and the town still burned. But here, in their little war, the crackle of small-arms fire and the explosions of grenades and mines had stopped just as suddenly as they had started; the G.I.'s still owned the street. The German attack had failed. The German tank had not gotten through.

Will was breathing hard. He felt himself trembling inside and hoped it didn't show. Phil Cohen came back with the G.I. from Charlie Company. "House is still secure," he reported. The G.I. nodded. He walked over to his friend, who lay on the floor shaking and gasping and whimpering slightly. Cohen put a tarp over the dead messenger. He lifted the man's shoulders and dragged him to the other room.

Now the G.I. held his friend's head in his lap and stroked his face gently. At the same time, he looked at Sommers and shook his head. He looked so very sad.

"Dead Jerries all over the place," said Gruber, who'd continued looking out the window. "They must've sent a battalion at us."

"A reinforced squad, anyway," said Phil, who had just returned.

"We got orders to go back and guard the C.P.," said Sommers. "They wouldn't have sent for us unless they needed us."

"No, sir," replied Phil. "We can't leave the C.P. undefended, but we can't leave this place undefended, either. For all we know, the Krauts might've taken the house across the street in that last fling. And there's just one guy left here if we pull out."

"Not only that, but we had to explode the mines to stop the Tiger and throw back their attack," said Sommers. "So we've got to get some more mines laid across the road, or any damn panzer that feels like it can come rolling down it like it was Main Street."

They were silent for a minute. For two minutes. For three. "Sir, may I make a suggestion?" asked Phil.

"Hell, yes," replied Sommers. "Nothing's ever stopped you before."

"We'll split up. You take the men back to the C.P. and tell Colina what's up. I'll stay here with a couple of guys and hold until you can send us some mines, somehow." Phil spoke fast and to the point. Will found himself nodding his head.

He heard a sound behind him. Turning, he saw the Charlie Company G.I. stand up after gently placing the head of his comrade on his heavy woolen scarf. The man lay motionless. In a moment, Will knew, somebody would drag him into the other room, where he would lie with the others.

"I guess I'm the only guy left from my squad now," said the other G.I. matter-of-factly. "I wonder if anybody's still over there." He motioned to the house across the street. He whistled softly. There was no answering whistle. He whistled again. Silence from the house. The man shrugged his shoulders. Just then, a faint wheeze floated across the open space.

The man jumped to the window. Hoarsely, he whispered, "Who's there?"

There was silence. Finally the voice came slowly, "Nobody …nobody…we…we're all killed…all killed." And the voice floated off into the night. But not before it had sent a cold shiver down Will's spine.

The voice had seemed so unreal, Will was wondering if he was still in the town of Damen, still fighting Germans, or if it was he who had floated off and was now in some Valhalla of disembodied spirits. But not for long. The sudden burst of a machine gun shattered the silence and sent everybody to the floor.

"Oh, my God!" said Gruber. Will looked at him, not understanding. Then he understood. He heard the squeaking of tank treads, the sound of a tank's motors, the popping of the rifles of the accompanying German infantry.

Instead of being frozen with fear, Will was goaded into action. He ran, crouching, into the other room, quickly dug into the ammunition box, and this time, after reloading his gun, he took as many sticks of Tommy gun ammo as he could stuff into his pockets. He dashed back into the main room. It had taken him only a second or two.

The panzer was close. The men at the windows were firing at the German infantry. The tank's turret was turning toward the windows of their house. This was it!

Will stood up and poured an entire clip of .45 slugs at the tank's turret. It was a futile effort. The turret continued turning toward them. The minute it stopped turning, it would fire. The 88 would blow them all to pieces. The panzer's barrel now pointed directly at the house.

The turret stopped turning.

There was a *flash!* A clap of pure noise—short, sharp. A ball of fire careened off the turret and spun into a building down the street. Will realized the Tiger tank had not fired! It had been fired on! His eyes stayed glued to the turret with its 88 pointed at him. He saw the slightest movement of the gun's barrel as the gunner started to swing it to meet the attack.

Will barely saw the flash of the antitank shell as it zipped low; like a fiery bowling ball, whipped down the street with immense force. It disappeared underneath the Tiger, and, at the same moment, there was an explosion from within the tank. The shell had been a lucky shot that had penetrated the panzer's underside! A split second after the explosion, the Tiger burst into flames.

Spontaneously, Will let out a loud cheer. And as he did, the others did, too.

Just as spontaneously, the cheer froze on Will's lips. Suddenly he felt clammy cold and nauseated. The others, too, fell silent, standing in horror, mute. Like everybody who has ever heard the screams of men trapped inside a burning tank, they would never forget them as long as they lived.

Will tried to put his hands over his ears, but it didn't shut them out. He was shaking. From the blazing Tiger came another sound, somebody hammering on the metal from within. The shrieks reached a crescendo, then they became weaker. A series of explosions inside the panzer mercifully ended them forever.

Will leaned against the wall for support. He realized he had not fainted. "Thank God. Thank God!"

Somebody was trying to force the door. "Open up!" shouted a distinctively American voice. "It's me! Colina!"

Cohen shot back the bolt, and the captain barged in. "Let's go!" he shouted. "We can't hold here any longer. Heard you blow your mines. We're pulling back and shortening our lines. Let's go! This burning Tiger'll hold the bastards back until we get clear. Come on!"

As the men left the house, Cohen and the Charlie Company G.I. dashed across the street to the other building. Before the Tiger blocked the street, there hadn't been any way to get across without coming under deadly German fire.

They quickly rejoined the rest of the men. Will heard the G.I. say hoarsely to Phil, "They were sure dead, all right. The guy what answered us must've been Hubert, the one lying by the window there with his arm blown off."

As they trotted back, staying as close as possible to the sides of the buildings, in the shadows, they saw no sign of the antitank gun that had knocked out the panzer. It had gone as if it had never been there, pulled out by its crew.

There were exchanges of passwords and countersigns as the little group came in. Now protected by the wall of a shattered building, the men heaved as their breath came in deep gulps.

Colina said to Sommers, "Okay, Dave. Let's bring the mine platoon back to protect the C.P. Krauts are all over the place. The Charlie Company guys'll join what's left of this squad here."

"There's only one," replied Sommers. Colina was silent. "Battalion messenger got it, too," said Sommers.

Colina nodded. "Okay, then, let's go," he said, his voice quieter now, more subdued.

As they started back, Will held onto the grease gun and slung his M-1 rifle on his shoulder. There was a jauntiness to his step that hadn't been there before, and a defiant look in his eye. Had he been alone, he would have run away at the first shot, but under the eyes of the men with him, with their support and their approval, he had fought the enemy. He had killed the enemy. He had survived to fight again. He was a veteran now, a veteran who knew he could beat the men he fought against. In that short battle for a small street in an obscure town, he had become the kind of soldier who wins wars.

5

It was a quiet winter evening at the governor's mansion. Sitting at one end of the polished mahogany table, George Pope and his wife had finished their dinner. The maid had cleared the table several minutes ago, but the governor made no move to get up. Instead, he leaned back in his chair and lit a cigar, then reached out and patted Cecily's hand.

She looked up and smiled at him. Her face was radiant. At forty-three, Cecily Devereaux Pope was a lovely lady. Her blondish-brown hair was cut short around her oval face so that her large brown eyes and turned-up nose showed to their best advantage, but it was her delicate coloring that gave her the beauty for which she was so renowned.

"I'd like to chat about Will for a minute," said the governor.

Cecily looked startled. "Will?" she asked. For all her loveliness and charm, Mrs. George Pope had never been known for being particularly quick-witted, but that was not why George had married her.

"Yes. Will," replied her husband. "He's a soldier in Europe, and there's a war going on there…"

"Are you making fun of me, George Pope? Of course I know our son is in Europe, and I know there's a war on. Everybody knows that. But what do you want to talk about?"

George Pope took a long puff on his cigar and blew out the smoke before he replied. "Cecily, I want to get him out of there."

Cecily took in her breath, preparing to tell her husband what she thought of that, but he held up his hand to forestall her and continued, "I know, dear. I know. He's in a nice regimental headquarters, just as he told us. He's perfectly safe. But I'm still uneasy, and besides—"

"Uneasy! You're worried sick, that's what you are! So that's your problem! You're upset about Will. That's why you don't sleep. That's why you pace the floor and can't concentrate. I should have guessed! You've been like this ever since Will went overseas. Why, George?"

The governor was taken aback at his usually docile wife's outburst. Then he realized his own worry and unusual behavior must be having its effect on Cecily, too. He'd have to calm her down before he could talk to her about what was on his mind.

He smiled his most confidence-winning smile and said, "Only because he's so young, darling. Remember, Will's only eighteen. He'd be a freshman in college right now if he hadn't been drafted. Just a freshman. You and I didn't go to Europe until we were out of college and married and your father gave us the trip for our honeymoon."

Cecily cocked her head. "Yes. That's right," she replied, and her husband knew she was trying to think out what he'd just told her. The innocent, puzzled expression made her damned attractive, he thought.

Finally she said, "Just how do you intend to get Will 'out of there,' as you put it, George?"

George Pope caught the note of suspicion in her voice. Cecily never trusted cleverness, and she disapproved of conniving.

He leaned forward and said, "Look, Ceci, dear, you remember, for a while, when Will was growing up, how he used to faint? And I'll bet you anything you want to, that he never mentioned that to the army doctors when he went in. Want to bet?"

The puzzled expression returned to Cecily's face, remained for a minute, then changed to understanding. "You mean you want to tell the army Will's a fainter so they'll discharge him. Is that it?"

The governor nodded.

"George, that's the worst idea I've ever heard. Besides, won't Will be just embarrassed to death? Imagine! For a thing like that to happen to a young boy like Will! Discharged from the army for fainting! He'd never live it down."

Pope was disturbed. He desperately wanted his wife to agree that he was doing the right thing—after all, Will was her son, too. But he didn't want to have to point out that Will was in terrible danger of getting killed unless they did something about it fast.

"Don't you want him home with us, Ceci? We missed so much of his growing up, didn't we? I was too busy building a political base. You were busy helping me. We left him alone too much…"

"He stayed with Mother…"

"Sure. But that's not the same thing. He's still a boy now. He'll be a man in a few years. He'll go to college. He'll leave home, get married. Don't you want to have him for as long as you can? Don't you want to have him home now? Before he goes away to college? Time's running out, darling. Suppose the war lasts a couple more years…"

Cecily Pope's mind worked slowly, but not that slowly. After all, she loved her son, too, and she felt just as guilty as her husband for having left him alone so much. She began to falter, and George Pope saw it.

He said, "Look, darling, if he's a fainter, it's not fair to the army not to tell them. Why, he could hurt his whole outfit. He's just a small link, but every one is needed. If important orders come to him to pass on and he has a fainting spell, the plans don't get delivered, or the troops don't get positioned properly, or whatever."

"I know!" exclaimed Cecily unexpectedly. "You're worried because of poor Jack Reynolds! That's it!" She shook her head. "What a dreadful thing. Such a fine boy… But remember, dear, Jack was in the front lines, the foxholes, or whatever you call them. Will's in a nice headquarters, and there's a big difference."

With a start, George Pope suddenly understood why his wife was so unconcerned about Will when she should have been worried to death, just as he was. He'd been married to her for twenty-three years, and he knew how her mind worked. "A nice headquarters"— that's what she'd said. And that's what she'd kept saying ever since they received that letter from Will. Of course!

As governor, he'd visited the National Guard units regularly before the war, and he usually took Cecily with him. Naturally, she'd remember those visits to their friend Colonel Tom Jacobs at his regimental headquarters! A beautiful white building, immaculately clean, filled with men in perfectly pressed uniforms, polite and respectful, neat and unhurried. And the building had plenty of space. It was a comfortable, nice place. As far as Cecily was concerned, a regimental headquarters is a regimental headquarters, and her son was privileged to be in one. She'd never dream that there was no resemblance between that gleaming white building and a dugout or bomb-shattered farmhouse close to the front, nor could she know that, although the antitank company was a part of regimental headquarters, they fought in the line with the combat troops except when they were out in front of those troops standing up to panzer attacks, laying mines…

No. To Cecily a regimental headquarters would always be a nice, white building, and that's where Will was, neatly uniformed and sitting at a desk.

On the other hand, I'll bet she misses him, he thought. "You mean you don't want your son home with us?" he asked aloud.

"Of course I do! You know I do!"

"Good," replied George Pope. "Because I've already called the White House, and they put me onto a man in the War Department who's going to arrange to have Will sent home for a thorough physical examination to see if he's fit to be a soldier. If he is, then fine, but if not, he'll be discharged, stay home with us until next fall, when his college term starts…"

Cecily's eyes opened wide. "You mean you've already done all that?" she asked.

George Pope nodded.

"Well, I suppose you know what's best." She sighed. "Still, I hope it won't embarrass Will."

Reassured, the governor smiled and patted his wife's hand once again.

★

Inside the C.P., the candles and kerosene lamps had been extinguished; the windows were wide open, and Will could see every detail in the room by the light of the flames that were now destroying a large part of the town.

Except for the constant repetition of instructions by the man talking on the radio, the C.P. was quiet. Major Rankin was resting on a cot in the corner.

Captain Colina told Sommers, "Better put your men two on and two off," which meant that each man would stand guard two hours, rest two hours, then go back on guard two hours.

After assigning the men, Sommers returned to Captain Colina. "Thanks for saving our lives, Captain. We were goners.

"We knew you were in trouble when you blew the mines," replied Colina. "So I located Joe Sumeric and got him over there as quick as I could. He sure took care of that Tiger."

But Sommers was looking beyond the captain at a man lying on a pile of old blankets on the floor of the C.P. He gestured toward the man. "That's Danny Sark," he said. "How long's he been here?" Sommers' voice was sharp. Sark's presence in the C.P. upset him. In the excitement of battle, he'd never missed him, and he knew he should have. Sark was one of his men, his responsibility.

Colina looked at the floor before he replied. "Dave, we've got a problem on our hands. Sark refuses to leave the C.P. I told him to move his ass out of here or I'd court-martial him till hell won't have it, and he said, 'Fine.' That would suit him just fine, he said, because in the stockade nobody'd be shooting at him anymore, and he'd like that. Then, Dave, I did something I've never done before. I pulled my .45 on him and told him if he didn't get going, I'd blow his head off. You know what? He just shrugged and said, 'Fine.' Said he didn't care.

"So Dave, I'm afraid we've got a sick man on our hands, and, dammit, we've never had this kind of crap in the outfit before! Never!"

Like everybody else in the platoon, Will overheard the conversation. At first he was embarrassed for Sark; at the same time, he felt superior to him. Then he began to feel contempt, almost loathing. That son-of-a-bitch, he thought. Hell, I am fighting my guts out, and this prick just lies here safe and sound, no good to anybody.

But as he thought about it a little more, Will was shocked by the realization that he would be very happy to do the same thing himself, to lie down on a pile of old blankets and turn the war off, shut it out, go to sleep. The temptation was almost too much for him to bear.

Sommers walked over to Sark. "Get up," he said. Sark rose to his feet. His helmet was off, and his blond hair fell onto his forehead. His freckled face with its turned-up nose looked frightened and defiant at the same time.

"What's all this about?" asked the lieutenant. "What's all this the captain's been telling me?"

"Yes, sir," replied Sark. "I ain't going to fight no more. I done my fighting on the ridge against them Tigers. We lost our gun. Everybody got killed but me. Then I laid mines on the streets, and the Krauts was shooting at me all the time.

"Now I've had enough. Can't take no more. I don't care if you shoot me or put me in the stockade. There ain't nothing you can do to me, Lieutenant, that's worse than me going out there again." He gestured toward the street.

Sommers looked at him in silence. Finally he said, "You know, you're not off your rocker, are you, Sark? You're completely rational. You've thought it all out, and you just refuse to fight. That's right, isn't it?"

Sark nodded.

Sommers stood rigid before the man who had had all he could take. Then the lieutenant seemed to relax. "Okay, Danny," he said. "I understand. It's been rough. And you know, Danny, we all feel like you do. Surprised? You shouldn't be. We'd all like to lie down and quit. Do you know why we don't? Because our friends are counting on us, that's why.

"You're only thinking of yourself, Danny. But you're not the only guy here, you know. What do you suppose would happen if we all lay down and gave it up, or if we all went off and just left you here? We haven't. We won't, either. You're one of us, and we'll all stand or fall together. We're fighting for each other. We're fighting for our friends. Can't you see that? We need you, Danny. We won't let you down. Are you going to let us down? Are you?"

The lieutenant's expression was friendly as he looked into Sark's eyes for a short moment before he turned and walked back to where Colina stood waiting for him. "Sark'll be all right," he said. "He was just exhausted, poor guy." His left eyelid closed for a moment in a guarded wink.

Colina nodded.

"How're we doing otherwise?" asked Sommers.

"So far we're holding the bastards," replied the captain. "But they're still fighting all over town. It looks like we've taken on two regiments of Waffen SS, the Tenth SS Panzer Division, and a couple of hundred Jerry paratroopers all at once. We're outnumbered about four to one, as close as anybody can figure."

Sommers nodded without smiling.

"Anyway, we've got everybody in the line, including the proverbial cooks, bakers, and company clerks. We're hanging on by the fingernail of our little finger."

During the conversation between Colina and Sommers, Dan Sark had remained standing where Sommers left him. He hadn't moved. Now he shook himself slightly and walked over to the two officers. He said, "Sir."

Sommers and Colina turned and looked at him without speaking. "Sir," began Dan Sark again, "I—I been thinking about what you said, and I'm sorry. I'm sorry I let everybody down like I done. It won't happen no more, sir."

Sommers held out his hand and shook Sark's. "As far as I'm concerned, it never happened, Danny," he said. Colina slapped Danny on the back. His relief was written on his face.

✪

Will did not even remember having gone to sleep when he was awakened with the usual taps on the soles of his boots.

"You take the window on the left," said Sommers.

Will began to pay attention to the sounds outside and inside the command post. Outside, above the popping of small-arms fire, he heard two sharp reports of an antitank gun. He heard shouting and machine gun fire and the flat explosions of Jerry grenades. He heard the other antitank gun. It shot only once, then its crew pulled it out of position before the enemy could return its fire.

In the eerie glow, men were fighting for their lives and were dying close to where Will stood. Inside, the radioman turned to Major Rankin and said, "The mines are making the Jerry tanks stop to remove them. That's when the guns and bazookas knock them off."

Major Rankin turned to Captain Colina and said, "Jack, I want to send one of your trucks back to pick up a trailerload of ammunition. One of your low-slung ton-and-a-half's has a better chance of getting through than one of our big brutes."

"Sure," said the captain. "Let's get Jack Diamond. He's the mine platoon's driver—only one left now."

Colina turned to one of the radiomen. He didn't have to say anything. The man nodded as he began asking a line company to send back Jack Diamond.

The captain grunted "Okay, Ceruti, you ride shotgun for Jack. The roads are covered by 88s, so you've got to get back before morning light. Regiment'll have the trailer ready for you, loaded with ammunition. Don't bring back any rations. Just ammunition."

A few minutes later, a hatchet-faced G.I., out of breath, entered the C.P. His left hand was bandaged. Will knew he must be Jack Diamond.

After Captain Colina gave him his instructions, Diamond said, "I lost my trailer, so I loaded my truck with mines. I think Murphy's truck should be okay, though. Where's Murphy?"

"Gone. Got it fighting with Charlie Company last night," said the captain.

Diamond's face never changed expression, but he took a long time before he answered. Finally he said, "Okay, I'll take his truck."

Just before they left, Major Rankin told Colina, "When they get back, have Diamond bring around his truck so we can get at his mines if we need them."

Will turned his attention to the street outside.

He realized immediately, more by instinct than anything else, that something was there that hadn't been there before. Will's eyes widened. There was a German soldier standing directly across the street in a long overcoat, his helmet squarely on his head, and his rifle held at port arms across his body. He was very young. He stood very still.

Will didn't know how long the man had been standing there, or where he had come from. How had he gotten so close to the command post? He was in the area Will was supposed to guard, and Will felt responsible. He raised his M-1 rifle to his shoulder and squeezed off two rounds. Both shots hit the soldier squarely in the chest and knocked him over onto his back. He never moved. He never let out a sound.

It was then Will realized the German must have been standing there terrified to death. Will felt confused and sorry he had shot him. That was an awful thing to do, he thought. But what else could I have done?

"What was that?" asked Colina.

"I just shot a Jerry," replied Will, nodding in the direction of the body lying in the street.

"Where'd he come from?" asked Rankin.

"I don't know, sir," replied Will. "All of a sudden he was just standing there, and I shot him."

Colina said, "Damn! He was probably sent to draw fire, so their forward observers could spot our C.P. and shell the hell out of us."

"No, Jack," said Rankin, "I think he just got separated from his unit and somehow stumbled into the wrong part of town. That happens all the time in this kind of a fight."

As Will continued to guard the C.P., he couldn't keep his eyes from wandering over to the body of the German soldier he had killed. It lay there like any other object in the street, like a stick of deadwood, or an empty shell casing. Yet only minutes ago it had been a living human being, another kid just like him; cold and scared, who stood on a street wondering how to keep from getting killed.

And I killed him, Will told himself and almost sobbed. He was from a crack SS outfit, though—I could tell that from his uniform. I'll bet that guy was a real hard-core Nazi fanatic. Volunteered for the SS to conquer the world for his damned *Führer*. Yeah. He and Hitler think the Germans are supermen who can beat us dumb Americans with their hands tied behind their backs.

Will smiled. The son-of-a-bitch sure was scared, his thoughts tumbled on. I shot his ass off, too. That'll show those Nazi bastards who they're up against! Supermen? Sniveling jerk kids who don't even know how to keep themselves alive for five minutes, that's what they are. Why, that scared little superprick never even shot back at me. I'm damned glad I spotted that little bastard, and I'm damned glad I shot his ass off, too.

He was distracted by voices in the C.P. Lieutenant Sommers was talking to Colina. "How are our two guns doing? Randolph and Sumeric still able to fire?"

"It's a miracle, but they're still going," replied Colina. "Antitank guns aren't supposed to survive this kind of a fight. But Randolph's cagey, cautious, and lucky. And the Polack is just the opposite. He's the most reckless, happy-go-lucky... You know, Dave, I think he enjoys this damned war, the son-of-a-bitch." But the captain was smiling when he said it.

Will woke up even though nobody had kicked the soles of his boots. Major Rankin was putting down the field telephone.

"How much ammunition did they send us?" asked Colina.

"Enough to last us about five minutes in a real good fight," replied the major.

Colina nodded.

"So let's hope we don't have a real good fight before we get out of here."

"Out of here?" asked Colina.

"I'll tell you about it now," replied Rankin. He led Colina off into the corner.

Will saw it was daylight. It was gray, but then all the days seemed to be gray. It was January, and it was cold. Will wondered why people had enjoyed going to Europe before the war. To him it was the crummiest place he'd ever been in his life.

G.I.'s were already coming in to pick up badly needed ammunition. It made Will think of his grease gun and his pocketful of clips. He had a pretty full cartridge belt, too, but he figured anything that gave him a better chance to survive was something he was going to hang onto. That was his life insurance.

Will now noticed that in contrast to the night before, the C.P. was filled with men, men coming for ammo, men making reports and then staying to rest awhile, and some just coming to make sure the C.P. was still there and functioning.

A sergeant came through the doorway wearing no helmet. His field jacket was open at the neck, and a bright red wool scarf was wrapped around his throat and hung down to his cartridge belt. He had such an air of assurance that Will knew he was not just another man coming for ammunition.

His face was thin. He had a little hooked nose, like a hawk or an eagle, and his mouth was wide in a big, open grin.

He walked over to the captain and said, "Hiya, Luigi! Thought you'd want to know I just lost my gun."

Colina turned and said, "How'd it happen, Joe?"

Will was watching, fascinated—he couldn't tear his eyes from the flamboyant figure with the perpetual grin and the flowing red scarf. This was Colina's "Polack"—Sumeric.

"Well," replied Sumeric, "She's been knocked around pretty bad these last couple of days. Guess she just got one too many. Ain't nothing but a pile of junk. Besides, Luigi, she got nothing to shoot. Ain't no more 57 ammo in this town."

Luigi? thought Will. I didn't think a sergeant could call a captain—

Then Sumeric saw Ceruti, who had just gotten up and was rubbing his eyes. Sumeric threw his arms open and said, softly, "Hey, little *paesano,*" as he went striding over to Ceruti and enveloped him in a bear hug.

For the first time in three days, Will felt his face crack into a smile. Sumeric's casual good humor was infectious. And the spectacle of the lean sergeant lifting the plump, round-faced Ceruti off his feet would have been amusing under any circumstances.

When he had both feet back on the ground, Ceruti said, "Hiya, Joe. Where the hell did you come from?"

"I came from the front, you dumb wop," replied Sumeric. "And all this time you been living it up back here in the rear echelons."

"Yeah, that's right, living it up," replied Ceruti. "We just went back and got you some ammunition, you dumb Polack."

"Yeah," said Sumeric. "I hear some of it's '03 ammunition. Thanks. What's wrong? Didn't they have nothing left over from the Civil War you could've picked up?"

"It's the same as M-1 ammo," replied Ceruti. "Different clip is all. Snipers use the 1903 Springfield rifle—you know that. Anyway, it's about all they got right now; so put it in M-1 clips and use it good, you dumb Polack."

"Why the hell didn't they do it for us? They ain't got nothing else to do back there but eat hot chow and go to USO shows. You could've showed them how."

"Bug off," said Ceruti, but he was grinning. They were obviously good friends.

Sumeric laughed. "Okay, Luigi," he said. "Go back to sleep, you high-living headquarters bastard."

Striding back to the middle of the room where Captain Colina and Major Rankin stood, Sumeric was still smiling when he said, "This has turned out to be one rough town, boss."

The sounds of firing from the street punctuated his comment, while both Colina and Rankin nodded.

"The boys figure on fighting this one out to the end, though," continued Sumeric. "They've lost so many of their buddies here, they'd rather die than let the Jerries have it now."

"We don't have much left to fight with," said the major.

"You're telling me," replied Joe. "That's why I figure we'll pull the hell out of here and leave the bastards holding the bag. So, Luigi, boss, anytime you're ready, just lead on. Old Joe'll follow you all the way back to Paris. I'll be drinking beer and chasing broads all over the Place Pigalle before anybody even knows we've gone."

Both Colina and Rankin smiled.

Sumeric's relaxed casualness was refreshing. And Will realized the captain was right: Sumeric was enjoying himself—this war was his element, it was what he was born for.

Sumeric wandered over to the open case of rations, fished out a breakfast K, and sat down against the wall. He took his trench knife out of its scabbard and neatly sliced the ration carton in half, took out the fruit bar, the can of powdered ham and eggs, and the envelope of powdered coffee. He stuffed the biscuits and other contents into his field jacket pocket for future use.

He then looked around the C.P. Other men had also begun to eat their rations, cold, as they had for the past three days. Sumeric reached into his otherwise empty gas mask case and extracted a blowtorch.

As he sat on the floor with the other men, Will ate his heated can of meat and thought how good it was to have warm food in his stomach. It made him feel less discouraged, some-how. "You're almost finished. How about letting me in?" asked Gruber.

Will scrambled to his feet. Joe was sharing his blowtorch with anybody who wanted to use it to heat their rations and coffee, and the circle had become large. In a minute, Will knew some officer was going to come and make them all disperse, but in the meantime, they might as well enjoy it.

He noticed that the mood inside the C.P. was already more cheerful. It was almost like a party. Yet from the town there were still the burps of burp guns, the rattle of light .30-caliber American machine guns, and the popping of small arms and grenades.

Joe Sumeric was chatting with everybody while he ate. Some of the other men were offering him the chocolate bars from dinner rations, or cans of cheese from lunch rations, and Sumeric was graciously accepting them. Everybody admired and liked him; of that there could be no doubt. The man was a popular hero in the regiment.

Will found himself liking him, too, even as he wondered how Sumeric could enjoy this war he loathed. To each his own, thought Will, and he realized again that war was something Joe was good at; something in which he excelled through some strange trait of character that Will would never be able to understand.

His thoughts were interrupted by the whistling of shells. As Will hit the floor with a bruising jar, he saw Joe Sumeric quickly turn off the blowtorch and lay himself comfortably on a spread-out blanket just as the thuds of the exploding artillery barrage blotted out all other sounds.

6

After the first fifteen or twenty shells, the German artillery slacked off and fired only one or two rounds every half hour.

"Hell!" said Captain Colina. "I thought they'd plaster us worse than that."

"I think they're a little short of ammunition, too," replied Major Rankin. "It's been a rough three days for both sides."

The radio operator turned to the major and said, "Able has only one light machine gun left, and it's almost out of ammunition."

Rankin sighed and said, "Okay. Let's send them a case."

Colina turned, pointed at Will, and called, "Hey, you! You're not doing anything now. I want you to take this box of machine gun ammunition up to Able Company."

Will looked blank.

"Remember the burned-out Tiger tank, where Carrington got killed?"

"Yes, sir."

"Well, it's three houses down from the tank. Just deliver the ammunition and come right back."

Will thought, That sounds simple enough.

He put down his M-1 rifle and picked up the shorter grease gun and slung it on his shoulder, lifted the heavy metal case with his left hand, and started through the doorway.

Except for an occasional rattle of small-arms fire, things were quiet. As he got farther away from the command post, though, Will could see in the daylight that there were still uncollected bodies everywhere, sprawled in the various attitudes of death, frozen in the positions in which they died: in doorways, in the streets, in the snow, lying on their backs or on their faces, crumpled in heaps or sitting, kneeling, gaping wordlessly.

Beside a house sat a dead German, with his legs under his buttocks, his head resting on his chest, arms at his sides, and a burp gun lying on the ground in front of him. He looked for all the world as if he had put the gun down carefully and was taking a short nap. Another lay on his side in the middle of the street with one arm raised, fingers outstretched, reaching for something that would elude his grasp forever. A storm trooper sat in a snowdrift with his eyes wide open, gazing intently at the street in front of him, as if he would always be vitally interested in what was going on there. The whole town reminded Will of a waxworks museum. The figures looked so real, yet so unreal at the same time.

Will hurried along. He didn't like being alone in this town. It was scary. He found the street, and he saw the blackened, silent panzer beside a blackened, silent house. He went trotting past it, one house, two houses, three houses. So far, so good. The door was slightly ajar, and he pushed it open gently with his foot and entered quickly.

Then he got a shock. Descending the stairway was a German soldier. He had on an overcoat with a cartridge belt around it. His rifle was slung on his right shoulder. He looked about twenty-five years old. His face had a pensive expression. It was a nice face, a kind face, and the man was as startled to see Will as Will was to see him.

In a fraction of a second, Will dropped the ammunition box, brought his grease gun off his shoulder, flipped off the safety catch, aimed the muzzle at the German's chest, and squeezed the trigger.

He thought he saw the first two or three slugs smash into the startled German's face. Then his head exploded, flinging gore in all directions.

Will had shot the man's head off.

Will stepped back out through the doorway into the snow and vomited.

He turned and ran as fast as he could back up the street. Behind him he heard rifles firing. In front of him, the occasional whine of a ricochet.

He kept running until he was back at the command post.

Will was disgusted and repelled by what he had done. Then he became angry at the German for being there in that house on those stairs. Yes! It was the German's fault. It was the German's fault that this thing had happened.

He stood outside the door of the C.P., heaving both from lack of breath and from the retching of his stomach. He forced himself to relax, remembered to put the safety catch back on his grease gun, and walked into the command post.

Captain Colina looked up and said, "That was fast. Did you deliver the ammo?"

Will was afraid his knees were shaking as he said, "No, sir." He caught his breath and added, "I got to the house, but there were Jerries there. I shot one of them and got the hell out."

"Can't be," said Colina. "We just talked to them." He looked at Will suspiciously.

Will replied, calmly now, "I can't help it, Captain. I went three houses past the burned-out Tiger and—"

The captain cut in, "What do you mean, 'three houses past the Tiger'? It's three houses before you get to the burned-out bastard! It's down from the son-of-a-bitch!"

Will replied, "Well, I guess I screwed it up." At that point, he didn't care. "But," he added, "I dropped the ammunition in the doorway. Third house past the burned-out Tiger tank, on the same side of the street. Maybe Able can take the house and get the ammo?"

Colina turned to the radio operator, but, as usual, he had anticipated him and was already trying to raise Able Company. Will put the grease gun down in the corner. It had saved his life by a fraction of a second. He could feel himself shaking inside.

Joe Sumeric had just finished his coffee. He walked over, patted Will on the shoulder, and said, "It was rough, wasn't it, Luigi?"

Will nodded.

"I know," said Sumeric. "It was fast and unexpected. You got good reflexes, kid!"

Will was flattered by the attention Sumeric gave him. He began to feel better.

"I'm Joe Sumeric," said Joe, sticking out his hand.

"My name's Pope," said Will. "Luigi Pope."

Sumeric looked startled for a moment, then threw back his head and laughed. "You're okay, kid," he said, and there was warmth in his voice this time.

Will saw Joe throw a covetous glance at his grease gun. All of a sudden, he realized he didn't want that gun anymore. It reminded him too much of the German whose head he'd shot off. It made him feel like vomiting again every time he looked at it.

"You can have that gun if you want it," he said. "I already bagged my limit of Krauts with it this season."

Joe reached out for the gun, picked it up, disengaged the clip, flipped out the shell in the chamber, and inspected the weapon very closely.

Will had reached in his pocket for the other clips and began handing them to Sumeric.

"She's okay," said Sumeric. "Thanks a lot. This baby can do me some good."

He slapped one of the new clips into the weapon and put the half-used clip with the others in his pocket, then said, "Yes, sirree, Luigi, baby, this gun ain't killed its last Jerry yet." Slinging the grease gun on his shoulder, Sumeric sauntered over to Captain Colina. "Well, Luigi," he said, "I guess I've had my little rest. Now I'd better get back to my boys. I left them with B Company. Guess we'll stay there. Anything special you want me to do?"

The captain turned around and said, "No, Joe. Just take care and get yourself and your boys back. I know you will. You're a good soldier."

Sumeric nodded and strolled out of the room.

Sommers walked over to Will, gave him a friendly pat on the top of his helmet, and said, "You sort of walked into this war right through the front door, didn't you, Pope?"

"Yeah, Lieutenant, I sure did. Would you mind if I went back and tried it again? Maybe I could find me a nice back door someplace and sort of sneak in easy-like."

Will and Ceruti sat in the corner of the C.P. It was almost noon.

"Do you think we're going to leave Damen?" asked Will.

"Don't know," answered Ceruti. "But if Joe thinks we are, I'll bet we are. He's a natural-born soldier."

Will smiled at the mention of Joe Sumeric's name. "Why does Joe call everybody Luigi?"

Ceruti grinned. "Because he can't remember anybody's name, that's why. Joe grew up in the same Italian neighborhood I did, and he says most of the guys were named Luigi anyway, so why not?"

"How come the captain lets him get away with calling him Luigi?"

"The captain can stand being called Luigi an awful long time before he can afford to lose a sergeant like Joe Sumeric. Anyway, they like each other, and the captain doesn't care what Joe calls him."

Will liked Ceruti because he was friendly and sort of happy-go-lucky with just enough conscientiousness to make him dependable. "You're from New York, aren't you?" said Will. He thought that was a good guess.

"You're damned right," replied Ceruti. "I didn't know there was noplace else till I got in this damned army, and from what I seen already, I ain't gonna waste no time getting back there, neither."

"What did you do before the army?" asked Will. Until he got drafted, he figured everybody his age was in school, but now he knew he could never take that for granted.

"I played the piano in a band," replied Ceruti.

"Wow!" said Will. His respect for Mike Ceruti soared.

"It was a nice little Italian place," continued Ceruti, savoring the memory. "Joe Sumeric was a waiter in the same joint. He speaks Italian real good for a Polack, but he was sure a lousy waiter. Always tried to make every broad that come into the place. Acted fresh with the customers—you know, like he calls the captain 'Luigi.' The boss fired him once or twice a week, but Joe always talked him into hiring him back.

Across the room the lieutenant sat talking to Captain Colina. Will glanced at them, then turned to Ceruti and asked, "How do you like Sommers as your platoon leader?"

Ceruti smiled. "I like him damned good," he replied.

"What did he do before the war?" asked Will.

"He taught high school English," replied Ceruti.

Will nodded. For some reason, it seemed the most natural thing in the world that a former schoolteacher should command a platoon of infantry on the line.

Just then, one of the G.I.'s, who was leaving after delivering a message, stopped and said, "My God! It walks! It talks! It crawls on its belly like a reptile! Jo-Jo the dogface boy! Now all I gotta do is collect me a crowd and sell tickets."

Will looked up and saw Jim Mahoney standing in front of him, even dirtier and more disheveled than usual. He scrambled to his feet. "I'll be damned! Jimmy! Back from the dead. How the hell you been making out?"

Mahoney grinned. "The same as everybody else. Champagne, chorus girls, caviar, the usual. Came back to see if you guys in the rear echelon needed anything."

Will smiled back at him. "My gun got knocked out, and they put me in the mine platoon," he said as casually as he could. "How about you?"

"The gun I was on knocked out two Tiger tanks, but the Jerries blew us to pieces on the way back to town, so we've been with Charlie Company ever since, sort of fighting as an odd squad."

"That's something, isn't it, that house-to-house fighting," said Will.

Jim made a face. "You can call it house-to-house if you want to," he replied, "but where I been it's more like room-to-room and corner-to-corner."

"You're telling me!" said Will.

"Anyway, Will, be careful," said Mahoney. "Before I come here, our lieutenant got hit bad. He was looking out a window, and a damn Jerry we thought was dead come to life and snapped off a shot. Went right through the lieutenant's chest. We cut the Jerry in half with a Thompson, but I don't think the lieutenant's going to make it."

"I thought all Charlie's officers were killed," said Will.

"This guy come over from Baker Company."

"They got a lot of extra lieutenants, then?" said Will.

"Naw. The guy was a sergeant in Baker Company, so when they made him a lieutenant yesterday, they sent him over to us. They made about three or four of our sergeants into lieutenants and sent them over to Baker and Able. That's the way the army does it, Will; in this outfit, anyway. When they give a guy a battlefield commission, they transfer him to another company."

Captain Colina walked over. He asked Jim, "Aren't you one of the new guys who came in with this one?" He pointed to Will.

"Yes, sir," replied Jim. "I'm in Whitey Woodall's gun squad, but Pope here's my buddy, like I told you when we come in—"

"Okay," said the captain, "I'm transferring you to the mine platoon. I'll tell Whitey."

"Thanks," said Jim. And Will realized Mahoney was the only person who hadn't complained about being put in the mine platoon. He'd actually thanked Captain Colina. He just didn't give a damn.

"Look, Jimbo, here's three clips," said Will. "I figure you must be almost out of ammo, and I've got most of mine." Jim stuck them into his belt. Then he sat down, removed his helmet, took a deep breath, and fell sound asleep. Gosh, thought Will, everybody's exhausted.

He scrambled to his feet as the lieutenant approached. "I guess you heard," Will told Sommers, "we got another man."

"Yeah," replied Sommers. "The captain told me."

"Before I forget, sir, do you know what happened to Gawalsky? The guy that came in your platoon with me?"

Sommers had to think a minute, fatigue obviously slowing his thoughts. "Oh, yes," he said, finally. "His gun was knocked out. The gunner was killed, and all the other men were badly wounded, so I suppose that means Gawalsky was, too. Some of the wounded were evacuated. The rest are at the aid station."

Will nodded. He felt sorry for Gawalsky for being hurt badly, but he envied him, too, for being out of combat now. Will hoped he would live.

"Are we really going to leave Damen?" he asked the lieutenant.

"Just as soon as it's dark," replied Sommers.

"What about the aid station full of wounded, Lieutenant?"

"When we leave this town we'll leave it with our wounded and our weapons. Or we won't leave it at all."

Major Rankin looked at his watch and said, "It'll be dark soon, so let's get set to haul ass." He walked over to the radio and hunched down to talk to the radioman. "Have all company commanders report to me here at the C.P."

While he waited for them to arrive, the major gave the orders to the mine platoon. They were simple: the line companies would come out one platoon at a time and make a forced march back to a wooded high ground near the city of Hagenor. There they would dig in and form a main line of resistance.

The trucks would transport the wounded and the head-quarters radio equipment together with the necessary staff. The truck convoy would pass through the files of infantry marching on each side of the road.

The mine platoon was to wait until everybody else had left, then they would pull out, stopping every hundred yards or so to lay mines across the Damen-to-Hagenor Road to delay any German mechanized pursuit. After they'd laid all their mines, they were to proceed up the road and join the First Battalion outside Hagenor.

The orders were greeted by silence. "Do you have any questions?" asked the major. They all shook their heads. Their orders were dismayingly clear.

The company commanders started coming into the C.P. while the major was speaking. Now Rankin waited until the battered, bearded, grimy, new arrivals had settled, strain and exhaustion showing in their deeply lined faces.

"Gentlemen, I've called you into the C.P. to give you the plans for our withdrawal from Damen."

A murmur arose, and one man stood up and said, "Look, Major, we've held this damn town for three bloody days against the whole German army. We want to stay and finish the fight, one way or the other. We'll either hold this town or die in it."

The major stopped him with an upraised hand. He spoke softly but firmly. "I know. We all feel the same way. But we're almost out of ammunition. The rest of this regiment and our other two regiments are in the same fix. They have to pull back; so do we. Division is at Hagenor. When we get there, we'll be closer to the ammunition, and we'll have a better chance to hold a line. Maybe even counterattack if the bastards give us the chance."

Rankin paused before he continued. "We stopped the Germans cold here at Damen for three critical days. We can't do any more. I think you men've lost sight of the fact that we're part of a division, part of an army. We're not just a battalion fighting our own private war. Our pulling back is not giving up. We've got to get back with the rest of the division so we can all fight together again. We've got to win. We can't stay here alone and lose. So no matter what you think, no matter how you feel, we're all going to be on the road tonight."

Nobody answered. The battle for Damen had become for them a furious personal struggle, an intense contest of wills that had made them lose their perspective. Now they understood.

No motors could be started in the town. That would have alerted the enemy that the battalion was up to something. The mine platoon pushed their truck out of Damen. Will felt the cold intensely. He had been inside too long and found it hard to breathe, and the effort expended in pushing took all the strength he had.

A couple of times they had to clear the bodies of dead German soldiers from the road so the truck could get by.

Will just kept pushing. He didn't even look where he was going. It was just push with one foot, bring it up, push with the other foot, bring it up. Purely mechanical motions. His mind was numb; so was his body. Just push with one foot, then the other foot.

When he heard the brakes catch and the truck skid to a stop, he looked up and saw they were out of the town and in the countryside.

On either side of the road, columns of infantrymen were moving past them in the dark.

There was no conversation. The men were exhausted from three days and nights of hard fighting, and the march back to Hagenor had just begun.

The road was icy. The men kept slipping and sliding, and now that his eyes had adjusted to the dark, it looked to Will as though they were spending as much time flat on their backs as walking. Still, they did not cry out—they did not even curse. They were that tired.

The truck convoy was waiting for the signal to start. First in the convoy were the wounded, then the trucks for headquarters, then the mines, apart from the rest. There were two or three Jeeps. Colina's was one.

At the last minute Randolph's antitank gun came bouncing across the field, pulled by its crew. Of the nine guns of the regiment, it was the only one left. It hooked onto one of the trucks, motors started, and the convoy moved off down the road. The infantry columns leaving Damen were thinning out; the flames of the town still glowed in the night.

Only eight men now stood on the icy road: Lieutenant Sommers, Diamond, Will Pope, Jimmy Mahoney, Jay Gruber, Mike Ceruti, Phil Cohen, and Dan Sark. Stiffly, they boarded their explosive-laden truck. Ceruti sat beside Jack Diamond so the lieutenant could be with his men in the rear of the truck to supervise fusing and laying the mines.

They started out slowly. Fusing mines in the dark on a moving truck was more difficult than they had thought it would be, and in their exhausted state the men were not up to it. Sommers had Diamond stop the truck. Then they were able to accustom themselves to the feel of the fuses and the mines. They fused six mines. Sommers and Gruber jumped down from the tailgate and placed them across the road.

While they were stopped, the riflemen had kept moving, trudging, sliding, falling, but going forward. After laying the first mines, the little platoon became aware of the complete silence that surrounded them.

Their truck was sitting on the Damen road all alone.

7

As the truck inched along, Sommers strained to see what lay on the margins of the road. So far there had been a large ditch on either side. After they had gone about a hundred yards, he called to Diamond to stop again, and they were able to fuse five mines quickly this time, since they had gotten the feel of it. In half a minute Gruber and Sommers had laid the mines across the road.

Will saw they had left the fields behind Damen and were on a road that went through wooded countryside.

As they continued forward, Gruber said, "Oh, hell, Lieutenant, let's cut and run. This ain't gonna do no good. All the Jerries have to do is lift the damn mines off the road. They know we ain't had time to booby-trap them."

Sommers replied, "Maybe you're right. Still, they can't be sure we haven't fixed them to blow up in their faces. Let's hope they take the time to check every single one of them before they pick up the bastards. I know I sure as hell would."

The platoon's progress was slow, stopping every few minutes as they did to lay mines.

When Sommers discovered that there was no longer a ditch on either side of the road, he said, "Okay, this time we'll lay five across the road and five on each side."

As Gruber slid off the tailgate onto the road, Phil Cohen said, "Why don't we cover the mines on the sides with snow? If a Jerry tank sees the mines on the road and tries to go around, he won't see the other ones, and they'll get him."

Sommers nodded, and they covered the mines carefully.

They reboarded the truck and started up again. There was still no sign of the line companies, who were far ahead of them. The eight men of the tiny American infantry platoon were on their own, all alone.

The flames of Damen receded in the distance. Only a glow remained. The men began to relax a little bit. "I think we've made it," Sommers said. "I don't think they know we've gone yet."

They started to breathe a little easier then. It was as if a collective sigh of relief had gone up from the platoon.

Will smiled to himself. He turned to Gruber and said, "I'll bet the Jerries're forming up for one hell of an attack on our positions in Damen. Probably right now. Want to bet?"

He heard Phil Cohen and Mike Ceruti laugh. Ceruti said, "Yeah. And when they come charging down the streets and nobody shoots at them, they're going to be so shook up, they'll go back to where they started from. They'll figure we're waiting for them with something real good this time. It'll probably scare the hell out of the bastards."

The others smiled in the dark. Will felt the cold again, but like everybody else, he was relaxed now. They were out of Damen. If it weren't for the fact that they had to keep laying mines, he figured he'd try to sleep. He thought, The lieutenant's right. I think we've made it. And I sure didn't think we would. God! What a relief—

Ziiiiiip! Crack! Ka-pow! It was sudden. It was unexpected. It was terrifying. They were under direct fire from an 88!

Even in the terror of the instant, the thought flashed through Will's mind that the shell sounded like somebody unzipping a large zipper. The explosion was slightly behind them and to the right.

Will flung a glance down the road and saw a Tiger tank entering it from the left, just past the last mines they had laid. The tank had not come from Damen. It had not come up the mined road. It had come from somewhere else, where it had broken through. It had seen them, though! And it was turning onto the road, where its 88 would bear directly on their truck, loaded with its mines.

Sommers instantly jumped to the front of the truck, whacked Diamond on the shoulder, and yelled, "Haul ass! Fast! Fast! Fast!" But it was not necessary. With the crack of the 88, Diamond had shifted down his gears and jammed his foot on the accelerator.

As they went around a bend, they heard another zip, followed by a loud explosion as the 88 shell landed behind them. The truck was flying along the road as fast as it could go without skidding out of control, while the men held down the mines.

Sommers realized that while their instinct was to get the hell out of there, their duty was to try to stop that tank from coming up the road. He shouted instructions to the men. They grabbed the mines and fused several in no time at all, either by the practice they had gained when the truck was standing still, or by an ability born of fear.

Stopping the truck was out of the question. They thanked God the road was a winding one through fairly thick woods, which partially hid them from view. They could hear the tank around the bend.

Will saw Gruber and Sommers talking. Gruber nodded and grabbed a mine, and the lieutenant yelled to Diamond, "Slow down, now!"

Sommers and Phil Cohen held Gruber while he leaned over the open tailgate and gently eased the mine onto the road as the truck slowed to a crawl. The mine followed them along for a few yards, then stopped in the middle of the road. They handed Gruber another mine, and he repeated the operation as they crept along, with their hearts in their throats.

They could see the long barrel of the panzer's 88 coming around the curve. They heard and felt the explosion as the shell hit the side of the road, showering the truck and the men in it with dirt and snow as the heavier steel fragments of the shell passed over them. The truck picked up speed for several minutes, then slowed down again, and Gruber resumed sliding the mines onto the road from the tailgate.

It was cold. Will felt numb. His job was to fuse the mines with Dan Sark after Jim Mahoney took them from under the tarpaulin and handed them to him. He and Dan fed them directly to Gruber, who was being held down by Phil Cohen and the lieutenant. A system was at work. It had developed in seconds.

From the road behind them came an unexpected sound: a dull explosion different from the familiar crack of an 88.

The men looked at each other. Had the tank hit one of their mines, finally? They decided not to try to find out but to keep going and to keep sliding mines onto the road.

After a while, there was still no sign of the tank. Or of anything else. The glow in the sky from the flames of Damen had gradually faded into total darkness as the Tiger tank was pursuing them down the road before it hit their mine.

Sommers was breathing hard as he said, "Okay. Let's catch up with the rest of the battalion now. We don't have time to slide any more mines."

The darkness was absolute. Will could not even see Jim Mahoney sitting next to him, and he could only hear Gruber gulping cold air. Diamond hadn't put on the truck's blackout lights. None of them had any idea what might be out there in the dark. The Tiger's attack on them had been so unexpected and terrifying, they didn't dare assume they were either alone or secure anymore. The night was their enemy.

They crept along, feeling for the road rather than seeing it. Jack Diamond's instincts were good at this. Finally, though, Lieutenant Sommers crawled forward and said, "Jack, let's put on the blackouts. We've got to make better time than this or the Jerries'll catch us on the road in daylight."

As Diamond switched on the lights, their dull glow gave the road in front of them an eerie look. It was just enough to allow them to see a few yards, but now Diamond could make out the sides of the road, and the truck picked up speed.

They saw it was snowing. It was a light snow, small flakes blown by the wind.

Coming around a bend, they narrowly missed slamming into the rear of one of the First Battalion's trucks. Sommers, sensing the questions in his men's minds, said, "That truck dropped back to pick up the stragglers. A lot of the guys on the road are walking wounded, and some of the others are so worn out they just drop. That truck is picking them up until they get back enough strength to get out and walk again."

When the big truck stopped the first time, Sommers jumped down and walked ahead to talk to the driver. When he came back, he said, "I told them if they needed any more space, we had some room here. They're doing okay so far, but they might take us up on it later."

Diamond cracked a little smile through his chapped and bleeding lips and said, "Lieutenant, they won't ride with us long. Nobody ever rides with us long. As soon as they find out we're sitting on a pile of TNT and likely to come under fire, they figure they can walk the rest of the way."

When Sommers climbed back into the rear of the truck, all his men were sound asleep, huddled against each other for warmth.

In fact, most of the infantrymen walking along the side of the road were practically sound asleep. The agony of putting one foot before the other, added to their terrible exhaustion and fatigue from the last three days' battle, had taken a dreadful toll. They were simply going through the motions. And, for some of them, their strength and will ran out. Without wanting to, they collapsed, falling by the side of the road with a hard thud and a loud clanking of helmet and rifle. They lay there, unable to move. If somebody hadn't picked them up, they would have died of exposure from the cold. They had reached their physical and mental limits. Both mind and body had ceased to function.

Will was hunched over, trying to keep warm. He was asleep and not asleep. His mental faculties were turned off, but the cold was so intense it would not let him actually sleep. In this haze, he heard voices and realized that something was happening. As consciousness began to creep back, he knew they must have arrived at their destination.

The other men were already getting off the truck. Will shook his head to try to wake himself up. He shook it again. Then he rose stiffly and jumped off the truck. Someone was telling Jack Diamond to take the truck behind the line they were forming. From what was being said, Will grasped that the platoon was joining Able Company of the First Battalion on the line. They were to dig in to defend a city they couldn't even see from where they stood.

The G.I.'s were in the open countryside. At least, in the dawn's half dark, Will saw no buildings or towns. Around him men were trying to hack holes in the hard ground. Some of them were too exhausted even to move—they were being prodded by their friends.

Sommers was placing his men along the edge of a field. He kept yelling hoarsely, "Don't dig your holes so close to each other. Spread out, dammit, spread out. Mahoney, get back a little bit. Hey, Sark! You can't dig there, it's too damn hard. Try over here. Hey, Ceruti, not under that tree. If a shell bursts there, it'll get you for sure. Hey, Gruber, dig deep."

Will found a spot and called to Sommers, "Can I dig here?" He didn't want to begin a hole and then have to abandon it to start all over again.

"Yeah, that's fine."

Will started chopping at the earth with his shovel. Damn, it was hard. After hacking through the frozen crust, he dug into good, soft ground, but as he got deeper, water began to seep into the bottom of the hole. Ice-cold water.

The cold, gray winter daylight now illuminated the woods and snowy fields. In the far distance there were a couple of small houses, probably farms.

"Hey! I ain't gonna get my feet into this damn water. It's freezing cold, dammit!" said Gruber.

"The hell you ain't," contradicted Ceruti.

"Keep digging. We don't have all day. We gotta be dug in quick. Dig fast," said Sark.

They dug. Then Will glanced behind them and saw a row of neat pillboxes, partially hidden by trees. "What the hell is that?" he asked nobody in particular.

"It looks like some old fortifications," replied Cohen. "Some sort of a defense line."

"What the hell are we doing digging these damned bloody holes for?" asked Gruber. "There's some beautiful pillboxes just a hundred yards back there."

"Yeah!" said Jim Mahoney. He'd been too cold to talk until then.

Some of the men started getting up out of their holes. "To hell with it. Let's use the pillboxes," said Gruber.

"No, you don't! Hold it right there!" shouted Sommers. "Nobody occupies those pillboxes. We dig in a hundred yards in front of them and that's our line."

The men were used to obeying, so they obeyed, but they didn't like it.

"Ain't that just like the army?" said Gruber. "Here we got beautiful fortifications a hundred yards away, and they make us dig holes." Grumbling, exhausted, they dug into the hard ground. It got to be noontime. It was still cold. Most of the men had learned that even though the bottoms of their holes were filled with icy water, they could build little ledges just above the waterline to stand on. Others, God knows where, found logs of firewood, which they put in the bottom of their holes to keep their feet out of the wet.

While the men were still settling in, frightened-faced young privates from the rear were dashing down the line, distributing rations and ammunition. After they left, each man had a fresh bandolier of cartridges, two hand grenades, and one K ration.

By now, some of the men were rolling themselves up in blankets beside their holes and trying to sleep. There was no sign yet of the German army.

Will Pope was too cold to try to sleep, even though he was so exhausted he didn't think he could stand. His feet had gotten wet and they hurt, but he was still putting off changing his socks. He knew he'd have to, but he just couldn't bring himself to take off his boots to do it.

Will had seen Sommers checking with the other men, who were already changing into dry socks. He hoped the lieutenant wouldn't see him. He even thought that if he got trench foot, he'd get out of the line.

"You got dry socks, Will?" asked Lieutenant Sommers.

Will nodded. Now he'd have to change, whether he was ready or not. "Where the hell are the damned Germans?" he asked.

Sommers smiled and said, "Guess they didn't expect us to fight them so fierce and hold them so long, Will. Guess they expected to roll right through our thin line and be halfway to Paris by now. Cut us to pieces, like they did our troops in the Ardennes when they first started. And after we stopped them so cold, they sure didn't expect us to pull back like we did. It was too fast and unexpected. That's why we've got a little time to get ready for them. But they'll be coming, Will. They'll be coming soon enough."

And he was right. At about four o'clock in the afternoon, the forward outposts sighted the enemy.

The Germans came cautiously. A few probing patrols at first. Then their infantry, spread out in battle formations and moving slowly; a few platoons at a time.

Even though they had a rough idea where the American divisions opposing them were and how far they had withdrawn, their respect for those divisions was now so great that they were not going to blunder into them and get another bloody nose. So the German army was strung out. Their movement was overly cautious. Now they began sending up the panzers to throw against the American line. They were sure the Yanks had no tanks left, anyway. Although they did not know it, they were setting themselves up for exactly the kind of situation the American commanders were hoping for.

Darkness comes early in Alsace in the middle of winter. And with the darkness that night came penetrating cold.

With a start, Will heard the familiar sound of tanks. Panzers! The squeaking, the clanking, and the roar of the motors were unmistakable. Now, in the dark, somebody was running along the lines shouting hoarsely, "Keep down in your holes! Keep down in your holes!" Let the tanks roll over you! Keep down in your holes!"

The tanks were moving and firing fast. The zipping, swishing, exploding 88 shells chopped up the silence of the night.

Will scrunched down into his hole as far as he could get. He slipped, and his feet splashed into the icy water at the bottom. He could hear the roar of the tanks' motors and he thought he felt the heat of their exhausts close to where he huddled, frightened to death.

The tanks rolled over the foxholes to within a few yards of the pillboxes. They fired their armor-piercing shells against the old fortifications, then turned and rumbled back to where they had come from, once again rolling over the infantrymen in their foxholes without doing any damage. But the old pillboxes were nothing now but smoldering piles of rubble.

Will poked his head up, but he couldn't see anything in the darkness. The tanks had left, believing they had knocked hell out of the American line. Now the German infantry would come screaming at him, flinging grenades and firing machine guns. Will braced himself, put his rifle to his shoulder, and was ready to fight.

But there were no more enemy attacks that night.

Still, it was a night of sheer hell. The cold was so intense Will did not think he could survive the physical pain of it. He kept kicking his feet together to keep the circulation going. Almost all the men had gotten out of their foxholes and were beating at each other to keep warm.

In the dark, Will heard someone whisper hoarsely, "I can't take it. I just can't take it."

Will thought, I can't either. No. I can't stand it. I—I want to die.

It even hurt him to breathe. The air was so cold it made his throat and lungs ache. He tried to run in place. Jim Mahoney was trying to do the same thing. Will heard Jim fall in the snow. His rifle and helmet clanked as he hit the ground. Will groped for Jim's hand to lift him up.

Then they beat at each other for a while. Neither said a word. Will felt the numbing exhaustion and excruciating pain enveloping him like the flames enveloped those German tankmen. Maybe they were luckier than he. He thought he envied them now. They were dead. They couldn't suffer anymore. Their pain was finished. His would last forever. He would never be warm again. Not until he was dead. Oh, how I wish I were dead, Will thought once again. Still, he endured. With all the means to kill himself, his bayonet in its scabbard and his loaded rifle in his hand, he continued to suffer the dreadful, bitter cold. His lips cracked open, his body shook, and his mind cried out in the agony of freezing exhaustion, knowing that there would be no relief to his torment.

The artillery on both sides fired sporadic barrages, exchanging several shells an hour. This did not even arouse any interest.

Trying to survive the cold that night was the main activity for the exhausted infantrymen of the Fifteenth Division.

Will heard Ceruti shout, "Mamma mia. I gotta get warm. I gotta."

He sensed movement. Ceruti was running.

The movement faded in the distance. He knew Ceruti was a brave man. He'd never consider running away from the Germans. Was he running away from the cold? Where? Where did he think he was going, anyway?

Will gave up. He was too cold to care.

The night lasted forever.

Finally, the faint grayness of the sky signaled the dawn. It was then that the runners arrived with the message that all officers and platoon sergeants were to report to battalion headquarters.

Still numb with cold, miserable and weary, Will thought about their situation. They did not have a platoon sergeant. In fact, they only had Lieutenant Sommers. They were really less than an understrength squad, when you came right down to it, but that was the story throughout the whole battalion. The officer ranks had been decimated, and most companies were down to platoon size; some platoons wouldn't even make full squads in a regulation-strength outfit.

Even though it was daylight, the sky was overcast. A heavy mist covered the field. Will had never seen such a completely bleak landscape in his whole life. And to make it worse, somewhere out there beyond the mist was the German army.

Will heard Gruber's voice. "Where the hell you been, Ceruti? Where'd you run to, anyway?" Will was glad Ceruti was back. It made Will feel good, somehow.

"I had to get warm," he heard Ceruti say. "I just had to. So I run off to find me a tank with its engines running, so's I could warm my hands by the exhaust. When I got good and warm, I come back. I feel better now."

"Wait a minute," Gruber said. "One of the reasons we're in such a hell of a fix is we don't have no tanks."

"Yeah, I know," replied Ceruti. "I didn't say it was one of ours."

★

The officers and platoon sergeants began returning from headquarters. In the heavy morning fog, the men of the mine platoon gathered around their young lieutenant.

Sommers said, "Okay, I've got two things to tell you. We'll start with number one, which is the situation we're in. The division's spread thin. Damned thin. All three regiments are in the line. Every battalion. Every company. Every platoon. Every squad. Every man. There's nothing in reserve. Nothing."

As the men around him nodded silently, Sommers looked into their faces, one by one. They were dirty and tired. Fatigue and cold showed plainly.

In that instant, Dave Sommers could realize something his men did not know yet. These men were no longer just a bunch of strangers thrown together by the chances of war, who stayed together because they had to, who fought together because they were ordered to. They were a platoon of infantry. They would fight long after he'd gone. He was proud of them.

Sommers smiled, "Well," he said, "we sure are some kind of outfit. Seven men. Dirty. Frozen. Beat. Looks like I've got me a bunch of lean, hungry scarecrows."

The men smiled back at him through their cracked lips.

Phil Cohen said, "What was the second thing you had to tell us, Lieutenant?"

"Oh, yeah," said Sommers. He looked at his watch. "The second thing is: in exactly ten minutes, we scarecrows're going to attack the whole damned German army."

By now the men of every ragged, understrength rifle company in front of Hagenor had received the same orders. Nobody questioned the command to attack. They just nodded their heads grimly. They checked their weapons. They counted their clips of ammunition. Some of them even smiled.

Then they began to unsheath their long knives.

When those gaunt apparitions rose out of the gray morning mist, they went forward with fixed bayonets, some trotting, some hardly able to walk, some supporting wounded comrades limping at their sides, some with their feet wrapped in blankets, many wearing dirty bandages, all with cracked, bleeding lips, scruffy beards, their jackets and trousers ragged and battle-stained. Faces hard and determined. Jaws set against their pain.

Yet forward they went.

And they swept all before them.

8

When Will Pope climbed out of his foxhole and followed his lieutenant into the mist that morning, Will still suffered from cold and exhaustion. He could do nothing about that. But ahead of him somewhere was another tormentor—the enemy—and he could vent his wrath on him now; on him he could let loose all his fury.

His rage drove him forward. Now he could come to grips with the cause of his misery—the Germans. He was attacking them as an infantry rifleman with A Company of the Triple Nickel. He was running faster now, eager to get to them to kill them, to make them pay for all his agony.

He stumbled as he ran through the smoke and mist. He lost sight of Sommers. German shells exploded behind Will as he plunged forward. Now, ahead of him, he heard the sounds of machine guns and rifles, which meant he was getting close to the enemy line. He bent low as he continued forward.

Now the mist was lifting in front of him, and he could see American riflemen already throwing themselves at the enemy with deadly effect.

A bandaged man who could hardly walk, knowing he could not make the last few yards to the German lines, hurled his rifle at them, bayonet first, like a spear, as he fell to his knees, then onto his face. Wounded men who had been supported by their friends now disengaged from the arms that held them and threw themselves forward, firing as they went.

Unable to resist such a savage American onslaught, the German troops were abandoning their line, streaming toward the rear, where they became entangled with other troops, trying to move forward.

Seeing the enemy running away from him gave Will a feeling of exultation that made him run after them even faster. He heard the single report of an artillery piece firing from his rear, the whistle of the shell passing overhead. He watched it explode ahead of him, cutting off the retreat of three German soldiers who dove to the ground to escape getting hit.

As soon as the smoke cleared, they got up again. But now they appeared confused, unsure what they should do next. They decided to turn and fire at the oncoming G.I.'s.

Will had been trained to shoot fast and to aim from the hip. He squeezed the trigger while the Germans were still raising their rifles to their shoulders. His shots knocked all three flat on their backs. Only one got up. He ran a few yards, then fell down and stayed down.

As he ran past them, Will looked to make sure they were dead and was surprised to discover they were just kids. Dead kids. It took a minute for him to realize these "kids" were about his own age.

Will had lost contact with the rest of the platoon as soon as they'd plunged into the mist when the attack began. Now, as he ran forward, he looked for Lieutenant Sommers. He spotted him, finally, up ahead leading a bunch of infantrymen. Will trotted faster to catch up.

A German shell was whistling in. It was going to be close. Will hit the ground hard. He covered his helmet with his hands.

The shell exploded.

The steel fragments swished over Will's prostrate body. Had he stayed on his feet an instant longer, they would have cut him to pieces. Will jumped to his feet and started to dash forward again.

Then he saw that the men with Sommers were going on, but the lieutenant was still lying on the ground.

Will ran toward him. Sommers was trying to push himself up. Every time he did, he flopped back down in the mud and slush, like a tired fish just dragged out of the water, or a wounded animal.

My God! thought Will. He's been hit. Now he saw Sommers' left leg. It looked like a tiger had been chewing on it. The trousers were ripped ragged, and blood oozed through the holes.

"Medic!" screamed Will at the top of his lungs. "Medic!" He looked wildly around him. "Medic!" he called again. There was one.

"Medic! Medic!" Will yelled. "Lieutenant's hit bad! Medic!"

"Okay, kid, take off. I'll take over from here," said the medical corpsman. He looked as grimy as anybody else. Hollow, sunken eyes, scruffy beard, dirt-lined face. What a sad face, thought Will. Will shook his head as the medic began cutting away Sommers' trousers. "He's the only lieutenant I got," said Will "And—and I'm gonna stay and make sure he's okay."

The medic nodded. "You can light a cigarette for the lieutenant if you want to," he said.

"I—I don't smoke," said Will.

Sommers spoke. "Don't worry, Will. I don't either."

"It's a dirty wound," said the medic. "Got some shrapnel in the calf and upper leg. Looks like it took in a lot of dirt and cloth from your trousers with it. Only good thing is, it don't look like it smashed any bones. And if it didn't you'll be okay, Lieutenant. But you gotta go back. They'll have to operate to get the shrapnel out." Then he turned to Will. "Okay, sonny, now you know. So take off. They went thataway," he said, pointing toward the advancing infantry.

Will touched the lieutenant on the shoulder and left. He hoped he'd find Jim, or Phil Cohen, or somebody he knew. He felt alone and leaderless on the battlefield.

Suddenly he was startled to see a group of Tiger tanks sitting in a field. He hit the ground, his heart pounding, his rifle aimed ineffectually at the panzers. But there were no crews in them. Later, somebody said they had run out of gasoline.

Will caught up with a small group of riflemen. They had gotten ahead of the rest of the battalion. With a single mind, they sat down by the side of the road to wait for the main body of infantry to catch up with them.

As Will sat there, the sun came out, and the sky became clear and bright instead of overcast and gray, as it had been ever since he'd been in the line. Other troops were arriving now, and the few men with Will had gone off to join their own squads. Will continued to sit where he was, thinking how good it was to see the sun, how good it was to feel its warmth, when he heard a roar above him. He looked up and saw a group of fighter planes streaking across the sky. It was flying weather. After they had passed over, he heard the clatter of their machine guns and the dull explosions of their bombs.

I hope they kill every bastard in the German army, he thought.

While the air corps planes were still strafing and bombing the retreating German columns, Jimmy Mahoney flopped down beside Will. "Is this your idea of spending a nice day in the country?" asked Jim.

"It's a living," replied Will. "You wouldn't want the army to think you're not earning your pay, would you?"

"I done earned my pay for the next hundred years, and that's for damned sure," said Mahoney.

Ceruti, Gruber, and Phil Cohen flopped down beside them. They had stuck together and had come looking for Will and Jimmy.

"Where're the others?" Cohen asked. "Where's the lieutenant? Where's Dan Sark?"

Will said, "I don't know about Sark. But Lieutenant Sommers got hit. Got a legful of shrapnel."

"Is he bad?" asked Cohen.

Will shook his head. "I don't think so. Medic said he'd be okay unless he broke some bones."

Phil Cohen said, "I wonder where the hell Danny Sark is. Any of you seen him?"

They all shook their heads. Since his breakdown, Sark had been shy and kept to himself.

"Okay," said Cohen, "we'll just have to hope he shows up. I don't want us to split up to go looking for him. We might not get back together." He took off his helmet and ran his hand through his curly red hair. "God, that sun feels good. I thought maybe it'd forgotten how to shine for the duration."

The others smiled. It was obvious to Will that Phil Cohen was the one they considered their leader now that Sommers was hit. Nobody had said anything. No vote had been taken. The matter had not been discussed. Yet Phil Cohen was their leader by unanimous consent. The men knew their lives were on the line. They had a choice, and they simply picked the ablest to lead them. It was part of their instinct for survival.

Will figured Cohen was about twenty-two or -three. He was tall, and his features were large but they went together well. Gruber had complained that Phil Cohen thought he was better than anybody else just because he came from a rich family in New York, and Will had to admit that sometimes Phil did seem to be a little bit too sure of himself. Even when Sommers was in charge, it was Phil who usually made the suggestions they followed. The rumor in Damen was that Major Rankin had offered Cohen a field commission, and Phil had refused it.

Phil reached out for his helmet and put it back on. He looked at the other four men and said, "I think the planes have done their job and gone home now. That means we'll be taking off again in a hurry, or I miss my bet. You guys set? You all got ammunition? Rifles working okay? No problems?"

They all nodded. In the distance they heard the officers

yelling, "On your feet! Hubba! Hubba! Hubba! Let's go get the bastards!" The infantry was moving forward again.

Phil stood up and shouted, "Follow me! And try to stick together!"

The riflemen of the Fifteenth Division lurched off once more into their attack, which continued to stagger on and on and on.

In the late afternoon, an exhausted Will Pope got out his shovel. The infantry was digging in for the night. The main line of resistance of the most forward elements of the U.S. Seventh Army was made up of their ragged string of foxholes.

Luckily, the Germans didn't know how few foxholes there were.

★

At the same time, in the headquarters of the U.S. Seventh Army, a major general, his two stars gleaming on his collar, was preparing to give an informal report to his superior, who probably knew the details of the situation as well as he did.

Major General Tom Jacobs had come up through the National Guard. He had commanded an infantry division at the front until he'd been relieved suddenly and transferred to the Seventh Army's headquarters. Here he was the assistant to Lieutenant General David Richardson, the plans and operations officer, who had one more star than he did. Jacobs sighed. If he hadn't had such a distinguished record, he'd have been sent home to obscurity instead of to the Seventh Army's headquarters. So even though it was unfamiliar territory, he'd decided to make the most of it.

Jacobs was stout and red-faced, which gave people meeting him for the first time the impression he was another one of those fat, jolly men who didn't expect to be taken seriously. They changed their minds fast. Stout and red-faced Jacobs might be, ineffectual he was not. His mind was quick and analytical; his judgment, superior;

his evaluation of situations, exceptional. In the eyes of the army, Tom Jacobs had only one flaw: he wasn't impersonal enough to sacrifice his men when that had to be done. He loved his infantry too well.

Jacobs stood outside the door to Dave Richardson's office, composing his thoughts. He still wasn't sure whether he liked Richardson. Dave was a cold fish; he'd never held a field command, having spent his entire career on one headquarters staff or another. But that was what he was good at—brilliant, in fact. At least everybody said so.

No feelings, thought Jacobs. Pushes units around like pieces on a chessboard. Successful as hell, though. Can't argue with that. So let's see how much I can learn from the son-of-a-bitch.

He knocked on the door, pushed it open, and walked into Richardson's office, which was a large, bare room with a desk, a few chairs, and a table covered with maps. Large chunks of plaster were missing from the walls.

Dave Richardson was lean and tall, and his body seemed to flow along the contours of the chair he sat in. He waved his hand in greeting to Jacobs, who couldn't help noticing how tired his chief looked. A lock of gray hair fell over Richardson's brow and gave his craggy, angular features the appearance of a beardless Abraham Lincoln.

Richardson had been in the U.S. Army all his adult life. He was one of the best strategists in the service, and he knew it. He excelled in everything he did, in fact—as long as human emotions were not involved. To him, logic was the only thing that counted. Outthinking the adversary. And he did it so well he was a three-star general now.

As a young officer, though, he'd been a pompous ass, and in social situations he'd always been a disaster. At parties he had no small talk and generally tried to find a similar soul to discuss more cerebral matters with; otherwise he was apt to sit in a corner somewhere until it was decent to go home. A lifelong bachelor, he was shy among women.

The war put him in his element. He'd been in the Seventh Army's headquarters since it was formed. He'd worked with its commanding generals, from George Patton, who was the first, to Alexander Patch, the present commander. Richardson had worked hard, planned strategy, deployed troops, developed tactics, yet he'd never seen a battlefield. His war was spent in his brain and in his office. His orders went forth, the results of those orders returned in triumph in the form of reports of battles won, enemy positions overwhelmed, enemy soldiers killed or taken prisoner, cities captured. To Richardson, they were figures on his scoreboard, ciphers that proved he was a winner. And that was all.

There was another column on the board: American casualties. But as long as the odds were in his favor, Dave Richardson was not overly concerned. After all, that was the nature of war. Men get killed or wounded. It was another statistic.

The German attack on his depleted troops in Alsace had taxed his abilities to their limit, though. It was a bad situation, and one not his fault. When George Patton had to rush his Third Army units north to hold the Germans in the Bulge, somebody had to fill in the gaps, and the Seventh Army was the logical one to do it. As a result, their lines were far overextended and undermanned when the Germans struck.

Jacobs surveyed his boss for a moment as Richardson waved toward a chair, inviting him to sit down. "Our infantry held them, Dave," Jacobs said. "The damned Germans threw everything they had at them, too—panzers, elite SS units, paratroops, panzer-grenadiers, their best Wehrmacht divisions…"

"I know, Tom," replied Richardson. "We can chalk up another one. Another time we beat the ass off the enemy."

"I know you mapped the strategy, Dave," Jacobs told the other man. "But when you get right down to it, the divisions had to fight it out on their own, all by themselves."

"So you tell me," replied Richardson. "The Third Division held like a rock. You told me so. The three regiments of the Rainbow

Division stood at the Moder River and flung back everything the Germans could throw at them. You told me that, too. The veteran Seventy-ninth stopped those superbastards cold and ate them for breakfast. But how about the Fifteenth, Tom? I just caught a German propaganda broadcast that said the Fifteenth Division has ceased to exist. I know that's not true, but the Fifteenth was hit damned hard, and I can't help wondering what sort of shape they're really in..."

It was Jacobs' turn to smile. "At 0800 this morning, Dave, the Fifteenth Infantry Division jumped off at Hagenor, right on schedule. And they routed an entire German army corps that tried to stop them. Does that answer your question?"

Richardson nodded without replying. Finally he said, "Good. I was sure they would. I wouldn't have scheduled their attack if I hadn't been. We deserved to win this one, Tom."

Jacobs shook his head slowly. "No," he said, "we didn't deserve to win this one. The Germans should have broken our lines and been halfway to Paris by now. The only reason they're not is because our soldiers fought like hell. They wouldn't give up. They didn't have your kind of cold logic, Dave, or they would have. We beat the Germans this time because when our infantry soldiers are in a tight spot and have to fight it out on their own, they're better than the Germans."

9

⸺◆⸺

The night was bitter cold. The excitement of the attack had worn off, and Will lay on the ground beside his hole and tried to sleep. His teeth chattered. He had hated to put his muddy boots into his sleeping bag. But he had. Even so, the blanket-lined bag gave very little comfort in such freezing weather. The ground was rock-hard and ice-cold. Will wished he were dead.

Somebody was shaking him. He must have been so exhausted, he'd dozed off. He looked up. Phil Cohen said, "Okay, Will. Your turn for guard."

Will scrambled out of his sleeping bag. He was stiff and sore, but it was good to stand. Jim Mahoney joined them, and Phil posted them behind a small, ugly, bare black tree. "You'll be relieved at four this morning," Phil said. "Keep a good lookout and be careful."

Will did not remember sleeping after coming off his guard with Jim Mahoney, but when he opened his eyes he was surprised to see the gray light of dawn. He slid into his foxhole and pulled his sleeping bag in after him. Lying on the ground was all right at night, with the darkness hiding you from enemy eyes, but daylight made you feel naked and exposed.

There was movement around him. He poked his head up and saw only the top of Mahoney's helmet. He called softly, "Jim. Jim. What's going on?"

"The same old crap. We attack the Germans again. This here war is getting damned tedious, if you ask me. Heard a guy say the Krautheads laid some mines."

Oh, oh, thought Will. He began to look around. His ears had unconsciously sorted out the sounds of the battlefield and concluded that both the heavy-artillery bursts and the small-arms fire were too far away to be a threat. The immediate vicinity was relatively quiet. Yes. Men were moving around. Not standing straight up, of course, but scurrying about, bent over almost double, with their hands touching the ground as they darted from one position to another.

Suddenly a danger signal went off in Will Pope's brain. Something in the scene alarmed him. There it was: a captain, making his way toward them. "Here comes trouble," said Will.

"The antitank mine platoon's supposed to be here with Able Company. Where are they?" Will saw Phil Cohen get out of his hole and touch the rim of his helmet in a casual salute, which the captain returned the same way.

"We got a job for you," said the captain. "There's a road that runs between where we are now and the German positions we hope to take this morning. Jerry mined the road last night."

Will saw Cohen nod his head slowly as the captain continued, "When we take the Jerry positions, we're going to need that road bad, to get the wounded back and to get ammunition up to the line. You understand?"

Phil nodded.

"So," said the captain, "that road has to be cleared of mines by the time we take the Jerry positions. Our attack starts in half an hour. Your platoon starts right now."

In front of the forward foxholes of the most advanced unit in the U.S. Seventh Army, the five men of the antitank mine platoon of the 555th Infantry crawled toward the enemy along the dirt road, each probing the ground in front of him with his bayonet. The five men stretched across the road in a straight line. They worked so silently, it would have been hard to tell if they were even breathing. But underneath their sweaters and field jackets the pounding of their hearts was like a concert of kettledrums.

In the middle of the road, now slightly ahead of the others, Phil Cohen held up his hand. All activity stopped. Without looking back at his men, Phil whispered hoarsely, "I've found a mine. Now watch what I do. See? I'm feeling around the base of the mine for trip wires. They're so thin you can't see them, and the Jerrys'll attach them to grenades underneath the mine. So if you just lift up the mine, it'll pull the pin loose on the grenade and blow your head off. See how carefully I'm feeling around the mine? See how slowly I go? I can trip the wire with the pressure from my hand just as easy as I can by lifting the mine. There! See? There don't seem to be any wires.

"Now look. I'm lifting the mine out of the hole very gently. If I missed a wire, it'll blow us all up. Gently, gently, gently. There it is!"

The sigh that went up from the platoon was audible. For the first time since he found the mine, Phil turned to his men. He smiled briefly.

"Listen carefully," he said. "We'd usually remove the fuses from these bastards, but we're not going to. The captain told me they've come across a new Jerry trick. As soon as you start to unscrew the fuse, it detonates the mine. So we're going to leave them at the side of the road without taking out the fuses. The engineers'll do it later. The main thing is to have the road clear."

Gruber hit a mine and removed it; so did Jim. Will's bayonet hit metal, clunk. He started to feel around the base of the mine. It had his full attention. He only heard the attack begin—he didn't see it. He searched for wires and hoped his fingers were sensitive enough to feel them after being so cold for so long. Artillery shells boomed and swished overhead, machine guns stuttered, rifles cracked and mortars whoomped all over the field. No. No trip wire yet. Almost finished. Shells were screaming into the field, and the riflemen who'd been dashing forward were now lying still, pinned down by enemy fire. Will slowly lifted the heavy, metal disc from its hole. He sighed.

"Pull back! Pull back! They're coming at us. We'll catch them in the open! Pull back! Pull back, so we can shoot the bastards good!" Will heard the shouting, but the meaning of the words didn't register in his brain.

He jabbed his bayonet into the dirt in short, shallow probes. He was doing it faster than he had at first. It was getting easier now. Cohen found another mine. So did Gruber. It would be Will's turn again in a minute.

There were no more charging G.I.'s. The mine platoon were by themselves, the only five men in the area. Clunk went Will's bayonet; he laid it aside and started feeling once more for wires.

Mortars were still churning up the field, machine guns were chopping up everything above the height of a short man's kneecap, and men were running past and flopping to the ground to make themselves more difficult targets. But this time the men wore field gray uniforms and came from the wrong direction. They shouted at each other in guttural-sounding voices in a strange language.

In the cold of January, Will Pope was sweating as he felt around the base of the mine. His mind was not entirely on what he was doing. Out of the corner of his eye he could not fail to see the German soldiers rushing past him. Nor could he fail to see the exploding shells or hear the crackling of small-arms fire. The G.I.'s must have been ordered to pull back. Yes. He remembered the shouts now.

We're all alone, thought Will. All alone on a mined road. Now I know how the old mine platoon felt just before they were wiped out. He was breathing hard. His heart was jumping out of his throat.

Like every man in the platoon, he'd been so intent on what he was doing—probing for mines and feeling for trip wires and concentrating on the demanding task in front of him—he had not grasped what had been going on around him except in a detached, unconscious sort of way. So now the platoon had no alternative but to continue to carry out their mission, acutely aware of the fact that they were five American soldiers all alone in the middle of a German counterattack.

"You okay, Will?" whispered Ceruti, who was lying beside him. Will nodded. He forced his eyes to focus on the mine. He started feeling around it again.

The German soldiers, intent on their own survival and alert only to danger to themselves, were paying no attention to the five men lying on the road.

Will was sweating again. As long as we keep on with what we're doing, he thought, they'll let us alone. They won't even notice us. But if we were to stand up suddenly, they'd shoot us all down so fast we wouldn't even know what hit us. Or if just one of us were to take a shot at them, we'd all be dead in a second. He prayed that everybody else had figured that out, too.

Now his hands began to shake, and he withdrew them from the mine. He took several deep breaths, concentrated all his attention and all his thoughts on the mine in front of him, and went back to work. The explosions kept tearing up the field, and the popping of rifles and machine guns was constant. Will tried desperately not to think what would happen if a shell hit the road.

The men in field gray who were still on their feet seemed to be falling back now. There was a lot of rushing around and some yelling in German. There were no more exploding shells or mortars, just the rattle of small-arms fire. The men in G.I. helmets and jackets had returned to the field and were driving themselves forward, firing from their hips as they trotted on and on.

Clunk. Another mine. Once more, Will put down his bayonet and started groping.

The gunfire was fading in the distance now. It looked to Will as if the G.I.s had already gone beyond their objective and were still rolling forward.

"Hey, there, you men," called a young officer from a group that had come up from the rear. "Good going, mine platoon. Nice work. But you have only five men. You'll take too long, so go catch up with the rifle troops. Our people can take it from here."

The five men stood stiffly on the road. They slung their rifles. "Good Lord!" exclaimed another officer, "Didn't they get any farther than that?"

"No," replied the first. "They've been feeling for trip wires and all that crap. Going by the book."

The other laughed. "Hell, we don't have to do that. Jerries never had time to booby-trap these bastards. All we have to do is lift them."

By now the platoon was moving again, and the words began to fade.

Will was angry and depressed. He knew Phil Cohen had been right to go cautiously, yet he felt like a fool after hearing those young officers talk like that. They'd dismissed the platoon—belittled them, even—after the mine platoon had done the dangerous work under enemy fire. And done it right, too, as they were supposed to. Damn those smug young officers!

They reached the top of the rise in front of them. Without a word, they turned to look back at the road, most of which they had cleared so painfully. There were soldiers on the road.

Nobody was shooting at them, and they had all the time they wanted. They were casually bending over to lift up the mines they were still finding, while the trucks waited in line for them to finish.

Will was about to turn back toward the front when there was a flash. An explosion! It set off another. And another in a chain reaction. Now their reports cracked the air. Mines were blowing up all over the road, and men were being tossed around like paper dolls in a high wind. Drivers were jumping out of their trucks and diving into ditches.

The group of fresh-faced young officers had been cut down by the first blasts and lay beside the road, looking like piles of bloody rags that moved only when the wind ruffled them.

Phil Cohen looked at Will for a brief second, and Will smiled. Then the platoon turned and headed toward the front and the advancing riflemen. Will felt good now. Phil had been vindicated. The platoon had done things the right way, and they'd been successful. So to hell with those fancy, smart-assed, know-it-all, rear-echelon bastards with their shortcuts. Those dead, fancy, smart-assed, know-it-all, rear-echelon...

Suddenly Will realized he was gloating because several Americans, men like him, had just been killed. He was horrified. Had he become so hardened, so callous? Had he? Had his values changed so dramatically that he considered death a suitable punishment for those who displeased him?

He had to think that one out.

He was glad Phil had been right, happy the platoon had been cautious, but that was all. Of course he felt sorry for the dead officers lying back there on the road. Poor bastards. They'd been so fresh and cocksure, like college boys. They never had the chance to learn that a battleground wasn't a playing field. They never would. Their lives were over.

Will wished there had been some way they could have botched up the detail without getting themselves killed. He realized once again that in combat, if you made a mistake, you died.

Catching up with Able Company wasn't as easy as Will had thought it would be. There were woods and scattered fields to cross, hills and streams. Will saw G.I.'s far away, still advancing. He heard artillery and small-arms fire, glimpsed patches of smoke-brown smoke, blue smoke, white smoke. He realized the little platoon was now trotting forward, crossing a narrow field between two stands of timber. They were in the open, and they could be seen. And there were bypassed Germans all over the place. The mine platoon began to run faster.

Phil yelled, "Hit it!" and dove forward onto the soft, muddy ground as the other four followed his example unquestioningly. Will heard the German machine gun firing, heard the whispering bullets pass over him. He heard an explosion. The gun stopped. Will looked up. Phil had thrown a hand grenade; now Gruber flopped forward as he arced another one toward the woods. Will saw the flashes in the pines. He saw Ceruti raise himself up and throw a grenade. Cohen was firing into the woods. So were Gruber and Ceruti. Then Jim Mahoney pulled himself up and threw.

Will pulled the pin of a hand grenade and lobbed it with all his might. He saw it hit the ground before it reached the trees, but it bounced into them as Will rose to his knees, firing his rifle.

He heard yelling from the woods. A German behind a tree was waving a white handkerchief at the end of a stick. Cohen stopped firing but motioned the others to stay down and stay back.

Still on his knees, Will heard Phil calling to the German and the German shouting back. Will's rifle pointed at the woods, at the white handkerchief. He saw movement. The Germans were coming out with their hands on their heads. He started counting them. "One, two, three. My God, they're young! Just kids. Six, seven. Those last two are wounded. That's all. Just seven of them left. I wonder how many they started with."

The fire fight with the Germans and their machine gun had slowed the platoon down, so they were more than glad to turn the prisoners over to a group of wounded who had been ordered to the rear.

"These guys won't give you any trouble," Phil assured the wounded men. "I think we've killed off all their elite superKrauts, and all we're hitting now is the second team, whatever they can scrape together."

The platoon was walking fast but not running or trotting, and Will was breathing hard. He knew they were getting close, though; among the other debris of battle there were now a number of freshly wounded men. In small groups, usually attended by a single medic, they sat glassy-eyed or lay still by the side of a road or path, wearing bandages. They made Will think of people who'd been injured in a bad automobile accident.

Then they came across clumps of dead Germans who had not been removed, and a few dead G.I.'s, and discarded ration boxes and piles of machine gun shell casings, discarded gas masks, packs, and mess kits. Suddenly Phil Cohen froze, with his rifle pointed toward a small hollow in the ground in front of him. Will drew up beside him. In the hollow were a group of German soldiers, sitting quietly, protected from danger.

The first thing Will noticed about them was that they were neatly uniformed and clean-shaven. Then he saw they were older men, probably in their forties, all of them. They're nothing but a bunch of German quartermasters, thought Will contemptuously. Rear-echelon bastards.

As soon as the Germans saw the platoon, they rose to their feet and began to bow and point toward their discarded helmets, indicating they'd surrendered already. *"Nazi kaput! Hitler kaput!"* they kept saying over and over again while they continued to bow to the G.I.'s, who kept their rifles trained on them.

Will was afraid he might start shooting these unarmed old men, and he knew that would be wrong, but he wasn't sure why.

As a man, the platoon turned and walked on, leaving the Germans standing in the hollow.

It was dark. Will felt the intense cold once more.

"Who goes there?" The shout was accompanied by the clicking of a light machine gun's bolt sliding into the cocked and ready position. "Mine platoon!" Phil Cohen called into the darkness. After the exchange of password and countersign, the platoon staggered into the Able Company position.

"I have two wounded men," said Phil. "I want to leave them with the medics, then find the CO and report." As they left, Phil said, "And keep a good lookout. There're Jerry patrols all over the place, including your rear."

Captain Wilkes of A Company was a tall, cheerful young man who, despite the recent bitter fighting, seemed relaxed. His manner was casual.

The command post was a small farmhouse. All the windows had tarpaulins over them, and tent tops covered the holes in the roof. Kerosene lamps and candles lit the room, and the air was heavy with their smoke. Three broken chairs and a table with a missing leg were the only furniture.

Phil Cohen seemed to have caught some of the captain's casual manner. As he finished his report, Phil said, "After dark, we heard a Jerry patrol go past. There were only six of them, so we followed, and when we thought we had a good chance to get them all, we opened up. Think we got them, too. But there was another bunch behind them. Lucky for us, they started shooting as soon as we took on their friends, or they'd have gotten us for sure. We barely got away in the dark as it was."

"You got a pretty lucky bunch, Sergeant? Lieutenant? Whoever you are. But, dammit, you should know the Jerries never send only six men out on patrol. You should've known they'd have the other half of the patrol stalking behind."

Phil smiled. "I know now. But we're only the mine platoon, remember? And I'm Private Cohen. I'm in charge."

Captain Wilkes snapped his fingers and said, "Wait a minute. Mine platoon. Mine platoon. Then that guy Sark was one of your boys."

Phil nodded. "He's been missing ever since the jump-off at Hagenor," said Phil. "What about him? Do you know where he is?"

"More or less," Wilkes said. "I'm afraid I don't have good news for you, though, except he'll most likely get the Congressional Medal of Honor. Posthumously."

The three men in front of him stared at Captain Wilkes, their exhausted minds trying to grasp what he'd just told them.

"Yeah," continued Wilkes. "He and your Lieutenant Sommers were together. They'd got separated from the rest of your boys in the mist. They'd just tied up with a couple of mine when a Jerry machine gun opened up on them.

"Well, it looked like they were going to be pinned down for a while, when this guy Sark jumps up and charges right at the damn gun all by himself, shooting as he goes, and he's lucky. Must have caught them reloading, so he's able to get close enough to toss a grenade and wipe the bastards out, almost.

"Anyway, he knocks out the machine gun, and your lieutenant and my guys come running up and just then some Kraut son-of-a-bitch wakes up and pitches a potato masher into the bunch of them. Your boy Sark jumps on it just as it blows. Saved them all."

The three men remained very still.

"By the way," continued Wilkes, "what happened to Lieutenant Sommers? Somebody reported he got hit."

Will cleared his throat. "I guess it was right after that I ran across him. He got a legful of shrapnel."

Wilkes nodded. "Well, you've got three men now, that's all. I'll split you up among my squads. We've been hit pretty bad."

Cohen shook his head. "Sir, we're a platoon of infantry— we fight as a platoon."

Wilkes laughed. "Three men? A platoon? Well, if you guys fight better that way, what the hell? I don't care. Let's see. My lightest squad is Johnson's. I'll put you with them."

Captain Wilkes had been studying the faces of the three men standing before him. Now his eyes darted from Cohen to Will to Jim. He paused before he said, "But you know, the guard roster's been made, and the guards're posted already. So why don't you guys go on over to the corner and get a little sleep. Hey?"

Will had unrolled his sleeping bag and wiggled into it wearing everything he had on except his cartridge belt, helmet, and rifle when the guard at the door stuck his head inside. "They's two guys out here what says they's mine platoon."

Ceruti and Gruber came in, both limping, their ripped trousers flopping over their combat boots, and bandages showing where their legs had been wrapped up.

Standing in the middle of the room, Captain Wilkes asked Phil, "Yours?"

When Phil nodded, Wilkes went back to what he was doing, the guard returned to his post; and Phil Cohen turned to Ceruti and Gruber. "What the hell are you guys doing here? Hey? Thought I sent you back to the medics."

Gruber said, "Hell, Phil, you know how the Medical Corps of this damned army works. 'Take two aspirins and see us in the morning,' right?"

"Wrong," replied Phil. "What happened?"

Ceruti coughed. "Well, Phil, uh, ah—we uh, figured three men ain't enough for you to take on the whole damned German army with, so we thought we'd give you a fighting chance, you know what I mean? Give you guys a little better odds."

Phil was shaking his head and smiling at the same time. "Did they let you come back, or are you guys AWOL?"

Gruber said, "Naw. We ain't AWOL. We told the medics our platoon was down to five men when we got hit, so if they sent us back to the hospital, the platoon'd show a forty percent casualty rate for the day, and that'd make a lousy statistic."

Ceruti cut in, "They patched us up and wrote out the papers for our Purple Hearts and stuff and let us come back. A medic told me most of the wounded who can still walk want to go back to their outfits, so they're letting them. We need everybody. They gave us some pills for the pain, so we can walk pretty good."

"We're jumping off again in the morning," said Phil.

Both men nodded. Ceruti smiled. "So we've heard."

Will Pope dropped his head back down on his blanket and closed his eyes. "'We few. We happy few,'" He murmured under his breath. "'We band of brothers.'"

Early the next morning the infantry resumed their attack on the Germans. The five men of the antitank mine platoon charged forward with the rest, but it was easier this time. During the night, the American artillery had come up and was now firing rapidly into the German lines. The big guns blazed away as the infantrymen went forward.

Even with all the noise and smoke, Will felt safer than he had before. Nothing could live under such heavy fire. He trotted forward confidently, always keeping Phil Cohen in view as the shells exploded in front of them. "This is more like it!" shouted Will to nobody in particular. The words had just left his lips when the artillery stopped, and he realized he was almost up to the German line. For a split second, his heart jumped into his mouth. He didn't know if he froze still at that moment or not, but now he was running through the smoke, firing his rifle as he ran, and feeling it jump in his hands. He remembered the simple principle: Keep the Germans' heads down in their holes with your rifle fire so they can't shoot at you until you're into their positions. Then you go in and destroy them with grenades, with point-blank rifle fire, with bayonets and trench knives, with rocks, any way you can.

The lines had formed again. Even though things were relatively quiet, Will dug his foxhole deep. The sun broke through the overcast sky just as he finished digging, and he realized it was almost noon. His spirits rose with the sun, and he actually felt cheerful.

The Germans who hadn't been killed had surrendered to the G.I.'s as soon as they'd entered their positions.

Will was about to shout to Jim Mahoney when Gruber called, "Hey, Will, some guy's going to thank you for that nice deep hole you just dug for him."

Will grinned at him, then asked, "How's that?"

Gruber laughed. "We're going to be relieved, I hear. Leastways, that's the hot rumor. A guy told me the 554th is already moving out of the line, what there is left of them."

"No kidding!" shouted Will. "When? When are they going to relieve us?"

"Ask a general or something," replied Gruber. "They ain't told me yet."

As the bearded, dirty, ragged, bandaged men of the 555th Infantry began to assemble behind the lines their relief had moved into, they were a pitifully small group, an insignificant handful when compared to the swarming G.I.'s of the new division's rear, who were setting up their supporting operations.

But Will didn't have long to stare at them before Phil Cohen was leading the small platoon off across a field still covered with snow, and Will realized they were alone again. After they'd gotten away from the hustle and confusion that always occurs when one infantry division relieves another, Phil stopped his four men at the far edge of the field, about a hundred yards from a pine wood. He smiled. "Well, you guys, we're going back to the good old antitank company. But we're going to have to walk a little, to the other side of the woods to a town. There'll be trucks from regiment there to take us the rest of the way.

"Okay, you two heroes, how the hell are your legs? Can you make it?"

Both Ceruti and Gruber grinned at Phil and nodded.

"Good," said Phil. "Now that we're out of the line, you're both going back for hospital treatment." He didn't wait for an argument but turned and led them off again toward the pines.

They were relatively safe, and Will felt a tremendous weariness as his body began to relax. He realized he was staggering. But when he looked at the others, they were, too—every single one of them. They were completely exhausted, but only now did their brains allow their bodies to react to it, when they weren't forced to stay alert in order to stay alive. They walked like men in a trance.

Somebody was shouting. It seemed to Will the shouts came from far, far away. But as his awareness returned, he looked up and saw a staff car parked in front of them, and a colonel standing in the road with his aides beside him. His voice was harsh and accusing as he yelled once more, "Where the hell do you stragglers think you're going? Hey? Hey?"

Phil was unsteady on his feet as he made his way toward the colonel. He saluted and had the salute returned. "We are not stragglers, sir," he said, having trouble keeping a note of defiance out of his voice. "We're a platoon of infantry, the antitank mine platoon of the 555th, coming out of the line as commanded, in good order, with our weapons and equipment. It just happens we're down to five men, and two of them are wounded, that's all."

The colonel nodded without replying, but for an instant, Will saw his expression soften.

Phil rejoined his men, and they started moving off again. Will glanced back at the colonel and saw the officer raise his hand to his helmet in a salute as the platoon swayed silently on its way through the snow. The colonel was still standing in the road holding his salute when they disappeared into the pines, like five shadows in the failing light.

Will Pope had been in combat exactly one week.

BOOK

2

ON SOME SCARRED SLOPE OF A BATTERED HILL

10

The Jeep's wheels spun in the winter mud as it entered the French village: a few crooked streets, a couple of dozen dirty stone buildings, and an unpaved square. Beside the driver sat a clerk from regimental headquarters.

Over the largest building on the square was a sign ANTITANK CO. 555 INF., and in front of the big, open door stood a guard in a clean but faded field jacket, with a rifle slung on his shoulder and a dented helmet pulled low over his eyes.

As the Jeep pulled up to the door, the clerk said, "Hi. Is the captain or exec around? I got tonight's password and countersign."

The guard smiled. "Hell," he replied, "we don't need no password. Division's in reserve. Ain't you heard?"

The clerk smiled back. He was used to this kind of an answer now—he got it in every town.

"Captain's inside," said the guard.

When the clerk came back out of the headquarters and got in the Jeep, the guard drawled, "Ease her out slow-like, buddy. Cause if you splash mud on my clean gear, I'll put one right through your gas tank for you."

The clerk waved his farewell as the Jeep slowly pulled away from the antitank headquarters, carefully avoiding a large puddle in the middle of the road.

✪

After the Fifteenth Division came out of the line and went into reserve, the walking wounded who had refused to leave their units went to the rear for medical treatment, and the men with an assortment of other illnesses caused by exposure and stress went with them, leaving the infantry companies bare.

For a few days during that winter, the towns and villages that billeted the three regiments of the division were like ghost towns. Smoke coming from the chimneys of a few houses and an occasional bundled figure hurrying stiffly down the street to relieve a companion on guard duty or to get a hot meal were the only indications of human presence. The few French civilians who had not left stayed inside.

In a house designated to billet thirty men, Privates First Class Phil Cohen and Will Pope were the only inhabitants. Ceruti and Gruber had gone straight to the hospital to have their wounds properly looked after, and the next day Jim Mahoney had to be carried out with a raging fever, unconscious from pneumonia. His utter disregard for taking care of himself had caught up with him.

The activities of the few men left in the company were limited to standing guard duty—the atmosphere was relaxed. But the officers and the headquarters staff were busy making preparations to receive the men and equipment they knew were already on the way. Phil Cohen had arranged to have the mine platoon excluded even from guard duty, so after getting warm and comfortable again, he and Will started passing the idle hours chatting when they weren't sleeping soundly.

The first things they talked about were the battles they had just come through, their small parts in them, and what was going on around them. Then they discussed the war in general and how stupid the generals were to let the Germans catch them like that, and afterward they spoke of their remaining companions, Ceruti and Gruber, of Dan Sark's throwing himself on a German hand grenade, about Sommers getting hit and Jim Mahoney getting so sick.

"By the way, how come you're such a friend of that nut Mahoney?" asked Phil. "He's a disaster."

Will was startled by the question. Even though there were a couple of chairs in the room, both he and Phil were sitting on a blanket in front of the fire. Will turned to look at Phil to see if he expected an answer. Before he'd become Jim's friend, Will would have automatically evaded the question by cracking a joke or making a flippant remark about hillbillies. But now, from the expression on Phil's face, his intuition told him Phil wanted to be his friend and was jealous of Jim. Will was pleased and flattered.

"Like you say, Mahoney's a nut," replied Will. "But there's a lot more to it than that. When I met Jim the first day of basic training, I was damned depressed. Do you know what I mean?"

"Sure," replied Phil. "Everybody is."

"No, no. I was more depressed than that," said Will. "Let me explain. You can see I'm not what anybody'd call good-looking; I had pimples all over my face until about a year ago. Besides that, I was awkward as hell, and I was afraid nobody liked me much. So I stayed to myself a lot. I got used to it, sort of. I got so I just loved to sit by myself. I'd read Shakespeare a lot, other things. But the high point of my week was Saturday—I'd go to the movies alone and sit through the main feature two or three times. I'd spend the whole afternoon there."

Phil didn't say anything, but Will could tell he was very intent.

"By the time I was a senior in high school, though, I'd made up for being so homely by telling jokes and making people laugh. And I always tried to be nice to everybody, anyway, and I started to get the feeling that the other guys might like me, even.

"Then it happened! I fell in love! Boy, did I ever! Her name was Maggie Donovan, and was she stacked! Her tits stuck out a mile, I swear. And she was beautiful, besides. At lunch in the school cafeteria, she smiled at me a couple of times. She smiled at me! After that, every time I'd see her in the street or in the hall, my heart would pound and I'd feel like the wind had just been knocked out of me."

"You had it bad all right," said Phil.

Will nodded. "Yeah," he said. "And because she'd smiled at me a couple of times, I got up the nerve to ask her to the senior prom last spring. My God! Was it only last spring? I figured dancing with her would be the closest thing to heaven there was. When I thought of pressing myself up against those boobs I got a hard-on like you wouldn't believe…"

"So?" asked Phil.

Will shook his head. "She didn't laugh out loud. No. She was too polite to do that. She even smiled at me. She was nice, but what she told me was that she and Jack Reynolds were going steady, so, of course, she was going to the prom with him.

"I died. It made me realize again what an insignificant jerk I was. Jack Reynolds! Of all the guys in the whole school!"

"Who was Jack Reynolds?" asked Phil.

Will bit his lip. "He was kind of my hero; the captain of the football team, the handsomest guy in school, and, dammit, probably the nicest. And do you want to hear the worst part? His father is my father's best friend! I didn't have a chance with Maggie, and that was for sure. So I started looking forward to getting drafted. I wanted to go right into the navy and get sent to the Pacific. It'd be exciting and glamorous, and I'd come home a hero, and Maggie Donovan would beg me to take her out, and I'd just look down my nose at her and say, 'Sorry, Maggie, you'll have to wait your turn with all the rest,' or something like that. Or if I didn't get in the navy, I'd go into the air corps. I've never been in an airplane, but I bet it'd be fun…

"Instead, they stuck me in the damned infantry! And it scared me to death. I remembered all those World War I movies I'd seen, with guys in the trenches getting blown up and bayoneted, and all that mud and slime. That's why I was so damned dejected that first day of basic. And nobody cared! Nobody gave a good, happy damn! And I just stood there looking like a lost puppy or something, I guess.

"And then Mahoney came over and said, 'Buck up, pal. You ain't dead yet,' or something like that. And I said, 'Don't bet any money on it, old pal, or you might lose your shirt.' And we both laughed, and I felt better right away—the more we talked, the better I felt, until I almost felt good. Can you beat that?"

Phil smiled. "Oh, I think that happens fairly often the first day of training. A bunch of guys get thrown together and each one feels a little lonely until he finds somebody he likes and feels comfortable with."

Will thought about that for a minute, then shook his head before he continued. "Anyway, Jim and I ended up bunking in the same hut and training in the same squad. After a while, I'd told him everything there was to know about Will Pope, and there wasn't anything I didn't know about James Davis Mahoney, either. For the first time in my life, I had a friend, a real, honest-to-God friend."

"You're a lucky fellow," said Phil. "There aren't many people who can say that."

Will looked up sharply to see if Phil was kidding him. He realized he wasn't, but Will had begun to assume that everybody had friends, now that he did. After he thought about it for a minute, though, he knew Phil was right.

"You were telling me about Mahoney," Phil said.

"Oh, yeah," answered Will. "He's not really a hillbilly, you know. I just call him that, and he acts like he is, but he's from a town so big it's almost a city. But it is in the Great Smoky Mountains, and the people in those parts talk like Jim does, even the ones who've been to college. If they don't, they put it on. They don't want anybody to think they're outsiders or something."

That made Phil smile.

"Anyway," Will continued, "Jim's paw, as he calls him, is a pretty big wheel up there in the mountains. And my father's a big wheel, too," blurted Will. "Maybe that's why I was afraid to make friends with the other kids. I thought they might want to hang out with me just because of my father." Then he gulped. He wished he hadn't said that.

"Your father's rich?" asked Phil. He asked it perfectly naturally, something, thought Will, not everyone could do.

Will shrugged. "He's a politician. But my mother's rich. She's a Devereaux, and they own the most part of a couple of counties." Again, Will felt like snatching back the words as soon as they'd left his lips. He knew he was trying to build himself up in Phil's eyes, and he knew he shouldn't say things like that, even if they were true. They sounded 'tacky,' as his mother would have said. He wanted to bite his tongue. He'd promised himself he'd never brag or let anybody know who his father was, and here he was, doing just that. He wanted so much for Phil to like him.

"So you and the hillbilly have something in common, then," said Phil.

"I guess so," answered Will. He sounded uncertain, though. He knew he'd made it sound as if he and Jim had a lot in common, but he knew they didn't.

"Jim's a hell of a lot better-looking than I am. You've got to admit that," said Will. He smiled. "He was even a beautiful baby, from what I gather. His mother doted on him, spent almost all her time with him. He was her only kid. Jim's father was an old man with grown children. He'd been married a couple of times before, but I think the wives died or something. Anyway, he was crazy about his young wife and let her do pretty much what she wanted to. He was damned well-off by the standards of the mountain folk, so he indulged her every whim, as they say. She spent all her time, just about, with little Jimmy.

"Jim worshiped his mother. I think he must have been a bright kid and cute—you know what I mean? So everything was as it should be, and the world was a perfect place."

Phil shook his head. "Devoted love between mother and child, a communion of souls." He shook his head again. "No, Will, it won't wash. Something tells me that's not what produces people like Jim Mahoney."

"No, it sure isn't," replied Will. "When Jim was seven years old, Jim and his mother got caught in a rainstorm while they were playing together in the woods. A few days later, the mother Jim adored died of pneumonia. That's not uncommon in those parts. But you can imagine the effect on the kid. He was devastated. Absolutely crushed. He felt lost and alone in the world. The only thing he'd ever loved was gone forever.

"And the hell of it was that his father was even more affected than he was! He didn't do anything but sit and grieve for his lost love, and he paid no attention to the boy at all. Instead of growing closer to his son, and trying to comfort this poor little kid, Jim's father withdrew into himself. They just got farther and farther apart until they couldn't possibly get back together again. That was when Jim changed, I think. His world ended when his mother died. He didn't care anymore what happened. Nothing life could ever do to him could hurt him more than that one, big, tragic thing.

"Later on, a lot later on, I think, his father came out of it and tried to make it up to him. He tried to love and to help Jim. He sounds like a fair, hardworking, and frugal man generally, but not what you'd call a pleasant man. Sort of dry and cold, if you know what I mean. Anyway, it was too late. Jim didn't give a damn. He wouldn't try to please anybody, least of all his father. He did whatever he felt like doing and didn't care a damn about the consequences.

"He's bright as hell, but he kept getting kicked out of school, and his father would give him a whipping every time he did, and that's the way things went. When he was older, he started spending his time at the pool hall or out fishing on the creek. And you know how good-looking he is? Well, he can really turn on the charm when he wants something, too. Like girls. I think he might have gotten a few of them pregnant, but Jim says he's not sure." Will smiled. "I'll bet you a dollar he did."

"Nothing he did would surprise me," observed Phil.

Anyway," continued Will, "his father got more and more fed up with him. He beat him more often and probably would have thrown him out except for the memory of his dear wife. That's what Jim says he called her all the time after she died—'my dear wife.' The old man never remarried, and on the day Jim turned eighteen, do you know what he did? Squire Mahoney marched right down to the draft board and demanded they take his son immediately. He told them he wanted them to put him in the army and make a man of him!

"They sure took him up on it, too, you can bet. Jim says most of the guys who turned eighteen lit out for the high timber and they had to go chase them, but you know how Jim is. He'll tell you anything that makes a good story. He didn't give a damn, anyway. Went right into the army and continued his same old way. He used to go AWOL all the time and just make it back before they caught him, and he never passed an inspection in his life, but what the hell? You know Mahoney."

"You really like him, don't you?" said Phil.

"I sure do," replied Will. "If it weren't for Jim, I don't think I'd have made it through basic. Taking care of the nut and trying to cover up for him took my mind off of why I was being taught to bayonet dummies and throw hand grenades and shoot the good, old M-1 from the hip and bandage head wounds and all that crap.

"And we talked a lot together. He told me his troubles, I told him my problems, the things I was afraid of, the things I liked. I'd never been able to talk to anybody about things like that before. I never felt that close to anybody."

Phil leaned over and squeezed Will's knee. "I hope you'll feel that close to me," he said almost in a whisper.

"I already do," replied Will. He was lying. He liked Phil, but he could never feel as close to him as he did to Jim.

Phil patted Will's leg, then squeezed his thigh, close to his crotch. It hurt, and Will stood up. "I've been talking too long," he said. "I've got to go to the latrine."

He wanted to get out of the room, but he wasn't sure why. He considered Phil his hero, much as he did Jack Reynolds, but he knew now that heroworship was a lot different from true friendship. Jack Reynolds had always been too busy with other things to become friends with Will, and as soon as things became active in the antitank company of the Triple Nickel, Phil probably would be, too. But right now, Will knew he didn't like the idea of Phil pinching his leg very much. It confused and bewildered him.

When Will returned to the billet, Phil was still sitting on the blanket by the fire, his arms around his knees. When he looked up at Will, he seemed a little embarrassed, although Will couldn't imagine why. After all, Will was the one who should be chagrined—he was the one who'd done the bragging, the one who'd told his most intimate secrets. It was time to change the subject. As far as he was concerned, they'd talked enough about Jim Mahoney and Will Pope. He said, "Phil, somebody told me you went to Harvard. Is that true? Then how come you're not an officer?"

Phil hesitated a moment, then said, "Maybe I like being a private without any responsibilities except keeping myself alive."

"Baloney! You take responsibility all the time. You took over the platoon after Sommers got hit. You know damned well you'd make a swell officer."

"All right, Will," replied Cohen. "It's this: I don't believe any man should be put above another man. I believe we're all equal, and I don't approve of a system that's based on somebody being better than somebody else just because he wears a piece of metal on his collar. So I'll remain a private, thank you."

Will scratched his head. His eyes widened. He almost whispered, "You mean you're a Red?"

Phil laughed. "No. I'm not a Communist, if that's what you mean. But I'm what they call a flaming Socialist. I have funny ideas, like I don't think it's right that most of the people in the world go to bed hungry when the world has enough to be able to feed them all. I believe…" He stopped and smiled at the expression on Will's face. "I see you agree with everybody else. My ideas are funny. Well, my friend and equal, that's why I'll never be an officer and why they'll never make me one, either."

Will shook his head. He thought for a moment. Finally he said, "Nuts. You'd make a damned good officer, and you know it. Don't you feel you have the obligation to be one? You're a leader— you're smart as hell. Don't you owe it to somebody or something to use the capabilities you've got? Don't the Socialists say 'From each according to his abilities,' or something like that?"

"'To each according to his needs,'" Phil finished. "Where in God's name did you hear that?"

"I read it someplace."

Phil was surprised by the extent of Will's reading. Like the others, Pope was just a kid. But he was obviously an educated kid.

"Anyhow, don't try to sidetrack me. I still think you ought to be an officer," said Will.

"It's an awful temptation," replied Phil. "I'll tell you a secret. Deep down, I'd love to be an officer. I like to take charge and lead men. But I have my principles. It's the system I refuse to support. I almost wish there were some way the army could force me to be an officer. Then I could do what I really want to and not compromise my beliefs. I'd have no choice. But the army doesn't work that way."

At that point, it was Phil who decided to change the subject. He'd said too much already. "You're bright and well educated, Will," he said. "Is there any special reason why you're a private?"

"Yeah. There sure is," replied Will.

"What is it?"

"I was drafted."

They both laughed, and that was the end of it.

Will jumped to his feet and yelled, "ATTENTION!" even though he and Phil Cohen were the only two men in the billet.

Striding into the room through the open doorway, Rankin, now a lieutenant colonel, said "At ease," in a normal tone of voice. Right behind him came a tall, lean officer wearing the insignia of a full colonel.

Both officers nodded at Will, which was the only acknowledgment they made of his presence, then went straight over to Phil Cohen. Rankin said, "Colonel, this is Private First Class Philip Cohen. Phil, Colonel Darlington, regimental commander of the 555th."

Phil smiled and extended his hand.

That was the end of the amenities. Rankin got to the point immediately. "Phil, I'm short of officers in the First Battalion. I'm even shorter of top-rate officers, but I've got carte blanche to do as I please about commissioning men from the ranks who can qualify.

"You qualify to a fare-thee-well. During the last German offensive, you brought a platoon out after clearing mines, shooting up German patrols, spearheading attacks, and everything else I can think of. You've been recommended for several decorations for gallantry in action and for valor. You're a college graduate, high I.Q., everything I want."

"We discussed it in the command post at Damen, sir," replied Phil. "As I told you then, sir, I'm flattered, but I'd prefer to remain a private."

"And I'd prefer to kick your ass right through the roof of this billet!" said Colonel Rankin. "But I'm not going to. Instead, I'm going to court-martial you for cowardice. How do you like that, Private Cohen?"

"Hey! Wait a minute. After all the nice things you just said about me, you can't do that. What the hell grounds do you have, sir? I—"

"I'm a colonel and you're a private, and that's all the grounds I need. As far as I'm concerned, by not accepting a commission, you're guilty. I might not convict you, Cohen, but it'll go on your record that you stood court-martial for cowardice in the face of the enemy, and won't that look swell?"

Will stood as if he'd been planted in the floor. He couldn't believe what he was hearing.

The silence continued as Phil and Colonel Rankin stared at each other. At last, Phil smiled. His smile widened to a grin, and he stuck out his hand to a now-smiling Colonel Rankin. "You win, Colonel," said Phil.

"Congratulations, Lieutenant," said Colonel Darlington, who had been standing as a silent observer during the exchange.

"Okay," said Rankin. "We've got an important slot picked out for you already. Colonel Darlington's here to make it official. You'll be commissioned as a first lieutenant and go to B Company as executive officer. Captain Wolfe of Baker Company is an old man and has arthritis so bad he can hardly walk. He got his boys out of Damen and led them in the jump-off at Hagenor, but that shot his wad. He's a retread from the First World War. Volunteered this time, but he never should have gotten a combat command. As soon as you're able, you'll take over from him, and he'll go back to a rear-echelon job, where he belongs.

"So now, Phil, you see why I pushed you so hard. Anybody I have who'd make a good company commander already is one. And, after the Ardennes and Alsace, nobody else has any officers to spare, either. So, Phil, congratulations."

"Thank you, sir," replied Phil.

"As exec of Baker Company, you'll have your own Jeep and driver. I'll have him pick you up here at, say, two o'clock this afternoon."

"That'll be fine, sir."

As the command car drove away from the billet, Will spoke for the first time. "Congratulations," he said, grinning broadly. "Now, what can I do for you, sir?"

"Well," replied Phil, "for starters, you can cut out that 'sir' crap."

★

Governor George Pope felt sorry for the stooped old man who had just sat down across the desk from him. Sam Reynolds had aged. The deep sorrow he felt was reflected in his tired eyes and sagging body. He seemed to have lost his keen enthusiasm for life, for the cut and thrust of politics that had brought the two men together twenty years ago.

The governor remained standing for a few moments. "It's just like old times, isn't it, Sam? Your coming by to tell me how to run the state."

Sam Reynolds shook his head. "No, George," he said, "I just came by to tell you how much I appreciated all you did when we got the news about Jack."

The governor held up his hand. "Sam, I wouldn't be governor if it weren't for you. So let's have no more of this kind of talk."

Reynolds nodded sadly. "Thanks, George. You know, they never found his body. He's still listed as 'missing in action.' That's the worst part for me—not knowing. It gives me hope without giving me hope. Deep down, I know Jack is dead. Yet, until they find him, I can't be sure. It's hell."

George Pope realized that anything he said would sound patronizing, if not hypocritical. He merely shook his head.

The two men sat silently for a few minutes. It was Sam Reynolds who broke the stillness. "I can't tell you how proud I am of you, George," he said. "I respect you tremendously for what you are doing."

George Pope lifted an eyebrow. He didn't understand what in the world Sam Reynolds was talking about. "What am I doing?"

"Your own son, Will. He's gone overseas as an infantry replacement, just like Jack did a few months ago. He might even be replacing Jack. And, George, we all know how close you are to the people in Washington. You could have had Will assigned to some safe job here in the States. Yet you let him go, just like anybody else."

George Pope was flustered. He replied. "Oh, uh, well. You see—"

"No, no, no," cut in Reynolds. "I admire you for it. I've always been right about you, George. I hope and pray nothing happens to young Will, and I'm sure it won't. You're fortunate, George. It looks like the war's finally winding down in Europe now; unless the Germans are crazy enough to fight to the last man."

"Dammit! It looks like that's exactly what they are going to do!" exploded Pope.

Immediately he felt embarrassed for his outburst. Or was his embarrassment due to something else? He didn't want to think about that.

Reynolds rose. "Will's going to be all right," he said. But his words lacked conviction. People used to tell Sam Reynolds that his son, Jack, was going to be all right, too.

After Sam Reynolds had left, George Pope slouched in his chair, thoroughly ashamed of himself. He hadn't had the courage to tell Sam that he'd already asked for his son to be returned from Europe.

Now he had serious misgivings. Once again, he wasn't sure he'd done the right thing. Wait a minute! he thought. Why can't Will be examined by an army doctor in Europe? If he's a fainter, they'll send him home. If not, it'll still take time, and the war will be that much farther along, and his chances will be that much better, and nobody'll say he came back because of political influence, or anything like that. Hell! Nobody here will even know about it, if he's okay. Then we'll have done the right thing anyway. He flicked his intercom switch.

"Mrs. O'Connor, please get me that fellow in the War Department, the one the White House put me onto…"

11

—

After Phil left that afternoon, Will was the only man remaining in the mine platoon billet. He was lonely, so he took a nap. After he woke up, he was even more lonely.

"Well, damn!" said Will. "Damn. Damn." The gray sky depressed him. The ugly village depressed him. The lousy old house depressed him. Having nobody to talk to depressed him.

He remembered that Sergeant Archie Randolph's squad had the billet down the street. He slung his rifle and started walking in that direction.

On the front doorstep, Will stopped. He wasn't sure whether he should just open the door and walk in or if he should knock first. He knocked. The voices inside fell silent. The door opened, and Archie Randolph stood there, smiling. "Come on in," he drawled. "Come on in and make yourself to home."

"Thanks," replied Will as he stepped hesitantly into the main room of the billet.

Around the fireplace sat the other men of Randolph's gun, all three of them. They looked up at Will and smiled. They were all young, lean, and athletic, and they shared a common characteristic: their faces were boyish, yet their expressions were almost always intense, as if they were concentrating all their attention on the work at hand—which they usually were. Now, though, they were relaxed, and Will felt almost guilty for having caught them off their guard.

"Come have a swig and set awhile," said Randolph, extending a bottle of cognac. Will tipped the bottle to his lips. The brandy burned his throat and he fought to keep from coughing. Now it burned his stomach. He hoped he wouldn't have to take another swig. He'd never drunk anything stronger than beer in his life.

"Now, what can we do for you?" asked Randolph. Archie Randolph was an amiable, soft-spoken country boy who never seemed to get upset about anything. He was so lightly built he appeared taller than his five feet, six inches. He had dirty blond hair and blue eyes and was polite to everybody. Yet he commanded an antitank gun that had knocked out six Tiger tanks and three half-tracks, officially, and actually more than twice that number—the Germans always removed their disabled panzers quickly, which made it difficult for a gun to get confirmed kills.

Unlike the dashing Joe Sumeric, Randolph was always calm under fire. Calm and calculating; playing the odds so carefully everybody thought he was just lucky. Of the nine guns in the regiment, Randolph's was the only one to survive the battle at Damen, and even now it could go into action on a moment's notice, with deadly efficiency.

Will broke his train of thought to answer, "Well, Sarge, you've got the only gun left in the regiment, and you know what? I'm the only guy left in the mine platoon, so I just thought I'd come over and get better acquainted. You know, as one survivor to another."

Randolph and his boys laughed. "That's real good," said Randolph. "Have another swig, and call me Archie."

His second swallow didn't burn as much, and Will began to feel the glow from the fire. He felt good. He told them about Phil Cohen getting a commission, and they said they knew he would all the time. They passed the bottle around again.

Will wasn't depressed anymore. He was enjoying himself, sitting on the floor by the fire talking to men he considered heroes and being accepted by them. They all talked a lot and laughed a lot, and Will felt mellow and contented.

Finally the bottle was empty, but they kept talking and laughing for a while, until Will began to feel sleepy. He got up but couldn't stand. He spun around and fell to his knees, then started crawling toward the door. The other four men roared with laughter, and Randolph drawled, "Whoa, babe. You got yourself a snootful, old buddy."

He and one of the others lifted Will up by his armpits and supported him through the doorway and down the street to his billet.

It was the middle of the night. Will woke up with the room spinning around him. "Oh, my God," he muttered. "I'm going to throw up."

The next morning, Will Pope opened his eyes slowly. There was a terrible stench in the room. His head pounded. He'd never felt so awful in his life. He didn't want to get up at all, but the smell forced him to sit on the side of the bed and contemplate the mess he'd made the night before.

"How in the name of hell could I have done such a thing?" He felt ashamed and degraded. "And what the hell do Randolph and his boys think of me now? I wish I'd never been born." He swore he'd never touch another drop of liquor as long as he lived.

There was no running water in any of the houses, so he went to the town pump to wash and start carrying back helmetsful of water to clean up the mess he'd made.

"Hi, Will!" The voice made him jump. Randolph stood in the doorway grinning. "How do you feel today? Didn't see you at chow, so I thought I'd come see what happened."

"I feel terrible," replied Will.

Randolph laughed. "At least you ain't dead or nothing," he drawled. "We was worried about you."

"Thanks," replied Will. "I guess I made a real ass of myself."

"Naw," replied Archie Randolph. "We all had a right good time last evening. But I come to tell you, guys're coming in. Some old men from the hospitals and some replacements already."

"Any of my guys?" asked Will.

Randolph opened his mouth to answer, but before he could, a large, powerfully-built soldier came striding through the open doorway. Will's eyes widened. The man was the neatest soldier he'd ever seen. His trousers were pressed, his field jacket clean. His helmet sat squarely on his head, and even his boots were spotless. He had a trim moustache. He was a handsome man. On his sleeves he wore the three chevrons and two rockers of a technical sergeant, which in the infantry meant he was probably a platoon sergeant. Showing a perfectly straight row of white teeth, he said, "They told me this is the mine platoon billet."

"Sam Bowden!" Randolph shouted the words. "By damn! Sam, how the hell are you?"

Bowden smiled as the two shook hands. "I'm just fine, Archie," he said softly. "And I'm back."

Randolph turned to Will and said, "Will, meet Sam Bowden. Sam's platoon sergeant of the mine platoon. Got hit by a sniper back in December while he was cleaning some mines off a street. Sam, meet Will Pope. He came in as a replacement at Damen, and he's yours."

Bowden stretched out his hand, and he and Will shook. Bowden was still smiling, but Will saw that his face was rugged and strong. His clear, gray eyes showed strength, too, as though he had a lot of iron in his backbone. The man was in his mid-twenties.

Randolph had stopped smiling suddenly and turned grave. He said to Bowden, "Sam, I'm sorry about your boys. Awful sorry."

Bowden simply nodded. Then he said, obviously having difficulty talking, "I—I heard they were wiped out in a minefield by artillery, but that's all. Can you tell me anything more about it, Archie?"

Randolph nodded slowly. "I'm afraid I can, Sam. But you gotta promise not to get mad or nothing."

Bowden nodded. "I just want to know. That's all."

"Well," said Randolph, "when the thing started in Alsace in January, our people found a field full of antitank mines right where they wanted to bring in some tank destroyers. So some officer sends your mine platoon to clear a path through the field so they can come through. So far, so good. Then another damn officer reads a report late and learns about the stupid mines. The bastard panics and calls in artillery to detonate the mines with shellfire."

"Good God!" breathed Bowden.

Randolph nodded. "Yeah," he continued. "A shell would hit a mine, and that mine would set off others—they tore the field and everything in it to pieces. Not one of your boys got out, Sam. They never had a chance."

"Our own artillery. Damn." Bowden's voice was sad and angry at the same time. Then he turned to Will and said, "So you're my platoon now, right?"

"Yes, Sarge," replied Will.

"Okay, let's get busy and clean this place up. It looks like a damn pigsty. I don't even move in until this billet is so clean I can eat off the floor."

Will thanked God that Sergeant Bowden hadn't arrived a couple of hours earlier.

At breakfast the next morning, Will saw there were more men than usual and surmised they were the returning wounded, and the new replacements. The night before he hadn't noticed. He had been too hung over. Spotting the familiar face of Archie Randolph, Will made his way over to his table and sat down. Randolph smiled. "Morning, Will. Feeling better?"

Will nodded, but he looked worried. "Tell me about Sam Bowden," he said. "The son-of-a-bitch had me cleaning the damn billet all afternoon and all night until I thought I'd drop. Man! We scrubbed. And scrubbed. I was so damned tired, all I wanted to do was drop to the floor and go to sleep. And you know what that bastard told me? He told me he wanted to know when I went on guard, so he could be sure to wake me up! And when I told him I don't pull guard because Phil Cohen got us out of it on account of we were only two guys, that son-of-a-bitch marches me right up to the C.P. and has a big guy put me on the guard roster of the Third Platoon, and I'm screwed if I don't get the two-to-four shift with some idiot that just came in and…"

But by now the whole table was laughing so hard Will stopped talking and grinned at them. He couldn't help chuckling as he asked, "What's so funny?" Then he added, "You know, I think that son-of-a-bitching sergeant's trying to make a soldier out of me."

After they'd stopped laughing, Will asked, "How can I find out when Lieutenant Sommers is coming out of the hospital?"

"Masters is back," Randolph drawled. "Ask him. He'll know, if anybody does."

"Who's he?"

"The first soldier of this outfit. Company first sergeant. I forgot he left before you come in. Got so sick back in December, they had to send him to the hospital. Somebody told me he had ulcers. Ain't that a funny one? Ulcers!" Randolph cracked a particularly broad smile.

Sergeant Masters turned out to be the "big guy" who'd put Will on the two-to-four guard shift the night before. Now, as Will stood before him, he saw Masters was, indeed, a big man, tall and well proportioned. And Will liked the man's face. It was pleasant, kind, and friendly, yet it would certainly be considered ugly by most people. The nose was too large. The lips too thick. The teeth too big. He realized, too, that Sergeant Masters must be ten years older than he. Masters had an air of relaxed confidence that permitted him to be amiable while conveying the fact that he would not put up with any foolishness, either.

"I'm glad you came by," said Sergeant Masters. "Now, what can I do for you?"

Will hesitated. Then he realized Masters was busy and would like him to come to the point right away. "I'm looking for news about Lieutenant Dave Sommers."

"Dave Sommers is in a hospital, but he's expected back. Unless we get some officer replacements, he might take over as executive officer of the company. And there was some talk of putting him in command of a heavy-weapons company. He trained in heavy weapons, you know, and he could probably handle that kind of assignment okay."

"Oh, gosh!" said Will. "I hope they won't do that."

"Chances are he'll be back to the antitank company. At least for a while. Is there anything else I can do for you?"

"Yes," said Will. "I came in with two other guys besides Mahoney." He was racking his brain to try to remember their names. Finally he got them. "One was named Gawalski and the other Mills."

He figured Masters would start looking through his records and files, but he answered after just the slightest hesitation, "Gawalski was on Johnny Wood's gun. They were knocked out during the panzer attack at Damen, as you no doubt know. Gawalski was pretty badly riddled with shrapnel and lost his left eye and most of his left arm, and they'll be pulling steel out of his left leg for a good, long time. He almost died. But he's already been flown out to a hospital back in the States."

Will nodded solemnly. "And Mills?"

Masters shook his head. "He was killed when his gun got knocked out. Sorry, Pope."

Will was doing some simple arithmetic. Of the four replacements who came into the company with him at Damen, one was dead—killed right after they came in—another was so badly wounded he was already back in the States minus an eye and an arm; Jim Mahoney was in the hospital seriously sick with pneumonia. So that left him the only one still out there.

After he left the sergeant at company headquarters, Will

figured being in the hospital during the battles at Damen and Hagenor probably cost Masters a battlefield commission.

And saved his life.

The sleepy little town was beginning to wake up fast. Replacements arrived—new antitank guns came in with their trucks, men returned from the hospitals, new noncoms showed up to take command of squads and platoons, and new equipment filled the supply sergeant's storeroom. Training began immediately. Almost before the new men jumped off the trucks that brought them into the village, they were out on five-mile speed hikes to keep them in top physical condition. The rest of their first few days were spent cleaning weapons and equipment and attending lectures and weapons instruction. Finally they'd drive out of town, then leave the road and pull into a muddy field, unhook the 57s from their trucks, and manhandle the guns into positions at the edge of a woods or any other cover. From there they would track vehicles driving along the road until it was dark. In the evenings, they'd clean the mud off and oil the guns.

The chow line stretched out for a whole block. Soon it would stretch around the corner as well. Kerosene smoke from the cooking stoves filled the air, and the clatter of armed men made the silence of the once-deserted village a memory. Like the other units of the Fighting Fifteenth Infantry Division, the antitank company of the Triple Nickel was ready for combat within two weeks after it came out of the line.

✪

Both Ceruti and Gruber returned to the mine platoon and were now sergeants; squad leaders. Ten replacements came into the platoon, greatly against their wills. All claimed they were natural-born gunners and wanted no part of the mine platoon, no how, no way— until Sergeant Masters brought them to attention and told them they'd been assigned to the mine platoon, they would serve in the mine platoon, and if he heard one more complaint, he'd make them clear mines from Alsace to Berlin with a bayonet jammed up their ass for good measure.

A third squad leader came to the platoon. He was a sergeant named Bob Brucker, and he was a quiet, formal sort of man. He didn't seem to want to do much more than he had to, and he didn't try to make any friends. He had cold eyes that frightened Will—they reflected a complete impersonality Will had never seen before and did not understand.

While the gunners were busy practicing, the mine platoon trained rigorously, unpacked and checked the new mines, went out and learned the practical aspects of laying a minefield, clearing a minefield, and protecting a minefield with their rifles.

Under the supervision of Sergeant Bowden, they developed into a disciplined military unit that could hold its own against any in the army. Sam Bowden was stern but he was fair, and Will decided he liked that.

When Will returned from Bowden's field exercises one day, he found Jim Mahoney sitting on his bedroll. Will's face lit up.

"What's going on around here?" asked Mahoney. "You guys stop fighting the war until old Jimbo comes back or something? I just found out you ain't done nothing the whole time I been gone. You ain't shot no Krauts, you ain't laid no mines, nobody's got themselves killed. Nothing!"

"Let me look at you, you gold-bricking son-of-a-bitch," replied Will.

Jim stood up and did a mock curtsy. Besides the fact he'd lost some weight, he'd changed. Will couldn't put his finger on it, but there was something different about his friend. Finally it came to him: Jim was dressed neatly—his trousers were clean and pressed, his hair was combed, his teeth were white. "Well, I'll be damned," said Will. "What do we have here? Hollywood's gift to the United States Army, I swear."

Will was joking, but he had to admit to himself that Jim Mahoney looked like a movie star now that he was turned out the way he should be. He expected Jim to come back at him with a wisecrack or to get mad and cuss at him, but he did neither. Instead, he blushed.

Will sat down. "What the hell happened to you back at that hospital?" he asked.

Jim didn't answer right away. He stared at his feet, he cleared his throat. Finally he said, "Oh, ah, I met a nurse. You see? And we cottoned to each other right off. She saved my life, Will. She's an angel. She's so sweet it hurts. Her name's Marylou Simpson. I'm a changed man. Can't you see it, Will? I seen the light. I'm in love, and I'm gonna marry this girl."

For a minute Will couldn't speak. When he could, he said, "Look, Jim, how old is this girl? If she's a nurse, she's got to be a lot older than you, and she's an officer besides. Hell! You're putting me on, Jimbo."

Jim shook his head. "No, Will, I'm serious. For the first time since you've known me, I'm serious. Sure, she's a little older than me, but that don't make me no mind. We're soulmates, Will. I ain't never known nobody so sweet and loving since my ma died. Straight from heaven, she is."

Will sighed. "Has she accepted your proposal of marriage?" he asked.

Jim smiled his old smile and said, "Some things is just understood, old buddy." He winked.

Will's eyes opened wide. "You mean you've been screwing her already?" he asked.

"Will, you're such a baby," replied Jim. "Hell, yes! We been screwing together like crazy! Every chance we got and in places you wouldn't believe possible! We're in love, you dummy."

Will just sat and shook his head.

Jim began singing softly to himself, "I just found joy; I'm as happy as a baby boy…"

"When are you tying the knot?" asked Will.

"Oh, after this damned war is all over and done with, I guess," replied Jim. "I don't reckon they let privates marry lieutenants—now, do they?"

"If you'd finished school, you could've tried for a commission. You're bright enough, God knows."

"To hell with it. This here war can't last forever," said Jim. "Now clear out and leave me alone. I got to write a letter to my true love."

That same day, two more men came into the platoon. Both were "old men" who'd served in the company since before Damen.

The first, Ernie Kitchener, at thirty-four was the oldest man in the outfit. He'd been a farmer before the war, been on a gun at Damen, fought with a B Company squad after his gun was shot to pieces. When they'd come out of the line, old Ernie had just stayed with Baker Company. That's where the army'd put him, so that's where he remained. The last time anybody from antitank had seen Kitch, he'd been in the cellar of a blazing building in Damen with a couple of B Company men, and the Germans were tossing grenades into the cellar, so nobody expected ever to see him again.

The day after Phil Cohen got to B Company, he was inspecting the platoons with Captain Wolfe when he spied the chunky, smiling old private whose face he knew so well. Phil's eyes popped.

Kitchener grinned and said, "Well, I'll be danged if it ain't Phil Cohen!" His smile faded slowly. A worried look replaced it. "Look, Phil, get outta them officer's clothes or they're gonna get you good, hear? Take off them bars before they finds out—"

Phil grinned back at his old friend. "It's okay, Kitch. I'm a lieutenant, fair and square. But what the hell are you doing here? We all thought you got blown up in Damen."

"You mean in that there cellar? Naw, Phil. I wouldn't be here if I'd have been blown up, now would I? What happened was, there was these big, old wine barrels in that there cellar, Phil. And me and them fellers from B Company just got ourselves behind them mothers, and the hand grenades didn't touch us even. After we was sure them Jerry fellers'd gone away, we got out quick. Just before the danged building falls in. It was burning pretty good, you know, and—"

"Okay. Okay. How'd you like to go home to antitank company, Kitch?" asked Phil.

Kitchener hesitated, then replied, "Not much, thanks."

Phil nodded. He understood. Both men had stood by their guns on the ridge outside Damen and faced the charging Tigers. Both had seen their guns destroyed and their friends killed in that hell of fire and steel. Given a choice, neither wanted to do it again.

"How about the mine platoon?" asked Phil. "That should be nice and easy, and you get to ride in a truck instead of marching, like you'll have to do if you stay in a rifle company. Dammit, Kitch! You're too old to march forty miles with a full field pack and a rifle and ammunition and—"

"Hold on, Phil. I ain't said nothing. I think the mine platoon'd be right nice."

So the platoon got Ernie Kitchener, and everybody was happy.

The platoon also got Harry Muller, and nobody was happy about that. Harry had shot his middle finger off on the freezing night they spent in the foxholes outside Hagenor. Most of the men thought he did it on purpose to get out of the line. Muller defended himself whenever he got the chance.

"It was a accident, I tell you," he'd say. "It could've happened to anybody. We was jumping in and out of our holes, and my rifle went off, that's all. Lucky I didn't blow my head off."

Will didn't care one way or the other, but the other men thought it was pretty crummy of Harry to get out of action that way, at a time when they needed every man who could hold a rifle.

Gradually, though, the incident was forgotten, and Harry Muller was accepted as a member of the platoon like everybody else.

The addition of Ernie Kitchener and Harry Muller brought the platoon's strength up to eighteen men, including Sergeant Bowden. They never counted their two drivers—they went with the trucks. They were supposed to have three squads of ten men each, plus a headquarters squad of six, but any infantry outfit that had been in combat for any length of time never regained its full strength, and eighteen men wasn't bad at all.

Since some of its units were due to go back on the line soon, the Fifteenth Division held an awards and decorations ceremony. As many of the combat platoons and companies as possible were trucked to the affair, which took place in a large field outside division headquarters.

The men to be decorated for bravery stood together apart from the rest. When each man's name was called, he stepped forward two paces, and the commanding general of the division, Major General Matthew Arnold Robinson, himself, pinned the medals and shook the hands of the recipients after his chief of staff read the citations.

Sergeant Joe Sumeric received the Distinguished Service Cross, second only to the Congressional Medal of Honor, for displaying extraordinary heroism against the enemy. He also received the Silver Star for gallantry in action and the Purple Heart for the assorted cuts and bruises he picked up in Damen.

Sergeant Archie Randolph received the same decorations as Sumeric, and his three men were each awarded the Silver Star. Captain Colina received a Silver Star and a Bronze Star. So did Lieutenant Phil Cohen, now executive officer of B Company. Quite a few men from the antitank company received the Silver Star for knocking out panzers at Damen, and Ceruti and Gruber each received the Bronze Star and the Purple Heart.

As the mine platoon stood at attention during the ceremony, Will Pope was moved deeply at the reading of each citation. But sneaking a look at Mahoney, he was ready to bet that Jim's thoughts were concentrated solely on how to get back to the station hospital so he could make love to Marylou again.

Sam Bowden seemed uneasy. He had trained his men hard, and they were fit, well-disciplined, and able. They were also violent young animals, armed to the teeth. Unless they could soon direct their passions against the enemy, they might very easily explode against each other.

At the end of the proceedings, General Robinson announced that three men would receive the Congressional Medal of Honor, the nation's highest decoration for valor. One of them was still in the hospital in critical condition; the other two were dead and would be awarded their medals posthumously. The last name on that illustrious list was the late Pfc. Daniel K. Sark, mine platoon, antitank company, 555th Infantry.

Even though he hadn't thought about Danny Sark for a long time, Will felt sad enough to cry, and he held back the tears with difficulty. The next instant, his sorrow turned to pride. He had actually known this hero who had charged a German machine gun single-handed, had thrown himself on a live hand grenade, taking its full blast with his own body to save the lives of a bunch of men he didn't even know.

Yes. He, Will Pope, could tell his children and his grand-children that he had been a comrade-in-arms of such a man. He would share his memories of the hero… But he stopped. His most vivid memory of Dan Sark was of him cowering on a pile of blankets, refusing to fight at all.

What could cause such a man to become a hero? Will would never know for sure, but he wondered if shame could have driven Danny to such heights of valor. Or pride? Or the desire to redeem himself? Or could he simply have lost his head for a moment and gone berserk? Or did he want to die?

No. It couldn't have been any of those reasons.

Then it dawned on him. It was rage. That German machine gun had been killing the men with Danny, and Sark just got so damned angry he had to do something. Yes, Will understood that. It was the same rage that had driven him forward during the attack at Hagenor. Will Pope, who'd never harmed a living thing before he arrived in Alsace, charging forward with bayonet fixed, shooting down those boys who stood in his way, firing clip after clip at the men in field gray, trying to kill them... Yes. He understood that kind of fury.

But it was a fury tempered with an instinct for survival. After all, Sark had the good sense to wait until the Germans had emptied their gun and had to reload before he charged in close enough to get them. So why would he throw himself on a German grenade? Will shook his head. Maybe Danny knew he'd be killed by the grenade anyway, so why not? No. He'd have had time to try to jump clear—he could have gone to ground, maybe into a shell hole. It would have been worth a try. It had a fifty-fifty chance.

And besides, he didn't even know those men... But he did! He knew Sommers! And back at Damen, Sommers had told him, "We won't leave you, Danny. We'll never let you down." And Danny didn't let Sommers down, either...

Will became aware that they were being marched off the field. The ceremony was over.

12

One of the replacements, a large man named Irv Donaldson, was the undisputed leader of the new men. He kept them in line and made sure they did things right and worked hard. He ran an organization within an organization. After a couple of days, though, it became apparent that Donaldson was a loudmouth and a braggart. "When they gonna let me at them Germans?" he'd yell at nobody in particular. "Wait till old Irv ties into them bastards. War'll be over, by God. Them sorry sons-of-bitches'll wish old Irv Donaldson'd stayed home, you bet."

He had a claque of three other replacements who egged him on.

At first, Will liked "old Irv" just because he was so dumb and so loud. He made Will smile.

After a while, though, Will grew disgusted by the way old Irv bullied the other replacements. He didn't like the attitude of superiority Donaldson exhibited toward them, which contrasted with his almost groveling obsequiousness toward Bowden, Ceruti, and Gruber, as well as his own squad leader, Sergeant Brucker.

Will had the combat veteran's scorn for untried replacements, anyway, so he avoided having anything to do with old Irv or any of the other new men. This irritated Donaldson, who began to show his irritation in various petty ways, making disparaging remarks about Will. "There goes that little snot Pope. He's a Pfc. Just like the rest of us, so why does he think he's such hot stuff, huh?" Or, "Pope over there thinks he's better than the rest of us, don't he? The son-of-a-bitch."

Will couldn't understand why he'd become the target of the bully's attention, and he didn't like it a bit. But he decided the best policy was to ignore Donaldson and his friends completely, and pretend not to hear his remarks. But although he wouldn't admit it, Donaldson's comments were beginning to annoy him, considerably. Every time he heard old Irv make one of them, his anger mounted, and he was having a hard time keeping control of his temper.

On the evening after the decorations ceremony, Will sat cleaning his disassembled rifle. He'd just finished inspecting its shining barrel when he heard Donaldson's voice close by saying, "There's that little snot, Pope. Just because he's one of the 'old combat men,' he thinks he's too good to fraternize with the rest of us privates. Don't you, Popie, old cock?"

Will didn't answer. He continued to run the oily cloth over the parts of his rifle. But Donaldson continued, "Pope didn't get no medals today, did you, Popie? So he can't be nothing much. That's what I say, hey?"

Will still didn't answer. He simply started to reassemble his M-1. But inside, he was seething. He'd grown to despise Donaldson, anyway, and he was damned if he was going to let the bigmouth ridicule him in front of the entire billet.

Donaldson stood over him. He had a coarse, lumpy face with a nose that was always red and cheeks that were often splotched pink. His mouth turned down at the corners, and his lips were thick, but for all his ugliness, he was a powerful, muscular man.

Almost casually, he thrust his beefy hands against Will's shoulders and shoved. "Too good to talk to me, hey? Too good to talk to good old Irv Donaldson, are you? Well, I'll show you. I ain't afraid of no little bastard like you. I don't give a damn if you been in combat or not. That don't mean nothing to me. No, by damn."

As he finished, he shoved Will again, harder than the last time, so that Will rolled backward on the floor.

"You just get out of my way when you see me coming," continued Donaldson as he walked away a few steps. By now, his hangers-on had begun to encourage him. "You tell him, Irv!" "Yeah! Yeah! That's the stuff. Who's he think he is, anyway?" "Go hit him in the mouth, Irv. He ain't nothing!"

Will sat up and finished putting his M-1 together. He took a clip out of his cartridge belt and jammed it into the rifle, shot the bolt forward, and flipped off the safety catch. He swung the barrel to point directly at Donaldson.

A sudden silence fell in the billet. Nobody moved. Nobody spoke. Will said, "I'm going to kill you, Donaldson."

Will's finger began to squeeze the trigger slowly and deliberately. At that moment, Jim Mahoney moved quickly between Will and Donaldson, so that Will's rifle pointed at him. Will clicked on the safety catch and said, "Get out of my way, please, Jim. I'm going to kill that bastard." Even as he heard his own words, they sounded like ice.

"No, you ain't, Will," replied Mahoney. "That'd be murder." He turned to Donaldson, who had remained planted to the floor without moving a muscle since the minute Will had aimed his M-1 at him. "Get out of here, Donaldson. Get out before I let old Will, here, shoot you like he should've."

There was a scramble as Donaldson and his "boys" made for the door, along with most of the other men in the billet.

"What the hell, Will?" said Jim.

Will lowered his rifle. He smiled. "I don't have to take any crap from that son-of-a-bitch," he told his friend. "He might be big and brawny, but this rifle makes us all equal. And I know what to do with it. Donaldson doesn't."

Jim Mahoney grabbed Will by the lapels of his field jacket and said furiously between clenched teeth, "Will! We ain't in the line, and he ain't no German, neither, you damned fool! If you'd have shot that big bastard, you'd have had your ass court-martialed for murder and spent the rest of your days in the stockade. Or gone before a firing squad!"

Suddenly Will realized what he'd almost done. He couldn't speak; he just nodded at Mahoney. He was scared. Damned scared. How could he have lost control like that?

Jim released his lapels. Will breathed deeply and unloaded his rifle. Finally, he said, "Jim, you saved my hide. Thanks."

Mahoney sighed. "God, Will! Don't do that again! What got into you, anyway?"

Will shook his head. "I don't know. I just don't know." He was only thankful he had a friend like Jim.

Will knew that Bowden was at company headquarters. He got to his feet. "I'm going to go tell the sarge what happened," he said. "He's got to know, and I'd rather tell him than have somebody else do it."

The inside of the antitank company headquarters was smoky, and the air was stale. Will coughed. In the daytime, all the windows were kept open, even though it was winter, but at night they were covered with blankets and tarps.

The meeting to discuss the next day's training had long been over, but several of the noncoms were still there, sitting around talking before going back to their units. Bowden and Archie Randolph were alone at a table smoking cigarettes and joking together. Archie wore his new medals—he looked like a general.

Making his way through the smoke, Will approached them slowly, not wanting to interrupt anything. He smiled as they raised their hands in greeting. Then he congratulated Archie once more. They shook hands. Archie grinned.

"What's up, Pope?" asked Bowden. "We got a problem or something back at the billet?"

Will shook his head. "I don't think so, Sarge," he replied. "But I sort of thought I'd walk back with you and kind of chat a little."

Both Bowden and Randolph got to their feet.

"See you later, Sam," said Archie. "So long, Will."

Bowden said, "Okay, Pope, let's go."

Outside, Will stopped. He told Sergeant Bowden exactly what happened between him and Donaldson. When he finished, he braced himself for the chewing out he was sure was coming. He was pretty certain Bowden could have him court-martialed for what he'd done.

Instead, Bowden just started walking, and Will fell in beside him. Neither spoke. At the town pump, the sergeant stopped and sat down on one of the stone benches. Will remained standing in front of him. Even though it was nighttime, he could see everything clearly by the silvery-metallic light of the moon, which made the scene look like a black-and-white movie.

Bowden looked up and spoke slowly. "You don't care much for, the new men, do you, Pope?"

Will shook his head. "No, not much."

For a minute or two, the sergeant made no comment. Then he picked his words as he said, "In most infantry outfits, there are usually more 'old men' than there are replacements. And the old men keep everything under control. But we've got an unusual situation in this outfit on account of the heavy casualties we took. Especially the mine platoon, because the platoon was wiped out and then reformed from scratch with you men from the knocked-out guns—you never did amount to more than an understrength squad, anyway, so now what's left of you are outnumbered by the replacements. It ain't a good situation."

Will stood silently, digesting the sergeant's remarks.

Bowden stood up and said, "But I'll tell you one thing, Pope, pulling a gun on them ain't the way to handle it. Not by a damn sight, it ain't. Now that you've learned to use that rifle, you figure it's a solution to every damn problem you run into, the easy way to settle things. But while you're in my platoon, you damn well better not do it again, you hear?"

"Yes, Sarge," replied Will quickly. He didn't know whether Bowden was just warming up, or if his lecture was already finished.

"I'll tell you something else, though," mused the sergeant. "Donaldson'll stay as far away from you as he can from now on. I think you've scared the piss out of the bastard. So you just keep your nose clean and mind your own business and leave the rest of the new men to me. Okay, Pope?"

"You bet, Sarge," replied Will, and in the moonlight he saw Bowden smile. Will smiled back. It was a smile of relief and of gratitude.

The next morning was cold. There was a mist and it was hard to see. Will was so worried, he could hardly eat his breakfast. Under his breath, he kept saying, "Damn that Jim Mahoney! Damn him to hell! How can he do this to me all the time?"

Jim hadn't been in the billet when Will returned with Bowden. Will figured he'd gone to pull guard. But when he'd crawled into his sleeping bag, he heard the crinkle of paper—he took it out, lit a candle, and read, "Will. Cover for me. I done gone to see Marylou. Tell Smitty not to worry about the Jeep, I'll bring it back. Your friend, Jim."

In spite of the note, Will slept soundly. In the back of his mind he expected Jim to be back by breakfast. But he wasn't, so now Will was really worried. He wondered what Jim meant by "Tell Smitty not to worry about the Jeep." Smitty was Captain Colina's driver. Good God, thought Will. He couldn't have taken the captain's Jeep? Then he realized that was exactly what Jim had done.

Will wondered what would happen when Bowden found Jim had gone over the hill. Will decided to tell Bowden that Mahoney went on sick call. Something to do with his pneumonia. Then Jim could handle it any way he wanted to when he got back.

At breakfast Will saw Smitty sitting a couple of tables away. Smitty was small and fresh, with a turned-up nose that made him resemble an elf. He was always making wisecracks, never at a loss for a comment on anything under the sun. As usual, he was joking and talking fast through his crooked teeth.

When he got up to go wash his mess kit, Will walked over to him. "Hi, Smitty," he said as casually as he could.

"Hello, Pope." Smitty looked surprised. He hardly knew Will.

"How's the captain this morning?" asked Will.

"How do I know?" replied Smitty. "He's gone to Paris on a three-day pass. Went right after he got his medals yesterday. Right now he's probably drunker than an Irishman and shacked up with the ugliest broad in France."

Thank God for that! thought Will. Aloud, he said, "I guess he took his Jeep."

"No, man," said Smitty. "I done finished telling you he went right from the binge yesterday. A whole truckload of officers went together. I brung back the Jeep and put her to bed. What do you want, anyway, Pope? You trying to sell a Luger pistol or something? You want a pass? You trying to get the key to the officers' liquor ration? What the hell is it, man?"

"Oh, nothing," replied Will. Smitty had finished washing his gear and was getting ready to leave the area. "Look, Smitty," he added quickly, "don't worry about the Jeep, hear? It's okay. It'll be back real soon—"

"What?!" screeched Smitty. "What do you mean? Where's my Jeep?"

"Calm down," said Will. "Everything'll be okay. Somebody probably borrowed it or something."

"You're crazy!" yelled Smitty as he began to run toward the barn that served as the motor pool for the headquarters vehicles. Will followed him.

Of course, the captain's Jeep was not there.

"What happened?" wailed Smitty to the sergeant in charge.

"Your friend took it last night," replied the sergeant. "He said you needed it urgent-like. An emergency. Real quick. And he signed for it all proper—"

"Let me see! Let me see!" said Smitty. He did everything but jump up and down.

The signature on the "out" slip for the Jeep was nothing but an illegible scrawl.

"Okay. Let's go get him!" said Smitty.

Will tried to laugh, but he didn't quite make it. A small falsetto squeak was the best he could do.

By the expression on Smitty's face, he could tell he was preparing to report the vehicle missing, alert all units to be on the lookout for the Jeep with the bumper markings. "HQ, I AT CO 555 Inf."

"Wait a minute, Smitty," said Will. "The Jeep'll come back. Just like I told you. Be patient."

Smitty's visage indicated he was thinking of all the things he was going to do to the Jeep-stealer when he caught up with him. They were not pleasant things. Will was becoming alarmed. "Remember, Smitty, as the bard put it,

'The quality of mercy is not strain'd,

It droppeth as the gentle rain from heaven,

Upon the place beneath; it is twice bless'd.

It blesseth him that gives and him that takes...'

"I don't understand a word you're saying," said Smitty. "All I know is somebody took my Jeep, and I'm responsible for that damned vehicle..."

"Will they make you pay for it?" asked Will.

"Damned right!" replied Smitty.

"Gee!" said Will. "That's good luck for you. Now they'll have to make you an officer so you can afford to give them all that money. Too bad it wasn't a Sherman tank. They'd have had to make you a general."

Smitty was not amused.

"Look, Smitty, don't get so worried," said Will. "I tell you somebody just borrowed the Jeep for a day or two…"

"Who?" demanded Smitty. Will shrugged. Smitty cursed. He was about to stamp out of the barn.

"Smitty!" called Will. "I'll tell you what happened. The Germans infiltrated during the night and made off with it. It's a 'combat casualty.' All you have to do is put in for a brand-new Jeep. How about that?"

"We ain't even in the line!" wailed Smitty. "If we was in the line, there'd be no problem. But goddammit, back here they won't even fill out the requisition! What they'll do is draw orders for a general court-martial for poor old Corporal Paul Smith!"

"I didn't know your name was Paul," said Will.

"Oh, shut up, dammit!" responded Smitty. He turned on Will and pointed his finger at him. "You knew about this! You knew about this! You're an accomplice. That's what you are. An accomplice to the crime, and I'm turning you in! How do you like that, Pope?"

Will had the vision of the commander of the firing squad asking him if he wanted a blindfold or a last cigarette.

Then he brightened. "Look, Smitty. I've got an idea. Let's go steal us another Jeep to replace the one the Jerries snatched. Regiment's just down the road a piece, and I'll bet they've got all sorts of vehicles sitting around. They'll never miss one little old Jeep. Never in a thousand years…"

"Nuts!" snapped Smitty. "I'm turning you in!"

A mud-splattered olive-drab streak flashed past them, just missing a truck before screeching to a stop a half inch short of the back of the barn. Jim Mahoney jumped out, jaunty and fresh as ever.

Will and Smitty stood speechless for a long second. Smitty's eyes bulged; his mouth fell open. Before he could recover, Will greeted Jim. "Thank God you got the Jeep back from those dirty Jerry infiltrators! Good work. Guess you had to chase them all the way to Germany…"

"No, Will," replied Jim. "I've been back to the field hospital." He turned to Smitty. "Thanks for the use of the Jeep, old pal. It saved my life."

Smitty was about to explode when Jim handed him a piece of paper. Smitty read it several times, then looked up and said, "Gee. This sure looks official, but why the hell didn't you go through channels? If you'd gone to Sergeant Masters, he'd have had me drive you back."

"Thanks, old pal, but everything happened too fast. Much obliged to you, though," said Jim as he tipped his helmet and strode out of the barn, followed by a very bewildered Will Pope.

Back at the mine platoon billet, Will looked questioningly at Mahoney and asked, "Okay, what gives?"

Jim reached into his pocket and pulled out what looked like a dozen pieces of paper like the one he'd given Smitty. He shoved them at Will.

Each was written on official hospital stationery and signed by the commandant. One stated that Pfc. James Davis Mahoney received emergency medical attention on that date, another said he was authorized to requisition transportation, another that he was allowed to be absent from his unit for medical purposes, another that he was to report daily to the hospital for treatment of a rare disease... There seemed to be no limit.

Will asked, "What in the—"

"Don't worry, Will. I ain't gonna use all them papers. Not all of them. It was Marylou's idea. Damned good, if you ask me."

"Who signed them?" asked Will.

"The name's there. Read it," replied Jim. "Colonel Samuel Jones."

"Colonel Marylou Simpson, you mean!" said Will. "Boy! You two really are soulmates! What a pair! If you ever do get married, I pray to God you never have any kids! What you two will produce boggles my imagination! Anyway, at the rate you're going, you'll both be shot by a firing squad before you get out of the army, so I won't worry about it."

"Gee, Will, don't be such a sorehead. What's wrong, old pal? Everything's just fine. Marylou and me caught up on our lovemaking. Smitty's happy—he's got his Jeep back. And Bowden don't even know I been gone. So take it easy. I'm home free."

Will had to smile. Jim was right. He'd made it once again.

★

After the incident with Donaldson, the replacements kept their distance from Will. They were afraid of him and didn't want to have any more to do with him than he did with them. They figured a guy who was liable to shoot them wasn't anybody they wanted to be around.

"Well, you sure got your wish," said Mahoney as they walked back to the billet, after noonday chow, their mess kits, with attached knives, forks, and spoons, jangling in their hands. "The new guys won't touch you with a ten foot pole. They think you're a weirdo-psycho-loonie hardcase."

"Good!" answered Will.

"Oh, cut it out, Will. Everybody blows his top once in a while. You was just a little more spectacular than most, that's all."

"What do you think of the replacements" asked Will.

"They're good old boys, except Donaldson's a loudmouth, and Gomez and Sullivan and Martinelli egg him on. They're just a bunch of flunkies. But I like the other guys."

Will nodded. He guessed that people were just people. Some were good, and some were bad, some were nice, and some were nasty, and all of them were all those things at one time or another.

"I wonder if Sergeant Bowden will ever get to like us?" continued Jim. "He's been real proper and all so far, but not very friendly."

Will shrugged his shoulders. He said, "You know why, don't you?"

Jim nodded. "Yeah," he replied. "It's only natural, I suppose. He misses his friends what were wiped out in the minefield. To him, they was the mine platoon, and we're just a bunch of recruits, and he knew Gruber and Ceruti as gunners, so they're outsiders, too. His boys are all gone."

Will nodded.

"I sure hope he'll accept us as 'his boys' pretty soon, though," said Jim. "It'll sure make things a lot more friendly-like."

★

The big room next to the headquarters was full of smoke and laughter. It was nighttime, just after evening chow, and many of the noncommissioned officers and a few of the "older" privates were playing cards, swapping jokes, and generally relaxing before they returned to their units.

Sergeant Bowden was there with Randolph, and so were Ceruti and Gruber, and Sergeant Masters. Joe Sumeric was absent without leave somewhere in the city of Nancy, where he'd gone right after receiving the DSC.

Will had just tried to smoke a cigarette, but he didn't have any idea of how to inhale, so he merely took a couple of puffs, blew out the smoke, and decided it was no thrill, so why bother? Finally he decided he'd had enough, and it was time to go home. He slung his rifle and left to return to the billet. He knew Jim was on guard duty with one of the new men, a freckle-faced, red-haired youngster named Trenton, whom they called "the All-American boy" for obvious reasons. He could have been right off a magazine cover.

The fresh, cold air felt good, and Will was glad to get the smoky feeling out of his system. He stuck his hand into his field jacket pocket to be sure he had some candles to read by when he got back. He'd read his paperback Agatha Christie mystery novel until Jim got off guard; they'd talk a while before they went to sleep; then Will would get up before midnight to go on guard with Hank Gray, another replacement.

When he got to the door of the billet, he heard noises inside—it sounded like a roughhouse was starting. He opened the door and stepped in. As his eyes adjusted to the dim haze, he saw that Donaldson and his gang were beating up one of the replacements. The rest of the men sat around intent on cleaning their rifles, or reading, or otherwise studiously avoiding having to take any notice of what was going on.

"Hey!" shouted Will. "Cut that out!"

All eyes turned to where he stood at the door. Donaldson stood up and dropped the arm that had been raised to hit the unfortunate boy he'd been picking on; his eyes suddenly seemed to pop out of their sockets, and the whites showed clearly. In that second, Will realized that behind his rough brutality, the man was a coward. His friends scurried away and sat down.

"What the hell's going on here?" demanded Will. He purposely refrained from unslinging his rifle.

Nobody answered. Then Donaldson said, almost in a whisper, "We was just going for a walk." And he and his three cohorts dashed through the back doorway away from Will.

The billet remained silent. The youngster Donaldson had been beating got to his feet. His face was bruised, and he bled from his nose. He was a boy named Brown; Will didn't know his first name. Brown rubbed his face and put his hand to his mouth. When he took it away to look at it, there was blood on it, too.

"Why the hell do you guys let those bastards do this?" asked Will. Then, for good measure, he swore. "Son-of-a-bitch!"

"D—D—Donaldson says I kicked him," blurted Brown. "I didn't. I stumbled over his legs when I come in. I didn't see them."

"Why didn't you guys help Brown?" demanded Will.

Nobody answered.

"Aw, to hell with you," said Will. He went over to his blanket and sat down.

The others began talking to each other in low tones. Will realized they were completely cowed by Donaldson's crew, and he felt sorry for them. Now he was damned glad he'd pulled his rifle on the overbearing bully. Donaldson was afraid of him, thank God. He lit a candle, got out his book, and started to read.

After a while, he looked at his watch. Jim ought to be back pretty soon. Muller was getting ready to go on guard with another new man, named Reilly, a nice kid who did everything wrong. He watched the two of them sling their rifles, adjust their helmets and go out to relieve Jimmy and Trenton. Just then, Hank Gray came over and sat down beside him. "You and me're on from midnight to two," he said, conversationally.

Will smiled at him and nodded. "That's right," he replied. "How's Brown?"

"Oh, he'll be okay. They'd just started on him when you showed up," replied Gray.

"Well, that's good," Will said.

"You know, Pope," continued Gray, "Jim Mahoney's been telling us you're an okay guy. You ain't no trigger-happy hothead like when you pulled on Donaldson. Jim says you just got mad, and you'd been used to shooting people and don't have to take no crap from nobody, that's all."

"In the infantry, you don't," Will said. He took a good look at Hank Gray. The boy was good-looking and intelligent, with straight features and clear, gray eyes, the kind of guy everybody likes immediately.

Hank was silent for a minute. Then he said, "Yeah, but Donaldson's got his gang, and one or two of us don't stand a chance against them. They know we won't shoot them. But you been in combat. You killed guys before, and they ain't going to mess with you none."

Will just nodded. He felt like telling Gray that Donaldson and his gang were yellow, and if anybody stood up to them they'd crumble. But he didn't.

Jim and Trenton came in from their guard duty. "Damn! It sure gets cold when you stand out there in one place for two hours," said Jim as he unslung his rifle and tossed his helmet onto his blanket. "Hi, Hank."

Gray acknowledged the greeting, then turned to Will and said, "So long, Will. See you at midnight."

Will nodded as Hank got up to return to his friend Pacini. It was only then that he saw Sergeant Brucker sitting alone in the far corner of the room, reading. Well, I'll be damned! thought Will.

Leaving Mahoney to take off his gloves, scarves, knit wool cap, and all the other cold-weather gear he wore, Will walked slowly over to Brucker. As he did, he realized he was a little frightened of him. The man was an absolute loner—yet he was a squad leader, and Will heard he had been decorated several times for heroism, which was the reason he was a sergeant.

As he stood beside Brucker, Will said, "Sarge, dammit, why didn't you stop those guys from beating up on Brown? You were here all the time."

Sergeant Brucker looked up at Will and replied, "Brown ain't in my squad, and them guys is. So why should I stop it?"

With that, Brucker returned to his paperback, and Will realized there was nothing more he could say to him.

As he made his way back through the billet, somebody tugged at his sleeve. He turned and saw Brown looking at him like an adoring puppy.

"I—I—I forgot to thank you for what you did," he said hesitantly. "Thanks for stopping those guys from killing me."

"Aw, forget it," said Will.

"Here. Have a cigarette," offered Brown.

Just then the door opened and Sergeant Bowden strode in. He looked around the room, sizing things up as usual. "Okay, you guys. In fifteen minutes we douse the candles and open all the windows. Can't breathe in this place for all the damn smoke, so get ready to turn in. Pope, come with me. I want to talk to you."

With that he turned and walked toward his room, which served as the platoon's headquarters.

"Yes, Sarge?" asked Will when Bowden had closed the door behind them.

Bowden looked at him steadily before he spoke. "That bastard Donaldson went and reported you tonight to Sergeant Masters for pulling down on him. Lucky I was there. I told Masters I'd take care of it here at platoon level, and he said, 'Fine,' so that's that. But why did he report you tonight? Any reason? You didn't go and do it again, did you, Pope? Because if you did, I'm gonna—"

"No, Sarge, I sure didn't," broke in Will. "And I've got the whole billet as witnesses. But I'll tell you what did happen." And he told him about Donaldson beating up Brown, and included the fact that Sergeant Brucker had been there all the time and had done nothing to stop it.

After Will finished, Bowden remained silent.

"I've got an idea, Sarge," volunteered Will. "Why don't we split those four guys up, just keep Donaldson in Sergeant Brucker's squad?"

Bowden stared at Will for a minute, then smiled. "You got more brains than I thought you did, you son-of-a-bitch," he said. "You're okay, kid! Now, let's get some sleep. Oh, hey! I forgot to tell you. Dave Sommers came back tonight."

"Forgot to tell me? Good God, how could you forget something like that, Sarge?"

"Sorry, Will. He's a first lieutenant now, and he'll take over as exec. But we're so short of officers he'll double as mine platoon leader when he has time. Anyway, he said to say hello, and he'll see you in the morning. You stand pretty high with him, Will, so I think with him as exec and me as platoon sergeant we can handle that bastard Donaldson without much trouble."

Will grinned. Now he stood in the doorway ready to return to his blanket to try to sleep before going on guard. "Thanks, Sarge. Anything else?"

"Naw," replied Bowden. "Except the division's going back into the line tomorrow."

13

The Fighting Fifteenth had been back in the line for several weeks, but the antitank mine platoon of the 555th had settled into billets behind the foxholes of the rifle companies. They occupied one of the dozen or so stone houses that lined the sides of a rutted, muddy country road, so it was almost like being in the rear, except they could hear the artillery in the daytime and small-arms fire as patrols clashed at night.

The guns still went out on exercises and occasionally set up to cover actual panzer threats, but none materialized. Somebody found a couple of minefields left by the Germans and sent the platoon out to clear them for practice until Bowden went to Captain Colina to have it stopped, and it was. "No sense in getting my men killed for no reason," he'd complained. "They're already trained. The next time they go into a live minefield, it'll be for real." So the platoon continued to live a pretty good life.

Even though it was close to the front lines, the town seldom came under shellfire, and several French families had already returned to their homes. If their houses were used to billet American troops, the entire family had to crowd themselves into one room, apart from the soldiers. At the beginning, they tried to have as little as possible to do with the Americans whose sleeping bags covered the floors of their houses, but after a few days their natural curiosity got the better of them, and they began to mix a little with the men, although their inability to speak English made communication difficult.

Between their daughters and the Americans, there was no such language barrier. Their efforts to understand each other succeeded famously. However, it seems that the affinity of young American soldiers for young French girls was not unknown to the U.S. Army. And apparently the army did not look favorably upon romance. It laid down the law. Lectures began immediately. Any complaints received from French civilians regarding the misconduct of American soldiers would be taken seriously and the culprits punished to the full extent of the military code.

This had its effect among the younger men. The lectures frightened them to death, and some of them wouldn't even talk to a French girl. That left the path clear for the older hands. Rumor had it that Private Joe Sumeric, busted earlier for stealing a Jeep and going on a three-day binge, was cozily shacked up with the prettiest girl in town and that the captain had an intimate arrangement with the lady of his house, whose husband was still away.

The mine platoon lived in a small house that contained no civilians. This was a disappointment to Sergeant Sam Bowden, who had to go all the way to the other end of the village to see the rather plain, middle-aged lady he'd set his cap for. "That's the way I like them," he'd told Colina. "Untouched and unspoiled. Tell me, who the hell else'd be interested in a broad like that?"

Will didn't know whether Bowden thought Jim's slips of paper from the hospital were genuine or whether he just looked the other way so as not to interfere with true love's course, but he let Jim take a Jeep to the hospital every evening. Sometimes he'd exclaim, "You gotta go to the damn hospital again, Mahoney? Why the hell don't they just give you a medical discharge and be done with it?" But then he'd smile. So Will wondered.

Naturally, Will was one of those on whom the lectures had the desired effect. "How come you ain't got yourself a girlfriend, Will?" asked Jim one day in the noon chow line.

"Ha!" exclaimed Will. "You've missed all the talks they've been giving us, you goldbrick. Do you know what happens if you screw a French girl and get caught? I'll tell you. She yells, "Rape!" That's what she does. Something about protecting her honor. But do you know what the army does? They hang you, that's what! So besides my not having any wild desire to get hanged, what do you think it would do to my father? Huh? It'd ruin his career, that's what. I can see the headlines now." And Will looked around to make sure nobody could overhear him.

"'Governor's son hanged for rape!'

"How do you think that'd look, Jimbo? Great, huh? It'd just kill my mother! So no way, nohow. I don't even nod my head at them when I pass them on the street."

"You're just chicken," said Jim. "But how come there's so many Frenchies here and there wasn't hardly none back when we was in reserve?"

"Because the army'd closed those towns off to civilians so they could take care of all the replacements and other crap coming in. They called it a 'restricted training area.' They didn't have room for any Frenchmen. But here I guess they figure if they want to come back home and get their ass shot off, let them."

Jim nodded. "Take it from me, old pal," he said. "You'll feel a lot better off if you go get yourself laid."

Will just shook his head.

The cry, "Mail call!" sent every man within earshot running to the truck parked outside the antitank company headquarters. Blalock, the company clerk, had jumped onto the tailgate and was already shouting names when Will arrived just in time to hear, "Pope, William!"

"Here!" he yelled.

Blalock tossed the envelope at Will's outstretched hand. "Gee, Pope," he said loudly, "It's from the governor! Maybe you got a full pardon or something." He laughed at his own joke.

"A circular to 'our brave men in the armed forces' is more like it!" Will yelled back. "The dumb politicians don't know we can't even vote yet." Everybody laughed at that.

"Cut out the wisecracks, Blalock!" shouted a sergeant. "Let's have the mail!"

This was the first letter Will had received from his father, who usually just wrote him notes at the end of his mother's letters. But this one was from his father, all right. The envelope was typewritten, and the return address was "Office of the Governor."

"Do me a favor, Jimmy," said Will. "Pick up the rest of my mail if I get any."

Jim nodded as Will made his way out of the crowd. If his father took the time to write him, it must be something important. "Oh, golly," he thought, "I hope nothing's happened. I hope Mother's not sick. I wonder if somebody's died, or if we've lost all our money, or if Dad's been kicked out of office."

Will had been walking toward his billet; now he was alone, standing in the street a block away. He couldn't wait. His hands shook as he opened the envelope. He read the typewritten letter quickly. It was the same kind most boys got from their dads, chatty and fatherly. All except the last paragraph. He read that one again:

"You know how proud we are of you," wrote the governor. "However, I'm sure you remember how you used to faint when you were young, and I'll bet you didn't mention that when you took your army physical exam, did you? You wanted to go into the service just like everybody else, and I admire you for it. But I don't think you are physically fit to be a soldier. You will be a liability to the other men who have to serve with you. Therefore, for the good of our country's war effort, I have arranged for an army doctor in the European Theater of Operations to give you a thorough physical examination to determine your fitness to continue to serve overseas, or even to serve at all. However, son, you must be honest and admit to him that you have, in fact, fainted on several occasions. Your mother and I are looking forward to seeing you soon."

Will was elated. He couldn't believe it. He was going home!

"Whoopee!" he shouted. He felt like singing. He wished Jim were there so he could tell him the good news. Will was touched. "My father must really love me to do what he's done. He must have had to pull an awful lot of strings to get a doctor to check me out over here, and he doesn't like to do things like that, either."

Now it was sinking in. "I'm going home. I'm going home," he kept repeating to himself. He felt a twinge of guilt about leaving Jim and his platoon, but it quickly passed. "To hell with it. I've done my part. I fought for Alsace. I deserve to go home, and by God, I'm going!"

He was sorry he couldn't take Jim with him, but Jim'd be all right. They weren't in danger anymore. Hell, they'd stay where they were until the war ended. Then everybody'd go home. He was just getting a little head start, that was all. If your father was the governor of a state, you ought to get some benefit out of it. Will smiled. He was happy.

The men started to return from mail call. "Hey, Will," said Jim Mahoney. "No more letters. Sorry. What did you get from your governor?"

Will was still smiling. "Oh, the usual crap," he said. "Just a circular."

Jim shook his head. "Aw, come on, Will. This here's old Jim Mahoney, remember? I know you."

Will put his finger to his lips.

"Your old man's gonna get you out of the army, ain't he, Will? I knew he would. No governor's son don't have to be in this here infantry. Nohow. No way. I'll miss you, though, buddy. I truly will."

"It's not absolutely sure I'll get out," said Will. "It'll depend on the doctors—a little, anyhow."

"Aw, you'll get out, all right," replied Jim. "And if I could get out now, too, I'd do it in a flash. So good luck to you."

Now Will felt even better.

A few days later, after Will had almost forgotten about the letter from his father, Blalock came looking for him. Peering at Will through the thick, horn-rimmed glasses that seemed to be *de rigueur* for any company clerk worthy of the name, Blalock said, "Pope, we got a message from the medical battalion. A doctor's coming over to give you a physical examination this afternoon. You know anything about it? You sick? Got VD?"

"Hell, no!" exclaimed Will.

"Well, whatever it is," said Blalock, "be at headquarters at 1400 hours today."

Will was so excited that afternoon, he couldn't wait. He'd already packed his gear in an old barracks bag, ready to depart, and at 1330 hours he left the billet and began to amble slowly toward the antitank company headquarters, trying his best to keep calm. Over and over again, he'd rehearsed all the things he was going to tell the doctor. That first battle, of course, when he'd fainted right on the battlefield at Damen. Then he'd go back to all the times he'd fainted before that... No! he thought. I'll leave Damen for last! That's the clincher! I actually fainted in combat! After that, there's no way they can keep me in this man's army! No way!

Then he thought, My God! I hope nobody else will be there when I have to admit that! He broke out in goose bumps. How embarrassing! But he knew he'd have to tell the doctor. Will wiped his brow. "Damn!" he breathed. "That's going to be damned unpleasant."

He switched his thoughts to the times he fainted in school. He planned to go over them all with the doctor—such as when he went out for football practice, and the left halfback got tackled so hard his nose bled, and the next thing Will knew he was flat on his back looking at the blue sky, with the entire team clustered around him. Now, that was embarrassing! And Will always wondered if it was one of the reasons he never made the team.

Once, he remembered, he'd passed out during a final exam. The room was too warm. That's what they'd said afterward. Actually, he'd been so worried and keyed up, he knew it was from that. He wondered if passing out in the heat counted. He'd done that during basic training. It was in August, and they'd had to march a long way to the rifle range under the hot sun. The only problem was that he wasn't the only one who'd passed out that time—half the company did. No. He'd better not use that one.

Let's see, thought Will. The doctor'll ask me if I faint. Or, maybe he'll ask me if I've ever fainted. And I'll say, 'Yes, sir, quite often,' or something like that. Then he'll ask me for specific examples, and I'll tell him as many as I can remember and, then, socko! The ridge outside Damen. Fainting in the face of the enemy! Oh, boy! Will rubbed his hands together. Then he stopped. A worried look crossed his face. Suppose he asks me if I ever fainted after that? He shook his head. No. Once is enough, anyway.

When he entered the company headquarters at 1345 hours, Blalock was in the outer office picking at an old, battered typewriter. From inside the executive officer's quarters, Will heard the sound of voices.

Blalock looked up and said, "Hi, Will. The doctor's already here." He turned and called, "Pope just came in, sir!"

Will had a sinking spell. He thought, My God! I hope Lieutenant Sommers isn't going to stay while I talk to the doctor! No, of course not. That wouldn't be ethical. There's something about a confidence between a doctor and his patient, I think.

Sommers appeared in the doorway. He was smiling, and his voice was warm and friendly as he said, "Hey, Will, come on in."

Will smiled wanly back and walked over to the lieutenant's door, where Sommers waited for him with his hand outstretched. After they shook, Sommers said, "Will, this is Doctor Ramsay. Just by chance, he happens to be an old pal of mine, but he's here because he has orders to see you for some reason or other."

The doctor was dressed neatly and looked like any other officer except for the black bag he had sitting beside him. He was about thirty years old, tall, with a small black moustache and straight black hair, which was already a little thin.

"By the way," continued Sommers, turning toward Doctor Ramsay, "why do you want to see Pope, here?"

Ramsay shrugged. "I'm not certain where it came from," he replied. "But there's some sort of a report that claims Pope faints or fainted or has some such problem."

Sommers laughed. "This damned army!" he exclaimed. "What'll they come up with next?"

"What the hell?" said Ramsay. "It gives us a chance to get together again and talk over old times, so quit bitching."

"Yeah," replied Sommers. "So let's get this nonsense over with, and I'll tell you some more about that hospital I was in after I got hit. Want me to leave you two alone?"

Ramsay shook his head. Will's heart plummeted.

"You got a fainting problem, son?" asked the doctor.

Will fidgeted. If only Sommers weren't there! Damn! He knew his lieutenant liked and respected him. Now what will he think? He cleared his throat. "Well, sir," he began, "you see, when I was in school—"

"I didn't think so," said Doctor Ramsay. "So we won't cause you any more embarrassment. You can go. But if you ever do feel like fainting or anything like that, put your head way down for a few minutes, okay?" The doctor wrote something on a piece of paper and waved to Will, indicating the interview was over.

Will was stunned. He croaked, "But sir…! But sir…!"

"It's okay, Will," said Sommers. "We know it's not your fault, so don't worry about it. I want you to know we're sorry the whole thing happened. If I'd known ahead of time what this was all about, I wouldn't even have bothered you." He turned to the doctor. "Right?"

"Right," replied Ramsay. "You go on your way, son. You look good and healthy to me."

Will stumbled out of the office like a man in a trance. He didn't even answer Blalock when he asked him if he had VD, and the sound of the company clerk laughing at his own joke irritated him.

Will felt let down and depressed. "How did I louse it up?" he asked himself. "How?" He'd lost his chance. He wouldn't be going home after all. If his father only knew how an army doctor at the front had translated his orders to give a private "a thorough physical examination" to determine whether or not he was a fainter, he'd lose his faith in the United States Army. And, by God, Will intended to tell him, too!

★

General Tom Jacobs stood in Dave Richardson's office enjoying the warm fire that blazed in the open fireplace. The room was still bare, but somebody had found a rug for the floor, and the chairs were different. They had a little faded tapestry to cover their bare wood.

A meeting had just broken up, and General Richardson had gone out with the other officers to say his farewells. Jacobs had stayed behind as usual to discuss things with his chief.

Tom Jacobs was beginning to like it in the rear. He walked from the fireplace to the large wall map filled with different colored lines and pins. He found himself enjoying pushing the units around, placing his reserves where he thought they'd be needed, deciding where and when to strike the enemy. "This is where I should have been all the time," he mused. "It's like a game when you're this far away from it. Back here, what happens on the field doesn't bother you, because you don't see it. You don't have to watch your men bleed and die; you don't have to visit an aid station and hear the moans and the screams of the horribly wounded men you sent into the meat grinder..."

Tom Jacobs remembered the feeling he'd had that last trip to the front as a division commander. He remembered it clearly. His casualties had been high. The Germans were fighting hard and were killing his men faster than he could replace them. They needed a rest, and he'd arranged for them to get one. That's why he was there that day: to make the preparations to pull his boys out. Then he got the orders. Instead of being relieved, his division was jumping off, attacking a superior enemy. He'd looked around at his dead and wounded; he'd asked the battalion commander with him, "Can you attack again?"

"If we have to, we will," came the reply. And that was when Tom Jacobs decided he wouldn't be responsible for killing men like that!

He'd driven all the way back to corps headquarters and stormed into his corps commander's office. When he pounded his fist on the desk, three coffee cups bounced, and one crashed to the floor. He remembered the startled expression on the corps commander's face, and he smiled. That expression gave Jacobs the incentive to shout, "You son-of-a-bitch! My line companies have been completely replaced three times in one month, and that's enough, dammit! You want us to attack? Fine! You go grab yourself a rifle and stick a bayonet on the end of it and come lead us, you bastard! Come lead us into those 88s that rip my men apart, platoon by platoon. Come lead us against their machine guns that shred whole rifle companies in minutes. Come on, you son-of-a-bitch, let's go!"

Well, he'd been relieved of command, of course. "Too emotionally involved with his men," that's what they'd said. Thank God his record was so outstanding that they couldn't just send him home. And now he was learning to be like his corps commander. And like Dave Richardson. He nodded his head. That's what makes them great generals. They don't have to share the suffering of their men. If they did, they'd never order another attack. And, of course, we'd never win the war, either. No, but there has to be a balance...

His thoughts were interrupted by Richardson's return. "Well, they've gone," he said. "That was a good meeting, though, Tom. No crises to resolve today, so let's relax."

"We can't afford to relax for long, Dave," replied Jacobs, stretching his arms. "Our big offensive starts in a couple of days now."

Richardson nodded. "My plans have all been approved. We're pretty much set. You know, Tom, this'll be our final push. This time we go all the way."

"I know. Getting started is going to be the bloody part—after that, I'm not worried. We'll go all the way, just as you say."

Richardson thought about that for a moment. Then he said, "You mean because the Seventh Army's going to make a direct, frontal attack on the Germans this side of the Rhine? That's what you mean by a bloody start?"

Jacobs nodded. "It has to be done. But it won't take our boys long, Dave. I say we'll be on the Rhine in two weeks. No. Less."

"Seventh Army jumps off on March fifteenth," said Richardson. "We've got our crack outfits spearheading—the Third Division, Forty-second, Fifteenth. We're going with our best. Can't afford not to if we want to wrap this thing up fast."

Tom Jacobs nodded. "Right," he said. But his voice had no emotion.

14

Early on the evening of March fourteenth, Will Pope came in from pulling guard. He unrolled his sleeping bag, took out a candle to put on the empty rations case he used as a table, then pulled out his Agatha Christie and laid it on top of the sleeping bag. He couldn't help chuckling as he glanced over at Jim Mahoney.

For the past three nights, Bowden had refused to let Jim go back to the hospital, despite his protests. "Look, Sarge, you knows how to read. Look at this. If I don't get no medical attention, I might die. You hear? Die! And you'd be responsible..."

Bowden was firm, and Bowden was stern. "Nobody leaves, dammit! I'm making bed check, Mahoney, and if you ain't here when I do, I'm gonna jam a bayonet up your ass so far you'll taste it for a month, so now shut up!"

That evening Will wandered over, as usual, to chat with Jimmy. He liked having him there, but he'd never say so. Jim'd kill him. "Still here, Jimbo?" he asked. "I thought you'd be back with Marylou by now."

The look he got told him Jim had lost his sense of humor. "What do you get for knocking off a chicken-shit sergeant?" asked Jim. "Thirty days in the stockade? Something like that?"

Will shook his head. "I think they shoot you," he replied.

"Damn!" said Jim. "Marylou'd never forgive me if I went and got myself shot."

"By the way, where the hell is Sergeant Bowden?" asked Will.

"At headquarters. There's a big meeting of some kind. All the platoon leaders and platoon sergeants. I don't like it. Something's up. First the sarge won't let me go see Marylou no more; then they have this here big meeting..."

"You worried, Jimbo? I don't believe it."

Jim was quiet for a minute. "You're right, Will. Nothing used to worry me, but now it does. I'm in love, and I worry all the time. I just hope this here army don't do nothing foolish that can get old Jim Mahoney killed, is all."

"No way, Jimbo," said Will. "We're just going to sit here nice and comfortable until the war's over—then we'll all go home..."

The door flew open, and Sergeant Sam Bowden stood there. All conversation stopped. The grim expression on the sergeant's face told them something important was up. Bowden looked steadily at his men, cleared his throat, and said in a voice filled with quiet drama, "Tomorrow morning at 0600, the division's taking off like a big-ass bird, and we're not gonna stop!"

In the absolute silence that greeted Bowden's announcement, Will felt his sense of security crumble.

"Tonight," continued Bowden, pausing for the word to take effect, "The mine platoon is going to clear mines in front of K Company. We'll move out with our gear, all our mines and equipment, everything. Don't leave anything behind. We won't be coming back. Every man will draw two bandoliers of ammunition, two hand grenades, and one day's K rations. Check your cartridge belts, your canteens, and your first-aid kits. Squad leaders, take charge of your squads and be ready to move out in half an hour."

Bowden turned to Ceruti and said, "Pull in the guards, tell them what's up, and get the platoon ready. I've got to get back to headquarters." And he turned and departed as quickly as he'd arrived.

Will felt as if somebody had just knocked the wind out of him. His heart was pounding, and his mouth was so dry he couldn't have spit if his life had depended on it. His hands were shaking as he rolled up his sleeping bag and started collecting his meager possessions. He'd been safe too long. He'd forgotten about the fear. But it was back now with a vengeance.

He looked over at Jim. For the first time since he'd known him, he saw fear in Mahoney's face. He saw his hands shake. Jim met Will's glance and shook his head. He wasn't smiling. He was scared, too. Will looked around him. The other men were getting ready. They'd opened up the box of ammunition and were helping themselves to the bandoliers of M-1 clips and draping them over their shoulders. Now Ceruti was breaking out the hand grenades.

Will found himself automatically reaching for a couple of bandoliers.

★

The terrain in front of King Company had been rugged. The Germans had two machine guns with perfect interlocking fire protecting the minefield, and they kept throwing up flares all night, so the platoon was never able to get near the mines. At three in the morning, they drove off to a small woods, where they unrolled their bedrolls and slept like rocks.

Will vaguely felt somebody gently kicking his ribs. He wiggled out of his sleeping bag, grabbed his boots, and buckled them on. All his actions were automatic. He rolled up his sleeping bag, tossed it onto the truck, and sliced his K ration breakfast open with his bayonet and began to eat.

Will's mind was still blank. If anybody had asked him, he wouldn't have had the slightest idea where he was or what he was doing. Gradually he became aware that he was in a wooded glen. Sounds began to register on his almost unconscious mind. A few rifle shots, a few artillery rounds, a short burst of machine gun fire. The firing was loud but sporadic, which meant the front was close by, but there was nothing serious in progress at the moment.

Will looked at his watch. It was 0500 hours! No wonder he was having trouble waking up! He'd just gone to sleep! Aloud he said, "Hell and damnation!"

He heard a chuckle to his right and looked over. There was Jim Mahoney. "So you're finally awake," said Jim.

Will replied, "Yeah. But why the hell am I? I just went to bed."

"We're going to go sit behind the First Battalion. That's our position for the jump-off. Sarge says they won't need us probably, but that's where we have to be just the same."

"Hell and damnation! Why can't we just wait here? We could sleep until they need us."

Jim laughed. "Will, you're too much!" he said.

Will was relieved to see Jim had gotten his spirit back.

A Jeep approached. On the rough, uneven terrain, the vehicle pitched and swayed like a bucking bronco. Sitting beside the driver, Lieutenant Sommers held on for dear life, his body moving like a rodeo rider's. When the Jeep pulled up, he jumped out. Bowden greeted him.

"Able's light for the jump-off," said Sommers. "They lost a patrol last night. You're going to fill in as an extra platoon for them, so let's get going."

As the men began loading onto the trucks, Sommers continued talking to his sergeant. "Sam, we think the Second Battalion'll relieve the First either tonight or tomorrow morning, depending on how things go. We'll get you back then. I hope."

They arrived at A Company just as it was getting ready to attack. Empty ammunition cases and ration boxes were scattered over the area. Radio teams were working; medics were setting up; officers were talking in clipped sentences; men were running off on vital errands.

Sommers emerged from the Able Company C.P., a large hole in the ground covered over with pine logs and dirt. He motioned to Bowden to follow him to the rear and bring his men.

At a protected spot about one hundred fifty yards behind the line, Sommers said, "Okay, Sam, here's the story. Captain Wilkes has already brought up his reserve platoon for the jump-off, so he wants you to stay here for now. But he may need you at any time. Take good care of yourselves, Sam, and we'll get you back as soon as we can."

They shook hands. Then as the mine platoon men stood silently beside the dirt road, Sommers got into his Jeep and led the two now-empty trucks off through the woods.

Besides Jack Diamond, the platoon had gotten another driver, named Shanker, who came in the same time they got their second truck. Will didn't know whether Shanker was a new replacement or had transferred from another unit, and he didn't care. He rode with Jack Diamond.

The men of the mine platoon sat or squatted in their small clearing among the pines. Nobody spoke as they listened for sounds that would give them an indication of what was going on. The men were looking at their watches. Will's indicated 0600 hours. "That's H-hour," he thought. "The attack should begin now." He heard the sudden crackling and popping of rifles and machine guns and could sense movement, just out of sight, of the G.I.'s going forward.

Then he heard the 88s. The familiar sound made him shiver.

They were in hilly and wooded territory, with clear spaces scattered among the pine trees. There were dirt roads and small streams, and there were little valleys. Except for the pines, most of the large trees were black and leafless.

The men in the mine platoon continued to listen to the sounds of the attack that they could not see—lots of small-arms fire, lots of artillery fire. The American guns had begun to support the attack as soon as it was under way. Now there could be no mistaking the infantry's intention to drive the enemy from the area.

Bowden turned to Ceruti and said, "I don't like the sound of it. It's a tough fight."

Ceruti nodded. "The Jerries've been dug in here for the last four years; this is gonna be a bitch."

"Yeah," said Gruber. "It's gonna be rough as a cob. That's why we're here: the good old Fighting Fifteenth. The army figures the Jerries missed a few of us, so now they're gonna give 'em a whack at getting us all."

It wasn't until around 1000 hours that morning that a sergeant came running into view yelling, "Mine platoon? Are you the mine platoon?"

Bowden looked up and said, "Yeah?"

"Get ready and come with me," shouted the sergeant.

The men rose and moved out quickly, rifles slung, bandoliers across their shoulders, hand grenades hooked onto their pockets or cartridge belts, K rations stuffed into their field jacket pockets. In a few minutes they arrived at the abandoned foxholes that had been the A Company positions before the jump-off.

Looking ahead, they could see trees and smoke; lots of smoke. The noise of firing echoed and re-echoed through the woods.

On the right, Will saw medics and stretcher-bearers bringing back the wounded. A few dead G.I.'s lay beyond the foxholes. Shell holes pocked the clear areas. Trees had been shattered, some reduced to stumps.

An officer came out of the A Company command post and spoke to Bowden urgently, "Look, Sergeant, we've taken heavy casualties. We've got a weak spot on our right between our men and Love Company of the Third Battalion. I want you to fill it. It's not wide, but I don't want to leave it empty."

Bowden said, "Right, sir," and the platoon moved out quickly.

Will tried not to look at the wounded coming back on stretchers.

There was very little wind. Will saw the flat layers of blue smoke floating in the air through the trees. Ahead, he saw puffs of white smoke.

"Where's Jim? There he is. Good." Jim was going forward cautiously, even falling a little bit behind.

Will could see the men of Able Company ahead of him, dodging in and out among the trees. He was closer now to the crackling and popping of rifles, the chattering of machine guns. Now he could hear burp after burp from the German automatics.

No mortars, though. No hand grenades. Too dangerous. Liable to hit a tree branch above you and kill you dead. More puffs of smoke ahead. The cracks of the rifles sounded flat now. More puffs of smoke. More. A yellow flash hit the trees ahead.

Hit the ground! That's an 88!

Crack! Will heard the explosion. Branches floated down from the splintered tree. Swishing bullets. The acrid smell of gunpowder.

Can't see now for all the smoke. His eyes stung from it.

Bowden was yelling, "Kitch! Kitch! Get over to the right. Make contact with somebody from Love Company. Find out where they are so we don't get in front of them! Muller! Hey, Muller! Go left and make contact with that Able Company platoon over there. You squad leaders. Spread out your squads. First squad to the right. Third to the left. Second in the center. Keep apart, you men. Keep spread out."

Will's mouth was dry. Where the hell is everybody? I can't see through all this smoke.

Eeeeeeee-ow! Ka-boom!

Hell! That's heavy artillery! That's not 88 fire. They've got big stuff back there someplace.

Will realized he was coughing from the smoke. He tried not to. He didn't want to draw attention to himself in any way. He just wanted to lie there and hope the shells and bullets would continue to miss him.

Ceruti and young Martinelli flopped down beside him. They were breathing hard. Rifles cracked ahead. The smoke got thicker. The shells screamed in faster.

Will didn't want company. His mind was frozen. He didn't think he could move. Or talk. Or think.

Ceruti said, "Hey, Will, look what we liberated."

Will saw that Ceruti had set up a light .30-caliber machine gun. Martinelli was already inserting the ammunition belt from the ammo case he carried with the tripod.

"If you keep your eyes open, you can pick up all sorts of useful stuff in a fight like this," continued Ceruti. "One of the new replacements, a kid, MacKenzie, picked himself up a beautiful Browning Automatic Rifle. It's a honey. Has a big chunk of wood out of the stock is all. Will, you stick with us. With this light thirty, we'll give the platoon some firepower. Bowden's taking the rest of my squad."

The forms moving through the smoke were almost out of sight ahead of them. The firing continued without let up. The three men rose to crouching positions. Ceruti held on to the machine gun. Martinelli carried the ammunition case. Will picked up the tripod.

They trotted forward, bent low. There were shell holes over the entire area. Shattered trees. Dead G.I.'s, some badly mutilated by the jagged, razor-sharp fragments of steel, called shrapnel, that had ripped them apart, severed legs and arms from bodies, gouged out chunks of flesh through ripped jackets and trousers. Others seemed to be sleeping on the ground, just napping until somebody came to wake them up. They lay where the German machine guns had cut them down.

The dead G.I.'s scared the hell out of Will. They scared him more than the heavy firing he could hear plainly. They frightened him almost as much as the shells. There was something about seeing a dead G.I. that Will could never get used to.

The three men hit the ground at the same instant. The roaring screams of the German heavy artillery blotted out all the other sounds. There was nothing they could do but pray, with their faces pressed into the dead, wet leaves.

Will's heart never stopped pounding. As the ground shook from the shock of the exploding shells, he felt tears in his eyes. He realized his impotence. There was not one damned thing he could do to save himself. If a shell hit him, he was dead. It was all luck. Just pure, dumb luck. Some guys get hit. Some don't.

He was only vaguely aware of the booming of the American artillery coming from their rear, almost unconscious of the whistling of American shells overhead. He heard the ragged popping of G.I. rifles. Short, steady bursts of machine gun fire. And he realized the ground no longer shook, and the screaming shells no longer came. Through the smoke, the forms of American infantrymen moved forward again.

Will got to his knees beside Ceruti and Martinelli. They had to advance with the attack. Ceruti nodded toward a slight declivity in the ground ahead of them. It was an ideal position for their machine gun. The small hole would protect them, and the gun would have a clear field of fire.

Ceruti started to his feet, but Will reached out and grabbed his shoulder and pulled him back. Ceruti settled on his knees with a questioning look at Will. Will couldn't think of anything to say. He knew they shouldn't go into that position, but he didn't know why.

From their left, three men from Able Company with their light machine gun dashed forward and jumped into the position Ceruti had wanted. They immediately set up their gun. One of the men started to feed it ammunition.

There was a bright flash. An explosion's roar. A German shell scored a direct hit on the hole that was supposed to protect the machine gun.

As the smoke drifted away, Will saw the three men sprawled there. One of them had been flung onto his back against a tree trunk so he was half lying, half sitting with his arms outstretched and his mouth and eyes wide open. His stomach had been ripped apart, and he lay gazing unbelievingly at his insides, which lay spattered in front of him, a pink and purple mess. A section of his large intestine was twisted around his leg like a big snake. Slowly the eyes closed and the mouth shut.

Another lay across the lip of the hole. His buttocks had been completely blown off; raw, shredded flesh was all that remained of his lower torso. The man never moved.

Beyond their position, the third man sat screaming at the top of his lungs. He looked as if a giant knife had peeled his scalp off from his forehead to the back of his neck. Will could see the bone of his skull gleaming white where it was not covered with the blood that was pouring out in red torrents.

Will felt the nausea and the clamminess and the pounding of his heart in his throat. He was afraid he would throw up or faint. He lowered his head and put his hand over his eyes and tried to think about something else.

He glanced up momentarily and saw a medic running through the smoke toward the screaming man. Just before the medic reached him, the man stopped screaming He sat very still. The medic checked all three men, looked back at no one in particular, saw Ceruti, shook his head, and left the position.

Will realized he was not the only one who was panting. Both Ceruti and Martinelli were breathing in short, labored breaths. Martinelli had tears rolling down his face. Will patted him on the back, then turned to Ceruti and said, "Mike, let's get the hell out of here."

"Yeah," said Ceruti. "Do you see a position for us, Will?"

"How about behind those logs? They're fresh. Artillery just chopped them down."

"Done," replied Ceruti.

They trotted to their right, put the machine gun down, and stretched themselves out behind the logs, facing the front. A tree blocked their view, but they didn't care.

The other men of the mine platoon were a good fifty yards in front of them and moving ahead fast. Ceruti turned to Will and said, "We gotta go forward! You see a position?"

Will looked. He turned back to Ceruti and said, "Anyplace away from those trees'll do. How about that bunch of shell holes over there?"

"Looks good to me," said Ceruti. "Let's go."

They were still breathless. Ceruti turned to Will and said, "You saved our lives. How'd you know the Jerries'd let go at that hole?"

"I don't know, Mike. I just didn't like the looks of it. It was too perfect."

"Yeah," said Ceruti. "You're right. They had it zeroed in. I should have known that. They're devils, those bastards!"

They continued the same kind of fighting the rest of the afternoon. Short dashes forward. Artillery barrages. Firing and being fired at. The word came that, at nightfall, the Second Battalion would relieve the First, so they dug in and formed a main line of resistance.

To the army commanders, the important thing that day was that the American offensive had not been stopped. To Will, the important thing was that he had not been killed.

15

When the mine platoon came off the line at about 1800 hours, Ceruti kept the machine gun and MacKenzie the Browning Automatic Rifle. Will was exhausted, hungry, and on edge. It had been a brutal day.

Lieutenant Sommers met them when they reached the area just behind the foxholes. The men of the Second Battalion were marching past them into the line in silent, well-ordered columns.

In a small clearing surrounded by pine trees, the men of the mine platoon sat down around their lieutenant, who was making small talk with Sergeant Bowden. The wind blowing through the pines sounded like somebody whispering in the distance. It muted the sounds of firing.

The squad leaders sorted out their squads and reported to Bowden. There had been no casualties. Will found it hard to believe, but there it was: no casualties to the platoon during the whole first day of the attack.

After the squad leaders returned to their men, Will heard Brucker talking to his men as the breeze caught his words. "Donaldson, you son-of-a-bitch, if you freeze up one more time, or don't do what I tell you to, I'm gonna fix your wagon good, you hear me? That goes for the rest of you bastards, too. You do what I tell you. When I signal 'go right,' dammit, you go right, and when I signal 'forward,' you go forward. You got that?"

Will saw them nod in the twilight. Brucker's words sent a chill down his back. The tone he'd used was cold, impersonal, menacing. Will shuddered slightly, the way he used to when he'd chance on a snake in the woods. He felt sorry for Brucker's men. Even for Donaldson.

Sommers had something to say, but he seemed reluctant to get started. He pretended to be listening to what the sergeant was saying, but by the fixed smile on his lips and the faraway look in his eyes, Will could tell he was thinking about something that had nothing to do with his conversation with Bowden. Finally Sommers took a deep breath and a step backward at the same time. He cleared his throat and said, "I've got some news for you you're not going to like."

He paused to let the words sink in, but he already had their full attention.

"Tonight at nine o'clock, the Second Battalion is jumping off in a night attack. Their objective is the Bitche-Hagenor road." Sommers paused again before he continued. "The area you attacked today was pretty woody, but in front of us now are some large, open spaces, even a few fields, and we think they're mined. So before the Second Battalion jumps off tonight, the artillery's going to plow up those fields pretty good and detonate any mines the Jerries put there."

Will breathed easier and leaned over to Jim Mahoney and whispered, "That's the ticket."

Jim grinned wryly. Just being there made him unhappy.

But Sommers wasn't through. "There's a dirt road that runs through the area, and they're not going to put any shells onto it because we're going to need that road badly after we take our objective; so we've got to be sure it's clear of mines, too."

Will knew what was coming, but, he thought, at least they wouldn't be clearing mines in front of the Second Battalion's night attack. They couldn't. Not with shells blowing up the minefields; he figured they'd go with the battalion, maybe fall behind them, since clearing mines took time, then get to the objective after they'd already taken it. And he was right.

"Okay," continued the lieutenant after he'd finished, "if there aren't any questions, try to get some rest before we take off."

Will felt depressed. That day's work had shown him that the German army was still in the field, still able to fight hard.

Jim said, "A guy told me King Company took seventy percent casualties during the first fifteen minutes of the jump-off. I guess most of them were from mines. Dammit! I'm scared, Will. I sure as hell don't want to die now! So please keep me from getting killed, will you?"

An officer came along yelling, "Okay, put out those butts, you guys! It's getting dark! Douse those cigarettes now, you hear? No more smoking!"

"Pompous ass," said Will as the red glows disappeared and the men started slicing open their K ration boxes and eating their cold dinners. Before they finished, Sommers and Bowden returned with a couple of the new mine detectors they'd just received. The men began getting to their feet and looking at their watches.

Martinelli came over to Will and said, "Pope, let's be friends, okay?"

Will was too startled to reply. He just looked at Martinelli uncomprehendingly.

"Today with Sergeant Ceruti," continued Martinelli. "You done saved us good. What I want to say is, to hell with that fat-ass Donaldson; I ain't gonna be part of his gang no more. I want to stick with you and the sarge and Mahoney here, with my own squad. Understand?"

Will smiled. He said, "Sure, Martinelli. Don't even think about it. Besides, Sergeant Ceruti tells me you're Italian, so you've got to be a good guy. He says all the good guys are Italians…"

Will turned to Jim. "So let's all be Italians, Jimbo. You can be Luigi Mahonetti, and I'll be Luigi Popelli, and—"

"Aw, come on, you guys, I'm serious," said Martinelli.

"Good!" exclaimed Will, sticking out his hand. They shook. "Us Italians gotta stick together," said Will.

Martinelli looked puzzled. He didn't know exactly how to take Will Pope—he couldn't ever tell when he was kidding—but he liked him, and the jump-off had taught him to stick close to the veteran combat men; he'd live longer that way.

When the Second Battalion jumped off in their night attack, the exploding shells lit up the sky, outlining the forms of the attacking infantrymen, while tracer bullets swarmed through the darkness like giant fireflies hurrying toward an unseen destination.

"I think we're walking into hell," said Will to nobody in particular.

"At least we ain't running," came a voice from the dark, which he recognized as Bowden's. "And I don't think we'll start our little walk in too big of a hurry, either."

"Amen," replied Will. He already felt better, knowing the big sergeant was nearby. He'd like to stick with him, if he could.

Bowden's next words dispelled that hope. "Will, you and a couple of the other old men'll start, so the new guys can watch you awhile before we get out too far. Then you and Mahoney fall back to cover our rear, and I'll put other rifles on the flanks and out in front as scouts."

"Okay with me, Sarge," replied Will. "Me too," came Jim's voice out of the dark.

✪

The night attack met tough resistance. It went slowly. The Germans hit them with heavy artillery and mortars and machine gun fire. Just before dawn, they launched a counterattack that was so furious it almost drove the Second Battalion back, but the battalion recovered quickly, and their automatic weapons slaughtered the oncoming Germans. From then on, the battalion swept forward to their objective, meeting only light resistance.

During the attack, the mine platoon worked on the dirt road as ordered. At first they swept it with the mine detectors—large, thick, plate-like objects attached to broom handle-type poles.

The men swung them back and forth over the area they were working, then moved on until the steady hum was interrupted by a loud beeping that meant there was metal in the ground that had to be checked out.

The men didn't like the detectors. They had to stand up to use them, and they made noise. So after about fifteen minutes, they threw them away and began crawling up the road, probing it with their bayonets, in the old tried-and-true method.

The shells that blew up all over the fields and woods also hit the road ahead of the platoon. If it had actually been mined, most of the platoon would have been killed, but after it was all over, Sommers' report stated the road had not been mined at all.

During most of the night, either Will or Jim Mahoney would dash forward to see how far the platoon had progressed, then return to tell the other, so they would not fall behind.

Now it was dawn. The battalion had taken their objective and the mine platoon had about a hundred yards to go when artillery shells started bursting around the area they were checking. After the explosions stopped, Jim motioned to Will that he was going up ahead to see what had happened. He rose and started his loping little trot toward the rest of the platoon.

Will lay concealed in the bushes, waiting. Thank God we're almost through, he thought. I'm so tired, I could go to sleep right here.

Mahoney came back and jumped into the bushes on the opposite side of the road. He whispered loudly to Will, "We took casualties that time. One of the guys hit was Gomez. Piece of shrapnel sliced him from his crotch to his belly button, and when Donaldson saw him just before the medics got to him, he vomited. Then he fainted and when he came to, he started carrying on like you wouldn't believe; weeping and wailing something awful. I think he's off his rocker. I think they're going to have to put him away…"

Even while Jim was speaking, Irv Donaldson, terrified and out of control, came running down the road as hard as he could run. A shell whistled in and blew up, sending him diving to the ground. Even after the smoke cleared, he just lay there, not moving, and Will thought he must be hit, except that he was breathing, and he'd shiver at intervals. Besides, the shell hadn't been that close, so Will knew Donaldson was just scared to death and couldn't move.

Will was thinking of going over to check on old Irv when out of the smoke came Brucker with his rifle in his hand. He wasn't running. He was striding deliberately to where Donaldson lay. When he reached him, he said, "Dammit! I said, 'Come back!' Didn't you hear me say, 'Come back,' you son-of-a-bitch?"

Brucker swung his rifle down so it pointed at Donaldson's head. He looked around to see if anybody was watching, and when he didn't see anybody, he pushed the front sight of his rifle under the rim of Donaldson's helmet and flipped the helmet off, leaving Donaldson cringing on the ground, bareheaded.

The next instant, Brucker pulled the trigger. The rifle jumped in his hand, and Donaldson jerked, twitched, and lay still. Then Will saw the brains start to ooze out from under his face. Brucker turned calmly toward the front and started back, walking as casually as ever, while Will lay paralyzed by the shock of what he'd just watched.

Brucker was almost out of sight before Will had the idea of shooting him. That was the only way to make sure he didn't kill somebody else, maybe even Will Pope.

He was too late. Brucker was gone.

Will saw the bushes rustle and part on the other side of the road as Jim Mahoney got up and loped over to flop down beside him. He was breathing hard. "Did you see that?" he asked.

Will nodded. "We should've shot the bastard," he said.

"Maybe," replied Jim. "I couldn't react that fast, though. I guess I was sort of stunned. I still am."

"Listen to me, Jimmy. Don't tell anybody about this. If Brucker knows we saw him kill Donaldson, he'll kill us too, without a qualm."

"I know," replied Mahoney. "That's why I'm scared. I'm scared of that bastard, and I don't know what to do."

They got up and started toward the front. As they walked along the side of the road, they didn't look at Donaldson lying there. They kept their eyes staring straight ahead of them, and they kept their rifles at the ready.

When they got almost to the Bitche-Hagenor road, they heard Bowden shout, "Over here!" and they turned and headed in his direction. "Keep away from them crossroads," said Bowden. "Jerries got it zeroed in and throw stuff at it all the time."

The men of the line companies were still digging in, and there were occasional shots. A German shell screamed in and blew up. Will looked around. In the grayness, he saw there was a ridge in front of them on the other side of an open field. Woods to their right and left. The road made a good line, one they could hold pretty well if they had to.

"Think they'll counterattack us again, Sarge?" asked Will.

Bowden shook his head. "Naw. They shot their wad with the last one. Anyway, the battalion's gonna take that ridge in front of us. Jump-off's set for 0900 hours."

"Where'd you come from, Pope?"

Will turned to see Brucker standing beside them. He wanted to tell him it was none of his business, but he couldn't speak.

"I said, 'Where'd you come from?'" persisted Brucker in his usual monotone.

Bowden answered him with undisguised hostility, "From where I sent him, Brucker. What's it to you, anyway? Go take care of what's left of your squad, and let me worry about the other men."

"I just thought he might've seen Donaldson, is all," replied Brucker. His voice hadn't changed in the slightest, but the words sent shivers down Will's spine as he thought, He must suspect something. He must've just remembered Jim and I were covering the rear. Now he knows. I sure didn't handle it very well.

Bowden asked Will, "You guys run into Donaldson?"

Will shook his head. So did Jim.

Brucker said, "Okay. I'll get going." And he left.

Will was wondering where Brucker was headed, when Bowden turned and said, "That son-of-a-bitch only has Muller and Trenton in his squad now. Gomez got hit real bad, and Donaldson's run off, so the lieutenant's sending Brucker back with a bunch of prisoners. I don't like it much, though. I'd rather have the bastard where I can keep an eye on him."

Will made his decision. He drew Bowden aside and whispered as softly as he could, telling him the whole story of what he'd seen happen to Donaldson.

Bowden remained silent for a minute. Then he said, "Brucker's got nerves of steel and a bucketful of medals to prove it. But he'd always worked alone before, and after he made sergeant he lost too many guys and, after a while, all his men started reporting on sick call, only they weren't sick. Something was wrong, so they transferred him, and that's how we got the bastard.

"I was supposed to keep an eye on the son-of-a-bitch, but in all the smoke and confusion of the last shelling we took, I lost him for a few minutes. I'll see it don't happen again, and I'll have the bastard court-martialed as soon as I can set it up. In the meantime, keep your eyes open, Will. Be careful and keep all this to yourself."

Bowden had spoken so fast, Will took a little time to digest all he'd heard. Then he said, "He's a psychopath, Sarge—" He was about to suggest Brucker be yanked out and locked up immediately when he was interrupted.

"Sam!" Lieutenant Sommers' voice was urgent. As soon as Bowden raised his arm and the lieutenant saw it, he made his way to him quickly, picking his way through the sprawled-out men of the platoon. "You're not going to be relieved," he said evenly. "The rifle platoons took heavier casualties than they expected, and they're scrounging every man they can grab. I'm sorry, Sam, but you're jumping off with the battalion at 0900."

"Yes, sir," said Bowden. His words carried no emotion. He liked and respected Sommers. Sommers had no choice but to carry out his orders. Bowden had no choice but to obey them.

The American artillery began firing. Will was already hacking a hole in the ground. He had butterflies in his stomach, but the digging kept his hands from shaking. As hard as he tried, he couldn't get his mind to adjust to the fact he was going into the attack again instead of returning to the safety of the rear.

Next to him Will heard Jim Mahoney lament, "It ain't fair! Damn them! We was supposed to be pulled out now. Let them damned Krautheads keep that there ridge if they wants it. I wouldn't give you two cents for it, and the damn army wants me to die for the son-of-a-bitch!"

"Let's stick together!" yelled Ceruti. "We fight as a squad!"

Whistles were blowing. The infantry were climbing out of their holes and moving forward, firing as they went. Will abandoned his half-dug hollow in the ground and began running forward into the field in front of the ridge as fast as he could. He kept his eyes on Ceruti, who was slightly ahead of him.

He zigzagged through the sparsely wooded field. He felt almost light-headed as he hit the ground at the end of each sprint, rolled to his right or left, then lay there long enough to catch his breath and shoot off a clip of ammunition before jumping to his feet to dash forward again.

He heard the popping of rifles and machine guns and saw bullets kicking up puffs of dust on the ground around him, clipping branches off trees, ricocheting off rocks. Will kept telling himself, "Don't pay any attention to all that. Just go by the book.

Run forward, hit the ground. Roll over. Shoot. Keep going. Keep your head down. Calm down, now. Calm down."

All he really wanted to do was lie there until it was all over. He looked up. He saw the explosions of American mortars hitting the German line on the ridge ahead of him. He heard the shriek of a German shell and felt the thumping, jarring, rock-splitting, dirt-spraying, shrapnel-flinging impact of its explosion. He figured that was about as close as one could come to him without actually hitting him, and as soon as the jagged steel fragments stopped cutting down everything in their paths, Will was on his feet, running forward again.

The American troops had taken the ridge. Their dead and wounded lay scattered all the way up the slope, the wake of an attacking infantry battalion.

Will Pope's chest heaved as he struggled to catch his breath after dashing, dodging, and crawling through terrain raked by bullets and blown to bits by explosives.

He looked around. He was in a large hole recently occupied by the Germans. All around him. G.I.'s from the line companies had taken over former Jerry positions, just as he had. Somebody was passing out bloody bandoliers taken off the dead and wounded. "God," thought Will, "there's got to be an easier way to earn a living."

Then he realized he'd made it. He'd survived once again. It gave him a thrill. Just surviving gave him a thrill.

"When Brucker comes back, we'll have fourteen men," said Bowden. He and Ceruti sat on the edge of Will's hole on the ridge.

"Who'd we lose?" asked Will. "I know about Gomez and Donaldson. Who else?"

"Brown got hit in the arm last night, but he ain't bad. They'll send him back to us, I reckon. Sullivan got it this morning during the attack. A mortar round knocked him ass over elbow. Don't know how he is. Nobody had time to stop to find out. Gruber got a medic onto him, so at least he's looked after…" Sullivan had been one of Irv Donaldson's gang. So had Gomez. That meant Martinelli was the only one of them left, and he'd turned out to be a good guy.

Will shook his head. "What now?" he asked.

Before Bowden could answer, an officer came down the line, looking for somebody. Gruber joined him, and they came over to Bowden.

"I'm Lieutenant Rodriguez, headquarters, Second Battalion. The exec from antitank is down there raising holy hell. Wants you guys back. Says there's mines all over the road, and they want to use armored cars, and how the hell come we're using specially trained troops as riflemen, and all that crap.

"Anyway, it shouldn't be too rough now. So to keep peace in the regiment, maybe you guys better go on back and report to your exec."

The platoon was resting among the pine trees beside a brook, where Sommers had left them.

"Where the hell have you been, Brucker?" Bowden's question was abrupt. The other men jerked their heads up to look at him.

"Eating hot chow back of the lines," answered Brucker.

Bowden thought for a minute, then said, "Brucker, your squad's too small to be effective anymore; I'm putting Trenton with Ceruti, and Muller with Gruber. You'll be my assistant. Stick with me all the time, and I'll let you know what I want you to do. Understand?"

"Sure, Sarge," replied Brucker.

Late in the afternoon, the platoon got orders again. "Damn!" swore Ceruti. "We're filling out another rifle company. I wish those bastards'd be more careful and stop losing so many men.

"Yeah," said Will. "I thought Lieutenant Sommers fixed it so we wouldn't have to do that anymore. I thought he told them we were specially trained troops and had to be ready to clear mines."

"Yeah, Will, that's right. He did," Bowden cut in. "But the line companies're taking such heavy casualties they're grabbing anybody they can get, and we're awful damned handy."

Between their attack that night and the one the next morning, Ceruti lit into Martinelli. "Hey! Martinelli! How come you got mixed in with Easy Company during that last attack, huh? I been looking all over for you. You got a habit of going off with them line company guys. Stick with your own squad, okay?"

"Yeah, Sarge," replied Martinelli. "Them guys looked like they know'd where they was going, is all."

"Okay, but don't let it happen no more, hear? Let's go, we're jumping off again. Let's go! Let's go!"

Late the next afternoon, Will was digging a foxhole. The platoon was going to spend the night on the line with Easy Company and come out with them in the morning.

Bowden came down the line looking for Brucker. Bowden was angry. But nobody could find Sergeant Brucker. Ceruti counted his men; they were all there. Even Martinelli had stayed with the squad this time.

Bowden told Ceruti to keep a lookout for his assistant, and he went off to find out how Gruber's squad had fared. He returned with the news that young Reilly had gotten it. He'd stayed on his feet too long during a dash forward, and a German machine gun cut him almost in half.

Then Bowden said, almost as if it were an afterthought, "They found Brucker, too. They found him by a clump of trees, dead. They ain't sure yet, but it looks like somebody put a whole clip of M-1 slugs into his back."

16

Will stood beside his half-dug hole, digesting Sergeant Bowden's news. Jim Mahoney was digging on one side of him, and Hank Gray on the other. The first shock gave way to relief. Will sighed. Thank God somebody got Brucker.

"Hey, Jimbo!" he called. "Did you hear that? Brucker's dead."

Jim looked up and smiled. He took off his helmet and said, "Mourned by all, I'm sure." He put his hand over his heart and asked, "Shall we have a moment of silence for the late departed?"

Hank Gray said, "I wonder who shot him? The sarge said he was full of M-1 slugs."

"I would have," replied Will. "I just never got the chance."

"You know what worries me about this here war right now?" asked Mahoney. "I'll tell you. We're moving too damned fast, and we're moving away from that there hospital that I calls home. Dammit! If we doesn't slow down a mite, I won't be able to make it there and back no more."

Will had to smile. Poor old Jim had been so worried about Brucker and the possibility of Brucker shooting him that he hadn't been able to think that much about his Marylou. But now he was back in full swing, and Will didn't want to hear about it.

Will dug out a little more of his hole, then stuck his shovel into the ground and said, "I'm going over to see what I can find out from Sarge."

He made his way over to where Bowden was making dirt fly as he dug his shallow trench for the evening. The sergeant had a pensive expression. He was thinking hard.

Will squatted beside him. Bowden continued digging. "Somebody saved the army a lot of trouble, right, Sarge?"

Bowden looked up at Will and nodded.

"When you came looking for him a while ago, you sure were mad at the son-of-a-bitch for some reason," ventured Will.

Bowden stopped digging. "Hell, yes!" he exclaimed. "I think that son-of-a-whore was shooting at me! I'd see dirt kicking up all around me, see? But not like it was coming from the Jerries. I'd turn my head, and every time there'd be Brucker right behind me with his rifle pointing at me, so I'd yell and wave at him, and he'd smile and wave back like everything was okay; then, five minutes later, the same thing'd happen. I was scared pissless, I can tell you! Here I'm leading my platoon against the Jerries, and one of my own men's trying to shoot me from my rear! How do you like them apples, Pope?"

Will shook his head. "Not much, Sarge." Then Will scratched his nose. "Why was he shooting at you, anyway?"

"Ha!" exclaimed the big sergeant. "You tell me and we'll both know!"

"Do you think he figured you knew about Donaldson?" asked Will.

Bowden shrugged. "Could be," he replied. "What I think's more likely is he figured he was my assistant now, so's if anything happened to me, he'd take over the platoon. If he could've shot me dead, he'd have been it."

"No way," said Will. The very thought made him shiver.

"That's not how he saw it," said Bowden.

"My God. That guy would've killed us all in time. Why, hell, Sarge, having a bastard like him in the outfit's like living with a rattlesnake. Whenever he feels like it, zap! There goes another one of us!"

"Yeah," replied Bowden. "Anyway, I'm gonna tell the captain the full story so's to make sure nobody calls no investigation or any crap like that. I don't know who shot the bastard, and I don't care. And Will, the less said about this whole thing, the better. You hear?"

"Yes, Sarge," replied Will. Deep inside, though, he couldn't help wondering who'd shot Sergeant Brucker.

★

After they came out of the line with the Second Battalion, the mine platoon kept on the move just behind the fighting. They were a mobile reserve, small but available at a moment's notice to go into a minefield or to fill in some depleted rifle company.

They usually sheltered in a woods. It gave them a feeling of security. They couldn't be seen easily, and they had trees to hide behind if they got jumped by Jerries. Still, they always posted guards and they always dug foxholes. If an infantryman thinks he's going to be in one place for more than five minutes, he digs a hole.

Will sat on the side of his hole and cursed his blisters. Jim and Hank Gray came over to sympathize. Ceruti and Martinelli came to join them. "Dammit!" said Ceruti. "We're all bunched up. One Kraut shell could get us all."

"What the hell," said Hank. "They'll get us all anyway, sooner or later, so why not make it easy for them?"

Carlo Pacini came over. He was in Gruber's squad, but he and Hank were pals. He'd heard Hank's remark and said, "Yeah. I come to help make it easy for them."

"Mamma mia!" said Ceruti. "What the hell am I gonna do with you guys?"

"Hey, Sarge," said Will, "tell us who shot Brucker."

"Aw, for God's sake and ours, leave it alone, Will," said Jim.

"You know they're liable to throw us into combat again at any time, don't you?" asked Ceruti. "So we've got to be ready."

"They've been liable to throw us in for the last two days. I've been ready, damn them!" said Will.

"Jumpy, Will?" asked Jim.

Will smiled. "I guess so. This waiting makes me nervous as a cat. I almost wish they'd throw us in and be done with it."

"I don't," said Jim.

"Yeah. Anything's better than combat," said Pacini. "There's a lot of things I'd rather be doing than this. I keep resigning from this damned army, but nobody pays no attention to me."

"Do you really think they'll get us all before we're finished?" asked Martinelli.

"Sure," replied Hank. "We all come in as replacements, right? Well, what do you think? The guy we replaced just decided to pack his bags one d.y and go home? Like hell!"

"That's right," said Will. "How many guys do you figure are still left that came over with the original Triple Nickel? Not enough to get up a good poker game, I'll bet."

They remained quiet for a few minutes, thinking that over.

"Yeah," said Jim Mahoney. "But remember, a lot of guys just gets wounded." A dreamy expression came over his face. "That's for me. Get hit, go back to the hospital, Marylou caresses my brow—"

"Aw, shut up, Jimbo," said Will. "Only the lucky ones get wounded."

"You know what they told us at the repple-depple back in Le Havre?" asked Hank Gray. "They told us there's only two ways out of the infantry: in a coffin or on a stretcher."

"You know what they told us?" asked Will. "They told us that if you last through your first day in combat, you'd be doing real good, and if you last a week, it'd be a miracle."

"Geez! They sure like to cheer you guys up before you get here, don't they?" said Ceruti.

"Yeah," said Jim. "So we figure it can't be as bad as they say it is. Nothing could be. Only, you know what? It's worse."

They all nodded.

"You guys worry too much," said Ceruti.

"That's right," replied Jim. "And when you're young and healthy, you shouldn't have to worry all the time. Not about dying. But we do."

"Well, there's one thing," said Will. "If this war keeps on the way it is, we won't have to worry about getting old, and that's for sure."

★

The two trucks of the mine platoon were traveling fast. They had already passed the other convoys; they passed the rifle troops trudging along the sides of the road.

The open countryside was pretty, yet Will sat ramrod still and glassy-eyed. He realized that at that moment their two trucks were spearheading the entire U.S. Seventh Army. There was nothing in front of them but the enemy. And the trucks showed no sign of slowing down.

Bowden hadn't told them anything, either. He'd just ordered them to move out. Whatever his orders, he was keeping them to himself. They'd left their small trailers loaded with mines behind. Each truck had only half a dozen, covered by a tarp on the floorboards.

The road they were on led straight toward some low hills. In front of the hills were open fields. At the crossroads ahead, another road turned to the right and followed along the edge of a wood.

For the first time since they started out, Sergeant Bowden turned around and spoke to his men. "I think that road to the right is the German border," he said.

As they passed through the crossroads, Will realized he must be entering Germany. It gave him an uneasy feeling. Yet, everything was quiet. They were simply driving into Germany, the homeland of the enemy.

"Oh, no. It can't be this easy. Those Krauts aren't going to sit still while we roll in through the front door. No way." He could feel his skin prickle.

Now he didn't like the looks of those hills ahead of them. No, not at all. He wondered what might lie beyond them. Or in them. And he didn't like all those woods, either…

Crack! The explosion was sharp and loud. The shell landed in the crossroads behind them. They were under the direct fire of an 88.

Jack Diamond skidded his truck to a dead stop in the middle of the road. Everybody on the truck jumped over the sides and into the ditches. Open trucks were cold and uncomfortable to ride in, but they were easy to get off of under fire. Shanker's truck, following them, had been knocked off the road by the concussion of the shell and was nose down in a ditch.

The men dashed into the trees as fast as they could run. They immediately began digging their holes there, where the woods concealed them from the Germans. Will's shovel was in the truck, so he dug with his bare hands.

The loud *crack!* of another shell was followed by a series of smaller explosions.

Will looked up. Diamond's truck had been hit by an 88. It was on fire, and the mines were going off. Thank God there were only a few.

Will crawled over to Sergeant Bowden, who was lying on his stomach at the edge of the woods, talking to Ceruti. He stretched out beside them and asked as casually as he could, "Sarge, what in hell were we doing, anyway?"

Bowden turned to him and said, "Making contact with the enemy."

"You're telling me!" said Will.

"No, I'm serious," replied Bowden. "Division didn't know how far back the Jerries had pulled, so they sent us on ahead to find out. My orders was to go until fired on."

"What?" exclaimed Will. "You're kidding! You've got to be kidding. Why, why those rotten, stinking bastards. Those atrocity-committing sons-of-bitches. Those—"

But before Will could really let loose about what he thought about "them," a couple of scouts from the lead line company arrived.

Bowden's report to them was brief and to the point. "The Jerries got 88s hidden in them hills ahead. Probably panzers. They're zeroed in on the crossroads."

The scouts went back to report to their commander.

Will looked to see if Diamond's truck was still burning. It was, but the fires were dying down now.

A few minutes later, one of the scouts returned with a captain and a sergeant. The captain asked Bowden if he'd had any casualties.

"No, sir," replied Bowden. "Just minor cuts and bruises to some of the guys in the truck that went in the ditch."

The captain said, "Okay, Sergeant. Good work. Now we want you and your men to take cover in the ditch along the road that goes off to the right. That's the road we're going to use, and you'll give us protection from any Jerry infantry that might try to rush the road to cut us off."

"Yes, sir," replied Bowden.

The captain smiled. "Okay, Sarge," he said, "we'll try to get some artillery onto those 88s for you. And as soon as I can, I'm going to send a patrol to find out what those Krauts really have got in those hills up there. Personally, I think it's just a couple of Tiger tanks trying to hold us up as long as they can to give the rest of their army a chance to form a line somewhere else. But we can't take a chance.

"Yes, sir," replied Bowden.

The mine platoon moved into position along the road. Ahead of them were the fields and the hills and the 88s. Behind them were the pine woods. They kept low and out of sight.

Will found Jim Mahoney midway down the road. They started to shelter in a ditch, then discovered it was full of water, so they pulled themselves up onto the bank and just lay there, rifles pointing at the hills the Germans held, ears straining for sounds of enemy infantry trying to approach.

It got dark. And with the night came the damp, penetrating cold. The mine platoon spent the night along that road. When the rifle companies swung onto it, the 88s raked it from one end to the other. Explosions shook the road. Chunks of dirt and rock flew in all directions. The riflemen pulled back and marched through the woods, parallel to the road but out of sight of the Germans.

All was quiet again.

A truck convoy showed up unexpectedly, and the targets they presented to the German gunners were too attractive to ignore. Trucks and Jeeps were blown into ditches—motors screamed; gears ground; men yelled; shells exploded.

Then silence.

Except for a few vehicles that weren't able to get out of the ditches and a couple that were blown to pieces, the rest of the convoy had gotten off the road and were well away.

Will had seen medics working along the road after the rifle troops came under fire, so he supposed guys had been hit.

Now he saw an ambulance nose down in the ditch.

It made him sad to see an ambulance in the ditch. There was something unfair about it. An ambulance shouldn't even be shot at. But when somebody climbed into the front seat and started to turn the motor over, the 88s began again, zipping in, swishing in, blowing the road to hell.

Will felt like screaming, "Leave that damn ambulance alone! Every time the Jerries hear something move on this damn road, they shoot!" But whoever it was had already gotten the hell out of the ambulance. He didn't try to start it again.

Will heard firing behind him. American artillery shooting at something. He hoped it was at those 88s in the hills in front of them.

In the dark he saw flashes on the horizon. He heard the distant chatter of machine guns and some popping of rifles. But the platoon's orders were to stay on that road and not let any Jerries come through them. So they stayed, sopping wet in the raw March cold, teeth chattering, wondering when the 88s would start to blow everything to pieces again, dreading that the next shell could be theirs, wondering if any of their friends had been killed but afraid to go look for them, because the Germans would hear them and start shooting again.

Will noticed the sky was getting lighter.

He said out loud, "With the dawn, if they're still there and we're still here, they'll wipe us out."

In another fifteen minutes, it was light enough to see.

In the ditch, the men of the mine platoon waited tensely. Nothing happened. Sergeant Bowden got up and stood in the middle of the road. He looked around him.

Still nothing happened.

Bowden went to the far side of the road and turned to the men.

"We're in Germany," he said. "Piss on it!"

And he did.

A battlefield that has not been cleaned up, even the remains of a minor skirmish, is depressing. That road was especially so in the early gray light of the half dawn.

Will Pope got out of the ditch, climbed onto the road, and looked around. He could still hear artillery and small-arms fire in the far distance, but along the road everything was quiet. The ambulance was still in the ditch. On the other side was a Jeep that had been sprayed by the shrapnel of an exploding 88. Ugly, black tire marks told the story of vehicles that had skidded into the ditch and gotten out again. Shell holes pocked the road and the field around it. Several trees in the woods behind the road had been splintered.

Will started walking back down the road toward the platoon's only remaining truck. Bowden and Ceruti were already surveying it with a view to getting it back onto the road. As his eyes darted back and forth, Will saw three half-hidden dead G.I.'s sprawled face down beyond the ditch. Farther on was an area where the medics had been working.

Bandages, dressings, empty plasma bottles, and discarded first-aid kits littered the ground. A few helmets and cartridge belts that had been removed from the wounded lay scattered with the rest of the clutter.

Will stopped. Among the debris was a rifle stuck into the ground with a helmet on top of it. Beside it lay a dead boy, his arms and chest soaked with blood. On the stock of his rifle was carved the word "Mother." As Will turned away, the carving affected him deeply. "Mother." That was the word the dead boy had so laboriously carved on the hard wooden gunstock.

The affection that boy had for his mother must have been great. And now what? It was forever gone. In the impersonal explosion of an 88 shell, all the love and tenderness between a son and his mother had been turned to heartbreaking sorrow that would last for as long as the woman lived who had borne that boy...

"Where's your helmet, Pope?" Bowden's words broke his thoughts.

Will reached up to feel his bare head. He grinned sheepishly.

"Guess I got it shot off in the war, Sarge," he replied. "I'll go find it. It's along the ditch someplace."

After fishing his helmet out of the ditch, Will realized he was still wet. He'd been soaked to the skin in the cold all night. He shivered. His combat pants, which he wore over his trousers, were sopping and muddy. He took them off and tossed them into the ditch, where they slapped heavily into the water.

Jim Mahoney had started a fire and was heating his coffee and warming his hands at the same time. Down the road, Bowden and Ceruti were winching Shanker's truck out of the ditch.

Will turned to Jim and said, "Damn! I thought sure we were all gonna get it last night. Didn't see any way we were going to live through that."

"Yeah," said Jim. "Spending a night under artillery fire, with shells blowing up all over the place, sure makes you think a lot. You know what I was thinking, Will?"

"I can make a good guess," replied Will. "It wouldn't have anything to do with one Marylou Simpson, would it?"

"Yeah," replied Jim, "it sure would. It's made me so I'm scared. Will, I'm scared all the time now."

Will reached over and patted his friend's shoulder. "Welcome to the United States infantry," he said.

"Before I met Marylou, I didn't give a damn whether I lived or died or got drunk or went to jail or what. But now I got something to live for. Something I got to live for. Now I give a damn, and I don't want to die. Do you understand a word I'm saying to you, Will?"

"Yeah," replied Will, "I think so. But I liked you better the way you were. You used to drive me crazy sometimes, but you were a hell of a lot more fun."

Jim smiled, gave Will a friendly push, and said, "Aw, go to hell, you damned yahoo."

17

The platoon stood in the road beside their one battered but serviceable truck, which Shanker continued to fuss over, even though he knew it ran.

Bowden quietly counted his men. There were now eleven, including himself. Ceruti saw him counting and walked over. "I can't find Martinelli," he said.

Bowden nodded, thinking. Then he strode off rapidly to where the three dead G.I.'s lay. He pulled them over onto their backs and looked at them closely.

When he returned, he gestured toward the three bodies. "I'm afraid I found Martinelli," he said. "We'll never know what he was doing over there with those guys, but there he is."

Ceruti tried to be casual as he walked over to jam a fixed bayonet into the ground and put a helmet on the rifle butt to mark the spot where Martinelli lay. But Will saw his hands were shaking. He saw his lip tremble.

"What do we do now?" asked Gruber.

The men wanted to go. Their surviving truck was in operating condition. Their mission had been accomplished—no Germans had stormed the road, and the rest of the division had gone far beyond them already. The road was quiet. There was no danger, but being there made them nervous. There were those dead G.I.'s lying around, and, until the Graves Registration people showed up to collect them, nobody would touch them. They'd all known Martinelli. He was one of their own, and the idea of him lying there gave them an uneasy feeling. In the distance, they heard the sounds of a sharp fight. The division had hit the Siegfried Line after they'd left the crossroads.

Sergeant Bowden saw how tense the men were. "Look, you guys," he said, "I got an announcement to make. I forgot to mention it before we took off so quick and unexpected-like, but Will Pope and Jim Mahoney both've been awarded the Combat Infantryman's Badge. Congratulations."

Will looked blank. Jim grinned. The other men shrugged their shoulders. Then Will threw up his hands in mock surprise. "Combat infantryman, you say? Oh, good Lord! And all this time I thought I was in the quartermasters."

The others smiled.

"It means ten bucks a month extra pay, Will," said Bowden. "Combat pay."

"I'll make a deal with them," said Will quickly. "I'll save them a bundle of dough. I'll trade them my ten bucks a month extra pay for a one-way ticket back to the States. Wait till the taxpayers hear about my generous offer. Too good to be true. Cancel the national debt. Better than war bonds."

Bowden grinned.

"Besides, I doubt if they'll need me here anymore. We're already in Germany now. Krauts're pulling back. Things should be a lot easier from here on."

The men were more relaxed now. Ceruti said, "I think it's just the other way around. I think the Krauts're going to fight harder now because we are in Germany. They'll be fighting on their own soil. Fighting for their homes."

Will winked at Jim, then said to Ceruti, "Fight harder? You mean things are going to get tougher now instead of easier? Oh, good Lord! Just when I was beginning to hope we'd make it, too."

But he was smiling. He really didn't believe Ceruti. Once they got through the Siegfried Line, it would all be over.

"Listen to that," said Bowden. "Sounds like they're hitting the Jerries with everything they've got."

"What do you reckon they'll want us to do now?" asked Jim.

"No telling," replied Gruber.

"Listen," said Will, "those are our guns, 57s, sure as hell! They're using them against the pillboxes, I'll bet."

"Yeah," said Gruber disgustedly. "Everybody's in the fight except us."

"That's fine with me," said Mahoney. "I hope it stays that way."

"Wait a minute," said Bowden. "Do you hear that?"

"Yeah," said Ceruti. "Something's happening. The noise is moving away from us. I can hardly hear it now. Not as much firing, either."

"What do you think it means?" asked Will.

"I'm not sure," replied Bowden. "It could mean a break-through. But I'd hate to guess."

Five minutes later, a convoy of trucks towing artillery pieces came down the road. As the vehicles came abreast of the platoon, Bowden yelled, "Hey! What's going on?"

One of the men on a truck heard him and shouted as they went by, "We busted the hell out of their line this morning! It's a rat race now, and we're trying to catch the rats!"

Bowden smiled a broad smile and turned to his men and said, "Hot damn! Y'all hear that?"

Before anyone could reply, a Jeep at the end of the convoy stopped and a lieutenant called to Bowden, "What outfit?"

"Mine platoon, antitank company of the Triple Nickel," answered Bowden.

"Good!" exclaimed the lieutenant. "You can come with us as far as we go, then you're supposed to go ahead and join the fun."

Bowden replied, "Yes, sir."

What was left of the platoon fit easily into their one truck. They rode for a good fifteen minutes until they came to the scenes of devastation. There had been one hell of a fight. There were the usual dead Jerries lying around. There were broken pillboxes. There were 88s that had been knocked out. The refuse of battle was strewn all over the landscape.

It wasn't long before they had to stop because there were so many prisoners jamming the road. The lieutenant got out of the Jeep and walked back to speak to Bowden. The lieutenant said, "Well, I think we can take it easy. I just got word that the Jerries are pulling all the way back to the Rhine. Looks like they're finished. This should really wrap it up. As far as my guns are concerned, we don't have anyplace to go in a hurry. We're trying to find out now what they want you guys to do."

Will had overheard the conversation and felt pretty good. He thought, "I bet this means the war's over." It was a beautiful day, and he began to relax for the first time since they started out.

The lieutenant was showing Bowden on his map where he should go.

"You end up in this town called Zellingheim, that's where regimental headquarters will set up. They're not there yet, but you guys go on ahead to the town."

"Check," said Bowden.

Their truck was all by itself again. It crept forward while the men kept their rifles aimed at the sides of the road. But they did not meet anybody at all until they came to a group of German soldiers holding onto a big, white flag as if their lives depended on it.

The truck stopped. Bowden got down. So did Gruber and Ceruti. Bowden looked at the Germans very closely, then said, "You surrender?"

The German in charge nodded his head vigorously, saying, *"Ya! Ja! Kamerad! Ja!"*

Bowden said, *"Haben Sie Luger?"* A German Luger pistol was more than just a trophy. It was an outstanding weapon.

"Nein. Nein," replied the German.

They had thrown their weapons away with their helmets in order to surrender. Bowden thought for a few seconds, then turned and said, "Okay, keep your white flag and go on back to the rear, with your hands on your heads."

"Bitte?" asked one of the Germans.

"Mit der Hand an der Kopf," said Bowden, pointing down the road.

"Ja, ja," replied the Germans, and they started off in the direction the big sergeant had indicated.

The platoon took the surrender of several other groups of Germans.

From a very far distance, they could hear small-arms fire.

"What's that?" asked Will.

"It's them damned SS and panzer-grenadiers," replied Bowden. "They're putting up last-ditch stands. Damned fanatics! That's what they are. Damned fanatics."

Sergeant Bowden stopped the truck outside Zellingheim, and the men entered the town on foot and spread out, rifles at the ready, but they saw no Germans. White sheets hung out of the windows, signifying surrender.

"Well," said Bowden, "We got here first, so let's pick us the best billet."

They chose a two-storied house near the center of town. Behind it were some woods; the whole town seemed to be built along one main street. The men took their bedrolls from the truck and threw them in the entrance hall, then searched the house, but there was nobody in it.

In less than fifteen minutes, two Jeeps arrived ahead of some large trucks. Regimental headquarters was moving into the town.

While some of the staff went to round up a couple of civilians to interrogate, the officer in charge came over to Sergeant Bowden and asked, "Mine platoon?"

"Yes, sir."

"Good. The rest of antitank is due sometime this afternoon. Did you notice a lot of dead animals on the road?"

Bowden nodded.

"And a lot of trees across the road?"

"Yes, sir," replied Bowden. "But it looks like somebody ahead of us chopped through them. A vehicle can get down the road okay. Only thing is, it's single file where the trees are."

"That's right, Sergeant," replied the officer. "But we'll have heavy traffic pretty soon, so I want you and your men to go back to where the road to this town begins and start clearing off the trees and animals. Make sure there're no Jerries in the woods. If you come across any, bring 'em into town here."

"Oh, my aching G.I. back," Will groaned. "Now we've got to go to work for a living." But he was smiling as he said it. He felt happy and relaxed and even a little bit cocky.

They had returned to within a mile of town when Will noticed a white flag stuck into a pine tree alongside the road. There were logs across the road at that spot, and the truck stopped so the men could remove them. Will was on the far side of the road, helping Jim pull away a log. On the other side, by the truck, he heard Gruber say to Sergeant Bowden, "I smell Krauts."

Will had never thought about it, but now that he did, he realized that you could smell the Germans by the odors of their tobacco and sausages. They were distinctive smells.

Without saying anything, Bowden motioned Ceruti and several other men to go into the woods.

Will and Jim finished removing the log and crossed the road. They had just reached the other side when they heard the cracking of M-1 rifles and the steady cadence of MacKenzie's Browning Automatic Rifle.

A burp gun went off, and German rifles popped and crackled. The Jerries were fighting back. Will and Jim Mahoney looked at each other, then started into the woods.

The trees made it hard to see what was going on. Will stood behind an evergreen and looked around. He heard shooting nearby. He saw some Germans running through a clearing. He shot at them from his hip with his rifle slightly extended. He fired fast, emptied his clip, then reached into his cartridge belt for another and jammed it into the breech as the bolt shot forward. He saw that several Germans had been hit.

One was writhing on the ground about twenty feet away from where Will stood. He was in agony. He kept pointing at his head and making a motion with his thumb, indicating he wanted someone to shoot him and put him out of his misery. Will felt sick.

A single shot rang out. The German jerked once and lay still. Now all was quiet again.

Will looked over to see if Jim had seen it. Jim had been kneeling behind a tree and was just getting up. At that moment, from the bushes nearby, a German soldier appeared. He did not have a gun, but in his raised hand was a blunt, clublike sword.

Will yelled, "Jim!"

Jim stood up and wheeled around, but as he did, the German's arm descended. The sword caught Jim Mahoney on the side of his neck. Jim went down backward. The German stepped forward, his arm upraised for another blow.

Will squeezed off eight fast shots. Each shot hit the German squarely. Each shot knocked him backward until he fell over on his back several yards from where he had stood.

Will was immediately at Jim's side. He lifted up his head. The blood was gushing out the side of his neck so strongly it was splashing. Will looked into Jim's face. He was alive but he could not talk. His mouth was full of blood.

But his eyes were looking straight into Will's, and they kept pleading, "Save me. Please save me… I don't want to die… Will, save me… I don't want to die."

But there was nothing Will could do. He was helpless. The color had left Jim's face. Will tried to fumble in his first-aid kit. He was on his knees, cradling Jim's head, his hands and trousers covered with his friend's blood.

Will looked down. The eyes no longer pleaded. They were sightless. The lips were white. The face was white. Jim Mahoney was dead.

As Will looked into his still, dead face, he had never felt so empty in his life. He felt drained of all emotion. His heart thundered in his throat as he felt a tear roll down his cheek, then another. But he was not crying.

He laid Jim's head gently on the ground. There was blood all over the leaves, but the huge gash in Jim's neck was no longer pumping it out.

Will stood up. He started stumbling toward the road. He felt like crying, but now the tears did not come. He was dry-eyed and dry-mouthed.

Lieutenant Sommers met him just before he got to the road. He had heard the firing and stopped to see what was going on. He was about to say something to Will, but when he saw Will's face, he shut his open mouth without uttering a word.

Will said simply, "Jim's dead."

Sommers put his arm around Will's shoulder and they walked together, silently, to the road. As they did, a couple of G.I.'s passed them, chattering excitedly.

"Look what I got off that last Kraut! A real Luger pistol Looks brand-new!"

"Neat! Neat!" replied his companion. "You're lucky! I didn't find nothing on mine!"

And Jim Mahoney lay on his back in the woods, his two legs resting on a log. He was as still and lifeless as a stone, his face drained white and his eyes open, staring forever at the limitless sky.

Will rode back to Zellingheim with Lieutenant Sommers. Neither one said anything. When they pulled up in front of the Rathaus, Sommers turned to Will and asked him very gently and kindly, "Will, are you okay?"

Will nodded his head. "Yeah," he said. "I'll be okay. Thanks for the ride."

He got out of the Jeep and went into the billet. The truck arrived, and the men started unloading. Several patted him on the shoulder without saying anything. Others managed to croak, "Sorry, Will," or, "Too bad." Most were silent.

But Will felt their sympathy, and he could feel his lower lip trembling as he went through the billet. He discovered a back door that led into the woods. He hoped nobody noticed as he went through it. Nobody went with him, and he had the fleeting thought that perhaps the woods were mined, but he didn't care.

And when he was alone in the woods, he slumped to the ground, buried his face in his arms, and sobbed his heart out.

BOOK

3

AT SOME DISPUTED BARRICADE

18

The weather in Central Europe in early April of 1945 was nasty. It was cold and damp, and it drizzled constantly. But inside Seventh Army headquarters, fires blazed in the huge fireplaces, and the atmosphere was almost relaxed.

Two G.I.'s carrying a wooden crate accompanied General Tom Jacobs as he entered Dave Richardson's office. Jacobs pointed to a corner and said, "Put her down gently, boys."

After the two men left, Richardson got up from his desk. "What the hell was that all about?" he asked.

"Brought you a little present," replied Jacobs. "Come take a look."

When he read the lettering on the case, Richardson cocked his eye. "Why, that's champagne. Good champagne. Where the hell did you get it?"

Jacobs smiled. "Wurzburg. I just got back from the front."

"Tom, I'm not sure this is right. We set a policy of not looting the Germans, and we've enforced it pretty strictly, too."

"Look, Dave," replied Jacobs, "if I hadn't salvaged a few cases of the good stuff, it'd be at the bottom of the Main River right now, so don't worry about it."

Richardson laughed.

"After they finally took the town," continued Jacobs, "the Fifteenth Division found bargeloads of the stuff down on the river. The G.I.'s filled their canteens with it before they moved out."

"Those boys'll be eating cold K rations with some of the finest vintages in the world," said Richardson. "What a waste."

"Oh, don't begrudge them a little pleasure, Dave. Remember, they still have a rough road ahead. We've smashed the Siegfried Line and crossed the Rhine, but the Germans are still fighting like hell, dammit. Look at Wurzburg, for God's sake. Every time we thought we had it, the Jerries sent troops up through the sewer system, and there'd be full-scale battles raging all over town again. It was a bitch. Look at all the other battles—"

Richardson waved impatiently. "I know it," he said. "And the hell of it is, the Germans'll keep on fighting until we've taken every city and town in Germany. And they'll fight for them all."

"What do you think about 'Festung Europa?'" asked Jacobs. "The Krauts're supposed to have a place in Bavaria or Austria somewhere stocked with enough guns, panzers, rations, and ammunition to last them another year. But the intelligence reports are mixed. Do you think the 'last stronghold of the Third Reich' really exists?"

Richardson shook his head. "No. I don't. Doesn't make any sense to me at all, but the army's treating it seriously, so I guess we'll have to, too."

"How seriously do you want to treat it, Dave? It's right in the path of the Seventh Army. They'll get there first. Should we change our plans? Tell them to slow down? Wait for reinforcements?"

Richardson shook his head again. "No," he replied. "They're going like hell. Let them go. The faster the better. Keep pushing. Keep attacking. Keep taking their cities, one after the other, until they've killed every damn German who still wants to fight. It's just a matter of time now. That's all. But it has to be done. And if there is a 'Festung Europa,' they'll take it in their stride. Just remember to mention it in a report once in a while."

After delivering that pronouncement, Dave Richardson smiled. "Tom, sit down," he said. "No. Not there. In my chair."

Jacobs looked uncertain as he plunked himself down.

"Tom, I've been in the army all my life. And do you know what? I've never had a field command. The army always said they needed me for planning and staff work. They said that was what I was best at."

Jacobs tried to look interested, but he thought, Why tell me this?

Almost as if he were reading his mind, Richardson went on, "Yesterday, Robinson of the Fifteenth Division got promoted to take over a corps. Five minutes later, I convinced the chief to give me command of the Fighting Fifteenth."

Jacobs rose in his chair. "You?" he blurted. He'd grown to understand and respect Dave Richardson during the time he'd worked with him, but he could never think of him as a field commander. He was strictly a desk general. "Dammit! If there's a division that needs a general, I'm the one who should get it."

Richardson smiled. "You're taking my place here at Seventh Army, Tom. You'll get another star out of it if you do as well as I think you will."

Tom Jacobs was confused. He scratched his head. "Me?" he asked. "Oh, no, not me. Look, Dave, I'm not cut out for this." But in that second, he knew he wanted Dave Richardson's job more than anything in the world. He'd just never believed there was any chance of his ever getting it.

"It's done," replied Richardson. "You know more about the job than anybody else. You're the natural choice. So now you're my boss, Tom. Good luck."

"Wait one damned minute," exclaimed Jacobs. "You mean you're willing to take a demotion in order to take over a division? Why, for God's sake?"

Richardson paused before replying, "I guess it's so that instead of having to say I served on the staff all my career, I can say I commanded one of the crack divisions in the United States Army, that's why."

Jacobs understood. Dave Richardson wanted some of the glory. Before the war ended, he wanted to make a reputation for himself as a "fighting general." Jacobs shrugged. Then he smiled. Now he'd get to keep that champagne he'd lugged all the way from Wurzburg.

After they left Wurzburg, the antitank mine platoon moved forward in the truck convoy that followed most closely behind the rifle companies, who were having to fight harder for every mile now.

Will Pope was thinking how hard the damned wooden seats were and how cold he was, when he heard the rain begin to spatter off his helmet again. He looked up and got a raindrop right in the eye. Now Will felt the water trickling down his back inside his field jacket. As usual, the truck was standing still in the middle of the road with a dozen others. Ahead of them they could hear machine gun fire and the steady booming of artillery.

Will shivered. The fields on either side of the truck were pocked by shell holes. He guessed the front was about a mile away, and he knew he wasn't in any danger, so he endured the discomfort without complaining. He'd much rather be cold and wet and safe than be cold and wet and shot at.

Sitting in the open truck in the rain, nobody felt like chatting, and Will's thoughts wandered. He remembered coming in from the woods late at night on the day Jim was killed—the other men had been waiting for him. They'd undressed him, washed the dried blood off him, scrubbed his clothes, and put him to bed. He'd asked, "What guard do I have tonight?" and Bowden had boomed, "No guard. No guard tonight. Regiment's pulling guard for us all." Will knew he was lying, and as he closed his eyes, a tear hit the pillow. He hadn't thought he had any left.

A couple of days later, Brown came back to the platoon with seven new replacements. Brown had been wounded so slightly he'd never even left the aid station.

One day in Zellingheim, Will asked Ceruti, "Where'd Sergeant Bowden get the Tommy gun? Looks almost new."

"He traded the supply sergeant an SS officer's sword for it," replied Ceruti. "It was a honey, too. Sarge figures a Thompson's a lot more practical, though."

Will felt his face flush. "Where'd he get the sword?" he asked as calmly as he could.

"Outside of town. Off one of them dead Jerries, I guess."

Will got up slowly and went to find Bowden. He was still inspecting the new truck. Will pointed to the Tommy gun and asked, "Sarge, how in the hell could you do a thing like that?"

"What do you mean?" replied Bowden. Then Will's meaning registered. "You mean about the sword?"

Will nodded.

Bowden patted Will on the back and said, "Oh, Will, it was just a trophy of war, is all."

"It was the sword that killed Jim Mahoney," replied Will. He hoped he sounded sufficiently accusing. He expected Bowden to be penitent. Instead, the big sergeant smiled and said, "Look, Will, suppose we felt like that about all them Luger pistols we been picking up. Hey? What do you think them Krauts use Lugers for? Decoration?"

Will was confused. He scratched his nose.

"I guess you heard about your friend Phil Cohen?" asked Bowden, obviously anxious to get Will off the subject of the damned sword.

"No," replied Will. "What about him?"

"He's gonna get the Distinguished Service Cross, that's what," replied Bowden. "For heroism during the jump–off. And get this! He's already been promoted to captain. Company commander of B Company! How do you like them apples, Will Pope?"

Will was smiling now. "I like them just fine," he said. "Now I've gotta go congratulate him. Where's B Company? Out in the woods still?"

"Yeah. They're still in the woods outside of town, but their captain ain't with them," replied Bowden. "He got hit at the Siegfried Line."

Will's heart sank to his toenails. "Bad?" he asked.

Bowden smiled and shook his head. "It could've been; it was close. But he was lucky, and they say he'll be back in a week or two."

✪

April 1, 1945, was Easter Sunday. Since the division was only waiting to cross the Rhine, the chaplains held an Easter service outside Zellingheim early that morning.

Will decided he'd go. He went early, and he went alone. He expected to find a handful of men there, maybe a couple of dozen. But as soon as he was on the road to the field where the chaplains had set up their altar, he thought he must have run into an army on the march. G.I.'s were streaming into the field from all directions.

Will had a hard time finding a place to sit. The field was covered with men as far as he could see, and the latecomers stood around at the edge of the crowd, while men kept arriving.

Like Will, they were the men who had just smashed the vaunted west wall of Germany, the men who had stood in Alsace against such dreadful odds and never faltered. They were men who had been close enough to death to know that "being" doesn't end with dying. With them that Easter, Will found the strength to accept death, if he had to; the courage to die, if he must.

That same Easter Sunday, they left Zellingheim to cross the Rhine at a place called Worms. It wasn't bad. They followed the assault troops. But the Germans were still fighting, and the division took part in a few minor engagements before it hit Wurzburg. Now, sitting in the truck in the rain with Wurzburg behind them, Will began to think of Harry Muller.

He had always tried to be nice to Harry Muller. He didn't care whether Harry had shot his finger off to get out of the line or not. Everybody else would always think he did, and Will felt sorry for him for that. He hoped he'd made Harry feel better in some small way, given him comfort somehow. Now he'd never know. Harry and young Trenton lay ripped apart in a ditch in a little town called Schwaningen on the Main River, a town the platoon had held for two days against five hundred SS officer candidates without taking any casualties until the end of the fight.

The Main River had separated them from the SS. Both sides did a lot of firing, the Germans with their mortars mostly, and the platoon with their light .30-caliber machine gun and MacKenzie's B.A.R. But despite the exploding mortar shells and burp-gun blasts, which were always answered by the platoon's automatic weapons and their M-1s, nobody got hurt. Will doubted if they did any damage to the Jerries on the other side of the river, either. As he told Lieutenant Sommers, who commanded their small task force, "This battle is nothing but a tale told by an idiot, full of sound and fury, signifying nothing."

However, the mortars did demolish Sommers's Jeep and Diamond's truck, which they thought were safe behind their C.P..

That was the only real damage before the American artillery began to soften up the town for an assault by a battalion from the Third Division. They had crossed to the German side at Wurzburg, downriver. The platoon had orders to remain in place along the riverfront so the Germans couldn't cross during the barrage. The army didn't want five hundred SS troops running around loose on their side of the Main.

But the first shells fell on the platoon's side of the river and blew everything they hit to pieces. It was terrifying. Muller and Trenton were out on guard, and they got caught in the first barrage with no place to shelter but a small ditch. It wasn't good enough.

Kitchener got hit, too. He got a piece of shrapnel in his leg from an exploding American artillery shell. It broke the bone, and poor old Kitch was in considerable pain, as well as being scared to death. "I'm thirty-four years old, you know," he moaned. "When you're old like that, sometimes the bones, they never heals. I might not never walk no more…"

"Hell! Kitch, you got a damn million-dollar wound, you old crock," said Bowden. "That leg'll get you a one-way ticket home just as sure as the devil eats little babies!"

It was both a miracle and a lot of good luck that the platoon didn't suffer more casualties than that. But once the American shells found their correct targets on the east bank of the Main, they really blew everything apart. Will found himself feeling genuinely sorry for the Germans on the other side of the river.

As soon as the artillery stopped firing, the riflemen from the Third Division went in. They cleaned out the SS in about an hour. As soon as the firing stopped and they saw American riflemen picking their way among the demolished buildings on the far bank of the river, the platoon prepared to depart. The town was in ruins. Debris cluttered the streets—entire walls had fallen in; roofs were shattered; bricks and loose stones were everywhere.

Will turned to Lieutenant Sommers and said, "You know, the Jerries shot at us for two whole days and never hit anybody. Then, in about two seconds, our own artillery knocks off two of our guys and puts a chunk of shrapnel into poor old Kitch. Some war! The Jerries miss you, but your own guys don't."

"Yeah, Will," replied Sommers. "I sort of thought I'd get us all out. Our orders were to keep the Jerries on their own side of the river, and I figured theirs were to keep us on ours, so that's what we both did, and nobody tried to cross, and nobody got hurt. I never even considered our own artillery falling short like that."

Bowden lined up the men and counted heads to make sure they were all there. Kitchener groaned as they laid him on the floorboards of the truck. "What shall we do about Muller and Trenton?" asked Will.

Bowden thought for a minute, then replied, "We'll cover them with ponchos or blankets and leave them where they are. The Graves Registration boys'll take care of them. That's their job."

In the late afternoon, twelve M.P.'s and their lieutenant arrived to take over the town from the platoon, who were to rejoin the antitank company at Wurzburg. Sommers took the lieutenant on a tour of Schwaningen to brief him on the situation and familiarize him with the terrain. A sergeant and several M.P.'s went with them.

When they returned, the platoon was in the truck, ready to go. Sommers was relaxed, glad to be leaving, but the M.P. lieutenant looked as if he had something on his mind. He turned to Sommers and said, "Lieutenant, I think that was a dirty thing you did."

Sommers looked startled. "What was that?" he asked.

"Leaving those two dead G.I.'s for my men to see. It scared them half to death, and you know it!"

At first Sommers didn't seem to comprehend what the other man was saying. Then it registered. He answered, picking his words, "You make it sound like I deposited them there as some sort of a grisly joke. Well, I didn't. American artillery killed them right where you saw them, and Graves Registration'll pick them up and bury them. You or your men never knew them, Lieutenant, but they were my men, my friends, so unless you want me to take your goddamn head off, you'd better shut up!"

The other lieutenant got red in the face. He didn't reply.

Sommers swung into the seat in the front of the truck. He motioned to Shanker to pull out.

"You know," Ceruti whispered to Will, "That's the first time I ever seen the lieutenant get mad."

Will remembered leaving poor old Kitchener at an aid station near Wurzburg. They left him lying on a stretcher in the rain, scared and alone, waiting for the busy doctors to find the time to attend to him. It had broken Will's heart.

Will had a hard time remembering he was an "acting" squad leader. He hadn't wanted the responsibility, but the mine platoon was supposed to have three squads, so he took the Third Squad with the understanding he could give it up whenever he wanted to. And while he was squad leader, he temporarily held the rank of sergeant.

Both Gruber and Ceruti acted as if they'd been squad leaders all their lives. They were good NCO's. Ceruti had decided he was going to stay in the army after the war. "Look, Will," he'd said, "I'm a sergeant. I got medals. Guys respects me. They looks up to me. How in the hell could I ever go back to playing a piano in a dumb joint like I done before? No way!"

Gruber was a married man. This surprised the hell out of Will for some reason. He just couldn't imagine Jay Gruber in a cozy little domestic scene. He found out later Gruber had to get married. His wife had a baby four months after they got hitched, and one month after that, Gruber joined the army to get away from home. Will once asked him, "Jay, what the hell are you going to do after the war?"

"I sure as hell ain't gonna stay in the damned stinking chicken-shit army like Ceruti," he'd replied. "And I ain't going back to being a clerk in a shoestore, either. I think I'll sign on a ship that's going out to China or someplace like that."

"You can't run away forever," said Will. He wished he hadn't said it. Gruber gave him a look that indicated he should mind his own business.

So Will spent more time with Ceruti and with Carlo Pacini and Hank Gray. Pacini was a clown, but it took Will a little time to get to know him. Ceruti had him transferred into his squad after Martinelli got killed. Will supposed it was because of the affinity of one Italian for another, but everybody liked Carlo.

Hank Gray's father was a mail carrier for the post office, which during the Depression was a very prestigious job. It meant he worked for the federal government. Carlo Pacini's was a foreman in a shoe factory, and they used to argue for hours about which job took more brains. Unlike most of the other men, they had both finished high school. Their mothers and sisters did war work, and Hank Gray had an older brother in the navy in the Pacific. Carlo seemed to have so many brothers and sisters that Will lost track of them all.

Will and Sergeant Bowden got along extremely well, too. Will was Bowden's pet for some reason, and Will didn't mind it at all. He respected his sergeant tremendously and was happy his sergeant liked him just as much. But after Will took over his squad, Bowden assigned him a replacement named Barrett, a short youngster with blond hair and blue eyes and a sense of humor. He had one fault: He was drunk all the time.

"Sergeant, I don't want this man," Will had told Bowden.

Bowden smiled and replied, "He's yours, Will. He's in your squad, and that's that. It's up to you to decide what to do with him."

Will understood. His sergeant was testing him to see how he'd handle a problem. He grinned back at Bowden and said, "Right." That was all.

He knew damned well that this Barrett could get them all killed if he got drunk and screwed things up in combat. "Imagine that little bastard in a live minefield, under fire!" The thought gave Will goose pimples.

As soon as he got the chance, Will gathered his small squad and told them to make sure Barrett got nothing to drink. If he did, Will told them he was going to have the whole squad court-martialed. "Aw, Sarge, have a heart," Barrett whined. Will just glared at him.

A day later, Barrett came to Will in tears. He said he couldn't take it without booze in him. Just being overseas in the infantry scared him to death. He begged Will to relent.

"You're sick, Barrett," Will replied. "You're going on sick call right now!"

He went. And he never returned.

✪

One day just before they crossed the Rhine, Captain Colina came to inspect the platoon. He'd never done it before. When he'd finished and was ready to go, he turned and, in a voice that was meant to be casual, said, "Pope, come outside with me a few minutes."

After they had walked far enough not to be overheard, Colina cleared his throat and said, "Pope, you and Captain Cohen were the only two men in the mine platoon billet for a few days after we went into reserve, right?" He glanced sideways at Will, who nodded.

"Well, something's come up. It might be a little unpleasant, so what you and I talk about now is just between the two of us, do you understand?"

"Yes, sir," replied Will, nodding again.

"While you two were alone in the billet, did Cohen do anything improper?"

Will thought for a moment. "Oh!" he said. "You mean about the guard duty. But I think Phil was right, sir. As he told you, there were only the two of us, and if we'd have gone on guard, there'd have been nobody in our billet, and anybody could have gone in and—"

"No, no, no! I don't mean about guard duty! "exploded the captain. "I mean, did he make any improper advances toward you?"

Will looked blank and shook his head. "I don't know what you mean, sir."

"Dammit!" said Colina. "Did he molest you homosexually in any way?"

Will was stunned. He was about to ask, "How's that again?" or "What?" or make some other delaying remark to give himself time to digest Colina's question and think out his reply. But he knew that would make him look dumb in the eyes of the captain, and he didn't want to do that, so he just remained silent, then replied, "No sir! Never! Hellfire, Captain! We're talking about one of the bravest men in the army, and one of the best friends anybody could ever have. Sir, this is the most ridiculous thing I've ever heard—"

"Okay, Pope, okay," cut in the captain. "I was sure it was like that, but I had orders to find out. You see, one of his men made a complaint. It's completely unsubstantiated, but we still have to check it out, and Colonel Rankin remembered there was another man billeted with Cohen back there, so I had to ask you. That's all there is to it. Anyway, Phil's one of our best company commanders, and we don't want to lose him."

"I hear we almost did," said Will. "On the battlefield, though. Not from some damn malcontent's complaint."

"Malcontent? Pope, where in the name of hell did you learn to talk like that?" asked the captain, shaking his head. Without waiting for an answer, he said, "You're right, though. At the Siegfried Line he got B Company around behind the German machine guns holding up the First Battalion's advance and attacked them from the rear. He led the charge himself, and he got hit just before his men took the German positions."

Will nodded. "You see?"

"Yeah," said the captain. "In fact, it was after Phil was carried back to the hospital the guy came up with his cock-and-bull story, the stinker. That tells you something about him right there. He waits until Phil's not around to defend himself. I think I'll tell Colonel Rankin there's nothing to it, and I'm sure he'll transfer the guy out of B Company. There's a lot of his type in this man's army, and the last thing Phil Cohen needs is to get stuck with one of them."

"How come they even take the time to fool with this kind of crap?" asked Will.

"I guess they've got to," replied Colina. "Anyway, keep the whole thing confidential, Pope. I wouldn't want any of this to get out. It'd only hurt Phil, and that wouldn't be fair."

"You bet!" said Will.

And that was the last he ever heard of it.

★

The trucks had gone ahead a few hundred yards while Will was reminiscing. They stopped again. Will shivered.

"Hey, Will!" called Sergeant Bowden.

Will saw the sergeant standing at the side of the road with Ceruti and Gruber. Will came off the tailgate and splashed through the mud to where they stood.

"What's up?" he asked.

"Ever hear of a place called Schweinfurt?" asked the sergeant.

"Don't think so," replied Will.

"Well, I'm going to tell you about it," said Bowden. "It's the goddamn ball-bearing capital of Germany, that's what it is. Every time our planes tried to bomb the place, they ended up with something like seventy-five or eighty percent casualties. Want to know why?"

Will wasn't sure he did, but he nodded his head anyway.

"Because it's a long way from the bombers' bases in England, and the Jerry fighters got a good crack at them, for one thing. But besides that, Schweinfurt's also the 88 capital of the world, that's why. The place is crawling with them."

Will felt like saying, "That's all very interesting, but what's it got to do with us?" But he'd been in the army long enough to know better.

Then it came to him. "Hey, Sarge," he said, "if they've still got those damned 88s they can use them against us, can't they? Talk about slaughter! Where's Schweinfurt?"

"Right in front of us, Will. Right in front of us. And our happy little platoon is now detaching itself from company headquarters and joining Easy Company of the Second Battalion so we'll be available for the assault."

"I think I want to go home now," said Will. "What time is sick call around this place?"

19

It was the first official reception after Easter, and Governor George Pope greeted each guest as a personal friend. Even though the party had to be held indoors because of rain, he was relaxed and smiling. After all, why not? It looked like the German armies were collapsing. The cigarette and gasoline shortages of the winter were almost over, and both spring and peace were on the way in.

He'd been upset when the Army Medical Corps reported his son showed no evidence of any fainting problem. But now everything should be all right. Will's chances should be considerably improved, the way things were going.

That reminded him of Jack Reynolds. The governor shook his head. Just after the snows melted in the spring, they had found Jack's body riddled with machine gun bullets, in the forward outpost where he'd died on the same cold December day that opened the Battle of the Bulge. Old Sam knew for sure now, but it meant that he and Sarah had had to endure the shock and grief all over again.

The governor quickly put unpleasant things aside and continued greeting and chatting with his friends. The receiving line had already broken up, and the governor could enjoy himself. "Would you like Bourbon or champagne, sir?" asked the waiter.

"Bourbon, of course," replied George Pope. Then, thinking better of it, he said, "No. Make it champagne today. To celebrate spring and toast the coming end of the war."

Those around him murmured their approval, and all took champagne. "Well, here's to victory and peace," said the governor, raising his glass.

As his friends nodded at him and started to sip the wine, an aide tugged George Pope's elbow. When he turned to him, the man leaned forward and whispered, "Sir, it's Mrs. Pope. I'm afraid she's fainted, sir."

When the governor returned after seeing his wife safely tucked in her bed upstairs, he went immediately to the group that had been with Cecily when she swooned. They looked upset. Pope smiled, hoping to put them at their ease, then said, "Relax. Cecily's just fine. A couple of the ladies are with her, and she'll be all right. But we all know she doesn't drink, and I doubt she's pregnant, so what happened?"

The group stood in silence, but after a few moments they began to glance nervously at a young army major, who appeared to be embarrassed. George Pope automatically turned his gaze in the young man's direction.

The major's face was only slightly familiar to him. The man was in his thirties, good-looking, with light brown hair and straight features. He was medium height, medium build, medium everything.

The ribbons over his left breast pocket showed he'd been overseas in Europe and been wounded, and the patch on his left shoulder indicated he'd been in a well-known infantry division. "Ah," thought Pope, "he has to be old Tom Jorgensen's boy. I heard he got wounded and sent home."

Tom Jorgensen was the Speaker of the state Senate and one of the governor's closest political allies. Pope smiled.

"You're young Jorgensen, " he said. "Welcome home, son. Your father's mighty proud of you, and we're all glad you're back." He continued to smile at Jorgensen, waiting for him to say something.

Finally the major replied, "Uh, thank you, sir. It's good to be back, sir." Then he hesitated a moment before he stammered, "I think

I said something I shouldn't have, uh, to Mrs. Pope, sir. I didn't mean to, uh, but, uh, it just came out, sir."

Still smiling, the governor said, "Well, son, you just tell me what you told my sweet lady, and don't worry about it. After all, we're practically family, your folks and mine, and if you tell me what upset Cecily, I'll be able to put things right." As he finished, he flashed an exceptionally winning smile, the one that always gained the confidence of any voter within its range.

"Well, sir," the young man said hesitantly, "we were talking about the war, and she was telling me about your son, who's in the army, and she mentioned he was in an antitank mine platoon somewhere in the rear. Uh, she seemed to be under the impression he was in a headquarters in Paris, or something like that, sir. I laughed and said, 'An infantry mine platoon?' and she said, 'Yes, that's right,' and then, sir, I guess I wasn't thinking. I told her I admired your son a lot and was glad I didn't have his job. I said it takes a lot of guts to clear mines in front of infantry attacks and that kind of thing. And, uh, that's when she fainted. I didn't mean to. It's just that, in the army, the rougher the outfit, the prouder you are of it. I didn't want her to think your boy was nothing but a rear-echelon type, not when he's in the thick of it."

"It's all right, son, I understand completely," said Pope in his most comforting tones. Actually, he was wondering how this idiot ever got to be a major.

"I uh, really respect your son, Governor," said the major. "I was in division artillery, you know, not nearly as rough." Then he had a thought. "But look, sir, a mine platoon isn't really a suicide squad, you know. It's just that nobody likes to fool with mines, and those guys are under fire a lot. But he'll come through okay. I really was just trying to build him up a little for your wife, sir, trying to make her feel good about having a real front-line soldier in the family and that sort of thing—"

"Yes, yes, of course, my boy," replied Pope, the smile still on his face. "Now, what you need is a good drink. The bar's right over there."

As he waved at the back of a vastly relieved Major Jorgensen, Governor Pope's face turned from genial to worried. "How in the hell am I going to calm Cecily down now? Good God! Why can't these young jackasses learn to keep their mouths shut? Unthinking nincompoop."

The morning sunlight streamed into the Pope bedroom. Standing fully dressed beside his wife's bed, George Pope was saying, "No, dear, I'm not going to telephone the White House. I don't have to. I—"

"George, you know I couldn't sleep at all last night. Oh, poor darling Will. All that danger!" Her lower lip began to tremble again.

George Pope cut in quickly. "Everything's all right. First of all, Cecily, the war's almost over, and Will's alive and kicking. If he were going to get himself kil—hurt, he'd have already done it during the hard fighting. Now he's practically home free.

"But anyway, darling, I've already made arrangements." He smiled at his anxious wife. "Remember my old friend Tom Jacobs? The officer in charge of our National Guard unit a few years ago? Well, Tom's now on the general staff of the Seventh army, and the Fifteenth Division is in the Seventh Army, and…"

★

In front of the tall, gray-haired general, the young officer replacements stood at ease. "Welcome to the Fifteenth Infantry Division," said the general, who had arrived only the day before. "I'm General Richardson."

After the usual words of indoctrination about their duties, Dave Richardson told the new officers, "Now, there are a couple of problems you're going to encounter. One is that men who've been in combat a long time become pretty independent, and discipline suffers. You'll have to find ways to establish your authority and lead the men gently but firmly back into the army way of doing things.

Your success will depend on how well you handle it, but for God's sake, use good judgment.

"The other problem is that anything the men throw away, wreck, or lose, they call a 'combat casualty,' and nobody's accountable for it. You can follow an outfit for miles by their discarded gas masks. The hell of it is we can't question losses sustained under enemy fire. How can we? Men's lives come before equipment every time, and that's the way it should be. But a lot of these so-called combat casualties are nothing of the sort, so see what you can do to cut the losses down. Are there any questions?"

The new second lieutenants shook their heads.

"Then Godspeed and good luck," said Richardson as he turned and left the hall, accompanied by his staff.

The saucy little nurse walking down the hospital corridor with her companion was obviously popular. Everybody waved to her. The other nurses called, "Hi, Marylou." The orderlies said, "Hello, Lieutenant Simpson," and Colonel Jones smiled and drawled, "Good morning, my dear."

Even though she was talking at a rapid rate, she interrupted herself to respond to every greeting. While Marylou was tiny, with dark, flashing eyes and auburn hair, her companion, Helen, was a more placid lady, tall and easy, blondish and thirtyish.

But the little one did all the talking. "It doesn't matter I haven't heard from Jimmy in eight days; the mail is all jammed up now; there's a big American offensive on, you know; Good Lord, Helen, don't you read Stars & Stripes? Anyway, Jimmy said if anything happened, his friend Will Pope would let me know. He has my address and everything.

"Just think, Helen! If Jimmy gets wounded, they'll send him here! Won't that be grand! Oh! I can hardly wait to see him! We're too far back now for him to come visit, aren't we? Maybe the hospital'll move forward, behind the Seventh Army…"

"How about right behind the Fighting Fifteenth Infantry Division?" asked her companion, speaking for the first time since they left the ward.

"Oh, wouldn't that be grand! Wait a minute—I've got to check the mail again, just in case." She giggled and darted into the small room that served as the hospital post office.

Helen stood waiting outside. Marylou would bring out her mail too, if she had any.

A minute later, Marylou stumbled to the door. When she looked up at Helen, her face was drained of color. She was trembling. In her hand was an unopened letter.

She handed the letter to Helen. "I—I—I can't open it." Her voice trembled as she said it.

The return address on the envelope said, "Pfc. William B. Pope." Helen opened it. She read it to herself quickly. Halfway through, she sucked in her breath. A tear started to roll down her cheek.

Marylou said, "Jim's dead." She didn't ask. She knew. Even as her lip trembled and the tears started to flow, she resolved not to show her emotion until she was alone back in the nurses' quarters. But suddenly she could hold it back no longer. She threw her arms around Helen and wept hysterically. Her body shook. Her sobs echoed through the halls.

★

Will Pope zigzagged toward the house as machine gun bullets kicked up chunks of dirt around him. He was at a suburb near Schweinfurt, the objective of their attack. Kneeling beneath a window, Will's hand shook as he groped for a hand grenade. He pulled the pin and opened his fingers to flip off the activating lever. He tried to count to five, got as far as three, then tossed the grenade through the open window and threw himself flat on the ground. He heard movement in the house, like somebody trying to run away.

He lay there for what seemed an eternity before the hand grenade exploded. When he rose and started to vault through the window, he forgot his bayonet was still attached to his rifle, and it hit the side of the window and toppled him back onto the street, where he lay sprawled flat on his back. He jumped up, glanced at the window, then turned and kicked open the door.

Inside, he jumped to his left with his back to the wall, covering the room with his M-1. He saw two dead Germans crumpled together in a corner. They were bloody, badly cut up, as men killed by hand-grenade fragments usually are. They'd tried to get away from the grenade before it blew up, but they hadn't been fast enough.

Bowden, who'd been covering Will during his last dash to the house, came through the doorway, breathing hard. He leaned against the wall. After he caught his breath, he asked, "Where's your squad, Will?"

"Hank Gray can take care of himself. I lost contact right after the lieutenant told us to fix bayonets. I never know where the hell MacKenzie is. Olsen'll catch up with us, and that's all I have."

Bowden nodded and said, "Yeah. Hank'll be okay. MacKenzie and Olsen, too. Did you see the Germans take off when we came at them with our long knives, Will? They don't care much for cold steel, and that's for sure."

"Huh," Will grunted. "I'm not so crazy about it myself, if you want to know the truth."

Bowden threw a glance at the dead Germans, then said, "This is as good a place as any to assemble. You wait here, and I'll go round up Gruber's and Ceruti's squads."

Right after he left, Hank Gray came through the doorway, lurched over to Will, and sat down hard, gasping for breath.

"You okay, Hank?"

Hank nodded. He was so winded he couldn't talk yet.

Gruber walked in with what looked like his whole squad. He waved his recognition to Will and Hank and sat down with his men without saying a word. By their squirming, a couple of the newer men betrayed their discomfort at being in the same room with two dead bodies.

Everybody sat listening to the battle raging in the city. For them, Schweinfurt had been an anticlimax; a nothing. The Fighting Fifteenth had been out of position, so the Rainbow Division made the main assault, and the Fifteenth was covering their flank. They could have missed it altogether, but they had a new commanding general who seemed to want to fight every battle there was to fight.

Bowden and Ceruti came through the door with a couple of Ceruti's men. Olsen was with them; he flopped down beside Hank. For some reason, Olsen could never remember he was in Will's squad. Ceruti's face was streaked with dirt. He wiped his hand across it. "Pacini's hit. So's Findlay," he said.

"Hit bad?" asked Bowden.

Ceruti smiled. "No," he replied, "hit good."

The other men grinned. They knew that meant Pacini and Findlay were okay.

"Remember how I always tell Carlo Pacini to keep his big ass down?" continued Ceruti. "Well, he didn't. Got a bullet right through the left cheek, just as clean as anything. The medic laughed like hell. Said Pacini'd be back in a couple of weeks. Findlay got it through the leg. Medic couldn't tell how bad it was, but he thought it might be a ticket home. Lucky bastard." Findlay had only just come in with the last bunch of replacements.

Gruber said, "Brown got hit. Jerry slug took off his helmet and creased his scalp. He was bleeding like a stuck pig. Said he knew he was gonna die. Medic told me it wasn't nothing. Just a crease. Head wounds bleed a lot. But Brown was sure scared to death."

"When the hell isn't Brown scared to death?" asked Hank Gray.

Will realized Hank was upset about Carlo Pacini's getting hit. Thank God he wasn't killed. Then Will smiled. That was just like old Carlo: Even when he got wounded, it was a joke. In his mind, Will could picture the medic and Ceruti sitting beside the prostrate Pacini, and both of them laughing like hell.

Will suddenly remembered MacKenzie. Damn. He cursed himself. He should've kept better control of his men, and he knew it. "I don't know where MacKenzie is," he said. "Did any of you guys see him?"

Nobody answered. "I heard a lot of B.A.R.'s firing, but I don't know if one was MacKenzie's or not. No way of telling," said Gruber.

Will got to his feet. "I'll go look for him," he said. "If he shows up, just keep him here."

The others nodded. Will slung his rifle and went into the street. He looked across the field they'd crossed during the attack. Shell holes dotted the muddy scene. Medics worked with the wounded. A few dead G.I.'s lay where they'd fallen. Will figured he'd look for MacKenzie someplace else.

He decided to check the other houses where the men from Easy Company had taken positions. MacKenzie had probably joined one of their squads, and, knowing that quiet kid, Will supposed MacKenzie would just stay wherever he was.

As he went from house to house, Will thought about MacKenzie. He always kept to himself. He spent all his spare time cleaning and oiling his B.A.R., and in combat he never missed an opportunity to use it. You could hear its steady, reassuring bursts whenever things got hot. He had no friends, but everybody liked him. He wrote to his father almost every day. Once he told Will his dad was a hero in the First World War, and he wanted to be like him.

When Will returned to the platoon without MacKenzie, they were already loading on their trucks. They'd done their job. Sommers wanted them back.

Sitting on the truck, Will leaned back and tried to relax. Nobody was talking now; the exhilaration of having survived another battle began to fade. Will thought, Too many guys got hit. Too damn many. And we had the easy part, too. We didn't have to

charge into the point–blank fire of those massed batteries of 88s—
the Rainbow Division did. But I guess after you've made it through
a few tough ones, you figure you can make it through them all, and
you start to get careless.

And that's when they get you.

The antitank C.P. was a large house in the outskirts of
Schweinfurt. The mine platoon moved in after Bowden reported
to Captain Colina, who was not pleased with the number of
casualties.

"That does it!" he exclaimed. "You guys are an antitank mine
platoon, and I'm not attaching you to any more rifle companies,
dammit! If they're light, then they're light, and I don't give a good,
happy damn."

Will smiled and unrolled his sleeping bag. He liked
Captain Colina, who reminded him of a little bantam rooster. He
always looked like he needed a shave, and usually he was puffing
on a cigar.

Will also knew the antitank company was lucky to have two
such fine officers as Colina and Sommers in charge, especially since
they got along so well. This was all the more surprising because they
came from such different walks of life: Sommers, the high-school
teacher from Minnesota, fresh-faced and young-looking; Colina, the
union leader from the Pennsylvania coal-mining region, tough and
compassionate at the same time, always thinking of the welfare of his
men. He'd known hard times in the coalfields, but he'd known
power, too. That made him an ideal company commander.

Will couldn't help wonder what Colina was like at home. He
knew only that he was a mine unionist, that he was married and had
a couple of kids. Will wondered what Mrs. Colina was like. Big and
fat, he supposed.

He mentioned this to Ceruti one day, and Mike laughed out
loud. "Mrs. Colina is one of the most beautiful ladies I've ever seen,"
he told Will. "Not that I've seen her in the flesh, but the captain

always kept her picture on his desk, when he had a desk, and man, is she a knockout! Hell, Will, he writes her every day of his life. He's crazy about her."

"How about when he was shacked up with that French broad back in Alsace?" asked Will.

"Oh, hell, Will," replied Ceruti, "the captain takes it where he can get it when he's this far from home, but that don't mean he don't adore that beautiful wife of his." Ceruti smiled. "It's the way men are, is all. You'll find out soon enough."

Now, in the C.P. at Schweinfurt, Will could see that Colina was worried. He was standing with Sommers in the middle of the big room. "Dammit, Dave," he was saying, "our boys've been working their tails off. The guns're too damned good at knocking out pillboxes and smashing buildings. One sniper, and they bring up a 57 to blast the whole place to pieces."

Sommers nodded. "Joe Sumeric knocked out a couple of Jerry armored cars yesterday. Poor bastards tried to recon down the road Joe was covering, and that was the end of them. At least Joe's using his gun like he's supposed to."

"I still don't like it, Dave," said Colina. "You know as well as I do, an antitank gun makes a prime target for Jerry artillery. The line companies're using them like tanks, and, dammit, our guns don't have the protective armor or mobility of tanks."

Sommers said, "I hear the boys are getting pretty good, though."

"Guess so," replied Colina. "To fight in the line this long and survive, they gotta be good. They're good or they're dead."

Colina and Sommers smiled at each other. But Will could tell they were worried about their guns. They were straining the law of averages, cutting it too close for comfort.

★

On April 13, the army in Europe received the news: Franklin D. Roosevelt, the President of the United States, was dead. A cerebral hemorrhage had suddenly ended a career most Americans thought would last forever.

"Good God!" Will hardly knew he'd said it.

"It's official. Happened yesterday," said Bowden. "We got the word from headquarters."

"This is awful," said Will. "Here we are in the middle of Germany, and the guy who sent us over here has just died. Good Lord."

"Don't worry, Will," said Bowden. "Nothing'll change. We'll go on fighting until we've beat the bastards. That's all."

Will nodded. He knew the government would continue to function as usual. It was just such a shock to think that Roosevelt was dead.

✪

"I've got some bad news, Will," said Colina. "They found MacKenzie." The captain paused to let his words register. Will nodded, waiting to hear the details he knew were coming.

"They found him in a shell hole with his head blown off. But his dog tags were still around his neck. They were held there by his shirt and undershirt, and his B.A.R.—the one with the chunk out of the stock—was right beside him."

Will could only nod. The captain put his arm around him and said, "Sorry, Will."

Will was thinking. MacKenzie was always such a quiet boy, and now he was dead. And nobody even knew about it until the day after he'd been killed.

It was Jay Gruber who came over to commiserate with Will. He was genuinely sorry about MacKenzie and said so, while the other men remained silent.

Gruber still griped about everything from the lousy rations, the lousy officers, the lousy Germans, and even the lousy weather right down to the lousy town they were in, whichever town it might be. But that was his way of expressing his displeasure with the way the world had treated him in general. It was mostly talk. In fact, he was steady as a rock under fire and one of the most competent noncoms in the outfit.

In Schweinfurt, the platoon got five new replacements, which brought their strength up to fifteen men.

Then they got a sixth replacement. He was Second Lieutenant Dan Bradford, and he'd come to take over as platoon leader of the mine platoon.

20

Will studied Lieutenant Bradford closely. He was standing in the middle of the room talking to Captain Colina, who had just introduced him to Sergeant Bowden.

The lieutenant was young. Will guessed about nineteen or twenty. He was short, about five-foot-four, and he was light, small-boned. He was a good-looking man, his face enhanced by a thousand freckles, and his hair was reddish-blond and very fine and very straight.

Will was disposed to like practically everybody, but there was something about Lieutenant Bradford that gave him misgivings.

Captain Colina was striding toward the door after telling Sergeant Bowden to take the new lieutenant over and introduce him to the platoon.

Will thought Bowden did it rather nicely. He said, "Men, I want to introduce Lieutenant Bradford. The lieutenant's taking over the platoon, and I'm sure you'll join me in giving him our complete support and cooperation."

The lieutenant broke in, "That's not necessary, Sergeant. As your platoon leader, I'm automatically entitled to your cooperation, whether you want to give it or not. I also expect your unquestioning obedience. Is that understood? And I want another thing understood, and understood right now. I am in command of this platoon, and things will be done the army way from now on. And you'd better get used to it quick, because I intend to whip this platoon into shape.

"I want all squad leaders to report to me right now. The rest of you wait until we're finished."

As Ceruti and Gruber and Will went up to the lieutenant, Bowden, who stuttered for the first time since Will had known him, introduced them. Will noticed that Bowden's hand was shaking slightly.

Will said, "Sir, I'm only a temporary squad leader. I accepted the stripes with the understanding I could give them up as soon as somebody else was experienced and qualified enough to take over, and I think now——"

Before Will had stopped talking, the lieutenant snapped, "Good. You're now a private. When a sergeant gets busted, he gets busted all the way."

Will didn't really care whether he was a private or a Pfc., but he was hurt.

He protested, "But Sir, I'm not busted——"

The lieutenant cut in, "You are busted!"

Bowden broke in. "Sir, Will is just relinquishing his——"

"Sergeant! You will give me your opinion only when I ask for it. And I am not asking for it. I just busted this man for insolence. Now let's reorganize our squads. Since the squad that was led by, what's your name? Polk? Oh, Pope. Since Pope's squad now has no leader, Bowden will take it over."

He then assigned the replacements to the squads.

He didn't assign Will, but after he finished, he turned and said, "You! Pope! You'll be my driver."

"I'm sorry, sir," replied Will, "but I don't know how to drive a Jeep."

"Don't you get insubordinate with me, Pope, or I'll throw the book at you," snapped the lieutenant. "I've had enough from you. Everybody knows how to drive a Jeep, so don't get funny. When I tell you you're going to do something, your only response is: 'Yes, sir!'"

Will mumbled, "Yes, sir."

The lieutenant then turned to Bowden. "Sergeant, are your mine detectors in good operating condition?"

"No, sir," replied Bowden. "We don't have no mine detectors."

"What happened to them?" asked Bradford.

"We lost them on a road back in France," replied Bowden.

"Well, Sergeant, I want you to know I hold you accountable for those mine detectors."

Bowden said, "Lieutenant, they was a combat casualty. We wrote them off the company books."

"Baloney! Everything you guys throw away or destroy you've been writing off as a combat casualty. That's the easy way. But it's not going to be done anymore in this platoon. Have you inventoried your mines? Know exactly how many you have?"

"No, sir," replied Bowden.

"Well, you're going to do it right now."

"We don't have no mines," said Bowden. "Lost them all. Used them all."

Lieutenant Bradford cut in again, "Where'd you get that Thompson submachine gun? You're not authorized to have one of those, Sergeant. You're supposed to have a carbine."

Bowden started to say something. Will knew that Thompson was dear to his heart.

Before he could open his mouth, the lieutenant barked, "You turn that Thompson in to the supply sergeant right now and draw a carbine. That's an order."

He addressed the platoon. "Looks like there's been no discipline around here. Things are sloppy. Well, get this, and get it good. I am in charge, and I repeat, things will be done the way the army wants them done. Be ready for a rifle and equipment inspection in half an hour."

As Bowden started to leave, Lieutenant Bradford said in a loud voice, "Bowden, you've been operating without an officer too long. Things have changed. You'll take orders now. Got that?

Bowden turned and said, "Yes, sir," as he went through the doorway.

Will heard trucks in the street and ran to see what was going on. The gun platoons were coming in. Will counted. "Yep. All nine guns. Good!"

Captain Colina walked into the C.P. smoking a cigar. He had finally arranged to get his guns back and get the men billets.

Will started thinking very seriously about Lieutenant Dan Bradford. He resented his throwing his weight around and acting like a horse's ass just because he'd finished Officers' Candidate School, but that didn't worry him. What did was that Bradford had never been under fire, and Will didn't know how the new lieutenant was going to react in combat.

He thought, There's no problem with a replacement who's a private, but this guy could be big trouble, because he's in command. He'll be making decisions that can get our asses shot off!

Which made Will think of the kid named Barrett whom he'd sent back on sick call for being drunk all the time. Barrett could have gotten them all killed, too. Will wondered what had happened to Barrett and went over to ask Colina. "Captain, I thought they might send Barrett back to us with the new replacements. Any word on him?"

Colina turned around and said, "Oh, hi, Will. No, he's not coming back. We got the word this morning. The medics say he's psychologically unfit for combat."

"Hell, who isn't?" said Will.

"Anyway, they're going to keep him in the rear, scrubbing floors or something."

"Maybe that's better for everybody."

The captain was about to reply when he and Will became aware that Lieutenant Bradford now stood beside them. Bradford said to Will, "Any time you want to speak to the captain, you do it through me. I want a direct line of command. Any communication with the company's headquarters will be through me. And only through me."

Will did not reply. He turned his back to the lieutenant and started to walk away.

Captain Colina stared at Bradford. "You hold it right there," Colina growled. "Will Pope can talk to me anytime he wants to. And what's more, Sommers has been telling me you've started riding your men. I want it stopped."

In a kindlier tone, he said, "Look, Lieutenant, when you get into combat, your life is going to depend on your men, and their's is going to depend on you. You've got to have confidence in each other, and respect."

Bradford was silent for a minute. Then he said, "I'll consider your suggestion, Captain."

But his voice was insolent, patronizing.

Colina's face turned bright scarlet. He put his cigar down on the table against which he was leaning. He took one step forward. And, it seemed, without even cocking his arm, his solid fist shot out landing squarely in the middle of Lieutenant Bradford's face. The lieutenant staggered backward. Colina took another step, pulled his arm back, and let go a smashing blow. Bradford hit the wall and slumped to the floor, stunned.

Colina walked back to the table and picked up his cigar. Bradford shook his head and started to get to his feet. When the captain saw Bradford stirring, he said in a loud voice, "Do I make myself clear, Lieutenant?"

Lieutenant Bradford was standing now. He rasped, "That's a court-martial offense, Captain. I'll see you get ten years."

The room was quiet. Sergeant Bowden had just returned with his new carbine and was standing by the door. He said, "I didn't see nothing, did you, Will?"

"No, Sarge, I didn't see a thing," replied Will.

Gruber said, "All I seen was the lieutenant fall over a chair."

Lieutenant Bradford looked around the room, then stumbled through the front doorway.

After Lieutenant Bradford had left, Colina said, "Will, I hear Bradford wants you to be his driver. Do you know how to drive a Jeep?"

Will replied, "No, sir."

"I didn't think so," said Colina. "Hey, Smitty, come over here a second." When his driver, Smitty, had come over, Colina said, "How'd you like to be Lieutenant Bradford's driver, if he comes back?"

"Not much, thanks, sir," replied Smitty.

Colina smiled and said, "Didn't think so. But this guy worries me. I'm serious when I say I want you to be his driver. And I want you to let me know what the hell he's up to and what he's doing. If it gets too bad, I'll yank him. Colonel Darlington and I are good friends. He'll lend me a driver from regiment in the meantime."

Will suggested to Sergeant Bowden that the men fall out for inspection since the half hour specified by Bradford was up. "Then," explained Will, "we can always say we fell out as ordered, but the lieutenant didn't show up. Otherwise the bastard might say we disobeyed him."

Bowden took the opportunity to call roll. It was a good way to connect the names to the faces of the replacements. He began with the "old" men: "Ceruti. Gruber. Pope. Gray." Then he continued with the ones who came in at Zellingheim: "Olsen. Browning. Crowell. Innis. Black."

Then the brand-new names: "Boticelli. Stern. McCrory. Russovitch. Pendergast." The last, "Pendergast," didn't get an answering "Yo."

"Where's Pendergast?" Bowden asked.

"He's around. Said he'd be right back," answered McCrory.

Just then, a corporal from headquarters came in, saluted Colina, and said, "Captain, you're wanted at regiment." He started to leave, then turned around and said, "By the way, Captain, I thought I ought to tell you there's a lieutenant down there talking to Colonel Darlington. He says you socked him. And he's got a replacement with him who says he saw it."

As Colina started toward the door, Lieutenant Sommers said, "Hold on. I'm going with you."

Bowden said, "So am I."

When they returned, Bowden winked at Will and Ceruti, so they knew everything was okay.

Later, when they were alone, he told them what had happened. When they entered the regimental headquarters, Lieutenant Bradford was there with the kid named Pendergast. Bradford's nose was red and swollen. It looked like a small tomato.

The colonel said, "Okay, tell me again, Lieutenant."

Bradford described how Colina had hit him twice.

Colonel Darlington turned to Pendergast and asked, "Did you see this?"

The replacement nodded his head and said, "Yes, sir."

Colonel Darlington looked at Colina.

Colina said, "I think there must be some misunderstanding."

Sommers said, "I was in the C.P. the whole time, and I never saw the captain even touch him." This was true. Sommers had been working on his papers and had had his back to them.

Sergeant Bowden spoke up, "Somebody said the lieutenant fell over a chair. Flat on his face. That must have caused his red nose."

Colonel Darlington hit his knuckles on the table. "Look!" he said. "I've got a lot to do. We're moving up again, and I don't have time for this kind of crap." He turned back to Colina and said, "Jack, get this thing settled at the company level, and get it settled quick."

"Yes, sir," replied Colina.

"Then," said Bowden, "we all left, and that was that."

Will asked, "Where's Tomato-nose?"

His question was answered quickly. Lieutenant Bradford, accompanied by Pendergast, entered the room and came directly over to them. The lieutenant glared at Bowden and said, "I've just promoted Pendergast to sergeant. He's taking over the third squad."

At four the next morning, Will heard the trucks of the gun platoons moving out and wondered where they would be going now. They were deep into Germany. Nuremberg, he had heard, was the next objective, and that was going to be a big one. The Nazis would put up a hell of a fight there. It was their "sacred" city.

Relations between Captain Colina and Lieutenant Bradford were, understandably, cold. Colina had told Bradford the night before that Smitty would be his driver; Bradford made no comment. Colina told him; he didn't ask him.

The situation troubled Will. He could not go back to sleep, so he started putting his boots on. It was 0415 hours.

The last of the gun platoons was rolling out.

Will lit a candle.

As soon as he did, he saw three or four other candles lit in rapid succession, so it looked like quite a few of the men had been awake but just hadn't gotten up yet.

The whole C.P. was stirring by the time Will went outside to heat his coffee. Even when he was billeted inside, he liked to do his cooking outside. It was what he was used to.

The previous evening, Lieutenant Bradford had assigned Will to Pendergast's squad.

After breakfast, orders came down that Colina and his antitank headquarters were moving in with regiment—the mine platoon would be attached to the First Battalion, and Lieutenant Bradford was to report to Colonel Rankin.

Bowden was standing outside the door when Smitty came out. He smiled at Smitty, took him by the arm, and said, without raising his voice, "If we get in a real good shooting fight with the

Jerries, Smitty, you get as far away from Lieutenant Tomato-nose Bradford as you can get."

Smitty replied, "Don't worry, Sarge, I read you loud and clear."

Five minutes later they were on the road, Lieutenant Bradford in his Jeep followed by the two trucks of the mine platoon. The one they'd lost at Schwaningen had been replaced quickly. What the army required now was mobility.

German resistance had eased a bit, but each town had its garrison that put up a fight. Usually, small detachments of SS troops were present to make them fight whether they wanted to or not.

At the First Battalion command post, which, as usual, was the large downstairs room of the town hall, Lieutenant Bradford went inside and reported to Colonel Rankin. Rankin walked to the open window, and Will heard him say, "Okay, Lieutenant, I want you to move out and proceed until you meet enemy resistance. Do you understand? Drive until fired on."

Bradford replied, "Yes, sir. But sir, I think we ought to draw some mines first. After all, we are the mine platoon. I couldn't make Captain Colina see it, but I'm sure you—"

Rankin interrupted him. "You listen to me, Mister Lieutenant, you just cut out all that crap about going back for mines. When I say, 'Haul ass,' dammit, you haul ass!" And he banged his fist on the table for emphasis.

Will smiled. Colonel Rankin was always considerate to the men under him; it was obvious Colina had briefed him on Lieutenant Bradford.

As their tiny convoy rolled down the road, Will moved over to Ceruti. "What did you do with your light thirty?" he asked.

Ceruti grinned. "Gave it to Joe Sumeric before the guns pulled out. Had it sitting outside the whole time. Thought sure old Tomato-nose'd spot it. But he didn't."

After driving several miles through open countryside, Bradford pulled his Jeep to the side of the road and motioned Bowden in the lead truck to pass him. As Bowden pulled even with the Jeep, the lieutenant yelled, "You go on ahead, Sergeant. My motor doesn't sound right; I'll bring up the rear."

Will thought, "Why, you dirty rotten son-of-a-bitch!"

Bowden remained stonily silent.

After Will had calmed down, he turned to Ceruti and said, "Looks like we got a yellow second lieutenant."

Ceruti nodded.

"Remember what happened to Brucker?" asked Will. "I'll make you a bet the same thing'll happen to Tomato-nose Bradford."

"Maybe," answered Ceruti.

"I wonder who got Brucker," said Will. He hadn't thought about it for a long time.

Ceruti turned on the seat to face him. "You mean you don't know?"

Will shook his head.

The truck continued to roll. "Aren't you going to tell me?" asked Will.

Ceruti shook his head. "If he didn't tell you, I'm not going to. It's better to forget it."

Will was puzzled. He sat in silence for a while. Slowly he began to realize what Ceruti was saying. Now he remembered. Jim Mahoney had been terrified Brucker would kill them both. Jim had felt Brucker was a more serious threat to them than the Germans because he could shoot them in the back. It had preyed on him like a nightmare.

Still, Will looked startled, "Jim?" he said. "I don't believe it. He'd have told me."

"Look, just forget it, will you?" replied Ceruti.

Will sat very still, thinking hard. He understood now. Jim had gotten the opportunity to eliminate that cold-eyed killer, and he'd done what he had to. It was unpleasant but necessary, like shooting a horse with a broken leg. It was nothing he'd ever tell anybody about.

Will turned to Ceruti. "You saw him do it, didn't you? You saw him shoot the bastard."

Ceruti nodded. "Jim never hesitated. Brucker got in front of him to get a crack at Bowden, and Jim put his whole clip right into the son-of-a-bitch's back. Didn't take more than a couple of seconds, and it was all over."

After half an hour, the platoon arrived outside a small village. The buildings were clustered around the main street and one or two side streets. Most of the houses were one-storied, but there were a few larger stone buildings near the edge of the town.

Bowden stopped the trucks and ordered the men to get down.

Lieutenant Bradford stomped up and barked, "Sergeant, why are you stopping the trucks?"

"Because there's a town up ahead," replied Bowden. "We'll go in on foot, spread out 'as skirmishers.' Town could be full of Jerry soldiers."

The lieutenant yelled at the men, "Get back in those trucks!"

He shouted to Bowden, "Sergeant, our orders are to drive until fired on. We haven't been fired on. So you get back in that truck and you keep going until somebody shoots at you. That's a direct order."

The lieutenant stamped back to his Jeep.

Sergeant Bowden got into his truck. Then he laid a hand on Jack Diamond's arm, got off, and walked back to the Jeep. He said, in a voice that was ice cold, "Lieutenant, you're our leader. You lead us into that town."

Bradford shouted, "Sergeant, you do as I say, or I'll throw the book at you!"

"You do, and I'll throw it right back in your teeth," replied Bowden. "Now you get your Jeep in front of this column and lead us into that town."

At that moment, from the buildings at the edge of town, a burp gun and several rifles opened up.

Everybody jumped into the ditch. Will thought, "Whoever those Germans are, they just got so nervous they couldn't wait any longer to see what we were up to." He figured there was one burp gun and maybe a dozen men—couldn't be any more. The firing had been enthusiastic but light.

Behind him he heard the Jeep turning around and heard Lieutenant Bradford yell, "I'm going back to tell the battalion we've been fired on!"

As the Jeep drove off, Sergeant Bowden stood up in the ditch where the replacements could see him.

He motioned to Ceruti and Gruber to take their squads to the left. He signaled Pendergast to the right.

When they got to within fifty yards of the buildings, on the signal from Bowden, the men fanned out in the fields. The German rifle fire was sporadic, and nobody got hit.

Bowden yelled, "Okay, open fire!"

They all started firing at the same time, shooting at the windows in front of them.

After firing off a couple of clips of ammunition, Bowden held up his hand and yelled, "Stop! Cease fire! Cease fire!" The Germans had stopped shooting several minutes before.

Bowden turned and shouted, "Ceruti! Pope! Gray! Follow Gruber and me. We're gonna dig those bastards out. Olsen, Browning, Crowell, Innis, Black. You follow us as support. Be ready to come in if we need you. The rest of you guys, keep us covered. Keep shooting at the windows until we get close. Then stop!"

They started across the field, trotting low to the ground, but nobody shot at them.

Will heard the popping of rifle fire behind him and saw bullets chip at the walls in front of him. If the replacements didn't hit him by mistake, he'd be all right.

It was over quickly in a ragged blast of grenades and a short volley of rifle fire.

The men lying in the field saw twelve gray-haired old men wearing the uniforms of the German Army march out of the town with their hands raised in surrender. Ceruti and Will were on one side of them, Gruber and Gray were on the other, and bringing up the rear was Sergeant Bowden.

White sheets fluttered from the windows of the town as the platoon's trucks rolled through it. Even though Will suggested that they'd been "fired on" and should stay where they were, Bowden just laughed. "That weren't no resistance, Will. We got to go ahead until we hit the German main line. Then Rankin's battalion can come up and clean out the bastards."

Hank Gray and young Olsen remained behind to guard the prisoners; the twelve old men who had done their duty and were happy the war was over for them.

Driving through rolling, open country, they passed several farms, but nobody shot at them.

They came to another town, and Bowden had all the men get out of the trucks and walk into it in two extended columns, their rifles covering the windows, ready to fight at the slightest sign of danger.

It was a large town. It was a pretty town, too, clean and scrubbed, full of small white houses with blue or green shutters and flower boxes with bright flowers in them. A German soldier with a white flag in his hands met them. Will figured he was about sixteen years old. He indicated that the garrison wished to surrender and motioned to the platoon to follow him. Flanked by Bowden and Will, he led them to the town square, which was filled with German soldiers who had just finished stacking their arms and were waiting to give up.

The buildings on the square were larger than the neat houses they had passed when they came into town. Some were three-storied, all were well-built, and several had pillared balconies. As Will continued to look around the square, he let out an involuntary gasp. From one of the balconies, swaying slightly in the breeze, hung the bodies of two elderly civilians with ropes around their necks.

One of the Germans, who spoke a little English, was already explaining what had happened: six SS troopers had arrived and given orders that every soldier there defend the town to the death. But two of the leading citizens had the courage to argue that resistance was futile and would only result in the needless destruction of their village.

The SS men had declared them to be cowards, unworthy to live in the Third Reich, and summarily hanged them from the balcony. But as soon as the American trucks came into sight, the six storm troopers had driven off.

The soldiers then decided to surrender to the Americans.

"Okay, Will," said Sergeant Bowden, "you wait with, what's your name? Boticelli? Okay, wait here with Boticelli and turn over the town and the prisoners to the next unit that shows up. We'll go on ahead and see if we can catch those damned SS bastards."

Will saw Pendergast tugging Bowden's sleeve.

Pendergast said, "Look, Sarge, before we move out of here, I want to go back to being a private."

Bowden replied, "No way. You're Bradford's boy. He made you a sergeant, and, by damn, you'll stay a sergeant until he unmakes you one, or until you get your ass shot off leading your squad someplace where you shouldn't ought to go."

Pendergast had more tenacity than Will had given him credit for. He said, "Look, Sarge, I'm sorry. That damn lieutenant would've got us all killed back there. You saved our lives. But look, Sarge, this guy Bradford told me his uncle's a senator, and if I just told the truth about the captain slugging him, he'd take care of me after the war. I just got here, Sarge. I didn't know no better."

Bowden replied, "Pendergast, that's between you and Bradford."

The trucks drove out of town, leaving Will and Boticelli standing alone with forty or fifty German prisoners.

It wasn't long before Smitty drove into town. Gray and Olsen were with him. They were relaxed and smiling after their pleasant ride through the countryside.

"Where's Bowden and the rest?" asked Smitty. "I was supposed to tell them to wait here for the First Battalion."

"They've gone on ahead," replied Will. "Chasing some SS that left just before we got here."

Smitty looked down the road that led out of town.

Will said, "I sure hope Bowden doesn't get into any trouble."

Smitty sat thinking about that for a few seconds. Then he turned to Will and said, "Okay, Will. Let's go get 'em."

The Jeep shot forward. Without taking his eyes off the road, Smitty said, "You-all don't have no lieutenant no more, Will. They yanked Bradford."

"Oh?" said Will. "That sure didn't take long."

"Yeah," continued Smitty. "Soon as we got back to battalion, Bradford starts telling Colonel Rankin about Bowden being insubordinate to him and he wants him court-martialed and all that crap. But when Rankin finds out Bradford went off and left his men under fire, he hits the roof! It would've done your heart good, Will, to hear him chew out Bradford!

"He gets on the phone to Colina. Tells the captain what happened, turns and tells Bradford, 'You're relieved of command of the antitank mine platoon. Go outside and wait.'"

"Then what happened?" asked Will.

"Rankin wants to bust the son-of-a-bitch to private. But it turns out Bradford's got an uncle who's a senator, and there'll be hell to pay if they bust him, so Rankin talks it over with Colonel Darlington, and they both agree he ain't fit to lead the mine platoon. You guys are out on your own too much. Same with the guns.

"So they figure they'll put him where he'll be under somebody who can keep an eye on him. Let him stay a second lieutenant, but transfer him to a rifle company. When I left to tell Bowden to wait for the battalion, they was talking about giving him to A Company. Heard Rankin say Wilkes was good at kicking ass, and he figured Bradford's butt would sure be sore before Wilkes finished with him."

Will smiled and said, "How long do you think Bradford'll last in an outfit like A Company?"

"I dunno, Will. What time is it now?" They both laughed.

Ahead of them they heard the popping of small-arms fire. Smitty slowed down.

An abandoned German command car sat in the middle of the road. Smitty went around it and came up to the two mine platoon trucks. He stopped just behind them. Both of the platoon's drivers came over.

Jack Diamond filled them in. "We run across their car sitting here out of gas, and the six of them bastards walking down the road. Bowden had the men fan out and close in, shooting. Jerries jumped in the ditch, but they ain't shot back yet, and our guys're already lobbing hand grenades into the ditch."

A series of exploding grenades terminated his talk. Then everything was quiet.

Led by their sergeant, the men of the mine platoon walked back to their trucks. Bowden was smiling.

He said, "It was like shooting fish in a barrel. The bastards was out of ammo, too. Funny how just because they was SS they could cow everybody in that whole town. There they was, giving orders and hanging people. And they didn't have a single round among them. Shows how scared them dumb Krauts are of these bastards."

Smitty told Bowden about going back and waiting for the First Battalion, which was fine with the big sergeant, who smiled as he listened to the driver's staccato sentences. But his eyes stayed fastened on the German command car.

When Smitty was finished, Bowden drawled, "Do you think that thing'll run on G.I. gas?"

As Will and Bowden rode back to town in the command car, Will filled the sergeant in about Bradford. Bowden simply nodded his head. He made no comment. He didn't even smile.

21

When they returned to the town, the First Battalion was there. Soldiers and vehicles and weapons filled the streets of the tiny village to overflowing. Bowden reported to Colonel Rankin, who congratulated him for taking the two towns and catching the SS before they could do any more damage. Rankin was warm in his praise. He never mentioned Lieutenant Bradford.

Making it sound almost like an afterthought, Rankin said, "Look, Sergeant, we've got a platoon of division Rangers with us and that's why I wanted you to hold up here. We want your trucks to haul them. Their strength's about two good squads, so there'll be no problem fitting them in two trucks.

"I'm going to send the Rangers on ahead to clear out the towns along this road until we hit the German main line of resistance. They'll start right away, and they'll be going fast."

After getting briefed on the mission, Sergeant Bowden returned to his men. "Pendergast!" he called. Pendergast stepped forward.

"Your boy Bradford ain't coming back," said Bowden. "I'll give you your choice. Keep your stripes and transfer to Able Company, or take a voluntary demotion to Pfc. and stay here."

Almost before the sergeant finished, Pendergast replied, "I'll stay, Sarge. I'd rather be a Pfc., anyway."

Bowden nodded. "Okay," he said. "Our trucks are going to take the point of the spearhead with a bunch of Rangers. I need two volunteers to ride shotgun for Diamond and Shanker." He paused and looked around at his men, who were shifting uneasily.

"Pope, you and Gray are the volunteers. Draw extra ammunition and grenades and be ready to move out right away."

Will watched the Rangers board the trucks. Instead of helmets, they wore wool knit caps. They had sweaters on under their loose-fitting field jackets. Most had Thompson submachine guns or grease guns, and each had a trench knife strapped to his right leg. Their faces were blackened, commando-style.

They took along Bowden's newly-acquired German command car with the understanding they would return it with the trucks.

A young lieutenant named Pierpont was the Rangers' leader. He and a couple of his men went ahead in the command car. Will rode with Diamond, Hank with Shanker.

They tore along the road, cleaning out German resistance in town after town, rapidly, efficiently, ruthlessly, until about four in the morning, when they came to a large, empty barn sitting by itself in the countryside. After they'd checked it out, the Rangers had the two trucks and the command car drive into the old, wooden building, and as soon as the motors stopped turning, everybody went to sleep in the hay.

Two hours later they all woke up, almost as if it had been planned. Before they'd gone to sleep, Lieutenant Pierpont had checked the men who had been wounded in the fighting for the towns they'd taken. Their injuries were all from German bullets, and most were superficial. Three of the men, though, were wounded badly enough to worry their lieutenant. After sleeping on it, he decided to send them back for medical attention. They went in the German command car.

The Rangers loaded into the trucks. Lieutenant Pierpont took a seat on Jack Diamond's spare gasoline tank. He leaned over Will, slapped Jack on his helmet, and called out, "Okay, Tiger, let's roll."

They were in the open countryside. On both sides were newly plowed fields with large shade trees dividing them. The trucks were moving fast.

There was nobody in sight, and Will was beginning to enjoy the tranquillity of the rural scene. It wasn't much different from the rest of the countryside they'd passed through, but it seemed more unspoiled. After bending sharply to the left, the road led directly toward a thick, wooded area.

Will became aware that the lieutenant was standing on the running board, looking around. He sat down and said, "Oh, oh. I don't like the smell of this." He turned to Jack Diamond and said, "Pull her over, Tiger. I think we'll hit those woods cautious-like."

At the same time, he motioned to the other truck to pull over behind them but to stay back.

The Rangers jumped over the sides and fanned out into the fields on either side of the road almost before the engines stopped.

Will said, "Jack, I'm getting out!" He ran back to a point between the two stopped trucks and dove into the ditch. Diamond did the same. All was quiet. Will thought he heard a cricket chirp in the field.

An instant later, the tranquillity was shattered. Shells screamed in and exploded on the road. Will covered his head with his arms and tried to wiggle his body deeper into the bottom of the ditch.

Crack!

That didn't sound good, Will thought. He smelled cordite and gunpowder. He smelled rubber burning.

Ka-booom!

Will looked up. A shell had hit Diamond's truck. The last explosion he'd heard, he supposed, had been the gas tank blowing up.

Will figured he'd better get out of that ditch. The Germans would have it under fire in a minute.

He yelled over to the other side of the road, "Hey! Jack Diamond! Get out of the ditch and into the field behind the Rangers!" Will was already on his way into the plowed field. He threw himself into a furrow and waited.

He looked around, trying to size up the situation as quickly as he could. The German artillery had hit the road in front of Diamond's truck. Only one or two shells had hit the truck, but it was completely demolished. Behind the wreck, Shanker's truck was undamaged.

Everything was quiet again.

Will knew the Germans were in the woods in front of them. He knew their artillery was behind the woods.

He heard the sound of a motor. He looked over his shoulder and saw that Shanker had reboarded his truck and was backing it up as fast as he could go.

Will heard shells whistle through the air. He yelled as loudly as he could, "Jump, Shanker! Jump!" Will saw the truck stop. He saw Shanker start to leap out. He saw a flash, and another! and another! as artillery shells hit the truck.

He saw Shanker's body fly through the air as if it had been catapulted by a huge slingshot. It landed in the field, bounced twice, and lay still.

Shanker's truck was torn to pieces. It looked to Will as if the three shells had been direct hits. He figured the Rangers would now begin moving back, that they'd pull out of sight and wait for the line companies of the First Battalion. But when he looked around, half of the Rangers had already gone forward into the woods, and the rest were not far behind them. Will wondered if the Germans had seen them go. He had not.

He heard the firing of Thompsons and grease guns: quick, short bursts. He heard burp guns and German rifles. On his right, he saw a group of about eight Germans come out of the woods and start running along the edge of it, toward the firing.

They're going to try to take the Rangers from their rear, thought Will.

He raised himself up on his elbows, sighted across the field, and began firing at the Germans. He fired his entire clip as fast as he could pull the trigger. He saw the Germans drop to the ground as soon as they realized they were under fire. He didn't know if he'd hit any, but he had slowed them down, stopped them from running toward the fight.

He had a fresh clip in his rifle, and he was waiting for the Germans to get up. Instead, he heard the soft whisper of Jerry bullets going over his head. He stayed as low as he could.

He sensed movement to his front, rose to his elbows, and fired. He was able to get off only five or six shots before the Germans hit the ground again, but this time he had seen only four or five of them.

Will heard movement behind him. He turned fast, his rifle pointing at whatever it was.

It was Hank Gray. He flopped down beside Will, breathing hard. He said, "Did you see what happened to Shanker?"

Will nodded. He spoke fast. "Hank, keep your eyes open. Rangers're fighting the Krauts in the woods, but there's another bunch of Krauts trying to get over to cut them off. I'm trying to stop them."

Hank became tense. He put his rifle to his shoulder, but there was no further movement. Will saw the Rangers coming out of the woods fast, keeping low. With them they had five German prisoners who were also running, but with their hands on the tops of their heads.

Will turned to Hank and said, "Okay, Hank, it looks like we're leaving the party. Let's get going."

In a few minutes they arrived, breathless, around the bend of the road, out of sight of the German observers.

Lieutenant Pierpont counted his men; the German prisoners sat by the side of the road in a circle, covered by Ranger Tommy guns. The lieutenant and several other Rangers who spoke German started asking the prisoners questions, but the Jerries shook their heads and wouldn't answer. They were both sullen and arrogant. The Rangers' job was to get information from the prisoners. That was the only reason they went into the woods to take them in the first place.

"Let's shoot one of them," said a sergeant. "Then the rest'll talk their damn-fool heads off."

"No. I don't want to do that," replied the lieutenant. "If the next one won't answer, let's hit him in the mouth with a shovel. After we do that a few times, they'll change their minds, the stinking Nazi bastards."

In approximately three minutes, the Rangers were getting good answers to all their questions, some through bloody lips and broken teeth.

Diamond joined Hank and Will. He was breathing just as hard as they were. The first to speak was Hank Gray, who said, "You know, I got to know Johnny Shanker pretty well the last few days, and he was a good guy. He and I were joking together just before the artillery started. When I saw him blown through the air like that, I think I went into shock. Am I in shock, Will?"

"No, Hank," replied Will. "You're shaken up pretty badly, though. But you'll be okay."

The Rangers finished questioning their prisoners.

"Sounds to me like their line's not very strong," said the lieutenant. "Regular run-of-the-mill Jerry troops. No crack units."

"Yeah," said a Ranger sergeant. "But we all agree there ain't no better soldier in the world than the Jerry."

"Yeah. You're right. And they got artillery, too. But what the hell. Rankin's boys can take on the best of them. Eat them for breakfast and never even burp."

The men all nodded.

Pierpont walked over to Will and said, "Thanks, soldier. We saw you pin down those bastards who were trying to cut off our line of retreat. Good work."

The riflemen of Able and Charlie companies began arriving. The First Battalion had been split, and Baker and Dog had gone off on a parallel road. The prisoners the Rangers had taken were starting back to the rear, under guard. Medics were attending two wounded Rangers.

Will walked up to Captain Wilkes and said, "Captain Wilkes, sir, I'm Pope from the antitank mine platoon."

Wilkes clapped him on both shoulders and exclaimed, "Sure! I remember you. Damn good to see you again."

Will continued, "I think you ought to report to Colonel Rankin we lost both mine platoon trucks out there."

"Yeah," replied Captain Wilkes. "Charlie Pierpont told me." He picked up the field telephone.

"Don't forget to tell him we lost Shanker, too," said Will.

Wilkes nodded. "He was the driver, right?"

"Yes, sir." Will stayed with the captain while he made the brief report. Just as Will was about to give his best imitation of a salute and depart, a lanky, gangling first lieutenant with a hard-bitten face came up to Captain Wilkes and said, "Sir, it's that new lieutenant, Bradford."

"Yeah?" said Wilkes.

"He's gonna be trouble. The little bastard's been raising hell about the equipment losses. Says he's gonna make the men responsible. Sir, you know how heavy all that crap is to carry after a few miles, and we come a long, long way, most of it on our own two feet—"

"I know. I know," said Wilkes.

"But that ain't the big problem, Captain. The little prick's been making fun of his noncoms in front of the men and telling everybody he's the only guy they take orders from and a lot of other crap. The sergeants're unhappy as hell, and we got a real bad situation building up, sir."

Wilkes nodded. "I know. The little bastard got his commission through political pull. Anyway, right after this one, I'll take care of the son-of-a-bitch, if I have to ram a bayonet up his ass and twist it."

The rifle troops moved out to attack the German line—the information the Rangers had given them indicated there was no reason to wait. Able and Charlie companies knew their business. They did good work. After about five minutes of sharp fighting, it was all over except for sporadic gunfire beyond the trees. Then they heard Baker and Dog companies working on their sector. It didn't take them long, either. The battalion had broken the German line in a total elapsed time of fifteen minutes.

Will saw prisoners starting back to the rear. He saw the medics setting up a battalion aid station where he had been fighting Germans an hour ago.

Will saw the two trucks; they were empty and proceeding slowly, as if they'd been sent to pick up a unit and weren't quite sure where they were going to find it.

The driver of the first truck leaned out and asked, "Rangers?"

"Who wants to know?" demanded Lieutenant Pierpont.

"Yeah, that's them," said the driver to his buddy.

As usual, Will slept, while the truck he was in rolled. He woke up when they stopped in a small town.

After everybody had jumped down, Lieutenant Pierpont came over and shook Will's hand. He smiled as he fumbled in the large pocket of his field jacket, then said, "Here. Take this as a memento of our joint operation."

"Thanks, sir!" said Will. "Thanks a lot!"

"Think nothing of it," replied Pierpont. "I got several."

In his hand, Will held a beautiful Luger pistol.

⭐

The mine platoon was in the same town as the regimental C.P. The division was moving fast now. The first thing Will noticed was that Bowden had his Tommy gun back.

"Hear we lost both trucks this time," said the sergeant.

"Yeah," said Will. "We drove until fired on, and they fired on us real good."

"Damned shame about Shanker," said Bowden.

Will nodded.

"What happened to my Jerry limousine?"

"Didn't the Rangers bring it back to you?" asked Will. "They used it to haul a couple of their wounded and said they'd return it when they finished."

"Fat chance," said Bowden. "I didn't want to let them have it, but I didn't have no choice. I'm afraid we'll never see her again, Will, but she sure were a sweet little baby."

"Amen," said Will.

⭐

The regiment kept moving forward, and the mine platoon fitted themselves into any empty seats they could find on the trucks and Jeeps.

After a couple of days, Sergeant Masters told Bowden, "Sam, I've found you two trucks. They're a little beat up, is all. How soon can you send back for them?"

"Right now," said Bowden. "You got an extra driver?"

"Sorry, Sam. Guess you'll have to pick one of your own guys."

Bowden picked Browning, who'd been through an army driver training course. To Will and Hank Gray he said, "Okay, you guys got the rough one last time. I'll give you an easy one: go back with Diamond and Browning and ride shotgun for them coming back."

They hitched a ride with one of the drivers going for rations and mail. But when they got to the ordnance repair shop, the trucks were completely disassembled. It turned out they'd been shot up so badly they were about to be abandoned when the mine platoon requisitioned them.

The ordnance sergeant was emphatic. "Look, I know they're for the antitank mine platoon of the 555th. I ain't arguing with that. But what I'm telling you is there ain't no way these here vehicles is gonna be ready in less than two days."

Will was worried. He didn't mind at all staying in the rear area for two days, but what would Captain Colina think? Or Lieutenant Sommers? Or Sam Bowden? They'd wonder where he was, that's what. Probably have him court-martialed for going AWOL. Probably figure he'd deserted.

During the two days they spent at Division, Will found an empty house for the four of them to sleep in, got some old, torn blankets and tarpaulins from the repair shop to cover them at night, scrounged some rations from headquarters crew, and tried to find out how the war was going.

He told Hank Gray what he learned. "The Russians are closing in on Berlin. Our guys are stuck on the Elbe River, wherever that is."

"Yeah," said Hank. "The Jerries know how to use the rivers pretty good. And they're making it tough."

"We got any rivers in front of us?" asked Will.

"The Danube," said Hank. "Heard some guys talking about how we gotta cross the Danube. Hell. If our army can't get across the Elbe, what makes them think we can get across the Danube?"

"Yeah," said Will. Now he had one more thing to worry about.

★

Will Pope stood in one of the chow lines of the Fifteenth Division's rear, so far behind the front he couldn't hear even the slightest sound of firing. He thought he probably ought to have returned to the company as soon as he found out the trucks weren't ready, but it was too late now. Every time he saw an M.P., he'd push his helmet down over his eyes and pull up his field jacket collar to hide his face. He was sure they were looking for him.

"Ain't seen you around before. You new?" Will jumped at the sound of the voice behind him, but when he turned around he found himself looking into the friendly eyes of a technician wearing greasy Army overalls.

Will smiled his relief. "I'm from the Triple Nickel, come to pick up a couple of trucks," he replied. "So I thought I'd stick around awhile and see how the other half lives."

"We lives lousy," replied the man. "Lousy food. Lousy billets. Lousy pay. Too much work. No USO shows. No nothing."

"My heart bleeds for you," said Will.

The man smiled. "How're things at the front?"

"Oh, the usual. Lots of laughs," replied Will. "How's the war going?"

"You just came from it. You tell me."

"How should I know? I been too busy shooting Krauts."

"Hey," said the technical man, "you one of the guys come to pick up them two trucks for antitank company?"

Will nodded.

The man laughed. "Them trucks come in all beat up. Then they was in the fire."

"What fire?" asked Will.

"Oh, we had a big fire last week. One of the damn warehouses next to the ordnance shop. Everybody's running around like crazy, and nobody knows what to do. The dumb captain we had is jumping up and down yelling, 'Do something!

Somebody do something! Even if it's wrong, do something!'

"So some guys throws a can of gasoline on the fire. Man, oh, man! It was just like being at the front."

Will smiled. "How come you guys're so dumb back here?" he asked.

"It just comes natural," replied the man. "Hell, if we was smart, they'd have put us in the infantry."

"Gee," said Will. "So that's how they pick you guys."

"Naw. Not really. It's just luck," replied the man. "I used to work in a filling station back home. All I did was pump gas and change people's oil and stuff, so the army figures I'm a motor mechanic. You see that sergeant over there? He was a janitor in an A&P grocery store before the war, so they figure he's a natural-born quartermaster.

"Sometimes we get misfits, though. Had one guy used to do the work of a whole damn maintenance section. Suspicious as hell, right? So they look up his record, and sure enough, it turns out he was nothing but an inexperienced college boy. Can you beat that? They transferred him to the infantry real fast, I kid you not."

By now they were filling their steel trays with lunch. The trays had neat divisions to separate the different foods, but the cooks slapped everything together. After they sat down, Will started to eat his mashed potatoes and discovered they were vanilla ice cream.

The technician sat next to Will. As they ate, he said, "One good thing, though, is we all learn a lot in this here army. Everybody learns a trade."

"Yeah," replied Will. "Too bad Al Capone's not hiring anymore. I'd fit right into the Chicago mob."

The man laughed. "At least you don't have to salute all the time up at the front. Man! Back here we spend half our time saluting idiot officers, and they spend half their time just walking around the place to make sure we're saluting them."

A master sergeant walked over to Will's new friend. He

greeted him briefly with a "Hi, Mike," then got down to business. "We'll be working all night again. Division's hitting some rough resistance, and we gotta get them vehicles running."

After the master sergeant left, the man said, "Dammit! I wish you guys'd be more careful. You got us working our tails off. What happened to your trucks, anyway?"

"They got blown to bits by German 88s," replied Will.

"Well, dammit, watch out next time, okay? Be more careful. Remember, I ain't got to see a movie for over a week now."

"Gee," said Will. "Things that rough, huh? I'll sure watch it, old pal. It'd break my damn heart for you to miss another week of movies."

"It's okay," said the man. "We're moving again, anyway. Been moving all the time now. It ain't like back in France, when the line was stable and we could set up and stay awhile. You know what I think? I think you guys're pushing them damn Krauts around too hard, that's what I think. Why the hell don't you slow down a little? Take it easy, dammit. Knock off for the weekends or something, okay?"

Will had to laugh. He realized the motor mechanic was a good guy, and he liked his sense of humor. He enjoyed kidding with him.

He also realized he wasn't even in the same war.

22

———

Moonlight streamed into the small house through the windows and through the holes in the roof. While his three friends slept, Will was awake. He was uncomfortable, and he still worried about being away so long. Anyway, this was the last night. The sergeant said the trucks would be ready the next day.

He thought he heard a movement in the other room. He decided it was probably the wind. Or maybe a cat or some other animal. Mice, maybe.

He might have fallen asleep, but suddenly he was wide awake. There was somebody in the room besides himself and his three sleeping companions.

Will was tense. His mind raced. Who could it be? A Jerry soldier? This far behind the lines? Not likely. A rear-echelon bastard looking for souvenirs? Maybe. A German civilian looking for food? Yeah. That would be more like it.

He might be armed, though, and he might panic and try to kill me if I surprise him, Will thought. Slowly and quietly, he reached under his thin blanket for the Luger he always kept with him now. With the pistol in his hand, he immediately felt more confident and less vulnerable.

Drawing it from under the blanket, he raised himself onto his elbow. As his eyes followed the pistol's short barrel around the room, he saw nothing. No movement. No shadows.

His eyes stopped at the open doorway to the other room. The house had been empty when he took possession of it. But he hadn't checked it since.

Will rose to a crouching position and tiptoed to the door. Rising to his full height, he pressed himself flat against the wall, then quickly slipped through the opening with his back still to the wall and his pistol pointing into the room.

From the corner there came a gasp, and Will's Luger swung instantly to point at whoever was there, but his eyes continued to search the rest of the room for other signs of danger.

He whispered, "Who's there?"

There was no answer.

"*Sprechen Sie Deutsch?*" he whispered.

After a moment's silence, a tremulous voice answered, *"Ja. Ich spreche Deutsch. Ich bin Deutsch."*

Will was startled. The voice was that of a girl. Under his breath he murmured, "Good Lord."

Aloud he said, *"Sprechen Sie Englisch?"*

There was a slight hesitation before the girl replied, *"Ja.* Yes. *Ein bisschen.* In school I learn a *bisschen Englisch."*

Speaking slowly, Will said, "What… are… you… doing… here?"

There was another pause as the girl tried to translate his words to herself. Finally she said, *"Ich schlafe hier, neh.* Sleep here. Before was *mein Haus, neh?* Now I come back, *neh?"*

Will thought, So this was her house, and now that the fighting's over and the town's quiet again, she's come back. Poor kid must be scared to death.

He smiled and whispered, *"Alles* okay. Don't be afraid. *Ich nicht* hurt you, okay. Not hurt you." But he still kept his back to the wall and his pistol pointed at the corner. He saw her get to her feet. They stood facing each other, neither one making a move.

Will could see the girl clearly in the moonlight. She could be anywhere from eighteen to twenty-five years old. She was slim and neatly dressed in a skirt and blouse. Her long, brown hair was combed and tied in a bow at the back of her head. Her nose turned up and the corners of her mouth turned down, and she had large, dark eyes.

Will had not seen a girl in a long time, and he thought that this was one of the most beautiful women he'd ever seen in his life. He felt his blood course through his veins faster and his breathing become harder.

He remembered she was German. She was the enemy. But he was armed and had friends available in the next room, if necessary. In all probability, she was alone and unarmed.

"Let's be friends," he said. *"Ich, du, Kamerade, neh?"*

"Ja, ja," came the girl's voice. *"Krieg kaput. Nazi kaput.* I, you friend now, *ja?"*

"Ja," replied Will. "Friends." He put the hand that held the Luger into his field jacket pocket, but he still kept a tight grip on the pistol, just in case.

"You were looking in the other room just now," he said, jerking the thumb of his free hand toward the door. "What were you looking for?"

There was silence. He wondered if she had understood him.

"Essen. Food. Look food," she murmured hesitantly.

Will reached into another pocket, where he kept a couple of D rations. U.S. Army field ration D was a large chocolate bar that could be carried on combat patrols and other missions where a man had to travel light. One D ration took the place of a meal.

"Schokolade?" he asked as he pulled a D ration out of his pocket.

Instead of answering him, the girl came forward and took the chocolate bar he held out. Eagerly, she stripped off the heavy waxed cardboard wrapping, bit off a chunk of the chocolate, and while he stood there wordlessly, she devoured the entire ration in a few seconds.

Obviously, she had been starving. Will let go of his Luger. He took out another D ration but motioned to the girl that she should wait before eating it. "Take it easy," he said. "Take it easy. You shouldn't eat so fast. It'll make you sick. Wait a few minutes. You can have this one, too, but take it easy."

Will wasn't sure, but the girl seemed to understand. She nodded her head, then motioned toward the corner where Will had found her and said, "Come. Come sit, *neh?*"

Together they walked over and sat down on the pile of old blankets. They were sitting very close together. Will felt the girl cuddle up beside him, and his heart began pounding in his chest. He felt a powerful, intense yearning as the girl laid her head on his shoulder.

Neither he nor the girl had spoken since they'd sat down. Will was trembling slightly and breathing hard from the violent feelings that were coursing through his body. He was eager, expectant, yet acutely unsure of himself.

The girl fumbled with her blouse for a minute, then, without speaking, began to caress Will's right hand with both of hers, making him more excited but less apprehensive.

She slipped his hand into her blouse and placed it on her left breast.

Will's heart pounded so hard he thought it would break a rib as he fondled the girl's soft, firm breast. She giggled. He kissed her on the mouth just as hard as he could. She kissed him back, and his tongue slipped into her mouth as he continued to feel her breast pressing against his hand.

They shifted to lie down on the blankets, and the girl's skirt slid up almost to her hips. Will put both arms around her. He was breathing hard. His hands shook as he unbuckled his belt. He pressed the girl close as he hugged her and felt her body against his.

It was thrilling, exciting, joyous. He could not have stopped himself if he had tried. The exhilarating emotion that swept over him was stronger than anything he'd ever felt. The pleasure increased and increased. Then came the ecstatic, sublime joy, the culmination of every gratification he'd ever known.

Afterward they lay together, with their arms around each other. Will felt fulfilled, satisfied, at peace. She was so soft, so lovely, so yielding. He dozed. Then he became pleasurably aware that the girl was fondling him. He caressed her. Again there was joy and happiness and rapture—it was heaven.

"*Schokolade?*" whispered the girl.

Will smiled as he gave her the chocolate bar. She ate it as hungrily as he had possessed her a few minutes ago.

Then they made love again. Afterward, Will lay in a contented doze.

"Well, I'll be damned! Will, you are a sly fox, you are! Shacked up right here under our noses and we never even knew it."

Will woke up with a start. Jack Diamond stood in the doorway, grinning. The gray of dawn already lightened the sky.

Will jumped to his feet. The girl turned her face to the wall.

"Jack, if you mention this to anybody, I'll break your neck."

"Relax, Will," replied Diamond. "It ain't none of my business, but damn good going, if you ask me. Just don't get caught, that's all. It's against regulations. Carries a sixty-four-dollar fine. 'Fraternizing with the enemy,' that's what they call what you just been doing. 'Fraternizing with the enemy.'"

Will pulled on his trousers and followed Jack into the other room, where Hank and Browning were just waking up.

Will had said nothing to the girl. He didn't want to say, "Good-bye." He hoped he'd be back. Hell! He had to be back. He didn't even want to go. All he wanted to do was stay with this girl, and if the army wanted to come after him and court-martial him, then that was okay, too; he didn't give a good, happy damn in hell.

But his devil-may-care attitude didn't last long. The reality and the routine of the headquarters town quickly brought Will back to his old, conscientious self.

✪

Will never saw the girl again, but he thought about her all the time. At first the thoughts gave him real happiness, an inner glow of satisfaction and contentment and pleasure that aroused him as they comforted him, that made him yearn to go back and hold her once more in his arms, to caress her again and again.

Afterward, he worried. He just knew he'd get an unmentionable disease, that his hair would fall out and he'd lose all his teeth, that he'd get sores all over and go crazy. But nothing happened. So he started to worry about whether he'd gotten the girl pregnant, and he worried about that for the rest of his life.

✪

The minute the two battered trucks pulled up in front of the headquarters of the 555th Infantry Regiment, Will Pope dashed into the building. He looked around, quickly spotted Captain Colina and Sergeant Masters and made his way toward them as fast as he could through the busy room.

He wasn't sure what kind of reception he'd get. He expected the worst. Colina and Masters looked up. Masters smiled. Colina said, "Hi, Will. What took you so long?"

"They were still working on the trucks, sir. Just finished this morning."

Colina nodded. "Okay, Will. Glad you're back."

That was all. Will was so relieved he couldn't believe it. Then a smile replaced his worried look.

"Sergeant, where'll I find the mine platoon? Bowden'll want his trucks."

"They've been with Easy Company ever since you left," replied Masters. "We're closing in on Nuremberg. Lots of Nazi fanatics holding things up, making the other troops fight like hell. Our casualties have been heavy, and the colonel made us lend the platoon to E Company in spite of the captain's objections."

"Any news on how they're doing?" asked Will.

Masters shook his head. "No, but the Second Battalion's been hitting damned stiff resistance, so that means Easy Company's catching it." He paused. "It's a bitch, Will," he said. "A real bitch."

While he'd been gone, Rankin had been promoted to full colonel and taken over as regimental commander of the 555th. Colonel Darlington had been made a brigadier general and sent to another division. Rankin's first battalion was now commanded by a Major Kevin O'Brian, a West Pointer who had been a company commander in the 553rd Regiment.

Back outside, Will joined the other three, who were sitting on their helmets by the side of the road. Suddenly Jack Diamond grabbed Will's arm and pointed at the headquarters truck that had just pulled up in front of the town pump. It was the mine platoon come back.

The men came off slowly. They looked battered. Their hands shook; their breathing was hard; and they kept licking their lips as their glittering eyes darted in all directions.

It made Will sick to look at them. Familiar faces were missing. "They'll turn up later," he thought. "They'll turn up. Maybe the rest of the platoon's coming on another truck. Maybe they stopped off to pick up rations or ammunition. Maybe."

The men sat down in the street. Sergeant Bowden remained standing. His face was drawn and haggard. Will came over to him. The sergeant said, "Will, you missed a beaut."

"I can see I did," said Will. "What happened, anyway?"

"We had to clear mines off a road. In the daytime. Under fire," replied Bowden. "You were lucky you missed it, Will."

Will saw that the sergeant was streaked with dust and dirt. His face, hands, and neck were grimy. His uniform was ripped and filthy. He needed a shave.

Will knew Bowden would never let himself get that disheveled unless there was no way to prevent it. Will could see he had been through an ordeal.

Sam Bowden took off his steel helmet, filled it with water from the pump, and poured it over his head.

The big sergeant said, "Things was fairly normal for a while. You know, the usual. We was another platoon for Easy Company. That was all. We got shelled and mortared and machine gunned. Jerry resistance has stiffened, Will. They're fighting like hell now.

"But we kept together. We held our own. Ceruti and Gruber and I kept the newer replacements under control. Kept them calmed down as much as we could. Know what I mean? No panic. They were doing okay, too.

"Then, all of a sudden, some bastard comes yelling for the mine platoon at the top of his lungs. And by the tone of his yell, I knew he wasn't looking for us to do us no good."

Will nodded.

"And I was right," said Bowden. "I sure was right. They'd run into a bunch of those fanatic Nazi bastards. But they was blasting them out okay. Got a couple of tanks up to shoot hell out of them. Krauts pulled back, it looked like. But when the tanks started down the road after the bastards, whammo, they'd mined the damn road."

Will nodded. "I think I see it, Sarge," he said. "I'll bet some son-of-a-bitch from Easy Company starts shooting off his mouth about how everything's swell because they've got the antitank mine platoon right there with them, and all that crap."

Bowden nodded, "You hit it, Will," he said. "That's the way she went. Only by now, the Jerries'd formed a strong line and were shooting anything that moved."

Even though he'd escaped the nightmare, Will must have looked sick—he could see sympathy in Bowden's eyes.

"Anyway," the sergeant went on, "The line companies covered us the best they could, and our artillery kept shelling the bastards. But we know there was mines this time. There was the bloody tank, half off the road to prove it.

"We was on our stomachs, inching along, probing with bayonets, hoping like hell the Jerries was keeping their damn heads down. Praying they wouldn't notice we was there. We could hear the rifles of the battalion behind us, shooting at the German line. We could hear the shells whistling over us to hit the Krauts. We could see the explosions on the Jerries.

"We had four guys on the road. The rest of us was along the sides giving cover and protection. We'd change off every few minutes. And no mines. Then Jay Gruber raises his hand in the air. Motions everybody to stop what they're doing.

"We all see him digging easy-like with his bayonet. We know he's found a mine. Nobody breathes, hardly. Nobody's paying attention to all the shooting that's going on around us. Nobody's paying no attention to nothing but Gruber probing around that damn mine.

"We see him feeling around the bastard for trip wires. We see him lift the thing out of its hole, real gentle-like. Then get to his knees and show us the damned mine.

"We all sigh and breathe again. We can hear a couple of guys behind us give a cheer. We find five mines there. Then we find four up ahead about ten yards. Then another five.

"And, Will, it was the hardest damn work I've ever done. Took us all morning. Every single damn mine had to be probed for and checked for trip wires and taken out careful. It was backbreaking. The only good thing was the Jerries didn't seem to tumble onto what we was up to. At least, they didn't open up on us. Guess the rifles of the line companies and the artill-y shelling was doing their job okay. And we was crawling low to the ground. We only got to our knees to take the mines out. And we didn't defuse the bastards, either. Left them piled by the side of the road for the engineers.

"I sort of figured that belt of mines was all there was. Didn't think they'd had time to bury any more. They hadn't even had time to booby-trap the ones we found. No trip wires. No grenades attached.

"I guessed we were home free. Told the boys to keep going, keep probing. I left Ceruti in charge and went to tell the CO of Easy Company that we'd found fourteen mines and removed them, and I figured that was it.

"I got back okay. Started to tell the captain about what we'd done. I told him the road leads right into the Jerry line and how far did he want us to go, when *whammo!* I hear an explosion on the road.

"I know something's come unstuck. I know there's been a catastrophe. I left the captain standing there and went whipping back up the road as fast as I could run.

"Just then, the Jerries really let loose. I dive into the ditch. Machine gun bullets are all over that road. I yell, 'Get off the road! Get the hell off the damn road!' But Ceruti's already got everybody off.

"Nothing can live on that road now. Whatever happened alerted the Krauts to what we was up to. I see three guys lying there. It was something I don't never want to see again. No way I can tell who they are. Blown to pieces, Will. Blown to bits. Their uniforms was nothing but rags. Blood and chunks of flesh all over the road."

Will felt sick.

"Another one's flopping around in the ditch. Couple of guys trying to get ahold of him. But he's moving and jerking too fast for them.

"Pendergast comes running back to me and says, 'Sarge, we got trouble.' He says it calm. But he's shaking like a leaf, and his face is white as a sheet.

"And the Jerry bullets're whizzing all around us. Kicking up a storm. He says, 'Innis or McCrory set off a mine. Don't know how for sure. Think he probed under it, and when he brought his bayonet up, it lifted the mine enough to set off a booby trap.'

"I said, 'Killed them?'

"Pendergast said, 'Yeah. Them and Black. Russovitch is the guy who's hit bad, too. I can't stand to look at him, he's so bad. Don't know how many mines the first one set off, but all four guys working the road got it.'

"Now our artillery was really letting go at the bastards. The shells was roaring over us and exploding into the Jerries good. I tell Pendergast, 'Okay, let's get the rest of the guys out of here.'

"Will, it was awful. Innes, McCrory, and Black lying there on the road blown to hell. Russovitch dead now, in the ditch. He was torn apart, too. Don't know how the hell he was able to thrash around like that for so long.

"Olsen's hit bad, unconscious. Gruber and Ceruti was both hit by rifle fire when the Jerries first opened up, but they was still going, trying to keep the other guys calm and starting to move them back. Gruber looked awful. Got a bullet through the side of his face. He was a bloody mess. But we got them all out of there. Back down the ditch. Carried Olsen. Gruber and Ceruti made it on their own."

Will became aware that both Captain Colina and Sergeant Masters had come out of the C.P. and joined them. Masters said, "Sam, come on in and report. We just heard about the mines."

The captain didn't say anything. He looked sad and shaken. Inside the C.P., Bowden told his story again. His report to Masters was given in an unemotional, matter-of-fact tone. After he finished, he summarized the casualties for the first sergeant:

"Lost four men killed by mines—Black, Innis, McCrory, Russovitch. Sergeant Ceruti and Sergeant Gruber hit by rifle fire, but they'll both be okay. Gruber's the worst, though. Got it through the face, the bullet went in one side and came out the other; took a chunk out of his cheek and a bunch of teeth. He looked awful, all swole up and bloody.

"Ceruti's still lucky as ever. Bullet went in his neck. Came out under his arm. Could've killed him for sure. But the medics said it missed all the vital parts and he'll be fine."

"Anybody else?" asked Masters, who had been taking everything down on his report.

Bowden nodded. "Olsen," he said, "He got a bad one. Medics wouldn't promise us anything. Said they'd guarantee Ceruti and Gruber were okay. Olsen, they weren't so sure."

Bowden turned to Captain Colina and said, "After we got off the road, do you know what they did, sir? The artillery forward observer calls for artillery, starting at where we left off. Spaced their shots to blow any mines that might have been there. Walked the shells right up the road as nice as you please. And it didn't take them no time at all.

"Now, how do you like that? We bust our ass. We lose four guys killed and three guys wounded. And all the time they could have taken care of the whole damn road with artillery."

Captain Colina shook his head. "No," he said, "if your guys can clear the mines off, we get the road intact. But if we have to use artillery, we plow it up pretty damn bad. You did a fine job, Sam. Have your men clean up at the pump, have a smoke, and get some rest. But be ready to move out if they need you."

Will started counting who was left. Browning was out—he'd gone for a driver. So there was Bowden, Hank Gray, himself, Pendergast, Boticelli, Stern, and Crowell. And that was it.

As they left the headquarters, Bowden turned to Will and said, "I'm making you a sergeant, Will. There's only seven of us now, and I'm going to run the platoon like a squad. I'll be the squad leader. You'll be my assistant. And we got five men."

Will just nodded his head.

"Hank Gray's the only other guy we got that's been with us since the jump-off. We'll make him a squad leader when we get replacements."

The other men were already washing at the pump, but they had that vacant, faraway look in their eyes that told Will they realized how close they'd come to dying and knew that the next time, death might not pass them by.

23

The battle for Nuremberg was hard-fought. Several times Colina got orders to send his mine platoon to one rough sector or another, but each time he found a good excuse not to. He figured the platoon had taken its licks already, and he was damned if he was going to send seven men into a minefield under heavy fire and lose the whole platoon again. It was too late in the game.

Sitting in his truck as it rolled into the captured city, Will saw it had been a beautiful place once; but not now. The rubble still smoldered. Civilians were already out cleaning the streets, removing roadblocks, sweeping up the debris, and they seemed almost friendly; relieved the war was passing beyond them.

In Nuremberg, it wasn't necessary to disperse the trucks and Jeeps into alleys or side streets, or to cover them over with camouflage. They parked right beside the curb, in plain sight. The two mine platoon trucks sat in the road outside the headquarters of the 555th Infantry Regiment.

"You figure we're going to stay here, Sarge?" asked Will.

Before Bowden could answer him, Lieutenant Sommers came out of the building and said, "Sam, we're taking off after the Jerries—we've got to keep pushing them. They've got SS units all over the place getting their regular troops organized for a stand, and we want to hit them before they can make that stand. You and Will ride with me awhile."

As they jumped off the truck, Will exchanged glances with Bowden.

The trucks looked empty, with two men on one and three on the other. Reading their minds, Sommers said, "You're getting replacements at the next stop. Meet my new driver, Corporal Halvosa."

After they were under way, Sommers turned in his seat and said, "We lost two guns; knocked out at Nuremberg."

Will's heart sank. Bowden asked, "Who?"

"Whitey Woodall got a direct hit from an 88," replied Sommers. Will saw that he was deeply disturbed and was trying to keep control of himself. He took a deep breath. Will thought the lieutenant might break down as he said, "A short mortar round landed on top of Joe Sumeric."

"My God!" exclaimed Bowden.

Will couldn't talk.

"It was a damned fluke. Never should have happened," said Sommers. "Joe was the finest soldier in the whole damned division. Just proves it's all luck in this war. There's nothing to stop the best soldier in the world getting killed by a stray shot or a bad mortar shell."

They drove in silence, each man with his own personal memories of a gallant warrior. To Will, Sumeric was everything that was glamorous in war. He had that devil-may-care attitude of men who believed they were indestructible. It was hard for Will to accept the fact he was actually gone. Then he remembered Ceruti and thought, Oh, my God! Who'll tell Ceruti? He felt a tear start. He wiped his hand across his face and breathed, "So long, Luigi."

Bowden was the first to speak. "How'd the captain take it?"

"Bad," replied Sommers. "I think he cried when he heard about Joe. And he's pulling in his guns. Told regiment they'd been abusing his boys and he was damned if he was going to lose all his guns that way. Rankin agreed."

They were still rolling through Nuremberg, but now they were in the suburbs, which were not as badly damaged. Soon they would leave the city behind them.

Moving out, thought Will. Moving out, again. And he realized that each place they left was a place to which they would never return.

Nobody spoke. Sommers sat looking straight ahead at the road. Halvosa was an old soldier, smart enough to know he was an outsider here and shouldn't butt in.

They were in the countryside before Sommers turned around again and said, "You'll spend the night in the next town. That's where I'll be leaving you."

Will and Bowden nodded.

Sommers said, "I mean, that's where I leave you. I'm going to take command of Dog Company."

"What!" yelled Will. "You can't do that!"

Sommers smiled at him. "Sure can, Will," he said. "I trained in heavy weapons, and I've had the experience of being exec of anti-tank. Besides, Will, I'll make captain out of it, and you can be damn sure no more heavy mortars'll land on our guns."

"You're going to leave us," said Will. He spoke like a man in a trance.

"Don't worry, Will," said Sommers. "I won't forget you guys. I'll see you around." He was trying to be casual, but his voice broke in midsentence.

Will turned to look at Bowden, who had remained silent. Will said, "Sarge. Sarge, what do you think?"

"I think Dog Company is mighty damn lucky, Will," replied Bowden. "Mighty damn lucky."

The truck with the replacements pulled up in front of the small country inn where the platoon had spent the night. The men on the truck were singing when they arrived, but it wasn't until the motors cut off that Will heard the words:

"Born in Kentucky,
Bred in Tennessee,
Went to school in Georgia,
Gonna die in Germanee."

Will had to swallow hard. Then he began to count heads. Twelve men. Damn good. Now they had nineteen men in the platoon, which was the most he could remember. He was mulling that over when he heard a voice in his ear saying, "Sergeant, baby, they told me you'd show me which end of my rifle the bullets come out of and tell me what's an 88 and explain what you use this here shovel for and—"

"Carlo Pacini!" Will flung his arms around him and gave him a bear hug. "Carlo! Welcome home!"

As they grinned at each other, Pacini said, "Look who's still a big-shot buck sergeant! My God, I spend a couple of weeks in an aid station, and what happens? I come back and find my friend, Will, drunk with Power, I'll bet."

Bowden and Hank Gray came over to greet Pacini just as warmly as Will had.

After the usual jokes about where he got hit, Pacini got serious. "This ain't the same platoon I left," he said. "There's too many guys I ain't never seen before and not enough guys I used to know."

While the platoon loaded onto the trucks, Bowden took Carlo aside and filled him in on what had happened since he got hit at Schweinfurt. It was a sadder-looking Pacini who climbed over the tailgate.

Will sat next to him. He remembered Pacini had been especially close to Ceruti. "You know Mike Ceruti's going to be okay?" he said. "He was lucky. He could have been killed, but he's okay, Carlo, so don't worry. Gruber's going to be okay, too."

"I know," said Pacini. "Bowden told me. But Will, I don't get it. All this fighting. All the casualties. Back in the rear, they're saying the war's just about over. That it's all wrapped up. But the other infantry and tank outfits are having the same deal we are. I hear they're fighting like hell all over Germany. And here we are, still taking casualties. Going south into what they call the heartland of the Nazis. How's the rear echelon figure the war's practically over? I don't get it."

In the early afternoon they arrived at a place that had been a prisoner-of-war camp. The rifle troops who had just liberated it were leaving. The officer in charge told Bowden to wait there until they knew where the platoon would be needed.

Will looked at the building. It was large, sitting all alone in the countryside. It was gray, four-storied, and had pointed towers on the roof. It had a great big courtyard in front and looked more like a school than a prison. Most of the prisoners were Russians. They were timid about making contact with the G.I.'s. But when the mine platoon started making fires in the courtyard, cooking coffee, and heating K ration tins, it was too much for them. Several of them came up, rather shyly. The members of the platoon offered them cigarettes, and the Russians took them. The Russians kept saying, "Me Russky. Me Russky. No Nazi. No Nazi. Me Russky. Me Russky."

The men laughed. Then they showed the Russians how their steel helmets came off the helmet liners and could be used for heating water, for cooking, for carrying, for shaving.

The G.I.'s and the former Russian prisoners communicated by sign language and by the little German they both knew, and they all laughed a lot. As they clapped each other on the back, they kept saying, *"Nazi kaput! Nazi kaput!"*

Captain Colina drove up, smoking a cigar. Bowden and Will went over to his Jeep and saluted for the benefit of the replacements. Colina smiled. "Well," he said, "How go things with my rear-echelon troops?"

Bowden and Will both smiled back at him.

"Sorry to break this up," said the captain, "But we gotta move. The front's fluid, but the Jerries are fighting. They fight and withdraw, fight and withdraw. They've been laying mines. Knocked out a couple of Jeeps and a truck. So now everybody wants the mine platoon."

Will asked, "Can't they take care of the mines with artillery fire?"

"Yeah, Will, but most of the mines are on the roads, and they don't want to make shell holes. Everybody's moving on the roads now."

"Where we going, Captain?" asked Bowden.

"Up behind the Third Battalion," replied Colina. "They lost a Jeep and a lieutenant with it, and they've been yelling for the mine platoon ever since."

"What do you think we'll hit?" asked Will.

"Scattered Volksturm and Wehrmacht troops with SS mixed in to make them fight," replied Colina. "Nothing serious."

In the cellar of the Third Battalion headquarters, the men unrolled their sleeping bags and spread them on the floor. Will felt relaxed because he knew he wouldn't have to get up in the middle of the night to pull guard now that he was a sergeant.

He sat down on the floor with his squad.

"The captain said we was his rear-echelon troops," said a replacement named Latham. "Are we rear echelon, Sarge?"

"Sure," replied Will. "We got a nice, comfortable cellar with a roof over our heads and nobody shooting at us. What could be more rear-echelon than that, for God's sake?"

A couple of the replacements scratched their heads. They could hear the artillery and machine guns firing. Latham's buddy, Silverman, asked, "How far away is all that shooting, Sarge?"

"Oh, I'd figure a half a mile," replied Will.

"Gee," said Latham, "then we're pretty close to the front lines. We never been this close before."

"Oh, boy. Now I suppose you'll want combat pay."

"Can we go up and see the front, Sarge?" asked another replacement, named Carlin. "Can we?"

Will shook his head. "When we go up to the front, son, it won't be to go sight-seeing."

"But, Sarge," said Latham, "the war's almost over. We might not get to see it."

"You're weird," said Will.

"Do you think we'll see any action before it's over?" asked Carlin. "My buddy MacDougall here says we won't. Will we, Sarge?"

Will said, "I sure hope not."

"It can't be that bad," said Silverman. "We just go shoot up a bunch of Germans, that's all. They're on the run. We shoot them like rabbits."

Will said, "Look, you guys, fighting Germans isn't like shooting rabbits. They're still the best soldiers in the world, so just pray you don't have to go mix it up with the bastards. That's all I've got to say."

The replacements were quiet for a few minutes. Then Carlin said, "Yeah, but Sarge, we been beating the hell out of them, ain't we? They can't be as tough as you say they are."

"I can take them on," replied Will. "But you can't."

An intelligent-looking replacement named Johnny Minelli said, "You mean because we've never been in combat. That's what you mean, isn't it?"

Will nodded. "That's exactly what I mean," he replied.

"Th—the Russians scared me," said a new man named Stanford. "They looked like crazy men, all thin and funny-looking."

"Oh, hell!" said a man called Benjamin. "Everything scares you. That's why Minelli has to take care of you all the time."

"Lay off him," said Stern. "He's liable to start crying again."

"Wait a minute," said Minelli. "Maybe Stanford's right to be afraid of them. They're probably fanatics like the Germans. All these guys are fanatics. Ain't that right, Sarge?"

"I don't know," replied Will. "Maybe they're like us."

Carlo Pacini sat down with Hank Gray and shook his head. "It's sure been a bitch, ain't it?" he said.

Hank nodded. "Yeah," he replied.

"You know, Hank," said Carlo, "we're the only two guys left out of our bunch of replacements that came in before the jump-off."

Hank nodded.

"You've changed, Hank."

Hank shrugged his shoulders.

"You've changed," repeated Pacini. "I notice it because I been gone. You're nervous all the time."

The two young soldiers sat without saying anything for a few minutes.

"You're right," said Hank finally. "It's like you say. There ain't many of us left. And when Gruber and Ceruti got hit, I realized I ain't got long to go. Neither do you."

"Yeah. But I got hit already. Maybe I'll be okay now."

Hank shook his head and said, "That's just wishful thinking, Carlo. You know that?"

Pacini nodded.

Sergeant Bowden came down into the cellar looking for Will. The other men were sleeping on the floor, wrapped in their blankets or bags. A few candles were burning.

When he didn't see Will, Bowden turned to go back up the stone stairs. As he did, he heard Will's footsteps and saw his shadow starting down. He waited until he reached the cellar, then asked, "Where've you been?"

"Out checking the guards."

Bowden grinned. "Looks like I'm going to make a sergeant out of you yet."

"The hell with that," replied Will. "This is the early shift. When I go to sleep, I don't intend to get up until tomorrow morning."

With one accord, the two men decided to go back upstairs. Now they automatically went through the open doorway of the farmhouse. The air felt good. Will stretched. He yawned.

Bowden stood still, and Will realized Bowden had something on his mind. Will waited for him to speak.

"I was talking to Masters," said the big sergeant after a long pause. "He told me what happened to your friend Bradford."

"You mean my good old buddy Lieutenant Tomato-nose?" said Will. He'd almost forgotten about the little son-of-a-bitch. "What happened? Couple of guys from Able Company decide to use him for target practice?"

Bowden shook his head. "Nope. Nobody from A Company even laid a hand on him, Will."

"So what happened?"

"Well, you know Captain Wilkes. He chewed Bradford out good a couple of times, told him he was a rotten officer and he was going to treat him like he would any other rotten officer, and he didn't give a damn if his uncle was the Secretary of War or the President of the United States. Told him if he didn't get his butt out of the dugout and lead his men into combat he was going to bust his ass if it took a court-martial to do it."

"Good for him," said Will.

Bowden nodded. "Well, the Jerries was retreating, and Able Company got orders to go marching after them. Wilkes assigned Bradford's platoon to lead the column. It was their turn.

"So Bradford gets in his Jeep and tells his driver to start her up. His platoon sergeant calls to him, tells him there's bound to be Jerries up ahead someplace, and he'd be a lot better off on foot in case they jump him."

Will nodded. The smaller target you presented and the less noise you made, the better your chances.

"Bradford says something like, 'When I want your opinion, Sergeant, I'll ask you for it,' and away he goes, Jeep and all.

"Everything's okay for a few miles. Then the lieutenant's driver tells him he don't like the looks of things and they ought to go back to the protection of the column—they's too far out ahead of them.

"Bradford tells him he makes the decisions and he'll decide what they do. Tells him there ain't no Germans for the next twenty miles. He hadn't even finished when his driver sees the bushes move along the side of the road ahead of them, then sees Jerry soldiers with burp guns and rifles getting ready to shoot at the Jeep. He slams on the brakes and jumps into the ditch at the same time the Jerries open up.

"But a couple of Jerry slugs catch Bradford. He topples out over the side of the Jeep onto the road. He's alive but hit bad. He starts to crawl back toward the column.

"Now, Will, the lieutenant's platoon saw what happened. There wasn't no way they could miss it, being as how they was only about fifty yards behind the Jeep. Now, you know damned well any good outfit would've rushed them Jerries and got their officer out of there. And Able is one of the best. Only it wasn't a Captain Wilkes or a Colina out there, or a Dave Sommers; it was Lieutenant Dan Bradford.

"The platoon just stays where they're at. The driver'd scrambled down the ditch by then and joined them. They sees Bradford on the road. He's trying to crawl, but he ain't doing it too good. He groans, 'Help me. Help me.' Then he sounds like he's crying. One of the men laughs, nervous-like.

"Bradford gasps, 'I command you to help me. I order you to help me... for the love of God, please—'"

"That was when a Jerry opens up on him with a burp gun. Another Kraut tosses a grenade onto the road. And that was all she wrote, Will. There wasn't much left of Lieutenant Daniel Bradford."

"Then what happened?" asked Will.

"Oh, then his platoon took the Jerries easy. Flushed them out with one B.A.R., they did. Hit a bunch and the rest come out with their hands up."

Will nodded. Now he felt sorry for the poor, stupid, arrogant little lieutenant. His own men had let him die out on that road without lifting a finger to help him...

Later Will wondered if Bradford had any friends. Certainly not in Able Company. No, nor in antitank, either. It made Will appreciate his own friendships with Sam Bowden and Hank Gray and Pacini. He realized the new men were trying to be friendly, too, and he felt flattered, but he held back. No, thought Will, I don't want any more friends right now. Not until everybody stops getting killed. But what the hell? I'll be gone, too. Nothing magic about me. I'll get killed right along with everybody else. Jim'll sure be glad to see me. And he smiled.

24

General Tom Jacobs had just finished his morning staff meeting and had a worried look on his face. His old friend Dave Richardson was trying too hard. The reports confirmed it. He was putting his infantry into dangerous situations unnecessarily, going for the brilliant victory and going for it at all costs. Trying to prove he could be as effective in his management of battles as he was in his management of staff meetings.

Jacobs had a request from Governor George Pope that he'd have to take care of, too. Dammit! he thought. I'm a general running a war, not a wet nurse to some runny-nosed kid. But he knew he owed George Pope a lot of favors, and besides, he liked the man.

He sighed. All his problems were centered in the Fighting Fifteenth, it looked like, and he had to do something about them.

General Courtney Jones came in after assigning the staff their duties for the day. Jones had taken Jacobs' place when Dave Richardson left and Jacobs succeeded him. From an old army family, Courtney Jones was neat, methodical, and efficient. With just a trace of gray in his hair, he looked much younger than his forty-six years. He was a handsome man.

Like many others, Courtney Jones had begun to realize that General Tom Jacobs had become one of the finest generals in the

United States Army. He'd forced himself to learn everything he could from Dave Richardson, and he could not have had a better teacher.

At the same time, Jacobs understood and sympathized with his combat soldiers. He was able to temper expediency with compassion, to synchronize head and heart. He never asked his men to do the impossible, and he never wasted their lives; yet he accomplished every assigned objective and was building a solid reputation because of it. If the war lasted much longer, he'd command an army.

Jones said, "Up north, they're stuck at the Elbe River."

Jacobs nodded. "We're going like hell everyplace else, though. It looks like the Germans are finally starting to fold."

"Yes, sir," replied Jones. "But look at the fight they put up at Nuremberg, for God's sake, and we know they're going to stand at the Danube."

"Last-ditch stuff, Court," replied Jacobs. "They're finished."

"What about 'Festung Europa,' their national redoubt?"

Jacobs smiled. "Propaganda, Court. There is no such thing. I've had it checked out real good, and it's nothing but the product of somebody's imagination. It doesn't exist, and it never did. So let's wrap this one up. We'll take the sons-of-bitches at the Danube and keep going. We'll go like hell now—they've got nothing to stop us with."

Courtney Jones nodded. He said, "Tom, let's talk for a minute about the Danube. The Rainbow Division's going to make the main assault at Donauworth. But now I hear Richardson plans to send one of his regiments over as a diversion. He knows there's Krauts in his sector downriver, and he's going to hit them. Harry Collins at the Rainbow doesn't think it's necessary. Says he can take care of those Krauts after he's over."

"I think so, too," replied Jacobs. "River crossings can be brutes. Why take the chance of losing a lot of good men if the job can be done without it?"

"I'll see if I can get it stopped," said Jones. "But it might be too late."

✪

"This is the life," said Will Pope. "Eating regular. Sleeping inside. Not getting shot at all the time. I've found me a home here with the Third Battalion. Just hope things stay this way."

"They won't, though," said Sam Bowden. "Nothing real good ever lasts very long."

Major Dunlap of the Third Battalion was coming over to where they were standing.

"See," Bowden said, "I told you."

"Sam," the major began, "our advance elements are on the Danube. We're going to make a crossing, and they want the mine platoon in the first wave. They figure the Jerries mined the far shore. You'll go with the First Battalion, so report to Major O'Brian.

"I hate to say good-bye, Sam. Rankin told me you were the best damn noncom in the regiment, and now I believe him. Good luck to you."

✪

On the bank of the Danube River, Sam Bowden fell in his men and called roll. As usual, he started with the old names, the ones he knew best: "Pope. Gray. Pacini." Then he continued: "Pendergast. Crowell. Stern. Boticelli." And then the new ones: "Stanford. Wilson. Janowitz. Minelli. Latham. Silverman. Carlin. Benjamin. MacDougall. Myers. Samovitch."

Afterward Bowden went to get the detailed plans for the night crossing. He left Will in charge.

In the half-light, Will looked around. Between the woods and the river was a clear, grassy slope, an excellent spot to launch boats. The Danube did not look wide. There was a current, but nothing to worry about. The river was grayish, maybe because of the time of day, but beautiful and blue the Danube was not.

On the opposite bank were thin woods and clear spaces with scattered clumps of trees. Will hoped it would be a dark night. It wouldn't be any fun to get caught under fire in the middle of the river.

The companies and the platoons of the First Battalion were divided into groups for the crossing, and somebody decided to put the mine platoon in two different boats; that way, the entire platoon wouldn't be lost if they were all in a boat that got hit.

Of the nineteen men in the mine platoon, Will had his squad of eight men to take over. In the dark, he sensed they were scared to death. They had to go off and relieve themselves every five minutes. "Calm down," said Will. "There's no need to worry…"

Will's little talk to his men was interrupted by the booming of artillery upriver, by the rattling of machine guns and the popping of rifles. Tracers laced the sky; shells exploded; flares flickered. It was a honey! If anything was ever designed to strike terror into the heart of a new replacement, it was to watch infantry assault a river at night.

Under his breath, Will muttered, "Damn!"

Aloud, shouting over the din of the battle taking place on their left, he yelled, "Okay, you guys! Settle down, dammit! Settle down! That's the Rainbow Division going across at Donauworth! They'll take the crap, and we'll get the gravy!"

The boats of the Fifteenth Division were being unloaded and put into the river. Will checked his men again to make sure he had everybody. He was crossing with A Company; Bowden and Hank with B.

They loaded silently. The boats began shoving off. Everything was quiet on their part of the river. The excitement was on their left, where tracers and exploding shells lit the sky. Ahead of the Fifteenth Division's boats was only the darkness of a silent shore.

Will thought, I think we're going to make it. They don't even know we're crossing. The calm of the river was beginning to have a tranquilizing effect on him.

He heard a swish above his head. Flares! Even before they popped to illuminate the sky and the river below them, Will knew they were flares.

Pop! Pop! Pop! The flares ignited above their heads, making the river, the assault boats, and the entire scene as clear as daylight.

A geyser of water from an exploding shell went up close to the side of Will's boat. When the water came down, it drenched them all. Then, they got another drenching, and another, as the water swished into the air, then splashed back down into the river.

The machine guns began. The steady cracking of the heavies. The burps of the burp guns.

The boats were going as fast as they could toward the shore from which the firing came. All they wanted to do now was get there; get out of the middle of the river where they were vulnerable and get to dry land where they knew how to fight.

Off to the right, Will saw an explosion. A shell had hit a boat!

Another! The Germans were using mortars and artillery on the landing craft!

Machine gun bullets stitched a white seam in the water ahead of Will's boat. He could see and hear the tracers hissing into the water. They were coming close! "Oh, God! Let's hurry! Hurry! Hurry!" he breathed. His heart pounded in his throat.

Then he thought he heard one of his men whimpering. He said, as calmly as he could, "We'll be there in a minute. Everybody take it easy. We'll be there in a minute."

A bright flash! A loud explosion! Another landing craft was hit but not sunk. It swerved off its course and almost ran into them.

Will heard the popping of more flares overhead. The others had slowly drifted into the water on their little parachutes. Then he heard artillery shells whistling overhead from the American side of the river. Behind him they boomed. Ahead of him they exploded. Their flashes were constant now. The explosions were loud. The boats kept going toward the shore while the shells whistled over-head unceasingly.

Will was looking ahead, watching the exploding American shells. He didn't notice they had arrived at the far bank of the river until he felt the landing craft jar to a stop. In that second, the men were on their way out of the boat.

German tracer bullets were still zipping overhead. Men were still being hit, and some troops were thrashing in the water.

The A Company squads that came over in Will's boat were already moving inland, firing as they went. Will counted heads. He had his eight men.

"Let's go," he said. "Keep behind the riflemen."

His men spread out and went forward. The small-arms fire was far ahead of them. So they continued to advance standing up.

Will never heard the mortar shells until they exploded. Loud. Sharp. And nearby. As he threw himself down, he could feel the blasts. He was on the ground, flat on his face, with his arms over his helmet. He thought, That was a killing barrage. I never heard them coming in. I don't know how I missed getting hit. Dumb luck; just plain dumb luck.

The riflemen were going forward again, but they were bent low and were not going as fast as they had before.

The relief of leaving the landing craft had been dispelled by the mortar shells. The men were tense, straining their ears for the slightest telltale swish above the crescendo of the river battle.

Will thought, I better check my men. Those mortars were into us. He looked around, straining his ears against the noise of combat. He got behind a tree and looked backward. He could hear A Company ahead of him, but he couldn't see anything behind him. He thought desperately for the names of the men in his squad. He called, "Stern! Stern!" There was no answer. "Minelli! Minelli!"

Then, during a pause in the firing, he heard a sob off to his right. He looked over. He could see the outline of a helmet. He dashed toward it, keeping himself so low that he was practically on all fours. He was right. It was a G.I., and he was crying. Was it one of his men? He patted him on the back and said, "It'll be okay, son, it'll be okay. Take it easy." He wanted desperately to see the man's face.

He said, "What's your name? What's your name, son?"

"St—St—Stanford," replied the other.

Yeah, thought Will. He's one of mine.

Four shadows came toward them, crouching low to the ground.

"Who's there?" asked Will.

"MacDougall."

"Carlin."

"Benjamin."

"Stern."

"Okay," said Will, "that makes six of us." He thought, There should be more, me and eight replacements.

He asked Stanford, "Are you hit?"

Stanford shook his head.

"Where are your friends?" asked Will.

Stanford pointed toward the left.

Will said, "Okay, let's go get them." He figured they were still too frightened to move.

"Wait here," he told the others.

He helped Stanford get up, and they headed in the direction Stanford pointed to. Stanford was unstable on his feet and walked almost like a drunkard. Will held him steady. Will almost tripped over a G.I. sprawled on the ground in front of him. He knelt down. The man was breathing hard. He was practically unconscious. He groaned.

"Medic!" yelled Will at the top of his lungs. "Medic!"

"Who is it?" he asked Stanford.

"Minelli," replied Stanford. "Johnny Minelli."

Will's heart sank. Of all the new men, he liked Minelli the best. He was fine and idealistic, and damned intelligent, too. He had a great future, if he lived. If he lived.

Two forms loomed out of the dark, red crosses standing out against the white circles on their helmets. They knelt by Minelli.

"He's hit bad," said one. "Stomach wound. Worst kind."

"I think we might have more guys hit," said Will. He looked at Stanford.

Stanford started off with Will. Then he stopped. He pointed. There lay two G.I.'s. They were ripped to pieces.

Will didn't even have to look to make sure they were dead. "Who are they?" he asked Stanford.

"Latham. And Silverman," replied Stanford without expression.

Will turned to Stanford and said, "Mortars?" realizing as he said it that it was a stupid thing to say—of course it was mortars. He had to get a grip on himself. He was just going through the motions. Stanford nodded.

"Okay," said Will, breathing heavily, "we were supposed to meet up with Sergeant Bowden and Hank Gray after we got away from the river. Let's pick up the rest of the squad and go see if we can find them."

Will returned to the medics and said, "Please take special care of Minelli for me. He's a good guy."

They nodded.

As he walked away, Will was thinking furiously, Minelli hit bad. Silverman and Latham dead. And they were afraid the war'd be over before they saw action…

Then Stanford tugged at Will's sleeve and held up his hand as if to say, "Wait a minute." Will stopped walking while Stanford stumbled back to where the medics were treating Minelli. He tapped a medic on the shoulder. The medic looked up. Stanford said, "Here, you might need this," as he put something into his hand.

Will heard the medic say, "What the hell!"

He hurried over to see what was going on.

Stanford had given the medic a bloody human hand, cleanly severed at the wrist.

25

They picked up the other four men and started inland. Will realized that Stanford had cracked. Mentally he wasn't with them anymore. A mortar shell must have cut off some G.I.'s hand and hurled it at Stanford. The poor kid just hung on to it, and when the impact of what he was clutching registered in his brain, he broke down.

Will's problem now was to link up with Bowden and with Gray's squad. The sky was beginning to get lighter.

Will heard himself challenged. "Who are you?"

"First squad from the mine platoon," replied Will.

"Oh? Somebody's looking for you. Just wait here."

That suited Will. He sat down and motioned Stanford and the other four to do the same.

Bowden showed up with Janowitz, Boticelli, Wilson, Myers, Crowell, and Samovitch.

"Where are the rest of your men, Will?"

"Latham and Silverman are dead," replied Will. "Minelli's hit bad."

Now it was Will's turn. "Where's Hank?"

"Hit in the leg right after we come ashore," replied Bowden.

"Bad?" asked Will. His heart beat faster.

"Don't think so," replied Sam. "He got a lot of small pieces of shrapnel in the leg but nothing to cause any real damage. He'll need blood, though; the medics were hooking up a plasma bottle."

"Thank God!" murmured Will. "Pacini and Pendergast?"

"Dunno," replied Bowden. "Lost contact with them, but I figure they'll turn up."

Will hoped so. Pacini was an old friend now, and Pendergast wasn't such a bad guy, either. Will turned to Bowden and said, "This guy, Stanford. Might be a good idea to ask the medics to have a little chat with him afterward."

It was now daylight, and Will could see Bowden raise his eyebrows. He frowned, nodded his understanding, and said, "We'll wait here for a few minutes to see if Pacini or Pendergast shows up, then go back to the river. There aren't any mines. First Battalion's hit tough Jerry resistance, though, and they're forming a line until we can get some artillery onto the Jerries and get our tanks across the river. Trouble is, we haven't pushed them back far enough to get the river out of artillery and mortar range yet, and all the bridges are blown."

Five minutes later, Carlo Pacini came loping up to the group and flopped down. Carlo had the left sleeve of his field jacket and shirt cut away at the elbow. Around his forearm was a bloody first-aid bandage.

"What the hell happened to you?" asked Bowden.

"Jerry bullet," replied Pacini. "Never felt the son-of-a-bitch. I waited to make sure Hank'd be okay, then I started trying to catch up. I was going ahead like nothing, when a guy from B Company says, 'Boy! You better do something about that arm before you bleed to death.' That was when I seen blood all over. We cut off the sleeve and put on a first-aid dressing."

Bowden shook his head. He said, "Damn, but you're lucky, Pacini. You seen Pendergast?"

Pacini shook his head.

"Okay, let's get back to the river. I'll tell these guys to send Pendergast back if he shows up."

As they walked, Will saw that Sam Bowden kept looking at him nervously. Will couldn't figure it out.

When they got to the Danube, everybody was moving off

upriver. "What's going on?" Bowden asked the master sergeant who seemed to be directing things.

"Everybody's going over opposite Donauworth. That's where the engineers are gonna put the bridges across. That's gonna be the bridgehead. We was just a diversion."

When they got to the bridgehead, the engineers across the river were stretching a bridge out from the far shore. It would take a while, so Bowden picked a spot for the platoon to wait.

Then he flopped down next to Will. Bowden was nervous. He said, "Will, I got some bad news for you."

"Oh?" replied Will. "What?"

"In the crossing last night, B Company lost their company commander."

Will thought for a minute. What Sam had said had not sunk in yet...

Phil Cohen! Will turned sharply to Bowden. He looked the question rather than said it.

Bowden nodded his head. "I'm afraid so, Will. Direct hit in his boat."

Will could feel the tears filling his eyes. He couldn't stop them. Grief is as instinctive as fear.

He was aware that Sam was patting him on the back. He was also aware that his lower lip was trembling, and he was about to really let go and cry. Couldn't do that! Maybe later sometime. But not now. Again he thought, Pure, dumb luck. Some guys get it, and some guys don't. But Phil! Why Phil?

As he sat there, he realized the last time he'd seen Phil was in early February, way back in Alsace, the day Phil left to go to B Company. Since then, Phil had become a first-rate company commander and won the Distinguished Service Cross for heroism. Will guessed Phil would have changed a lot. But maybe not. Still, it had been such a long time.

February! That wasn't even three months ago. Yet it seemed to Will he had lived a lifetime since February.

Will breathed out. He was aware that his breath had been pent up inside him, but he thought he was in control of himself now. He turned to Sam and said, "And the Elements so mixt in him, that Nature might stand up and say to all the world, 'This was a man!' "

Bowden nodded his head and said, "Amen, brother."

Will's spontaneous reaction was to laugh. But what came out was a big, loud sob.

Will became aware through the blur of his tear-filled eyes that the bridge work was progressing faster than he thought, and it would soon be finished. He began to pay attention to where he was and what was going on. Bowden had led the platoon onto a rise that overlooked the river. They were sitting in the same kind of thinly-wooded area as the one they'd landed in during the night. Will nodded approvingly. They were out of the way, yet they could see everything that went on. And the woods gave some cover in case of a surprise attack.

His gaze fell back onto the bridgehead itself. It was a good area for building a bridge, but it was awfully exposed to any kind of artillery fire the Germans might throw at it. Men and vehicles were already starting across, even though the engineers were still finishing the last stages of their work. It was beginning to look routine.

Without warning, Will heard the familiar scream of German shells. He heard and saw the explosions hit the staging area. He was lying flat now, even though the shells were landing on the other side of the river.

The shells blew up part of the bridge. They killed several men on the landing site. Then the shelling stopped as quickly as it began.

The engineers were able to fix the bridge. Somebody removed the dead soldiers.

The German guns were no longer in position to shell them, and the army was coming across. The stream of vehicles seemed endless, and Will knew the platoon would not be left alone for long.

A Jeep drove up. Captain Colina jumped out and walked over to Bowden. "How'd it go?" Colina asked.

"Rough," replied Bowden. "You heard about our casualties?"

Colina nodded his head.

Then he and Bowden walked down to the riverbank. They spoke for about fifteen minutes. When they returned, Colina said, "Men, meet the army's newest commissioned officer, Lieutenant Sam Bowden."

All the men smiled. Will said, "Congratulations, Lieutenant!"

Captain Colina continued. "Lieutenant Bowden'll take over the Second Platoon of Baker Company. Baker lost their company commander last night. Phil Cohen. A damned good friend and a fine guy. Everybody's sick about it. Lieutenant Stransky of the Second Platoon is taking over B Company, and Bowden will take Stransky's platoon."

Will felt his heart sink. Bowden was the soul of the mine platoon. Will could not imagine the platoon without him.

The captain was saying, "Sergeant Pope will take over the mine platoon as platoon sergeant."

Will sat up with a jerk.

For the first time, Colina noticed Carlo Pacini's bloody, bandaged arm.

"You had that looked at by a medic, Pacini?"

"No, sir," replied Carlo.

"Well, dammit, get your ass back to an aid station. You can lose your arm from gangrene if you don't have it taken care of."

Pacini replied, "Right, sir," and left to find the aid station.

Will went to the captain's side, and they walked off a little bit from the men.

Will said, "Captain, before I take over the platoon, I want you to know I'm not even a good squad leader. I lost three men crossing the river."

"It wasn't your fault those men got hit, Will," replied Colina. "Besides, you're the only one left."

Will raised an eyebrow.

"You're the only one left that's come with us all the way from France. You're the most combat-experienced man in the platoon now. And the best. So you'll take over."

"Yes, sir," replied Will.

Bowden departed with Captain Colina. As the captain got into his Jeep, he turned to Will and said, "Wait here with your men, Sergeant, and we'll get instructions to you as soon as we know what's up."

After the Jeep left, Will realized again how much he and everybody else had depended on Bowden. Will thought, "I got big shoes to fill. And I got little feet."

Will walked over to Stanford, who was sitting propped up against a tree. Will said, "Okay, Stanford, please get up a minute."

Stanford rose, and Will knew he would do whatever he told him to. Will looked into his blank eyes and said, "Stanford, I want you to walk back to the aid station. The place where all the medics are, see? I want you to tell the first medic you meet that your platoon sergeant sent you back. Got that? Your platoon sergeant sent you back."

Stanford nodded his head. He slung his rifle on his shoulder and started walking toward the bridgehead.

Will looked at his platoon—eleven men now, including himself. He had forgotten to ask the captain about Pendergast.

Will and his men sat and watched the truck convoys crossing the river. They saw the artillery pull into a field to set up their guns. Will saw tanks crossing the bridge, an armored division on the march. He could tell by the way they handled their tanks that they were good. There was nothing timid about them. They moved fast, eager to join the battle. They were unbuttoned, and the tank commanders were sitting on their open turrets. Will liked their flair. Later he learned he'd watched the Twentieth Armored Division cross the Danube.

After the tanks had crossed the bridge, Will could hear them fanning out into fields beyond the artillery, which was already firing. The loud booming seemed to echo and reecho as the guns blasted away. They fired for only twenty minutes. Then the guns fell silent, and the gunners started cleaning up.

They didn't move out, though. They didn't seem to be in any hurry.

"Do you think the Germans'll throw counterbattery fire at our artillery?" asked Wilson.

"Wouldn't think so," said Will. "I hear the infantry's moving fast now, and I doubt the Jerries have any artillery set up anymore."

He smiled at them and said "And the mortars are way out of range now."

"Where do you think we'll go from here, Sarge?" asked Carlin.

"Yeah," said Myers, "where do we go from here?"

"I don't know," said Will. "We'll go take the next town in front of us, I guess. And if we survive that, we'll cross the next river, storm the next hill…"

The men nodded their heads. They didn't comment or ask any more questions. They'd become a subdued, pensive group.

Will looked at the sky. It was starting to get dark. The troops had been crossing the river all afternoon. He turned to his men and said, "I bet we spend the night here, so make yourselves as comfortable as you can."

After it got dark, Will lay on his back and watched the stars. It was a clear night, and the stars were beautiful. They were well to the rear, in the middle of artillery and anti-aircraft batteries, so it was out of a sense of duty more than anything else that Will posted his men on guard duty that night. Five shifts of two men each. It worked out perfectly.

Will slept soundly. At about three in the morning, everything was quiet. The booming of distant artillery could be heard faintly. Will smiled to himself and rolled over. Then he heard the voices of the two men on guard talking to each other in the clear night. They were far away from where Will lay, but he could hear them distinctly.

"Do you think Sergeant Pope'll ever get so he accepts us as the real mine platoon?"

"What do you mean?"

"Well, I think he misses his friends. From the old platoon. The guys he jumped off with in the Alsace. The guys that got it at Wurzburg and at Schweinfurt and Nuremberg and—"

"Yeah. I see what you mean. He thinks we're just a bunch of recruits, something like that?"

"Yeah."

As the voices faded, Will felt a lump in his throat. The familiar words had been like ghosts come back from long ago. From very long ago.

26

Will hadn't seen the tall, sad-looking general walking along the riverbank on the morning after the assault. The general's eyes had taken in every detail, though, every corpse and every wrecked boat. He'd talked to the wounded at the aid station, and they'd replied through swollen lips, stared at him through puffed-up eyes.

Dave Richardson walked back to his waiting staff car. He got in and signaled the driver to start. Richardson felt physically sick and emotionally drained. Now that he'd seen what those neat lines and arrows on his maps meant, the suffering they represented, the agony and misery, he made his decision.

He shook his head. He'd gone to the front only because Tom Jacobs had ordered him to go. Tom told him his Danube crossing was unnecessary, nothing but a waste of good men's lives by an ambitious commander's futile attempt to gain glory. "Go see what your egotism cost," Jacobs had said.

When General Richardson returned to his headquarters, he wrote his request to be relieved of command of the Fifteenth Infantry Division. He then began to compose his letter of resignation from the United States Army, in which he had served for twenty-five years.

★

Early the next morning, after making its way over the Danube on the pontoon bridge, one of the trucks left its convoy, cut across the field, and stopped. The driver, who was a sergeant, yelled over, "This the mine platoon? The 555th?"

"What's left of it," replied Will.

The driver smiled. "I come to take you up to Regiment, Sarge. Hop in."

Will loaded his men in the back of the truck and he got in front with the driver. As the truck returned to the road and continued its journey, Will could hardly wait to ask, "What's going on? What's happening up front?"

"Lots," replied the sergeant. "Jerry army's pulling back. We've been using all our trucks to haul rifle troops after them as fast as we can go. The Forty-second Division's got their trucks on the Autobahn, and they're headed straight for Munich."

"Wow!" exclaimed Will. "Isn't that supposed to be the heart of 'Festung Europa?' Aren't they supposed to fight like hell for Munich?"

"That's what they say," replied the sergeant. "But I think it's a lot of crap. What the hell they gonna fight with? We done took most of Germany already. We done took all their factory towns."

"But," continued Will, "I heard they got enough stuff stashed away down here to last them a year."

"That's a lot of crap," said the sergeant.

Will thought, I'll bet he's right, too. Yeah! I'll bet he's right. He turned to the driver and said, "Looks like this has turned into a rat race."

The driver smiled and said, "Yeah, sure looks like it, but I'm damned if I know where the rats are racing to this time."

They both laughed.

It wasn't until the early afternoon that they found regimental headquarters. Will went in to report. He asked for Colina. The captain running things thought Colina was out with his guns. They were going forward pretty fast.

"Mine platoon? Oh, yeah. We thought we were gonna need you. There were some mines laid up the road apiece. But we made the Jerries clear them. We figured, they laid them, they can pick them up."

"Great!" said Will. "I'll endorse that policy anytime you want."

The captain laughed.

"Main problem we're having now is taking care of all the Jerry prisoners that're coming in. It's a brute. Jerry resistance seems to be collapsing all along the way. Rainbow Division's having some fighting outside Munich, but it's pretty spotty. Mostly SS types. That's about all we're hitting, too."

The captain looked a little sad and said, "But guys are still getting killed. The war's still going on. You're just as liable to get your ass shot off today as you were yesterday. But, Sergeant, look. I don't know what to do with you guys right now, since the Jerries are picking up their own mines, and the line companies don't need reinforcing—they're going like hell. So why don't you just stay with us, and we'll use you where we need you?"

"Sounds good to me, sir," replied Will.

Just then, Colonel Rankin came in. When the colonel saw Will, he smiled. "You're Pope from the mine platoon," he said.

"Yes, sir," replied Will.

"Glad to have you back," said the colonel. "Now, to keep things straight, you go around the corner and draw tech sergeant's stripes. Jack Colina told me you're in charge of the mine platoon now, so get those stripes on." The colonel smiled again, made the "V" for victory sign, and strode off to continue directing the activities of his now extremely fast-moving regiment.

At first, the supply sergeant said, "Naw, I ain't gonna open up my stocks just for one lousy set of stripes. Too damn much trouble. I'm getting ready to move again. Storehouse is closed."

"Look," said Will, "Colonel Rankin gave me a direct order to draw tech sergeant's stripes, and I'm gonna draw them if I have to tear this damn place apart and you with it."

The supply sergeant said, "Okay. Okay. Damn! I hate dealing with you tough young sergeants."

After Will had gotten his stripes, he said, "Now I'll need a needle and thread." The sergeant supplied them without a murmur.

"By the way, you don't happen to have a Thompson submachine gun, do you?" asked Will.

"Yeah, I got a whole case of them. But I ain't issuing any. Not unless you got a requisition."

Will thought for a minute. Then he reached into his pocket and pulled out his Luger pistol. He laid it on the tabletop in front of the supply sergeant. "How's this for a requisition? Even swap?"

The sergeant's eyes lit up. He smiled and said, "Hmmm." He hesitated another moment. Then he said, "Yep! That and your M-1 rifle will get you one Thompson submachine gun." He came back with a Tommy gun that was clean and well oiled.

"Now," said Will, "how about some ammunition? I'll need a couple of clips."

"You didn't say nothing about no ammunition," said the sergeant.

Will picked up the Luger and pushed its clip release button. The pistol's ammunition clip shot out into his hand. He put it in his pocket and returned the Luger to the table.

"How many clips you need?" asked the sergeant.

"Oh, give me about five or six," said Will.

When he had the clips for his Thompson, he put the full clip back in the Luger.

"You're gonna like that baby," said Will.

"You bet your sweet life," said the sergeant. "And I'm gonna get to take it home. You're gonna have to turn in your Thompson as soon as the war's over."

Will smiled and said, "That's okay by me. I won't need it anymore as soon as the war's over."

Will returned to find his men sitting in the street. He hadn't left anybody in charge, simply because he didn't know who to leave in charge. He wanted to keep the squad leader jobs open for Hank Gray and Carlo Pacini, and unless they got replacements again, he couldn't justify having more than two squads.

"Okay, you guys, come with me," he said. The men rose and followed him.

Will remembered a building with a large courtyard on the outskirts of town. They could rest there and still see what was going on in the street without being in anybody's way.

As they filed into the courtyard, Will fumbled in his pocket for the list he had made of the names of his men. He called roll: "Boticelli. Janowitz. Wilson. Stern. Crowell. MacDougall. Carlin. Benjamin. Myers. Samovitch." They all answered.

"Okay, let's make ourselves comfortable until they need us," said Will.

The men sat down in groups and began to chat. Will sat by himself. After a while, several of the men got up and came over to him. They all smiled. Will grinned back and said, "Sit down."

Myers said, "You know, Sarge, when we first got assigned to the mine platoon, we griped a lot. We told them we didn't want to be in no mine platoon, no way, nohow. We was really raising hell about it, too, until Sergeant Bowden tells us to shut up or he'll have us all shot at dawn." Myers smiled. So did his friends.

Will thought, Oh, hell! They want a transfer.

"What we want to say," said Carlin, "is that we didn't mean it. We're damned proud to be in the mine platoon. And Sarge, we're damned proud to serve under you."

"Oh?" said Will. He thought that he wasn't following this too well.

"Yeah," said Stern. "We been talking to guys about things what happened before we come in. They still talk a lot about Damen, even though most of the guys come in afterward. They talk about how the nine guns of the antitank company stood up to a panzer division. And how they stopped them. And threw them back, too.

"And how they lost eight out of their nine guns doing it. And you was there. You was the only survivor out of your gun crew. The only one left. That's why they put you in the mine platoon."

Myers cut in. "They say the mine platoon was the last one out of Damen. And you left sliding mines under Tiger tanks what was shooting at you with 88s!"

"And they say you guys've already had three trucks shot out from under you since the jump-off."

Will had to think for a minute or two. They were right, he supposed. But they made it sound a lot more heroic than he remembered it. He nodded.

"So when we tell some guy we're in the mine platoon, we don't have to say no more. We're proud to be in the mine platoon and damn glad you're our sergeant."

Will smiled. "Thanks," he said. "And I'm happy to have you in the platoon." They all smiled back, and Will realized, with embarrassment and misgivings, that he was a hero to his men.

Then Wilson spoke for the first time. "You know, Sarge, what bothers some of us, though, are the names missing from the roll call you just read. Latham. Silverman. Minelli, Stanford. They were all friends of ours. Came in with us. And we got to know Pendergast real good, too. They say Sergeant Gray'll come back pretty soon. And so will Pacini. But our friends never had a chance. It was their first fight. They just got here and got killed."

Will nodded. He said, "Yeah, I know."

"But I guess you lost friends, too, huh, Sarge?" said Carlin. "Lot of guys got it since you come in."

Will reflected. He said, "Yeah, all the guys who were here when I came in are gone. All the guys who came in with me are gone. Guys who came in after I did are gone. But I've never even been hit. So the law of averages is bound to catch up with me. I can feel it in my bones. My time's run out, and there's not one damn thing I can do about it."

✪

Courtney Jones shook his head. "I'm sorry about General Richardson," he said.

Tom Jacobs nodded. "I kept telling Dave those weren't toy soldiers he was playing with. They were men who bleed and die. But to him, casualty reports were always just that: reports, numbers, so many killed, so many wounded, so many missing. Statistics. The cost of doing business. Well, dammit! You can't do business like that. I guess that's why I had to make him see what his innocent little diversion at the Danube cost in suffering and agony."

Jacobs was silent for a minute, reflecting. Then he looked up and said, "You know what happened, Court? Dave Richardson was just too damned decent a man not to be affected by what he saw. And he was too intelligent not to know he was the only one to blame for it. That's what happened!"

Jones was silent. He'd just remembered something. He said, "You know, with Dave leaving and everything, nothing ever got done about the Pope boy. Your order transferring him here never went through."

Jacobs was annoyed. He had a lot to do, and he was enjoying his work. But the war would be over quickly now, and George Pope would be governor for a good, long time.

"Okay, Courtney," he said. "There's only one thing to do. I'm going up to the Triple Nickel and see the boy, bring him back with me. There've been too damn many slip-ups on this detail. I'll take care of it once and for all."

✪

Colonel John Rankin, West Point Class of 1934, presently commanding the 555th Infantry Regiment of the Fifteenth Division, was pleasantly surprised to receive a visit from General

Jacobs, Plans and Operations Officer of the Seventh Army. He knew exactly who General Jacobs was, of course, but he didn't know why he had come to visit a regimental headquarters. That was most unusual.

General Jacobs didn't keep him wondering for long. After the conventional pleasantries, Jacobs smiled and said, "I guess you're curious as to why I'm here?"

Colonel Rankin nodded at the same time he replied, "Yes, sir."

"Well, I've come to see an enlisted man in your regiment. His father's a friend of mine. He's worried about the kid. The boy sounds like one of those weak sisters who's afraid of his own shadow. He's even been known to faint on occasion, according to his dad."

The two officers were sitting on chairs at right angles to each other in the makeshift office Rankin had fixed up. The colonel leaned back almost far enough to upset his chair, smiled at the general, and said, "Sir, we don't have men like that in this regiment. We're the Triple Nickel of the Fighting Fifteenth. My men've smashed to pieces every German unit that's ever opposed them. You don't really think we're harboring a bunch of delicate little sissies that'll run every time they hear a loud noise, do you?"

Jacobs had to smile. He liked this Colonel Rankin, and, along with everybody else in the army, he had a great respect for the fighting abilities of the regiments of the Fifteenth Division. "It is sort of funny," he said. "But there it is. My friend doesn't say in so many words that his son's a weakling, but it's there between the lines. Anyway, I might take him off your hands if he's as big a mess as I think he is."

"All right, General," replied Rankin. "Do you have his name?"

Jacobs nodded. "William B. Pope," he replied. "Here's the full details." He handed over the paper with Will's serial number and MOS and other pertinent data.

Colonel Rankin handed it back with a startled expression. "I won't need this," he said. "I know Will Pope. He's just down the street, and I'll have him here in two shakes."

He called out the door to one of his men. "Hey! Sergeant! Send for Pope of the mine platoon. Tell him to get his ass over here on the double!"

Colonel Rankin looked confused. He was trying to remember what he could about Will Pope. He'd come in as a replacement at Damen. That was the battle that had made Rankin's reputation, so he had a warm spot in his heart for any man who fought for him there. Besides, Pope was a survivor—that was for sure. And Colina thought highly of him. Rankin shook his head. Finally he said, "General, I take it you're expecting a whimpering, runny-nosed little kid?"

Jacobs nodded. "I expect so, from what his father told me."

"What would you say if I were to tell you Pope is the platoon sergeant of the mine platoon? Suppose I told you he fought in Alsace and Wurzburg and Schweinfurt and Nuremberg; took a squad across the Danube in the first wave?"

"I'd say either you or his father don't know this boy very well, or we're talking about two different people," replied Jacobs.

"Sergeant Pope, sir," announced an aide.

After the introductions, Colonel Rankin left Will alone with General Jacobs.

In front of the general stood a lean, tough-looking platoon sergeant, the kind of infantryman Jacobs knew and loved. His helmet was dented. It was black from sitting on so many open fires to heat water. An M-1 cartridge belt circled the man's waist, even though he had a submachine gun slung on his shoulder. A couple of hand grenades hung from the breast pockets of his stained field jacket. His trousers had crusted mud still clinging to them. A trench knife stuck out of his combat boot.

General Jacobs was confused. This wasn't the boy George Pope had told him about. Not by any stretch of the imagination.

This is the wrong man, thought Jacobs. They sent me the wrong man.

"Is your name William Pope?" he asked.

"Yes, sir."

"Are you Governor George Pope's son?"

The sergeant cocked his head. "What's that got to do with anything, sir?" he asked.

"Are you?"

The two infantrymen took each other's measure. The sergeant nodded. "Yes, sir," he replied.

The general wrinkled his brow, scratched his head, and looked doubtful. Finally, he smiled. "I'm a friend of your father's," he said. "And I'm having you transferred to my headquarters on special assignment."

"Why?" asked Will.

"Because your father wants it that way. That's why."

Will didn't reply. He was thinking. If he left now, there'd be nobody to take care of his men. The mine platoon would be nothing but a bunch of replacements who couldn't last a minute if they hit anything serious. Or the army'd put some little prick like Bradford in charge of them, and they deserved better. They were good guys and they deserved a fighting chance. Only he could give it to them. It was his responsibility to stay and look after them.

"Suppose I don't want to transfer?" he asked. "Can you order me to?"

"You're a sergeant," replied Jacobs. "And I'm a general. You're damned right I can order you to!"

The two men glared at each other without speaking. Will realized he couldn't argue with a three-star general. He'd lose that one for sure. But there might be some other way. He remembered how persuasive his father could be whenever he came up against tough opposition. And, after all, he was his father's son, wasn't he? Hellfire, yes! That's why he was in this jam.

Will smiled. "Were you ever in the infantry, sir?" he asked.

Jacobs nodded. "You bet your life I was," he replied.

Will's smile broadened. The pride the general had put into his words told Will he had a chance. He said, "Then, sir, I'd like to appeal to you as one infantryman to another.

"Put yourself in my place. Would you want to transfer out of the Triple Nickel into a rear-echelon headquarters after fighting halfway across Europe? Would you, sir?"

"Why not?" asked Jacobs. "The war's almost over, so why not transfer? It won't make any difference, and it'll make your father happy."

It wasn't going to be so easy after all. "Sir," Will said, "my platoon are all replacements. I'm the only thing that holds them together. Sir, if it's like you say, and it won't make any difference, my place is with the mine platoon. They need me. Your headquarters doesn't."

"Worried about your men, are you?" asked Jacobs.

"Yes, sir," replied Will.

"They'll be all right," said the general. "You don't have to concern yourself with them now. I promised your father I'd transfer you, so that's that. Start getting ready to leave."

"We could tell my father you had me transferred, but I refused. He won't know any better," said Will.

He saw the general hesitate.

Will spoke slowly, and his words were sincere. "You know, I'm the only one left in my platoon, sir. Would you have me break faith with the dead? Would you? I owe it to them to stay until the end. I'm proud of being a combat infantryman. Leave me my pride, sir. My place is here."

General Jacobs didn't answer Will for a long minute. Finally he said, "I don't know what you were like when you left home, but if I ever have a son, I want him to be exactly like you are now."

Then he turned and walked through the doorway without looking back.

After the general left, Will went out of Colonel Rankin's office and into the main headquarters where he found Sergeant Masters standing near the radios.

"I'll bet you've come to ask me about your trucks," Masters said to him. "Well, they're way the hell up front hauling rifle troops as fast as they can roll, so forget it."

"Fine with me," replied Will. "What else's new?"

Masters grinned. He'd obviously been under a lot of pressure because of the rapid advance and attendant confusion, and he was relieved to find somebody who wasn't demanding something of him. He said, "Let's see. First, congratulations on taking over the mine platoon. It'll be good working with you, Will. Second, in case you haven't heard, Colina's just been promoted to major. He'll be leaving to go join General Darlington's outfit as a battalion commander."

"I'll be damned," said Will. A few weeks earlier, he'd have jumped with disbelief and cursed the gods of war for depriving him of his captain. Since that cold January afternoon when Will found himself dumped on the antitank company doorstep like an orphan, he and Colina had fought their way through a lot of miles together. And all he could say was, "I'll be damned."

At the same time, he realized he'd miss his commander. He'd miss the security of knowing he was there, experienced, capable, caring. So now one more person he'd learned to depend on was leaving, and as he stood amid the bustle of a headquarters that was preparing to move forward, he felt alone again.

"I'm glad I caught you, Will," came the familiar voice.

Will's frown disappeared. He grinned and held out his hand. "Congratulations, Major Colina," he said, "but what's this I hear about you leaving us?"

"It's true," replied Colina as they shook hands. "I'm leaving, but since you worry about these things, I want to tell you now the officer taking my place is a real fine guy. You'll meet him in a minute. He is Captain Tirado—Joe Tirado. Commanded a gun platoon in the

554th, been wounded a couple of times and decorated with the Silver Star. He's a real crackerjack, Will."

"He sounds good, sir," replied Will, "but as far as I'm concerned, nobody can ever take your place."

"Thanks, Will. That means a lot to me. But you look sad. Worried?"

"I guess I'll worry as long as the war lasts," replied Will. "Whenever you have people shooting at you, there's always the chance one of them'll get lucky and hit you. And now I've got a whole damned platoon to worry about as well."

Just then a slim, dark-haired young captain came over to them and said, "Major, I don't think it'll make any difference at this point, but they're not going to replace those two guns we lost at Nuremberg."

After Colina introduced them, Will was glad he'd filled him in on Captain Tirado's combat record. Otherwise he might have had misgivings, because Tirado had the Latin good looks of a matinee idol.

Will hesitated, then said, "We'll give you our fullest cooperation, sir. You can count on us."

"Thanks, Sergeant," said Tirado. "I'm going to need all the help I can get."

⭐

The next day, the Rainbow Division took Munich. Before they began their assault on the city, they had taken a place called Dachau, reported at first to be a prison camp. But the word got around that it was much more than another prison camp.

The Seventh Army commanders decided to show as many troops as possible exactly why they were fighting. So on the thirtieth of April, Will and his platoon loaded onto trucks with other G.I.'s from the headquarters of the 555th Infantry Regiment and went to Dachau.

Dachau had just been liberated. It was pretty much the way the Rainbow Division had found it. A few inmates were still there, those who were still alive. Will looked into their emaciated faces and their sunken eyes. He was not prepared for this. None of them were.

Will and his men walked past the ovens. They walked past the stacks of dead, piled on top of each other like cordwood. They walked past the railroad trains loaded with bodies.

Will Pope felt sick. He had been certain that war was the worst possible pestilence on the face of the earth. He hated it. There could be nothing worse.

Now he changed his mind. Here defenseless human beings had been tortured, starved, beaten—finally gassed to death and burned in the ovens. Will thought, There are things worse than war. This is worse. Much worse. Infinitely worse.

It was a sobered and reflective Will Pope who started to walk back to the truck. But even as he walked away, he couldn't get Dachau and all it meant out of his mind. I've seen a lot of awful things. I've killed a lot of men. But I've never seen anything like this—a factory that produces dead bodies just like other factories produce soap or automobiles. Without emotion. Without pity.

Will had been shaken, and his thoughts were disturbing him profoundly. Are we all capable of such cruelty? Am I? Is one bastard like Hitler all it takes to bring it out? Or might it come out by itself? How close to the surface is it?

"You look shook up, Sarge. You're white as a sheet."

Will turned. A young soldier from the Rainbow Division was standing beside him, and he realized he was at the gate of that place, and the soldier was on guard there.

He replied, "Aren't you shook up?"

The boy nodded.

Will asked, "Were you in on the taking of this place?"

"No, but I come in right afterward."

"What happened to the sons-of-bitches in charge of this place?" asked Will.

"They tried to run away, but our Rangers went after the bastards and brought them back. They slashed them open with their trench knives and busted their faces with rifle butts, they was so furious. Then they turned their Tommy guns on the sons-of-bitches and really ripped them to pieces."

"Good," said Will.

Will looked back through the gates. He said, "You know, if we'd have taken places like this as soon as we got into Germany, instead of now at the end, I think we'd have killed every German we could've laid our hands on. I think we'd have annihilated the whole damned race of them."

"You know, Sarge," said the soldier, "you're talking like a Nazi."

Will was shocked at himself. It had been so easy to slip into that way of thinking. He nodded at the man. "You're right, son," he replied. "You're right as rain. I guess it's something we all have to watch out for."

He waved good-bye and continued walking toward the truck. But he thought, The Germans alone aren't to blame for this. We all are. The sins of any man are the sins of us all.

27

With nothing to stop them, the U.S. Seventh Army rolled on. The division's motor trucks crossed the Austrian border into the beautiful Tyrol Mountains. In a valley surrounded by majestic, snow-capped peaks, the 555th Infantry Regiment settled in. It was then that Will Pope realized that nobody was shooting at him, and he had nobody to shoot at. It hadn't sunk in before. It was a strange feeling.

The civilians were friendly. The girls were beautiful, the men were old, and speaking to Austrians was against regulations. To the girls, the men of the 555th paid a lot of attention; to the regulations, they paid none.

The town that was host to the antitank company of the Triple Nickel was the most charming place Will had ever been in. It gave him the feeling he was living in the middle of a very pretty picture postcard.

But the war was still on. Germany hadn't surrendered. And Will Pope began to worry about whether he might have to fight in these mountains that were so lovely to look at but would be such absolute hell to do battle in.

He decided he wanted to have a talk with Sergeant Masters. He knew Masters's first name was Peter, and he wondered whether he ought to continue calling him Sergeant Masters, or if he should call him Peter, or even Pete. After all, Will was a tech sergeant now, almost Masters's equal. Will mulled it over as he walked down the quaint, exceptionally clean street to the company C.P.

Masters was relaxed. For the first time in three months, he'd caught up on his work. Now there were no more casualty reports, no after-action reports, no equipment losses to be replaced, and his morning reports were routine. He welcomed Will's visit. He was delighted to have somebody to chat with to break a schedule that was becoming increasingly boring.

"Sit down, Will. Sit down," he said, getting up from his desk and coming around to sit beside Will on one of the two soft armchairs on the other side of the room.

Masters poured them each a canteen cup of K ration coffee. "We'll be getting better rations pretty soon," he said. "They just haven't caught up with us yet."

"Are we going to have to fight around here?" asked Will. Masters shook his head. "I shouldn't think so," he replied. "I'd say our fighting days are over unless this damned 'Festung Europa' pops up someplace. But, hell! We've taken all of Bavaria and sent our patrols scouting all over Austria, and, Will, it don't exist. It's nothing but the biggest propaganda con game of the whole war."

Will liked the sound of that, but he remembered he had more tangible matters to discuss. "I heard a rumor that Johnny Minelli died," he said.

Masters nodded. "He never left the aid station. There was nothing they could do for him. His insides was shredded to pieces."

Will sighed. "Of all the new men, he was the best, and he was a nice guy, besides. He was the only one who took the trouble to look after that creep, Stanford... By the way, what about him?"

"The guy who went off his rocker at the Danube? That the one you mean, right?" asked Masters.

Will nodded.

"They're going to have to put him away for a while. Seems he's had what they call 'emotional problems' for a long time. They would've most likely discharged him in the States, except they been sending infantry replacements over so fast they never caught up with him."

Masters saw the grieved expression on Will's face. He knew he was still thinking of Minelli. "Did you hear about Pendergast?" he asked.

Will shook his head. "More bad news?"

"Hell, no!" exclaimed Masters. "He got captured by the Jerries right after the Danube crossing. Seems he just got ahead of everybody else and they took him."

"That's not bad news?" asked Will.

Masters laughed. "No. It sure ain't, because you know what? Our guys liberated him the next damn day. And you want to hear the zinger? All liberated prisoners of war get sent home to their loved ones! Get it, Will? Your boy spends one day as a POW and gets a one-way ticket home. He's already in Le Havre waiting for a boat."

Will had to smile. Pendergast hadn't come into the outfit until around the fourteenth or fifteenth of April, and now he was on his way home already, while it looked as if Will Pope would be here for a long, long time. It was ironic.

"Do you have any more good news?" he asked Masters.

The big sergeant thought for a moment. "Well," he said, "I've got some that's both good and bad, but mostly good. We got a letter from Ernie Kitchener. He's still in the hospital in England. He likes all the old boys in the ward with him, of course, but he'll be going home as soon as he's well enough. Trouble is, he's gonna have a crooked leg and a limp for the rest of his life. It'll get him a pension, though, and shouldn't keep him from going back and running his farm."

Will shook his head. "Old Kitch was afraid of that," he said. "He was afraid he'd never walk again."

"Oh, it's nothing that serious," replied Masters. "He'll walk just fine, with a cane. Just think how distinguished he'll look, Will. He'll be a war hero for life."

Will smiled. He guessed Masters was right. When a guy walks with a cane, it reminds everybody he received his wounds honorably, fighting for his country on a foreign field.

"Speaking of heroes," continued Masters, "you know Bowden put Ceruti and Gruber in for Silver Stars for getting their men off the road there at Nuremburg, even after they were both hit. They got the decorations, all right. But you want to hear something funny? Gruber's from a small town, and only a few other guys from there went in the service, and they ended up in the quartermasters or the shoreside navy, and Gruber's the only guy from the whole town who's seen action. Not only that, but he's been wounded twice and decorated for bravery. Well, the local newspapers picked it up, and now he's the town's one and only genuine war hero. His picture was on the front page of the paper and everything. When he comes home, the mayor's gonna meet him and give him the key to the city, and everybody's falling all over themselves to present gifts to him and his family. They're all just as proud as Punch to have a real live hero from there, and they're gonna do it up brown."

Will laughed. "I wonder how old Jay'll take all that?" he said.

"He'll take it damned good," replied Masters. "They've already elected him to the town council and a lot of other crap."

"When'll he go home, though?" asked Will. "The way Sam Bowden talked, he was hit pretty bad."

"It did look bad," said Masters, "but that was all. It wasn't nothing serious, except they have to do some plastic surgery to make old Jay pretty again. It won't take long, and when they're finished he'll be as good as new. Then home to the parades and the speeches."

Will smiled and shook his head at the same time. "Of all people! Jay Gruber! I wonder if it'll change his outlook on life?"

"I think it'll be pretty hard to keep on griping about everything after your own hometown makes a hero out of you," said Masters.

"What about Mike Ceruti?" asked Will. "He's from New York, and that's one place that's not going to pay a lot of attention to you just because you got shot up and they pinned a bunch of medals on you, and that's for sure."

It was Masters' turn to laugh. Then he replied, "No. Ceruti's already got accepted into the regular army, though. He'll go on recruiting duty for a while, then go to a permanent post in the States. He's a good man. The army thinks highly of him. He's getting married, by the way."

"What?!" the words flew out of Will's mouth.

Masters nodded. "Yep. Going to marry an English girl he met while he was in the hospital there. After they get better, the patients get passes to go into London, and that's where he met her. They'll marry as soon as the war's over. She's a real good-looker, I hear, and awful nice, too."

"Well, I'm damned," said Will. "Why the hell couldn't I have gotten hit? I'd have gone back to a nice, clean hospital, and I'd have met lots of nice, clean nurses and English girls and—"

"Will, you could've got your damned leg took off like Findlay, too!" said Masters. "Or your head like MacKenzie, or—"

"Findlay lost his leg?" asked Will. "We all thought it was nothing but a ticket home. We weren't even sure he was hit that bad."

"He's back in the States, all right," replied Masters, nodding his head. "But he's minus his right leg."

Will was silent. Findlay had come in just before Schweinfurt. That was the only real action he saw. Just that one fight. And damned if he didn't lose his leg in it.

Will remembered poor little Brown got hit the same time Findlay did at Schweinfurt. It was a head wound that bled a lot and scared Brown to death. "How about Brown?" he asked.

"Got a scalp crease? That the one? There wasn't nothing to his wound, but the kid kept carrying on like you wouldn't believe, so they decided not to take any chances, and they sent him back to the States for observation. Now I hear he's fit as a fiddle, chipper and happy as a pig in the mud."

"I hear my pals Gray and Pacini are on their way back here," said Will. "Is that so?"

"Yep," replied Masters. "They're in a repple-depple someplace, but nobody's rushing nothing no more, so God only knows when we'll see them again. Neither one was hit very badly, you know, just enough to be Purple Heart heroes when they get home."

Will realized he wouldn't even be that. He'd never gotten hit, he'd never been decorated for bravery. But so far he'd survived, and he figured that was plenty good enough for him.

It wasn't until a day later that Masters came looking for Will to tell him he'd just gotten word that young Olsen died a few days earlier in a hospital in England. Another Nuremburg road casualty. Even though he'd hardly known Olsen, Will was sad, not only because Olsen had died, but also because he'd forgotten all about him, forgotten even to ask Masters what happened to him…

✪

Completely defeated and occupied, Germany surrendered unconditionally on May 8, 1945.

In the quaint village in Austria, Will heard the news from Captain Tirado. "The war's over, Will! It's over!" he shouted. As the words sank in, Will scratched his nose. The whole terrible thing had just petered out while they sat in a pretty little town in the Tyrol.

The captain was on his way down the street to spread the word to the other platoons. Will needed time to think. In an automatic gesture, he slung his Tommy gun onto his shoulder and started walking. He walked out of the town and came to a path that went up the side of a hill. He kept walking up the path, climbing until he arrived at a small plateau that overlooked the valley.

Will sat down on the grass and contemplated the scene. It was a pleasant, sunny day, and on all sides were the green and purple snow-capped mountains.

As he looked out over the valley, he saw dairy cattle on the slopes. He heard the cowbells clanking. He saw immaculate small chalets on the hillsides, the quiet town below him, the stream running through the valley, the small bridge over it.

Nothing in this picture had been scarred by war. It was the most beautiful scene he had ever set eyes on in his life. And the most tranquil. It was a world at peace.

Will breathed deeply. He felt so happy, he wanted to embrace everybody on the whole face of the earth. He had made it! He had survived. He was still alive. He remembered reading that Winston Churchill once said, "The most exhilarating thing that can happen to a person is to be shot at—and missed." Will experienced that feeling a thousandfold.

But soon the intoxication of survival left him and it was a sobered Will Pope who sat on the grass. He had never expected to survive, because he didn't think he could. He'd prepared himself to die, and now that he was going to live, he felt almost disappointed. More than that, he felt guilty. He felt guilty for having survived.

In the battle for Alsace, when he first thought he was going to die, he kept asking himself, Why me? Why me? Why me? Now that he knew he had survived, he kept repeating the same words, Why me? Why me? Why me?

He'd expected to join his dead friends, but death had rejected him. He was confused. I'll visit their graves, thought Will. Yes. That's what I'll do. I'll take my mother and father. I'll tell them, 'There lies Jim Mahoney, the best friend I ever had. He was killed when he most wanted to live. He was so terribly in love. But that doesn't say even a part of it. And there lies Phil Cohen, the finest of us all. He was commissioned on the battlefield in France. Decorated for heroism, wounded at the Siegfried Line. Killed leading his men in the assault on the Danube River.'

Will waved his hand in an unconscious gesture. 'And all the others,' his thoughts continued, 'the kind sergeant named

MacAllister who sent me for ammunition and saved my life, perhaps on purpose. And his gunner, Jones. And Hays and Faulkner. And that great and wonderful soldier named Joe Sumeric. The enemy could never kill him. No! Never! But a short mortar shell could and did.'

Will was standing now, and the tears were streaming down his cheeks. 'There they all lie. Trenton, the All-American boy, and poor Harry Muller. The quiet kid MacKenzie—they found him in a shell hole with his head blown off. Gomez and Martinelli and Sullivan. And the poor replacements who never had a chance, Silverman and Latham. And Olsen, who died in the hospital. That nice Johnny Minelli, with his insides shredded. Innis and McCrory, blown to pieces by mines with Black and Russovitch.

'Poor Reilly. Carrington and Kilbride, men I hardly knew. And Johnny Shanker, flung halfway across a field because he tried to save a truck. And Danny Sark, who threw himself on a live grenade to save a bunch of men. Irv Donaldson, Brucker, and Bradford were bad guys in their different ways. But it doesn't matter anymore. They're all dead now.'

"Yes. I remember them all. Every single one."

His tears dried, and Will's thoughtful look returned. He had to accept the unexpected prospect that he would live.

But, he thought, surviving is what life is all about. Before you can accomplish anything, before you can use that power God gave to you to do good or to do evil, you have to stay alive. And war makes it so terribly difficult that if you last longer than anybody else you feel you've succeeded in something even if you had very little to do with it. It gives your life a special edge.

And as he sat on that hilltop with his arms around his knees, the hard look he'd acquired began to soften, and the aged expression on his face began to fade. The bloom of youth was returning like the spring after a long, cold winter, vigorous and virile, nature restored and renewed.

Finally Will smiled. He stood up in the late-afternoon sunlight and, as he started down the hill, Will Pope felt a hundred years younger than he had before and a thousand times happier than he had ever been in his life.